The Last Days of Ray Cobb

Vagrant Mystery Book 3

Brad Grusnick

KDP PRINT ISBN: 9798838045201

INGRAM ISBN: 978-1-7326018-1-9

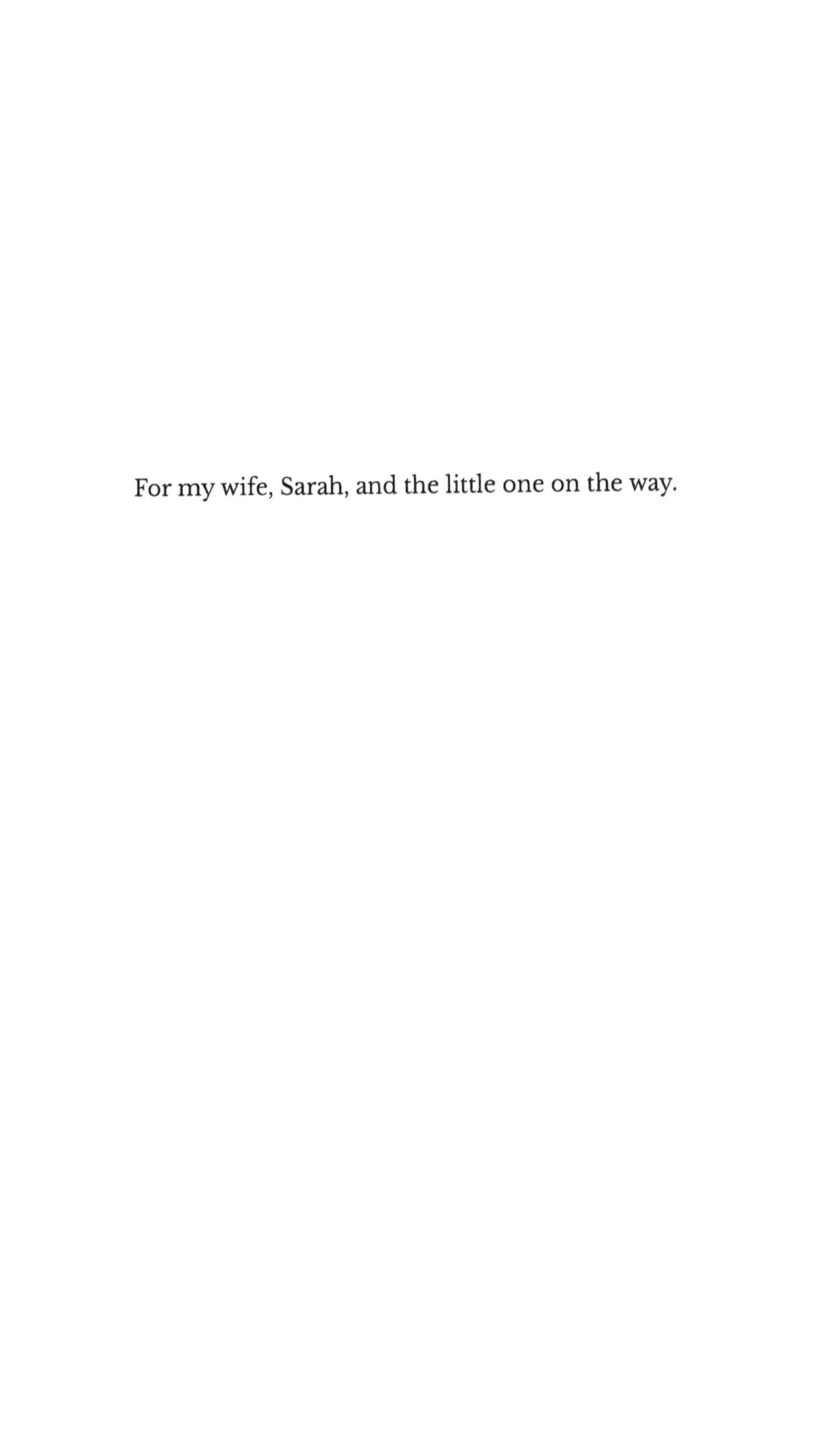

For my wife, Sarah, and the little one on the way.

<u>**Vagrant Mystery Series**</u>
The Last Will and Testament of Ernie Politics
The Last Dance of Low Seward
The Last Days of Ray Cobb

Watch for more at strangescribe.com

1

"Propinquity."

"Hmm?"

"Propinquity. It means an affinity or kinship," Detective Hsu said, his face glued to his phone.

"Great," Nick sighed.

He had only been partners with Hsu for a week. They weren't exactly bosom buddies. On paper, David Hsu was a good a cop. College grad. Detail-oriented. Loved the hell out of paperwork. But his social skills sucked. Like his need to read his "Word of the Day" out-loud every morning, no matter what sort of environment they were in. Under the on-ramp of jammed cars honking to squeeze onto the 101 freeway, Nick could've used a break from the vocabulary lesson.

"It can also mean nearness, either physically or psychologically," Hsu said. He put his phone away and looked both ways down Juanita Avenue. "You think anyone had *propinquity* with the victim at the time of death?"

"Pretty sure they all did," Nick said.

The short stretch of Juanita between Beverly Boulevard and the 101 had become a mini-version of Skid Row over the years. A small group of homeless people who the gentrified Arts District had pushed into the underside of Silverlake's hipster haven.

The tiny tent city was the homeless equivalent of upscale living. If there was an economic tier in street residency between a fifteen-dollar tent bought at Target and Section 8 housing provided by the city, the structures on Juanita fit the bill.

Tents tethered together with tarpaulin and cardboard boxes. Pressboard stolen from construction sites to set up a makeshift latrine. The sheer innovation of the homeless who had put the mini-subdivision hovel together was impressive. A few of them were feats of engineering and architectural genius. Each tent-house built on Juanita was going to be there for a while. Even if a bad El Niño came through, some of those makeshift houses would withstand the weather better than the mudslide-prone mansions in Nichols Canyon.

What the residents of Juanita Village had to worry about was the body. The victim was inside one of the smaller tents. The "owner" was in custody, but he swore up and down he had an alibi from the night before, complete with witnesses. He'd told the girl she could sleep there if she needed to. It seemed like a hollow gesture for a man who looked like he didn't give a fuck about anybody. The corner of Wilshire and Alvarado, where he claimed to have slept the night, had several security cameras. Nick and Hsu would know soon enough if his story checked out.

He must have been confident that the girl was too far along to give him any action. Some guys were grossed-out about that sort of thing. They're happy to pick through festering garbage for a stained baseball cap, but God forbid they have sex with a beautiful woman just because she's growing a life inside of her.

Scratch that. *Had been* growing a life inside of her.

Her life was gone. Whether the baby's heart still beat was anybody's guess.

"We may be looking at a Caesarian kidnapping," Hsu said. A search of the area hadn't come up with an aborted fetus.

"That sounds made up," Nick said. He knew Hsu would elaborate, no matter what his response had been. It was his way. If Hsu had read about it within the last five years, he would regurgitate it to anyone in the nearby area. Nick had made the mistake of going out for a beer with Hsu on the first day they were assigned together. *Jeopardy!* was playing on the TV above the bar. The guy had an explanation for every fucking answer. And yet, the only thing Nick had retained was that priapism was the medical term for an erection lasting over four hours. How that ended up in a discussion about a quiz show he couldn't remember. Though he had a vague recollection it had started with an answer about Grecian wine.

"It's rare, but becoming exceedingly common. Usually premeditated. In the old days, it was called a hysterical pregnancy. There was a lot of preparation that went into keeping up the illusion. Now, all a perpetrator needs is access to a social media profile and a sonogram. For months, a woman can post about how she's expecting. When the time comes to produce the child, they go into a panic, find a pregnant woman, and take the child by force."

"Sounds a little Manson Family to me," Nick said.

He regretted it as soon as he'd said it. One of these days, he might get Hsu to play along with his sarcasm.

And on that day, he'd buy a large cake.

With buttercream frosting.

And those little flowers on it.

Today wasn't that day.

"Oh, no. The murder of Sharon Tate and her unborn child was more of a ritualistic sacrifice than a crime of envy. In Caesarian kidnappings, the death of the mother is merely a by-product of her housing the unborn individual the kidnapper wishes to abscond with."

Abscond was the "Word of the Day" yesterday.

Nick wondered if there was going to be a day where Hsu didn't use one of his new vocabulary words.

"Have you had enough of a breather?" Nick asked.

"I'll be honest," Hsu let out a sigh, "for as detached as I try to be, this is hitting close to home. If you don't mind, I'll conduct more interviews."

The murder hitting too close to home was the extent to which Hsu talked about his life off-the-clock. There were pictures of his pretty Korean wife on his desk. All of them were of her alone, standing in front of some landmark — Stonehenge or Golden Gate — nothing of them together. It was as though she'd brought her husband along on her vacations to serve as her personal photographer. Either that or she had similar pictures sitting on her desk of him, alone, in the same poses.

Nick still wasn't sure if her name was Jin or Jen. Hsu only mentioned her in passing. Which Nick found strange because Hsu had once gone on for an hour about the migration patterns of the North American pronghorn antelope. Nick also knew Jin or Jen had been sick, causing Hsu to take an extended leave of absence from the force. When he came back, he was assigned to Nick Archer.

Willie Grant, Nick's former partner, had asked for a transfer after he'd accused her of leaking the details of a high-profile investigation to the press. This was only hours before she stopped a young entertainment assistant high on psychedelics from putting a bullet in Nick's brain.

Nick watched his new partner approach the homeless witnesses, each of them spooked by the yellow tape and uniforms. Street instinct was to disappear when the cops showed up, but they wanted to know who it was in the tent. By the time they'd realized it was an outsider and not a member of their little community, they were stuck being held for questioning.

There was bruising around the girl's neck where she had been strangled and held down. He didn't see any hair or skin under the fingernails. The victim hadn't gotten a hand on her attacker. If she had, the medical examiner was going to have to do some digging for it. There would be plenty of DNA evidence to collect, but the tent looked dirty enough that every piece pulled would come from someone with a record. Those who lived on the streets didn't do a great job of avoiding the law. A better bet would be to watch the hospitals for anyone coming in with a newborn in distress.

Nick emerged from the tent and made a beeline for Hsu.

"Anyone report hearing a child crying?"

"Haven't asked."

"If our perp meant to keep the baby alive, it was making noise. And at that hour, a child's screams would wake up the block."

There was probably more he could learn from the body, but he didn't want to go back into the tent. Forensics would give him plenty to go through later. Then he could examine it without the mixing smells of shit, body odor, and rotting viscera.

Juanita looked like an ancient excavation site. Cordoned off with yellow tape, each of the tent structures stood empty, their residents held for questioning. Forensic techs in full blue pajama suits took detailed photographs of each, the most attention paid to the torn-apart woman by the freeway. Each of the structures would be cataloged and stripped, some of them taken apart and boxed up. These people's homes would be destroyed because they lacked permanent addresses. Rights pertaining to search, seizure, and private property were non-existent because they lived on the sidewalks. Nick hoped he could get enough of a story out of some of them before they realized what was happening.

No one thinks about how many rights they retain just from the ability to close their doors. In all the time Nick had spent trying to understand the street community and how they lived their lives, he would never really relate to them. He would always be one of the normal people. The "haves." A cop who can steal their property and mark it as evidence just because they slept on the wrong block.

Among those waiting to be questioned was a Hispanic man, about twenty-five years old. Dark clothes, faded, but coordinated. The emblem on his Yankee cap was grey from dirt, but the bill remained crisp and unbent. He kept getting on and off a BMX with scuffed paint, holding onto it to make sure it wasn't heaped into evidence with anything else. A uniform was watching him, scolding him from hopping onto the seat, afraid he would bolt from the scene. Nick could see the man trying to play it cool, but his eyes were darting toward the lean-to made from Rite Aid shopping carts. Colored bungee cords held the structure together. He jumped any time an officer or tech got too close. That house was his.

"What's your name?" Nick asked.

"You guys gonna be done here soon? I got to get my work uniform, man," Yankee Cap said, not answering the question.

"You're probably not going to get back in there today unless we find something definitive in the next half hour."

"I didn't have nothin' to do with this, all right. Weren't even here last night. Was at my mom's."

"Can she confirm that?"

"No. She wasn't there, otherwise, I wouldn'ta been."

"Doesn't make for a great alibi. You know whose tent that is?"

"Thought that guy said it was his, um... Yusuf... the Muslim-looking guy."

Yankee Cap nodded in the direction of the tent's confessed owner. Nick was glad Hsu wasn't with him at the moment. He would've made an irrelevant comment about Muslim not being an ethnicity.

"That's not what I asked," Nick said.

"People come and go. I was only staying for a few days 'til I got a new place," Yankee Cap shrugged. "Can't I get my clothes and go? I'm gonna be late."

"A few days, huh? You got a driver's license?"

"All right, shit. I'm gonna reach for my wallet. Don't shoot me."

"You see my gun out?" Nick asked.

"I watch the news. You don't need no excuse."

Nick held his hands up in supplication, away from his service weapon. Yankee Cap pulled out his wallet and tossed it over. Nick flipped through the worn flaps. Not much in it but a bunch of club cards, a Costco employee I.D., and a California driver's license. He snapped a picture of the license with his phone.

"Forno Garcia," Nick read. "Forno? You get teased a lot as a kid?"

"What the fuck for?"

"No one clever enough to call you Porno?"

"What's the law say about grounds for police harassment?"

"Meant nothing by it, sorry. My mouth moves quicker than my brain sometimes."

"Okay, you saw it. Gimme it back."

Nick flipped to the back flap and noticed there were eight crisp hundred-dollar bills inside.

"Costco pays pretty well, huh?"

"Man, what the fuck?" Forno took a step forward, but the uniform was quick to block his way. "You looking for a bribe, dirty pig?"

Nick closed the wallet after replacing the I.D. and put it back into Forno's hand.

"Hsu," Nick called across the tape. His partner made some last notes with the haggard woman he was interviewing and trotted over.

"Yeah."

"This is Forno Garcia. My partner, Detective Hsu."

"You want a handout, too?" Forno asked Hsu.

"Forno, did I take any money from your wallet?"

Forno counted the bills. Twice.

"No. Don't mean you won't later."

"Is that the confirmation you needed?" Hsu asked, "I've got a few more I need to get to over there."

"Have the unis do it," Nick said. "I think we've spotted a person of interest."

Forno's eyes darted back and forth between the two cops. They could see he wanted to bail and wanted to bail hard.

"Okay, Forno, it's honesty time," Nick glanced back at Forno's tent. It was next in line for photographs and cataloging. Forno was huffing and sweating. "Whatever you got in that tent is now potential evidence in this case. We're going to pull down each of those tarps and canvases that you probably spent days stringing together, and we're going to find any dirty little secrets you might be hiding. Maybe even a murder weapon."

"I didn't kill nobody! I just—"

"Want to get to work. I know. You typically get your paychecks in cash?"

"How much did he have on him?" Hsu asked.

"Eight Franklins. Foil strips."

"Legit money," Hsu said. "You don't believe in banks, huh?"

Every conversation Nick had ever had with Hsu had been strained and awkward. Hsu was in cop-mode now. He knew how to mirror his interviewee. Even his posture had changed. A by-product of years spent in Vice.

"Since when is it a crime to have money?"

"It's not, as far as I know," Hsu said, "Just a matter of how you got it. That's enough for a down payment on a small apartment. If I had that kind of walking around money, I'd upgrade my living arrangements."

"Obviously, you haven't looked for an apartment in L.A. lately. Probably live in Valencia or some shit."

"Chino Hills," Hsu said.

Forno watched the crime scene techs move one tent closer. "There's nothing in there. Don't take my tent apart, man," he whined, "That's all I got."

"That license expired two years ago and my guess is that permanent address expired with it," Nick said. "The way you were twitching at the officers milling around your tent made me think it was more than just a crash pad for you. So, you see how I might be suspicious with your handful of lies along with your lack of an alibi and wallet full of cash?"

"That sort of information might even make you a prime suspect," Hsu added.

"I just live on this block. I didn't do nothin'."

"Who else lives on this block that we don't know about?" Nick pointed over to where the girl was found. "Whose tent is that, really?"

Forno stared at the detectives with a pleading look in his eyes and took a deep breath.

"I dunno," he mumbled.

Nick turned to Hsu. "Rock Paper Scissors?"

"I grew up playing Odds and Evens," Hsu said. "I would prefer odds."

"Suit yourself."

In unison, the detectives held out their fists.

"One, two, three, shoot."

Nick held up two fingers, as did Hsu. Evens.

"Winner's choice," Hsu said.

Nick turned back to Forno, smiling.

"All right, Forno, you don't know anything. But somebody does. You want to point us in the right direction?"

Forno was watching them carefully. His brow scrunched up in confusion, wondering what the cops had decided with their little game of Odds and Evens.

"Under the overpass on Virgil. Zeke been there forever. Knows everybody who sets up down here. Everybody that comes and goes on the regular. Thinks he's king of the fuckin' mountain, but he ain't nothing but a troll under a bridge."

"What's Zeke look like?" Nick asked.

"Hunched back. Dreads. Muthafucka looks like some kinda Igor George Clinton," Forno said, "Can I go?"

"Well?" Hsu asked.

Nick looked at Forno, who was twitching to get back on his bike.

"I'll look for Zeke," Nick said.

"You sure?" Hsu asked.

"Yeah, I'd rather be out here."

Hsu nodded.

"Forno, we're going to head downtown and make sure you've got your story straight," Hsu said. "I can call your boss to tell him you'll be late."

"Am I under arrest?" Forno asked.

"Do you want to be?"

"No."

"Then get in the squad. I'll even buy you lunch. We'll put your bike in the trunk."

Forno hung his head, but did what he was told.

After the car had pulled away, Nick turned back to the scene and scanned the tents. He could interview every person living on that street until he was blue in the face and come up with nothing. With a murder this brutal, there was one guy he knew who would have his ear to the ground. A guy who would take an interest in a woman's uterus being torn open, her body left to rot in a dirty tent. But that guy was long gone. And Nick only had one connection to him left.

He dropped it into the inside pocket of his suit coat every morning and didn't touch it again until he emptied the contents at night. The last thing Nick needed his new partner to see was that he was carrying around a second phone. The type of phone that was notorious around Vice and Narco as hard to trace. It would raise a lot of questions Nick couldn't answer.

"Got a tip on a witness," Nick called to the closest uniform, "Heading over to Virgil for a bit."

He could feel the stares of the detained homeless as he passed. People who wanted nothing more than to be left alone. People like Ray. As Nick made his way up the street, he could feel the burner phone thumping against his chest with every step.

He should have snapped the SIM card, broken the thing in half, taken a ferry to Catalina, and dumped it over the side into the ocean. Instead, Nick kept it with him, waiting for it to ring. Waiting for the man at the other end to ask for his help.

But as far as Nick knew, Ray Cobb was already dead.

2

Everyone who came out of the Big Bear Lake Dollar Tree looked like they were a single paycheck away from joining the trio of homeless men on the bench outside. Three men for whom only the bond of homelessness could bring together. A grandfatherly type surrounded by plastic bags, clutching the butt of his cigarette for dear life. Another stretching into middle age, silent, dressed in tattered hunting camouflage. The third was in cross-country ski tights that had seen better days and a faded Gore-Tex jacket. He was regaling the other two with an itemized receipt of all the toiletries he'd just scored for under ten bucks.

Ray kept his distance from the three stooges. They were the first and only homeless he'd seen in the several weeks since getting into town and were probably territorial. Even with fresh clothes, they would've spotted him from a mile away. The tourists and winter travelers did their shopping at the Stater Bros. supermarket across the way. Most patrons ignored the stooges, afraid to confront their own financial cliff.

And then one didn't.

The kid had acne, a hawk's beak nose, and a crooked smile. He braced himself against the cold and gave each of the stooges a handshake. They liked him. They knew him. He handed each of them a crumpled buck before shuffling across the slush to his rusted red VW beetle — the old model — the one that didn't look like it came out of a vending machine.

Three tries and the engine wouldn't turn over, but the look on the kid's face through the salt-speckled windshield didn't change or get frustrated. To Ray, he looked like someone who'd had some trouble early in his life, but was trying to stay positive in a world where second chances were shit. The kid got out of the car, popped the hood and pulled up his sleeves to keep the oil off of them.

He almost felt sorry for him. Until he saw his arm.

Getting a glimpse of Bear tattoos around town had proven fruitless. Even with the heat blasting in every bar and restaurant, long sleeves were pervasive.

Ray watched the kid slam the hood and then the bug sputter away toward town. He'd abandoned Low Seward's Audi deep in the woods when he'd arrived and had no way to follow. The stooges were going to come in handy after all.

"Hey," Ray said to any of the three stooges who would listen. It seemed as good an opening gambit as any.

"What's your problem?" Gore-Tex asked. The other two turned their attention toward Ray, but it didn't seem like they were the talkative types.

"Nothin'. Just that guy, that one with the bug. He dropped his wallet in the slush when he got in his car."

"Give it to us, we'll get it to him," Gore-Tex said, stretching out his hand.

"Not to insult you or nothin'," Ray said, putting on a dumber vernacular than usual, "but I'd rather hand it off in person."

Gore-Tex gave him a look up and down.

"Cops give you that shiner?" Gore-Tex asked. Ray could see him testing the waters. Searching for some story behind the fresh face in the mountains. Last thing Ray wanted to say was that a fat, naked man had given it to him in a tub.

Ray chuckled.

"My old lady. Caught me with some strange a few nights ago. Didn't even have time to wash the pussy stank off my dick, you know?"

The joke broke the suspicion. Camo Stooge chuckled.

"I hain't washed in so long, probably got the last three pussies still on mine," Camo Stooge giggled through his missing teeth.

Gore-Tex still wasn't sure.

"Your lady built like a line-backer?"

"Not when I met her, but boy did she balloon," Ray said. "I was looking for a fuck that wouldn't crush me underneath her."

"Strange you'd run away to here of all places. Where you from?"

"Lucerne Valley. Just got on the 18 and drove. My piece of shit truck died about halfway up. Seemed like a good place to stop. Figured I might get some seasonal work."

"Ain't nobody hirin'," Old Stooge finally spoke up.

"You got a name?" Gore-Tex asked.

Ray stretched out his hand. "Leon McBride. Leo."

Gore-Tex hesitated, then shook. The other two followed suit. None of them gave their names.

"Deuce works at the Grizzly Manor. Breakfast place up the road. Maybe he'll buy you a pancake for your good deed," Gore-Tex said.

Ray stepped off the curb before they could ask any more questions.

"Watch yourself out here, *Leo*," Gore-Tex said, the name said between clenched teeth, "colder up here than it looks."

He'd wandered down Big Bear Lake's main street several times since he'd arrived. It was a typical small town, speckled with the trappings of a tourist culture. A strip of bars and restaurants the locals worked in, but never ate at. Shops full of coffee mugs and novelty t-shirts. Every corner emblazoned with the familiar brown bear found on the California state flag. There was no sign of the actual predators lumbering through the streets.

Most of the bears in town were standing upright and carved out of wood. The sculpture in front of the Grizzly Manor Cafe was no different. Selfie-ready for adventurers in ski gear before they made their way up the mountain. Ray huddled on the small wooden porch outside in the biting wind, waiting for a table with a group who looked like they'd spent their night with a bottle of Woodford Reserve and a jacuzzi.

The inside wasn't what he was expecting. It was a single room. Griddle open for the patrons to see. Tables smashed together with barely enough space for the waitstaff to squeeze between them. A small counter wrapped around the back of the room. Hundreds of bumper stickers lined the walls in place of wallpaper. Most of them advertising Los Angeles institutions like Amoeba Music and Whiskey A Go Go.

"One?" the tattooed girl in the ripped Ramones tee asked.

"Yeah. Mind if I grab a seat at the counter?"

"Wherever's open. Go for it," she smiled. Either the girl was a better actress than any he'd seen in Hollywood, or she genuinely enjoyed her job.

Ray plopped down as close to the grill as he could and shook the snow off of his stocking cap before setting it down next to his cutlery.

"Coffee?"

He nodded to the woman behind the counter and blew into his hands to warm them. Deuce had taken over the grill from the morning prep cook and was grinning and jiving to the radio as he tossed down slab after slab of frozen hash browns. Pancakes worthy of the gods stacked up on a plate next to him as he ground up salt and pepper into the sizzling potatoes. He wore a stained sleeveless white t-shirt and bandana to hold back the sweat. The Bear tattoo snaked up his forearm.

After she delivered his coffee, Ray pulled a wad of crumpled bills out of his pocket and smoothed them out on the formica counter before shoving the folded bills back into his coat. It was the universal homeless symbol for *I can pay. Don't kick me out*, but nobody seemed to look at him sideways.

"So, what're you best at?" Ray called over to Deuce, who was folding diced onions and peppers into some scrambled eggs.

Deuce kept his eyes on the food, but smiled. "I'm good at everything. Close your eyes and point to the menu. You won't go wrong."

Ray smiled, keeping his tone light, "C'mon, I'm down to my last bills. Make it worth my while."

Deuce looked up from the grill and gave Ray a once over. "You got it, boss."

"What're you having?" the server asked.

"I got him, Tina," Deuce said.

"All right then. Just gimme a holler if you need a refill."

Ray took a big sip of his coffee and she topped him off before heading back down the line.

Blueberry pancakes browned to a perfect gold. Bacon crisp, but not burnt. Scrambled eggs that melted in his mouth. One of the best damn breakfasts he'd had in a long time.

"If you make the rest of the menu half as good as that, no wonder the locals keep coming back."

"Most of the tourists won't bother waiting in the cold. Their loss," Deuce said, "I take it you didn't come up here to enjoy the fresh powder?"

"My butler is waiting in the car. I only dress like this in diners to throw gold diggers off the scent," Ray said. He winked at the server and paid his tab.

"I'd trust you to tip better than those snow hounds any day of the week, honey," she said after counting the extra cash Ray'd set on the table. He was nearly out of scratch, but knew no one talked to a bad tipper.

"Figured I might go native a while. Change of scenery."

"Should've come in the summer. Not as much work, but you won't freeze your balls off," Deuce said. "Order up!"

Ray pointed to his swollen eye. "Circumstances beyond my control."

"I hear that."

Ray stood up and put his hat back on. He downed the last of his coffee.

"I'm sure there are plenty of places for Muffy and Buffy to get a cocktail in this town, but I'm going to need something strong to warm me up later tonight. Where do the locals drink around here?"

"Depends on the night, but Murray's is where we go on Tuesdays. Cheap tappers."

Ray shoved up his sleeve as he went to shake Deuce's hand.

"Maybe I'll see you there. Thanks for the chow."

It was there. A flicker. Pupils dilated. For a second. Then covered by a smile.

"See you around," Deuce said. He went back to the grill without another word.

The last of Ray's cash bought him a single bottle of beer at Murray's and his patience bought him his first glimpse at freedom.

Deuce pushed through the doors of the bar like he was waiting for a firing squad on the other side. Ray nodded to him and gestured for him to sit down.

The kid sat down next to him ordered a Coors Light, but didn't drink. Just sat and slowly peeled the paper label off the bottle.

"So, what now?" Ray asked.

Deuce whispered under his breath, "We gotta stick together."

"Whatever you think this is, or whoever you think I'm with, I'm not," Ray said. "You ever seen it before? I mean, on someone other than you."

"Yeah," Deuce said, "Once."

3

Violence is not the answer.
  Violence is not the answer.
  Violence is not the answer.

Imani repeated the phrase in her head as she made her way down the block to the market on Vernon Avenue. George Washington Carver Middle School seemed to have bi-weekly seminars about how their bodies were going to change. How they needed to check themselves before letting their emotions get the best of them. Blaming gun violence on raging hormones.

Everybody in her class knew what was going on. They didn't need some lady from the LAUSD in a non-threatening blouse to tell them so. Imani had breasts by the end of fifth grade and had spent two years trying to hide them from the world. Having someone come in and give an assembly about how growing pubic hair would lead to more violence was bullshit. Especially in her neighborhood. Boys on her block didn't need their balls to drop before they dropped casings on someone.

But no matter what she told herself, she knew sometimes violence was the answer.

"Hey girl. What you doin'?"

She pulled down on the bottom of the baggy sweatshirt she was wearing and pushed past the corner boy hovering at the entrance to Vernon Market.

"I'm twelve," Imani said.

It had become her standard response. Growing into her body early hadn't just attracted the attention of the boys in her class. Everywhere she went, she could feel the gaze on her bubble butt and tiny waist. As she followed the gaze up her chest, she saw the surprise when they reached her baby face. Though that didn't deter some.

"Don't bother me none." The corner boy laughed, but didn't pursue her into the store.

The man behind the counter moved his eyes from the small TV to see who'd come in, then back to his show. Imani was in the store most days, but the two had never learned each other's names. All the counter man knew about her was that she didn't shoplift. All she knew about him was he always looked her in the tits when taking her money.

She was careful not to trip on the missing floor tiles. She used to run her hand along the shelves as she made her way to the back coolers, but once had put her fingers into something sticky near the magazines and now kept her hands to herself. Banners above the coolers advertised 40s of Old English for five dollars, 16oz for a buck. The things people actually needed, like diapers and cleaning supplies, were marked up.

Imani sorted through the Wonder Bread on the dirty shelf, looking for a loaf that wasn't smashed to nothing or opened by someone palming a couple slices. She found one that appeared to be intact. She swung it from the twist tie, the enriched white flour swatting against her leg.

Slim pickings in the meat department. Pimento loaf, watery ham. Everything had a bright orange price tag on it, several dollars over market value for near-expired lunch meat. She slipped a package of bologna off the metal spindle and gave it a once over. The black, dot-matrix expiration date was gone, but the glue on the plastic was sealed.

The counter man took her crumpled ten-dollar bill. He stayed quiet, leaving her to stand there biting the inside of her lower lip as she eyeballed the Snickers bars, knowing Darius would count the change. He threw the meat and bread into a black plastic bag.

The corner boy didn't hit on her again as she left, but she could feel his eyes on her until she disappeared up the street. She never understood that about men. Animals driven by their pricks. She didn't need to be a full-grown woman to know that.

"What you get?" Byron asked as she shut the gated door behind her with delicate ease. Her little brother was waggling his legs against the worn cushions of the couch, the backs of his heels scuffing the bare carpet.

"Shut the fuck up," she said in a harsh whisper, one glance toward the back bedroom.

"Well?" he asked, shutting off the TV he'd been watching with the sound off.

"Sandwich stuff."

"I don't want that," he whined, quiet.

"You don't have a choice," she said.

He followed her into the kitchen and leapt up on the counter, sitting next to the stove.

"Why didn't you get like a can of chili, or even mac and cheese?" he asked, his legs waggling on the counter with the same pent up energy they'd been using to abuse the couch.

Imani grabbed his ankles before the backs of his shoes could hit the pressed wood cabinets a second time.

"Let go of me," he puffed up, wiggling out of her grip.

"You know he's trying to nap."

"He's awake. I can hear him."

"Don't matter."

"Fine."

"Good." She let go of his legs. "Get off there and grab me the spread."

Byron shoved off the counter, his feet hitting the cabinet with a loud bang. Imani gave him a harsh stare, but he shrugged at her and opened the fridge.

There wasn't much. A few condiments. Cheap beer. A couple of McDonald's hamburgers in a brown sack that were probably no good. Their momma might microwave those for dinner when she got home.

Byron plucked the mayo jar from the door and flipped it into the air. Every damn thing he touched turned into a projectile. Imani snatched it out of the air before it hit the ground and bounced off the old linoleum.

"Looks like there's only a few dollops left. Mac and cheese woulda been better."

"You got money for butter and milk?"

"If we went to the Ralphs, we would."

"You gonna explain to him why he had to wait?" Imani asked, focused on collecting as much of the generic mayo from the side of the jar as she could.

"It ain't that far away," Byron said, under his breath.

"When you're old enough to do the shopping, you do whatever you damn please."

She slapped a couple of slices of bologna onto the white bread and handed it to him.

"You know I don't like the crusts," he said.

"That's all you get for the night. You don't eat 'em, don't you dare put 'em in the garbage for momma to find when she gets home from work."

He pulled the brown strips off the top of the sandwich and took a bite of the white goo. The Wonder Bread stuck to the roof of his mouth and Imani watched him try to tongue it free before he stuck a finger in.

"Don't worry," he said, his mouth full and smacking, "I'll give 'em to Zaps."

Byron pranced out the front door, slamming the security gate behind him before darting next door to feed the neighbor's dog part of his precious dinner.

Imani stood stock-still in the kitchen, waiting for the fallout from the whirling dervish of Byron's exit.

The house was quiet for the eternity of ten shallow breaths.

Swallowing hard, Imani opened the cabinet above her head with the care of a safecracker and pulled a blue plastic plate free from the stack in the cupboard. She pulled two slices of bread from the bag and placed them on the plate, handling each of them like antiques as she spread them with the remaining mayo. Pulling twice as much meat for the sandwich as she had for Byron, she lowered the other slice of bread on top as delicately as a Jenga piece.

Violence is not the answer.

She didn't knock. Just pushed the door open. It always creaked. There was no stopping it.

Darius was sprawled on top of the sheets. His boots tossed next to the bed, a dirty t-shirt dumped on top. There were oil stains on his work pants, some of them new enough to rub off on the bedding. One arm flopped over his eyes to shade the sunlight coming through the threadbare curtains. A cigarette was burning down between his fingers.

Imani tip-toed to his bedside and slid the plate down next to the ashtray. She stood there for a moment, looking at him. Should she take the cigarette out of his hand? He could burn the house down. Or worse, burn his fingers, wake up, and look for someone to blame for his pain.

"You need somethin'?"

Imani jumped at the sound of his voice and went for the door. Her mother's boyfriend hadn't moved. The arm was still slung over his eyes and the cigarette burned ever closer to the filter. Imani left the room, the door creaking behind her as she closed it.

Her legs were shaking as she went back into the kitchen. Pressing her eyes shut to hold back the tears, she squeezed her hands into tiny fists, then spread her fingers wide. Staccato breaths went in through her nose, a faint whistle through the dried snot. She opened her eyes and fixed them on the door she'd just closed. Watching and waiting for it to fly open. Ready for another afternoon it would take years to forget.

Zaps was barking in the yard next door, hoping Byron would feed him again.

The door didn't open.

Imani steadied her shaking hands and slapped a single piece of bologna onto a single slice of bread. No more mayo. She folded it in half and took a bite, her dry mouth having trouble breaking down the processed food.

She knew she'd have to eat better.

She wasn't just feeding herself.

She was also feeding the tiny life Darius had put inside her.

4

Nick yawned deep. He exhaled a high-pitched grunt as he closed his mouth and shook his head. Sleep had been a luxury over the past few weeks. It came in minutes rather than hours.

The dreams were never the same, but the cast of players remained unchanged. The tongueless vagrant with his neck nearly garroted through. A young Hispanic man in an argyle sweater hovering over him, eyes wild. His head explodes in slow motion. The taste of grey matter in his teeth. The face of the sultry redhead in the cemetery morphed into his mother's hollow, dying eyes, accusing him of not being there when she passed.

Sunlight reflected off the concrete of the overpass and blinded him. He put a hand over his bleary eyes and looked at the complex built into the hollow formed by dirt and concrete. The cars overhead crawled through rush-hour traffic, slowed by the yellow crime scene tape a block away. Commuters hoping to get a glimpse of a gory detail they wouldn't see on the evening news.

Nick vaulted the fence and started up the dirt incline. He stopped halfway up the hill. Nick didn't want to get so high he had to crouch and couldn't defend himself in case of attack. He'd learned the hard way to know where all the exits were.

Before he could say anything, a mountain of clothes pushed aside a tin door. Forno's description of Zeke wasn't far off. A parade float of dreadlocks cascaded from his head. Dark brown cylinders between the dull colors created enough negative space that it looked like Zeke was wearing a firework as a hat. His long grey beard grew down and around his face, with no clear division of where the hair ended and the beard began. He hunched down so far it looked like his head was growing out of the middle of his chest. He had a steaming mug of tea in his hands, holding it in front of him like it was keeping him balanced. The smell emanating from behind the tin doors let Nick know it was probably a homemade privy. That or another torn open girl was rotting inside.

"Shay 'bou dat girr," Zeke croaked. Between the Creole dialect and Zeke biting down on his lower lip with loose-fitting dentures, it took Nick a second to parse out that he'd said, "Shame about that girl."

"Didn't see you down at that crime scene. You take a peek before we got there?"

Zeke laughed out a noise that sounded like a mix between a cough and a belch.

"News travealls fay," Zeke said.

Nick wished there was a Google Translate for Mumblemouth.

"And who told you?"

"Word go by on'a win' down here."

Nick's lack of sleep wasn't helping his mind process Zeke's dialect. He was going to miss something.

"The wind have a name?"

Zeke laughed again. "Naw. Not today. But, you DNA bawys done gon' hay a feel day wit dat one."

"What do you mean?" Nick asked, both for clarification and to make sure he'd heard Zeke right.

"Dat'un down 'ere a whore how. Whore tent more like," Zeke laughed.

"Street brothel?"

Zeke nodded affirmative.

"Any regular clients?"

"Oh, sure," Zeke said, "You gazin' on one here n' now."

"Had you been with that girl?"

"What I heard, too itty-bitty," Zeke said, making a gesture with his coffee mug and other hand of a sizable ass in front of his face.

"Anybody you know who might've been with her?"

"Hafta see a pitcher."

Nick pulled out his cell phone and crept up to where Zeke was standing. They looked like a unlikely pair standing there under the overpass in the early evening. Nick zoomed in on the girl's face, hiding the other atrocious things done to her.

Zeke pulled out a pair of glasses. Both lenses were different sizes, one of them a bifocal. Tape held mismatching stems together. Nick got close enough to realize that most of the smell wasn't just coming off the homemade privy.

"Looks like you need a new prescription," Nick said.

Zeke laughed, "You funny, cop."

He squinted at the picture, grabbing Nick's wrist to move it out of the sunlight. Nick was going to have to remember to wash thoroughly. Zeke didn't use any hand sanitizer coming out of the shithouse.

"Seen lotta girr come true here. She new."

"Who owns the tent?"

Zeke took off his glasses and put them into the pocket of his ratted wool coat.

"Now ye askin' d'rye question," Zeke said, "What innit fo' me?"

"New glasses?"

"These'ns work fine."

"How about I let you keep your house intact?" Nick said.

"Whoa dere. You done gone from sweetie pie to meany poo rye quick."

"I don't like people using murder victims as bargaining chips."

"Fair 'nuff. Fair 'nuff. Dunno who got the deed, but Applebox, he run 'nem girrs."

"Applebox have a real name?"

"Sure 'nuff, but I ain't know it."

"You got a description? Where he holds up?"

"Now don' go gettin' all meany poo 'geen, but cain't say," Zeke said, "You know how 'tis? Zeke no snitch. Ain't never be. Ain't never gonna."

"You already told me his name. Isn't that snitching enough?" Nick asked.

"That was fo' the girr. She don' need no mo' dead end. She diffin't."

"Different how?"

"She Ayida Weddo's girr."

"Not Applebox's girl?"

"Sho nuff. Dis here gonna get worse. You wanna know why I talk so right quick? Don't nobody cross Ayida Weddo. Ears everywhere."

"Where can I find this Ayida Weddo?"

"You don't find her. She find you. *She* a ghost."

Nick didn't think he was going to get anymore out of Zeke. Once he'd started talking about the supernatural, there wasn't much Nick could believe.

"Anything else you want to tell me?"

"One ting might hell you a bit. Applebox like 'em farmer's marks."

"Thought you weren't a snitch?"

"Ain't. Everybody like 'em farmer's marks. Fresh fruit."

"No detailed description for me, then?"

"I helpfoo, ain't stupid."

Zeke took a sip of his tea and went into his tent. A signal to Nick that the interview was over. For all Nick knew, Zeke could've been hiding Ayida Weddo in that complex, five feet from where they'd been talking. But Zeke had given Nick some valuable information and didn't look like he had any plans to pick up shop and move.

Nick pulled out his phone as he made his way down the dirt and dialed Hsu.

"Hey. Float the name Applebox to Forno. See his reaction."

"Got it," Hsu said. "Anything else?"

"In your time in Vice, you ever heard the name Ayida Weddo?"

"Nope. But, I'll run it through the system. Anything else?"

"That tent was a street brothel. Lots of clients. See if Forno was one of them. If we can get another girl, maybe we can I.D. our victim."

"You heading back in?" Hsu asked.

"I'm going to see what else I can get out here. Is the tent's owner stewing somewhere?"

"Naches is working on him," Hsu said.

"Once they're done cataloging and photographing everything, they'll pack up the whole tent as evidence. If that's his primary residence, he'll either give his name to claim his property later, or move on and set up another one," Nick said.

"If he's smart, he'll disappear," Hsu said.

"We're going to have a lot of disappearing witnesses on this one, huh?" Nick asked.

"I'm sure we've lost a handful already."

"I'm going to wrap up here and make one more stop. I get any more witnesses, I'll send 'em your way."

"Where you headed?"

Nick heard Zeke cough something up and spit it out.

"Gonna go pick up some fresh fruit."

"That guy."

"That guy?"

"That guy."

Deuce nodded to the man in the corner of Nate's Place. The man's hair receded like Lake Mead in a drought. The bad dye job was twenty years into an unending mid-life crisis. He was wearing a letterman's jacket for Miller High Life. Under it, a red polo shirt and khaki pants. He was singing along to every single song that came on the jukebox.

Every. Single. Song.

At the top of his lungs.

"That guy?"

"Yeah, for fuck's sake, Leo, that guy," Deuce said.

Ray Cobb made a conscious effort to respond to the name "Leo." He took a deep breath in.

"What's his drink?"

"Jack and RC Cola with a splash of orange juice."

"Fuck off."

"I told you he was weird. They stock RC here for him special," Deuce said.

"Seriously, stop fucking with me. Not in the mood."

The lunch crowd had yet to saunter in. The town was still waking up from their hangovers the night before and the bar was nearly empty. Deuce flagged down the bartender and ordered a Reggie Special. Without a beat, the bartender poured a shot of Jack Daniels, cracked open a can of RC from the mini-fridge, and splashed it with orange juice from a plastic decanter.

"Anything else I should know?"

"Yeah," Deuce wiped his smile clean, "Don't piss him off."

Ray snatched the drink off the bar as Deuce tossed down a couple of bills and took a seat.

"Can I join you?"

Reggie waggled his fingers at the drink Ray held in his hand. Ray set it down on the table within arm's reach and went to pull out the chair across from the balding weirdo.

"I don't remember asking you to sit down," Reggie said before snatching up the drink and taking a hefty sip.

Ray looked over at Deuce, who had his back to the table, hunched over a half-full pint of skunky domestic pilsner.

"So, what does this drink buy me?" Ray asked.

"Nothing," Reggie said.

The song on the digital jukebox changed.

"Ohhh, I love this."

He played the opening drum beat of *Take the Money and Run* on the table, sung out the "WHO-WHO" along with the band, then slid the empty glass across the table.

"I'll take another, though," Reggie said, "But on your dime. Not his."

"And if I don't have the money to pay for another one of your little concoctions?"

"Then you can live with that tattoo on your arm for the rest of your life. Never knowing when someone is going to show up and remove the arm it's attached to," Reggie said without threat.

It was all Ray needed. Confirmation. After weeks of searching, he'd finally found the path again.

Three weeks in the snow. Ray couldn't believe he'd been in Big Bear that long with no answers. No knowledge of what went on outside of the frigid mountain hamlet. For all he knew, there was a manhunt underway for his arrest. Retribution for his involvement in a string of deaths. All it took was a dead movie star's stolen car to set him on a new track. Ray had abandoned Low Seward's Audi almost as soon as he'd gotten into town.

He was surprised the slick coupe had made the winding drive through the snowy mountain pass without snow chains. It was under a couple of feet of snow as far into the woods as it would go. He didn't want to get caught sleeping in it. Once he'd reached the frozen lake, the flurries had started, and Ray regretted his hasty decision to venture into the mountains and search for the man who'd placed him into involuntary servitude.

Winter in the mountains.

Homeless in unfamiliar territory.

No resources. No allies.

Seemed like a good idea.

"You've got five minutes," Reggie said, "And you can't get it from him."

Ray walked over to the bar and sidled up next to Deuce.

"Let's go," Ray said. He wouldn't play this fucker's little drinking game. He was back on the right track.

Deuce kept his eyes on his beer and shook his head "no". The kid feared the eccentric asshole. And as Deuce was the only other person in town he'd met with a Bear tattoo, he had reason to believe that fear was real.

Ray turned his attention to the bartender.

"How much for one of those shitty cocktails?" he nodded over to Reggie's table.

"For you? Six bucks," the bartender said.

"And for him?" Ray asked, thumb thrust over his shoulder at the cocky asshole sitting alone.

"On the house."

"I suppose there's not a transfer of that privilege knowing where the drink is going?"

"Nope. And if you attack anyone in my bar, I'll have you arrested."

Ray squinted his eyes in confusion. Why the hell would he assume that would be Ray's first instinct? Ray wasn't the first participant in Reggie's little game.

"Four minutes," Reggie said. He was shaking his shoulders along with the opening guitar riff of *Abracadabra*. "Ooo, rock block."

Ray scanned the tables in the back of the bar. No one had left an errant tip under a ketchup bottle or accidentally dropped a bill searching for change. A group of teens played pool in the back, but they were all sipping waters and looked like they'd had enough trouble scrounging together a buck fifty between the four of them for a game of eight-ball.

"Be right back."

Ray swung the front door open and stepped out into the cold.

A couple in matching snow gear were walking in from the parking lot. Ray knew the type. In their own little world, oblivious to those less fortunate than themselves, but adventurous enough to take in a bit of the local flavor before making their way to the craft brewery in downtown Big Bear for some gourmet jalapeño poppers. They were going to be a tough mark, but were more likely to be carrying extra cash than a local. The woman had her hands in the pockets of her down coat and the guy was twirling the key fob to his car around his finger like he was Wild Bill Hickok.

Ray stopped them just before they pulled open the glass door to the bar.

"Excuse me?" Ray asked. He put on a lighter tone. A nervous voice. What panhandlers called the "I never do this, but—" voice.

"Yeah?" the guy said, still in stride.

"This may sound stupid, but I ran out of gas, just down the mountain a piece. Didn't think it would take me as much to get up here, but traffic... any chance I could get six or seven bucks from you for a gas can and a gallon to get back up here?"

"Sorry, pal, heard that scam before."

The woman remained silent, but squished up against her man.

"Shit, listen, you're right, but just one sec," Ray said, the clock ticking in his head. "You see that guy in there?"

Ray pointed at Reggie, who waved back with a crooked smile.

"I bet him I could convince the next people who came into the bar to give me some cash because he talks shit all the time about being the most persuasive asshole on the planet."

"Can't help you," the guy said, annoyed.

"All right," Ray shrugged, "But you'll regret it when he's singing at the top of his lungs while you're trying to enjoy your Chablis."

The couple pushed past Ray into the bar.

Ray stepped off the curb into the parking lot. He glanced inside to confirm the couple was engaged in deciding on their drink choices before he bolted for the BMW. It was the only one in the lot whose logo matched the key fob the guy was swinging in Ray's face. The woman's purse hadn't been slung across her shoulder and the brown leather strap snaked across the floor mat where it was hastily shoved under the passenger seat.

He tried the door handle.

Locked. That would've been too easy.

Ray didn't need to glance back at the window to know that the clock was ticking. There weren't enough cars in the parking lot to mask him breaking the BMW's window and grabbing the purse without alerting passersby. Most people had already made their way up to the mountain for the day and he'd be an easy I.D. He'd get the information he was looking for, but would probably get arrested. He scanned the lot.

Someone had run into the handicapped parking sign when they'd pulled out in a drunken stupor. The crooked metal was attached to a piece of concrete worn down by people dragging it back and forth, but never actually throwing it away or replacing it. Ray placed his hands at the bottom of the sign and heaved. The cold metal dug into his hands and the strain did something awful to the scars at this belly, but he could lift it. He set it down and jogged back into the bar.

"Your parking lot isn't exactly a hotbed of activity," Ray said as he bellied up to the bar. "You sure you can't float me just this once? It'd be in your best interest."

"What'd I tell you the first time?" the bartender said.

"Fine." Ray turned around and beelined for the kids playing pool.

"Hey, I'll buy your next ten games if you tell me what you drove here," Ray said.

"Why? You in the market to buy a car?" a scrawny kid with black hair asked.

"You want the games or not?"

"Ford Fiesta," one said.

"Jeep Cherokee," said another.

"Anybody else?" Ray asked.

The two girls shrugged, brought there by their dates.

Ray darted back toward the front door.

Reggie called out, "Two minutes," as he passed.

He ran for the sign, grabbed it, and dragged the concrete through the snow. Hefting it hard, he flung the sign through the windshield of a rusted Toyota Tacoma. The shattering glass and cheap alarm brought the bartender running, but Ray had already disappeared.

"What the fuck?" the bartender screamed, "You fucking asshole, I'll kill you!"

He turned back to the bar just in time to see Ray's heavy breath fogging up the inside of the window, flicking the lock on the door.

Ray then strolled around to the back of the bar, poured a heavy shot of Jack into a tumbler, topped it off with RC and orange juice, and sauntered back over to where Reggie was sitting. He set the glass down, out of breath.

"Clever move," Reggie said. "How did you know it wasn't my car?"

"I didn't care," Ray said.

The bartender was slamming his hands against the doors, threatening Ray, begging the BMW couple to do something about his being locked out, but they were paralyzed by what the crazy beggar might do next.

"I'll be in touch," Reggie said.

"Good," Ray said, then turned to Deuce. "Time to go."

"Are you fucking nuts, Leo? I come in here all the time."

"Plenty of other bars in town."

The bartender had given up on the front door and was running around to the side door by the pool table where Ray had gotten back inside.

"Pool's free as long as he's out there," Ray called to the kids at the table, "Booze, too."

The dark-haired kid flicked the lock on the door as his buddy grabbed beers and quarters out of the register. The idiots didn't have the sense to leave like Ray and Deuce, who were already disappearing through the parking lot.

6

Nick wandered between the white tents. He was pretty sure if someone had murdered a girl a few miles away, they wouldn't be shopping for fresh fruits and vegetables, but killing someone without care led people to do strange things. A few years before, the Santa Monica police were tracking someone with a mobile pet grooming business. The only way they caught the guy was that all the victims had pets with a recent haircut. It was strange where patterns emerged when you went looking for them.

Expecting Applebox to be browsing through the Red Delicious at this market was a long shot, but if he frequented the markets enough that Zeke called it out, someone else could give him the description that Zeke withheld.

"Strawberry?" a middle-aged Hispanic man asked. He held a plump, red heart in his hand for Nick to try.

"Thanks," Nick said. He took a bite and pink juice dribbled down his chin. The vendor knew his fruit.

"Six a pint, two for ten."

He scanned the rows of pints. Strawberries blended in an intricate color pattern with blueberries, raspberries, and blackberries. Nick wanted to pick out a pound where the color matched the intensity of the berry he'd just eaten. The others didn't look as good. Nick's guess was the vendor plucked the finest ones out to give as free samples, then unloaded the less favorable berries once someone had a taste. It was a tactic heroin dealers had been using for decades.

Nick peered down the aisle. There were at least four more identical berry stalls. If he felt obliged to buy a pint from everyone who offered him a free sample, he'd have an empty wallet and three days worth of strawberry shits. He decided to just ask.

"You ever see a homeless guy around here, goes by the name of Applebox?"

"Lots," the vendor nodded.

"How often?"

"Lots of homeless."

"Ah." There was an obvious language barrier. "Okay, thank you."

All Nick had was a street name. It seemed like an obvious and kind of stupid idea, but he headed straight for the apple vendors.

"Those Pink Ladies are best right now," the woman behind the table said.

Nick picked up one of the firm fruits and gave it a slight squeeze. The skin had the high shine of a marble floor.

"I'm looking for someone. Maybe you can help me."

He put down the apple and pulled out his badge. After speaking to several vendors, Nick realized there was no underground fruit conspiracy network. The farmer's market folks weren't the cop-hating hippies of old. They were organic farmers looking to make a buck outside the supermarket system. Most of them probably still functioned only because they got a small government grant.

"Hope I can help," the woman said. She brushed the wisps of blonde hair out of her face.

"Guy who calls himself Applebox. Likes to frequent these things. Probably a homeless guy."

She took in a deep breath and gazed up into the sky as if she was searching for a memory there.

"Jeez. Don't really get a lot of folks names, honestly. What does he look like?"

"I have no idea," Nick said.

She laughed and put her hands on her hips.

"Doesn't give me much to go on."

"Yeah, well, this is the job. A big maze with lots of dead ends," he said. "Anybody ask you for left over boxes?"

"Not really. If you're looking for a homeless guy, they're more likely to ask for a free sample than an empty box. They stay away from food cartons because the residual whatever in them attracts bugs."

"Most of these street nicknames are inside jokes, anyway. My guess is it has nothing to do at all with apples."

"He comes to this farmer's market? There's a bunch of 'em."

"Again, no clue."

"Okay. Sure you don't want to buy some apples?" she smiled.

"No offense, but if I bought something from everyone I questioned today, I'd have a condo full of rotting fruit by the end of the week."

"Worse things to spend your money on."

"Thanks for taking the time," Nick said. He turned to go.

"Hey, don't know if this will help, but there's this guy. He doesn't come every week, but he never seems to turn the homeless away from his table. He's always talking to them. Honey guy."

"Honey guy?"

"Yeah, you know, a guy who sells honey. Honey guy. Every market has to have a good honey guy. One time he tried to buy bees off of me."

"You sell bees too?"

"No, but bees keep my orchard pollinated. Told me he'd give me a good price if I captured a queen for him. Not that

I know how to do that, so I turned him down. If he doesn't have apple blossoms, his bee vomit wouldn't taste like my bee vomit."

"Bee vomit?"

"That's really all honey is. Sweet, precious bee vomit," she smiled and took a bite of one of her own apples. "Makes these seem more appetizing, right?"

"You have an interesting sales technique," Nick said.

"Buy a dozen and I'll give you the organizer's card. Help you track the guy down."

"You won't do it out of the kindness of your heart?"

"Girl's gotta make a living."

"How much?"

"Cop rate. Five bucks."

Nick handed over five ones. She threw twelve hand-picked apples into a repurposed grocery bag and handed them over. Then she pulled her purse out from under the table, dug through her wallet, and handed Nick a business card.

"California Farmer's Market Association," Nick read, then looked up. "I could've just Googled that, couldn't I?"

"Yep," she said, "But now you have the benefit of some healthy food."

"Sneaky." He pulled out his own wallet and slipped in the card, then handed her one of his own. "Just in case you run into honey guy before I do."

"You got it. Enjoy the apples."

Nick smiled and slung the bag over his shoulder before walking away.

Bee vomit.

That was a new one.

7

Early afternoon sunlight squeezed through the bare trees and made the fresh snow sparkle like glitter. The whirr of a chainsaw echoed through the empty forest, the sound growing in intensity as it ate into the raw wood, white from lack of exposure to the elements. Flecks of bark curved the dark of the nose and eyes, but every other cut created the texture of fur. Small clawed hands took shape, hugging the bear's torso as though the creature had just consumed a large dinner of grubs made from the wood chips flying from the rotating blade.

The motor idled as the sculptor admired his work, assessing where to finesse the next etch. Master wood carvers can see where the edges need to be. Where the application of varnish later in the process would play games with light and shadow to create the illusion of depth and expression in the dead thing.

Xavier Malkin shut the engine off and set the small carving chainsaw down in the snow when he saw Reggie's car pull into the driveway. He heard the car door slam behind him as he used a piece of sandpaper to detail the edges of the chainsaw's rough work. The sunlight reflected off his scalp through his thinning blonde hair as he wiped away sweat with his sleeve.

Reggie had a pink smoothie in a 32 oz. BPA-free bottle and was shaking it up. He handed it over to Malkin, who unscrewed the top and took a big chug.

"What did you find out?"

"He's not exactly subtle," Reggie said. He was chewing his way through one of the red Twizzlers he clutched in his fist. A typical Reggie lunch.

"Learned that from the bathhouse," Malkin said, more to the bear than Reggie.

"The asshole put a concrete sign through Art's windshield and locked him out of the bar. Took everything I had in my pockets to calm Art down and convince him not to call in the sheriff. It was more than enough to cover the cost of the damage, but I don't think Art will hesitate to seek his own justice if he sees Cobb in the street."

"I told you not to play any of your games with him."

"I wanted to see how smart he was for myself," Reggie shrugged.

"He must be impatient."

"Should've killed him as soon as he got into town."

"What good would that have done?" Malkin asked. He swatted the sawdust from his gloves and shoved them in the back pocket of his jeans.

"You can't control him."

"Maybe," Malkin said, "but he's proved resourceful so far."

"Resourceful? Do you know how much he's cost us?"

Malkin pulled the carving knife from his belt and straddled the sculpture. He edged the blade along the dark sockets of the bear's eyes, thin strips of wood peeling off like warm butter.

"We have more money. Have you, perhaps, thought about it from a different angle?" Malkin said.

Reggie bit into another Twizzler. He swallowed, then used his thumb to mine a piece of chewy red goo from one of his molars.

"I'm all about the power of positivity, but you want to tell me how a homeless man taking down a huge revenue stream is a positive?"

"Your answer is in your question, my friend." Malkin curved the blade up along the bear's mouth, turning the maw of teeth into a menacing smile. "In the short-lived rollout, the drug already left a trail of bodies. It was supposed to be a suggestive hallucinogen, designed to make problem children like our Mr. Cobb more pliable. Our chemist was more concerned with his prey than creating a reliable product distribution system, and our enforcer used honor and superstition to guide his decisions. Ray Cobb did nothing for us but systematically expose each of these flaws. One homeless man was all it took to root out the bugs. Sure, we had to abandon the operation and the remaining product was confiscated, but I chalk it up to R&D. It was a drug trial that didn't work."

Malkin dug the knife deep into the top of the log, carving along the edge of the ear. His hand slipped, and he took a significant chunk out of the top of the bear's head. He cursed under his breath and tipped the sculpture back to get a perspective on its face. The gouge out of the side was hardly noticeable, but it gave the bear a lopsided look.

"Until today, he had no way of finding us. We control the narrative."

Malkin closed the knife. He pulled the gloves out of his back pocket and stretched the safety goggles down off of his forehead. With one pull of the cord, the chainsaw roared back to life.

"What next?"

"If we expose ourselves to him without an advantage, there's no telling what he could do. As you've seen, he's unpredictable."

Malkin revved the chainsaw up to full power and pressed the blade into the neck of his ursine creation. Sharp chains cut clear through the wood in a swift motion. The intricately carved head of the bear spun off the log and flopped into the snow. He split the remaining body of the log, set the chainsaw down, and tossed the pieces into a pile of scrap wood he would later use for his fire.

"I'm aware you can't fix some mistakes," Malkin said. "However, some mistakes can be opportunities."

He took another large gulp of the protein smoothie, put a heavy log up on his carving block, and shaved off the grey bark to get at the malleable meat underneath.

8

"He's exercising his right to remain silent," Hsu said.

The owner of the tent where they found the girl had given his name as Yusuf Veli at the crime scene. Veli gave a statement to the police about his whereabouts the night before and had said that he'd given the girl permission to sleep in his tent. It would take them a few days to sort through any video footage they could get from the area to verify the alibi. Now that Nick and Hsu had him in an interview room, he hadn't said another word.

"Anything out of Forno?" Nick asked.

"He no longer works at Costco. Hasn't for a few months, so that was a lie," Hsu said, "Search of his tent came up with the usual street contraband. No weapons. Drug residue. Forno's habit doesn't result in a lot of stockpiling."

"You confront him with it?"

"Just with the lie. He admitted to it quick. But that's all he admitted to. Still claims to have never seen the girl before."

"What about the cash?" Nick asked.

"Told me it's all the money he has in the world. Doesn't believe in banks," Hsu said. "Can't say that I blame him."

"What he gave me on Zeke was good."

"From where I'm standing, all it got you was some fruit," Hsu said. As usual, there was nothing behind the comment. He was just stating a fact. Hsu was always short on subtext.

"Ayida Weddo?" Nick asked.

"Not in our database. But I looked it up. Voodoo Fertility Goddess. Known as the wife of the Sky God, called The Rainbow Serpent. It's actually an interesting—"

"So, not someone we have an address on," Nick cut Hsu off before he listed off the entire Voodoo pantheon Wikipedia page.

"Likely a nickname, just like Applebox. The mad ravings of a man who lives under an overpass," Hsu said.

"You got anywhere to be tonight?" Nick asked.

"Already called off my dinner plans. You?"

"Nope," Nick said. "Go back to Forno and see what you can get on Veli. I'll see if I can get this one to open his mouth. He hasn't asked for a lawyer or to be released, so we might catch him in something."

"You know of some interrogation technique I'm not familiar with?" Hsu asked.

"Good Cop, Annoying Cop."

"We know you're not the former, might as well be the latter," Hsu headed toward the other interview room.

"That was actually pretty good," Nick said to himself. There might be something to this partnership yet.

He opened his bag of apples and pulled out two.

In the interview room, Veli kept his head down when Nick opened and shut the door.

"I'm sure my partner told you this, but since we've taken custody of your residence, we're going to have to hold you until we can verify your alibi."

No response.

Nick set an apple on the table in front of Veli. He shined the other against his shirt and took a loud bite. Sweet juice dribbled down his chin. He wiped it away with his sleeve.

"Mmm," Nick said, mouth full, "That's good. Pink Ladies, they're called. Just came from the farmer's market. I like the farmer's markets. Fresh fruit and veggies. Better for you. You get to them much?"

Veli shifted in his chair, but said nothing.

"That one's for you, if you want it."

He took another noisy bite. Nick hoped aggravating Veli into talking would work.

"My partner likes you for this. Your tent. Your stuff. It'd be a quick trial. State would have you dead to rights. The jury selection would just be for show. Sure you don't want that apple?"

Veli shook his head. Nick tried not to let his smile show. He was one step closer to words.

"Of course, if it wasn't your tent, and you were covering for somebody, you still wouldn't be out of the clear. You know how they excavate dinosaur bones?"

Veli's brow furrowed in confusion. It was what Nick wanted. Keep him guessing.

"They dig a little to get the top layer away, then they go at it with these little brushes. Dusting. Patient." He bit into the apple again. "Then, over time, they reveal the bones. If a certain spot is really hard, they go at it from a different angle until they loosen the dirt and it crumbles. If they used any bigger tools or a heavier brush, they could damage the bones. Saw that on The Discovery Channel."

The suspect settled back into his chair.

"Just kidding. What I know about dinosaurs I got from *Jurassic Park*."

Nick set the apple core on the table next to the untouched piece of fruit.

"See, here's where we're at. Whoever killed this girl, they're our dinosaur bones, right? And you? You're the dirt. You're the tough dirt right now. But if I brush in another place, I'm still going to knock loose the information I need. You're going to crumble. Like dust. Or something. I don't know, that metaphor got away from me. Point is, if you don't tell me what really happened last night, someone else will. We've got your neighbor, Forno, next door. Found a ten-dollar bag of something nasty in his tent and I'm sure he'd roll over on anyone to avoid the mandatory minimum on that."

Veli began shuffling in his seat. If nothing else, Nick was getting under his skin.

"Okay, so forget the dinosaur thing. Too abstract. I get it." Nick gestured to the apple on the table. "Right now, you're this guy, plump and juicy. Shiny. And we're going to take little bites out of you until you're nothing but a core. And what do we do with apple cores? We throw them away."

Nick grabbed the apple core and did a hook basketball shot to the garbage can in the corner. He missed. By a lot.

"That probably would've been cooler if I'd made it," Nick said. "You know a pimp named Applebox?"

Veli stopped moving and straightened up before he knew what he was doing.

Ding! We have a winner!

Nick picked up the other apple and took a tiny bite out of the top. He set it back down in front of Veli.

"See what I did there? I brushed a little of the dust away," Nick said, pointing to the apple.

"You mean you took a bite?" Veli said in his thick Turkish accent, unable to hold back any longer.

"Yeah, you're right. That's why I hate metaphors. Or are they similes? English is a weird language."

"What are you talking about? Shut up. Please, shut up!" Veli snapped.

"My partner is better at this than I am. He's already got a full confession from Forno, who said he saw you last night. I couldn't get anything out of him... ah, fuck. I wasn't... forget I said that."

"I know what you are doing. I am not stupid. Forno saw nothing."

"Fine. Give me the actual story and I'll leave you alone."

"It is like I said. The girl asked me to sleep there, I said yes. Then I slept down at MacArthur Park. That is the story."

"You usually let women sleep in your tent out of the kindness of your heart?"

"No, of course not. I thought she would..." His eyebrows went up to finish the sentence.

"You can't be that hard up. Pregnant tail? Unless you're into that sort of thing. What I hear is that you're running a skin ring out of that tent?"

"*I* am not."

"*You're* not? But someone is? You, what, rent space?"

"Something like that."

"So, no clients last night? There was no room at the inn, so you provided your manger?"

"What?"

"It's a bible ref—you know what? Now I'm annoying myself. Let's cut the shit. Applebox runs girls out of that tent. Something went wrong last night. He told you to give us a story, right?"

"I am not aware of anyone called Applebox."

"Forget the name. Does that sound right?"

"I am not giving you any reason to arrest me."

"You've already given me a reason. See, I couldn't softly brush away the dirt, so I—"

"Stop with the dinosaur nonsense!"

Nick stopped and smiled.

"You're an accessory on this. I can charge you right now. Or you give me a bargaining chip."

"I told you, I do not know anyone that is called Applebox!"

"But do you admit it's not your tent?"

Veli stayed quiet.

"Come on, Yusuf, don't clam up on me now."

"I told you what I told you already. I think I am finished talking."

"If you're afraid of someone, we can make them go away."

Veli shook his head.

There was a knock at the door. Hsu. Nick hoped he'd been watching. He got up and answered. Hsu pulled him into the hallway.

"I see you broke his vow of silence," Hsu said.

"Forno give you anything else."

"No. It seems he was doing nothing but protecting his stash. Didn't know Veli except in passing. Didn't know the girl. I'm ready to cut him loose."

"The name Applebox got no reactions from him?"

Hsu shook his head. Nick wondered whether Zeke had fed him a load of shit.

"I still think we can get something out of Veli. Someone put him up to that story. Someone he's afraid of. He doesn't know what he's doing, otherwise he would've lawyered up a long time ago. How do you think I should play this?" Nick asked.

"Lay it out," Hsu said, "His story. His tent. His body. He doesn't give us a name, we arrest him for the murder. He can stay silent if he wants, but talking is the only thing that will help him now. If he knew he could get up and walk away, he would have already."

"You want to do it?"

"No. He doesn't trust me," Hsu said.

"Okay. Let's hold Forno for a bit, see if time alone gets him jumpy. He's gone as soon as he's out the door." Nick pulled the business card he'd gotten at the farmer's market out of his shirt pocket and handed it to Hsu. "While you're waiting, could you give this guy a call? Ask him about who has rented space for a honey booth over the past few months. Get a list of names."

"First apples, now honey? Is there a method to this madness?" Hsu asked, taking the card.

"Nope," Nick said. "Forno leave any of that pizza?"

"A slice or two, but it's cold."

"I'll take it."

Hsu jogged around the corner and grabbed what was left. The cheese had congealed and there was a smear of marinara sauce on the plate, but Nick couldn't be sure of the last time Veli ate.

He went back into the interview room and slid the plate across the table. Veli eyed it with suspicion.

"Sorry it's cold. I can order a fresh one if you'd like."

"Is there meat on this?" Veli asked. "I'm a vegetarian."

"You'd think living on the street, you wouldn't be picky."

Veli scowled. "I have not always lived on the street. Sometimes one has to bear the burden of their principles."

Nick wanted to dig into Veli for his tone, but all he said was, "It's just cheese."

Veli picked up the first piece with ginger care, but it was gone before Nick could blink. The second went the same way. Nick tossed the paper plate into the garbage before Veli could eat that, too.

"How'd you end up where you are?" Nick asked.

"Same as everyone, I suppose."

"You don't seem crazy. Or like an addict," Nick offered.

"Life picked away at me. Wish I could do some of what the others do on the street. At least the addicts can forget their lives for a few minutes every day."

"But you have principles?"

Veli nodded.

"Have you applied for Section 8?"

"The rotten city is how I got out there. Tax nonsense once I became an official citizen. They began garnishing my wages. Soon, there was nothing left. Kicked out of my apartment. So, I bought a tent. Saw the tent cities all over the place, nobody telling anyone to leave, so I figured, why not?"

"I get it. Gentrification is driving everybody out of downtown. People are looking for anywhere to hang their hats."

It wasn't something Nick was saying to empathize. He'd recently driven through the neighborhood he'd grown up in. A place where he once had to be careful walking home from school. The lot where his childhood home once stood was now a fourplex of modern condos, the ground floor studio starting around $1.5 million. The mini-mart down on the corner of Washington was now a cold-pressed juice stand. Instead of finding people homes by making housing affordable, advocates were looking for a way to make sleeping on the street legal. If anyone had any illusions about the growing income disparity in America, all they had to do was walk a street in Los Angeles.

"May I go? I have told you what I had to tell you. It is not my fault the girl died," Veli said. The desperation in his voice was growing. Nick could see he realized he was in deeper than he thought he'd be.

"I want you to look at it from my perspective, Yusuf. The tent is yours. You claim you spoke to the victim the night before, but you don't know her name. Never seen her before, yet you let her sleep in your tent. No one sees anyone else go in or out of that tent last night. The next morning, the girl is dead. Not just killed. Torn apart. I want you to take one step back for a moment. What conclusions would you draw from this situation?"

Veli's eyes flicked back and forth at the ceiling. Nick could see he was taking in all the information. It was time to go in for the kill.

"There's no guarantee we can verify your alibi for last night. And even if there was, it's going to take us weeks to get that info. Right now, I can have you arrested for trespassing and vagrancy. And from what you told me, maybe even tax evasion. And in that time we hold you, we'll be gathering evidence in a murder case against you. Tell us whose tent that really is. Think about the girl. Does covering for what happened to her meet with your principles, too? Who are you covering for?"

Veli grabbed his face and rubbed it until it was red. When he placed his palms on the table, his eyes were bloodshot and full of fear. Then he spoke. Low and quiet.

"I was looking for work at the Jollibee. When they rejected me, I went begging for change to get back on the train. This man comes up to me and holds out a bill. He tells me all I have to do is go down to MacArthur Park, walk around, then come back to Vermont and tell a story."

"And you'd never seen him before?"

"Nope."

Nick slammed his hands down on the table and stood up, flipping his chair over.

"Stop fucking lying! Why the fuck would you cover for someone you never met and take the rap on a murder like this? Why would a murderer trust a random stranger with his alibi? And most of all, why the fuck are you so fucking scared of him?"

"You saw what he did to her!" Veli yelled back. "I am supposed to trust that will not happen to me?"

"What *who* did to her?"

"I," Veli took a breath, "I use the tent sometimes. Have sex with the girls. They are cheap. Last night, I came up to get some pleasure. This man tells me the store is closed. I put up a fuss, but he is frightening, this guy. He does not need to tell you twice. He gives me this story to feed you in the morning. Tells me my next five pumps are on the house. I know him, but he is not who I usually deal with for the... pleasure. But I swear, I did not know. Please, I do not... if he finds out...," Veli started crying.

"Name."

"Do not make me..."

"Name."

Veli clutched at his shirt like he was looking for any sort of comfort. "Sketch. Calls himself Sketch."

"Real name."

"I do not know it."

"Name."

Veli shifted in his seat. Nick held eye contact.

"He has got this blade he uses. One of those... butterfly knives. Did not think he would use that knife to do something like this."

"What's he look like?" Nick said. He was still standing, his hackles up.

"Black guy. Little taller than me. He has got this weathered face, like he is old, but his hair is perfect, no gray."

"You just described half the population of Inglewood."

"His hands," Veli said, like he was remembering all the sudden. "It must have taken him a lot of practice to get good with that knife. His hands, covered in tiny scars."

"That I can work with," Nick said. "Where can I find him?"

"I do not know. I have seen him all over."

"Like where you live? Down by the 110?"

"Once or twice."

"Where else?"

"Do you want a list of every place I ever seen him? People do not spend all day standing still."

"Okay. It's a start."

Nick put his chair back, grabbed the garbage can from the corner of the room, and went to the door.

"So, what now?" Veli asked.

"You saw what he did to that girl. Someone carved her into nothing. And you still lied to me. You and your principles can fucking rot."

Nick slammed the door behind him.

9

Water swirled around him. He thought it was the bathhouse, but it was too murky. Dark and green. Somehow her hair kept her curl as it swayed in the dirty depths. He could see the tips of her fingers. So tiny. Stretched out. Asking to be pulled up and away. But he couldn't reach.

Da—

Ray bolted awake, sweating. He wiped his forehead and his hand came away drenched.

Two days.

Deuce had been missing for two days. They had pissed off Reggie. Deuce might already be dead.

Ray had no choice but to wait for him to return. After the incident at the bar with Reggie and the bartender, he was staying as far away from the sheriff's office as possible. Though no one had come knocking on the door of Deuce's trailer looking for them, Ray wasn't about to offer himself up on a silver platter. When he went to the Grizzly Manor to see if Deuce had been coming in for his shifts, the hostess told him Deuce had been out sick for a couple of days. When Ray asked if Deuce had made the call, if they had heard his actual voice over the phone, it elicited some odd looks and he figured pushing the issue would put him on law enforcement's radar. He went back to visit the Stooges, but they hadn't seen Deuce either. Gortex was giving him the third degree about the wallet he'd supposedly returned. Ray could tell that they had their suspicions about his involvement with Deuce's disappearance as well.

That was all he had. A month in Big Bear and he'd exhausted all of his contacts. He never thought he'd say it, but Ray missed L.A. At least there he knew how to solve problems. Here, he was nothing but a stranger in a strange land. He had no choice but to wait.

Sleep only happened by accident. Now that Ray's only ally had disappeared, it came only out of sheer exhaustion. Dreams flooded with images. Benny 7-11, Deuce, The Bear, then—

His mind morphed the face into something else, someone from a distant and forgotten time. Dull thuds from his conscious mind took the helm and shoved him out of REM sleep.

The sound was something else, though. A pounding. Nails through plywood.

Ray sat up on the makeshift bed that also served as the dining room. The inside of the trailer was dark. Darker than usual. The orange-yellow glow of the nearest streetlight usually burned bright on the corner. Many tenants had complained about the brightness and had moved. Deuce, being the happy-go-lucky guy he was, had no problem paying less rent for an undesirable plot. Anyone who had spent a stint in lockup knew that a buzzing artificial light was nothing to complain about. The curtains on the trailer were thick polyester, but the light snuck into the gaps.

Now the light was gone. The trailer was pitch black.

Ray flipped open the curtains with one finger to see if the light had gone out. Something was blocking the windows. And that wasn't the only problem.

The pounding had stopped. And the trailer was moving.

If Deuce had returned from his sabbatical in a hurry, ready to hitch his trailer to a truck and pick up stakes, Ray could understand. But why would he board up all the windows?

Ray tried the door. The handle wouldn't budge. Someone had shoved something in the keyhole from outside and broken it off. He couldn't get enough leverage to slam his body against it. The trailer was canting backwards.

Beneath the trailer, he could hear the tires turn from plowed blacktop onto packed snow. They'd gone off-road. Wherever they were taking him, it was away from civilization.

Ray looked for the small fire extinguisher from beside the kitchen cabinet. It was gone. How long had it been gone? Wouldn't he have noticed the bright red cylinder missing from its berth?

Ray grabbed his boots and yanked them on without lacing them up. He kicked out at the window. There was more holding them there than a few nails. The wood didn't budge.

Then the trailer stopped.

A panicked person would have banged on the windows and door. Calling out for help. Ray wasn't one of those people. The boards were there for a reason. Outside, he could hear a set of footfalls crunching in the packed, frozen snow. A hand cranked up the trailer from the hitch on the back of the truck and another person drove the truck away. Then, nothing.

Except a familiar, unpleasant smell.

The trailer was on fire.

Flames hadn't reached the inside of the trailer yet, but the distinct smoke from burning insulation was filling the cabin with rapid intensity.

Without thinking, he went for the handle to the door again, but it was white hot and singed his palm. He wrapped his hand in the blanket he'd been sleeping on and pushed down on the handle, his shoulder heaving into the metal door, but it still didn't give.

He took a deep breath in to yell for help, but his lungs filled with airborne tendrils of roasted fiberglass and tore at his throat. He pushed into the back bedroom of the trailer, Deuce's private space, and flung open each of the windows. All of them had a plywood barrier, edges charring where the flames grew.

Whoever had trapped him inside had been watching him. Watched him drift into the heavy sleep of an emotionally exhausted being. Boarded up the trailer efficiently. A calculated move. Well planned.

His brain went to elementary school. What to do in case of fire. Get low, smoke rises. Smoke inhalation kills more than fire does.

Ray crawled to the trailer's tiny bathroom and dunked the sheet around his hand into the blue water of the portable sewage system. He wrapped the sheet around his face, blue fragrant water dripping down his neck. He was running out of time and air. The doors and windows weren't an option.

Skylight. The thick bubble of heavy plastic that never let in enough light. Ray used to stare up at it before he fell asleep, wondering what the point of it was. Now he hoped it would serve one lifesaving purpose.

Coughing, Ray scanned the darkening trailer for something to get through the sealed dome in the ceiling. Deuce didn't clean enough to waste money on a broom or mop. He'd have to get creative.

Above the stove were long pressboard cabinets. They covered the ventilation shaft which kept the tiny gas heater from bleeding carbon monoxide into the trailer. Ray opened the cabinet and pulled down hard. The flimsy hinges bent, but didn't break. He could feel the black smoke clinging to the inside of his lungs. With each deep breath, it was like he was inhaling the flames that were engulfing the trailer. How had he not heard sirens yet? Even in the middle of the woods, someone had to have noticed the blaze.

Blind and certain he was about to lose consciousness, Ray gave the cabinet door one more sturdy yank and the soft brass bent free. He climbed up on the counter, his feet kicking away the black metal claws of the stove's burners. Gripping the base of the board, he shoved wildly at the ceiling. The cheap wood stuck into the particle board, missing the skylight, now obscured by thick smoke. Ray would've cursed if he wasn't holding his breath.

The echo of the ceiling suddenly changed and Ray knew he'd found pay dirt. It took everything he had left in him. All of his senses had become completely overwhelmed. The floor appeared to be coming up at him through the smoke, the haze bending reality. His arms felt like gelatinous tentacles that had separated control from his brain.

The skylight gave way and smoke billowed up and out. Flames licked the edges of the melting plastic, devouring the new oxygen. With what felt like his final breaths, Ray grabbed the edge of the now doorless cabinet. All of his arm hair singed off from the flames that had crawled up the side of the trailer. With his remaining willpower, he hefted himself through the hole, unlaced boots dropping from his feet.

His elbows created an anchor as he took in deep breaths of fresh air through the wet and fragrant towel. He could feel the hot aluminum siding through his shirt, threatening to bake the skin on the underside of his arms. He pushed up through the pain in his hands, freeing his legs from the trailer. Stumbling to the edge, he rolled off through the flames and slammed hard into the ground. The fire had melted the surrounding snow, but the dirt was still hard under the thin layer of mud.

There were no gathered masses. No other trailers in sight. All he made out was a nebulous form standing over him.

"Hello, Ray."

Ray couldn't tell whether the figure had actually said the words, or if it was a manifestation of his smoke-filled mind. What he did register was that the apparition had a similar build to the man he'd left for dead in the bathhouse. And he had called him Ray.

Not Leo.

Ray.

A coughing fit took over. He couldn't get enough air into his lungs. His vision blurred and faded.

Then, all was dark.

"Any luck identifying the girl?" Hsu asked, throwing away his cup from The Coffee Bean. The two had little in common, but they both agreed Starbucks sucked. Gourmet burnt crap.

"Nothing yet," Nick said. "If she was a prostitute, there's a chance she was trafficked overseas without a passport. Could have been reported missing a long time ago. Or missing in another city entirely. We may have to dig deep on this one."

Nick had spent most of the previous afternoon and evening trying to identify the victim, but had come up with nothing. He'd taken a couple more than the recommended dosage of Tylenol PMs to get to sleep and was now paying the price in grogginess. He made Hsu drive down to 51st and the 110 freeway.

On the bridges crossing the 110, tent cities had sprouted like lichen on boulders. Underneath, cars grid-locked in a standstill honked in futile fury, while FastPass commuters sped above in the overhead express lane. Sandwiched in the middle were tiny villages of lean-tos and encampments. If Veli was a resident of this little community, Nick would know they were on the right track. After the story he'd fed them about a knife-wielding pimp, he thought they'd float the name Sketch in Veli's neighborhood, see what sort of bites they got.

Hsu didn't believe it from the beginning. He'd assumed that because Veli had lied to them at the outset, he would continue lying to them. Tension between the police and the public had always been a problem, but the plagues of unarmed black men being shot across America in recent years had heightened the tension to a taut wire ready to snap. Fewer people were willing to speak to the police. Or if they did, there was no way to trust their information without additional corroboration. *Fuck the Police* was a theme that never seemed to lose its luster.

Nick woke up a little when he saw two police cruisers and a flatbed truck parked in the middle of the street, blocking off traffic. Two uniforms had set up tape and a small blockade. There was a group of homeless outside their tents hurling curses at what looked like a couple of handymen taking apart a bright purple structure.

It looked like an ice shanty. Those portable tiny houses that fishermen would set up on frozen lakes. Not much to them. Plywood walls. A simple roof of tin. But this one was nicer. It had windows, the trim painted white. The purple of the rest of the wood belonged in a teenage girl's bedroom rather than on a shack under a busy overpass. The door had a lock on it. A small luxury.

When the handymen removed the roof, Nick could see that it had small solar panels. Not much, but enough to power a few lights and maybe a hotplate or a television. The shack had been assembled with care. And with capital. Whoever was living in it either didn't build it themselves, or had used every bit of their life savings to make sure living on the street would be comfortable.

"If you don't calm down, I'm going to arrest you," a uniform said to one of the louder protesters in the homeless crowd.

"You have no right to take that. If you don't want it here, fine. Let me take it apart. That's my property," the man said. He wasn't yelling, but he wasn't calm either.

"Sir, it has been here for six months on city property. We can do whatever we want with it," the uniform said.

"That's fascist horseshit, and you know it!" the man yelled.

The uniform turned his head, trying to ignore the man screaming inches from his face. His clenched jaw told Nick he was begging the protestor to do something else. Any reason to take him in and shut him up.

Nick and Hsu went up to the officers supervising the demolition and flashed their badges.

"May we offer assistance?" Hsu asked.

"Naw, we got this," the uniform said.

"What's going on?" Nick asked.

"Order from the mayor's office. Hazardous illegal structures. No building regulations. No permit. No zoning."

"The tents get to stay?"

"We've cleared them out before, too. But a few days later and it's back just the way it was. At least we can confiscate these. Been doing it all week. That asshole down there built a ton of 'em," the uniform said, nodding to the man who was cursing his fellow officer as fascist.

"How many exactly?"

"Fifty? Hundred? Seems like we find a new one every few days or so. Dump is full of 'em."

"Mind if we remain in the area for a while, just in case you need anything?" Hsu asked.

"You got a shinier shield than me, Detective. Do what you like," the uniform said, more weary than sarcastic.

Nick and Hsu shared a look, both of them knowing to focus their attention on the loud protester. If he had actually built these structures and was out among the homeless population fighting for their rights, then he was someone the community could trust. And trust breeds information.

"Are you their bosses? Who gave you the authority to do this?" the man spit out at Nick and Hsu as they approached.

He had a well-maintained hair cut, the sides shaved, pomade greasing down the top, which was combed and parted. Manicured stubble graced his jawline and he wore a pressed dress shirt under his studded leather jacket. Wire-rimmed glasses gave him beady eyes. He had a row of safety pins in each of his ears. Large brown gauges expanded his earlobes. Nick had trouble holding in his sarcastic comments when he met someone with those stupid plugs. He wondered how many of them thought about what the stretched-out hoops would look like when they were at retirement age.

"We're here on an unrelated matter," Nick said. "What's your name?"

"Fuck you, that's my name."

Hsu held his hands up in supplication, "Now, sir—"

"I'm trying to give these people a home. Don't you understand that? A little hope. They aren't much, but four fucking walls go a long way to helping someone feel human again."

All right, so the guy cares, Nick thought. It didn't change his opinion on the guy's choice of ear wear.

"We have nothing to do with this, but we need some info on someone who used to live down here. You help us and we can look into getting these structures put back up."

"I don't think you can change the zoning laws in an afternoon."

"Don't tell 'em nothin', DC," one of the homeless men behind the hipster scoffed before heading back to his tent.

"DC?" Hsu asked.

"If you want to look up my non-profit, whose money built these homes, it's registered under Richard Cretu. I did everything by the book."

"Except get the permits," Hsu said.

"Permits would've defeated the purpose," DC yelled. "Each structure is unique. This isn't cookie-cutter building we're talking about here. I want people to feel like it's their home. You know what? I'm not telling you anything else. You won't help me do shit."

Nick could've punched Hsu for antagonizing the guy, but he tried to keep his cool. Focusing on getting justice for the dead girl was the only thing keeping him from throwing up his hands and walking away.

"We just need to confirm an alibi. Do you know a guy named Yusuf Veli?"

"No."

"This guy," Nick pulled out a picture he'd taken with his phone of Veli stewing in the interrogation room. DC glanced at it quick.

"Sure. Didn't know his name."

"He live in one of your houses?"

"Oh shit," DC said as if suddenly remembering something, "I have to go. I have to warn the others. Fuck, why didn't I think of it?"

DC pushed through the dissipating group of homeless behind him and went for his truck. Nick moved to follow, ready to run after a potential suspect, but Hsu grabbed his arm. Nick nearly swung on him before he saw Hsu was pointing down the freeway across traffic to where several other shanties speckled down the 110. DC was on the up and up. He was Paul Revere-ing down the highway to let the rest of the residents know the British were coming.

"Just going to let him go?" Nick asked, more angry than he would've liked.

"Mr. Cretu doesn't appear to be avoiding the police in any capacity. I have a feeling if we need to find him again, we won't have any trouble," Hsu said. He reached for his wallet and pulled out a twenty.

"Does anyone here know Yusuf Veli?" Hsu asked, holding the bill in the air.

Three dirty figures stepped forward. A woman with crimped platinum hair and gray teeth led the pack.

"Pink tent. Hasn't been there for a few days though," she said, eyes hungry for the money.

Nick grabbed the bill from Hsu and tore it in half. He handed her a piece of the ripped paper.

"What the shit?"

"Show it to us," Nick said.

She snarled at them, but beckoned them to follow.

"Why you talk to them, Bleach? You wouldn't want them goin' through your shit," a guy called from his hotplate.

"You wanna give me twenty bucks to shut up? No? Then, eat my dank pussy."

She stood in front of the tent and held out her hand for the rest of the twenty.

"Was he here the night before last?" Hsu asked.

"No. But he's here most nights. Will be back tonight if you wait, I bet," Bleach said, her hand still outstretched.

"Ever heard of Ayida Weddo?"

"What kinda stupid name is that?"

"Applebox?" Nick asked.

"Nope."

"How about a guy named Sketch?" Nick placed the rest of the bill in her hand.

"You want my Rolodex?"

"Hands covered with scars?"

"Dunno," Bleach walked off, calling to the rest of the encampment as she went, "Any you fuckers got some scotch tape?"

Hsu looked over at Nick and shrugged. "Can't say we're getting the most reliable interviews in this case."

"You want to do the honors?" Nick asked.

"Not particularly," Hsu said, "but this is what we signed up for."

Hsu reached into the small leather satchel he always carried with him and pulled out a couple of pairs of gloves, booties, and masks. He held them out to Nick, who took them and put them on.

"Expecting to catch Ebola in there?" Hot Plate called from his tent.

"Shut up or we'll look in your tent next," Nick called back.

He hovered in the doorway. There wasn't room for both of them in the tent and the uniforms at the other end of the encampment were finishing their business with the shanty. They wouldn't be around to cover the detective's backs.

Nick was glad Hsu took point. Even though Veli hadn't been in the tent for a few days, it still reeked of dirt and sweat. There wasn't much to go through. Piles of clothes. Random books and papers. Veli didn't appear to be a collector like most people on the streets. Whatever he'd gathered together, he'd put there to survive day to day instead of hanging onto items of sentimental value.

Nick's condo didn't have knick-knacks either. Other than a handful of his favorite paperbacks salvaged from the fire, the overflowing garbage and the unmade bed, it still looked like the floor model used to sell the building. A storage unit in North Hollywood contained everything they had recovered from his childhood home — which was nearly everything his mother had accrued over the past fifty years. When he'd put her in the hospice facility and packed it all in the U-Haul, there was a part of him that knew he wouldn't look at any of it again until his mother died. He still hadn't looked at it. She'd been gone a month, and he'd done nothing with the storage facility other than continue the automatic payments on his credit card, even though he knew ninety percent of it was going to end up in the dumpster and would eventually end up in one of these tents as a vagrant treasure. When he thought about the cycle of life like that, it was a hell of a downer.

"Wouldn't it be nice if all searches were this easy to carry out?" Hsu asked as he flipped through the pages of the random books gathered by Veli's sleeping bag.

"I'm sure if Veli got the right ACLU lawyer involved, what we're doing is technically illegal. Privacy rights and all that," Nick said.

"Though it would be easy for the city to claim these tents as city property just as they are doing with the shanties," Hsu said, "The tent cities have become such a scourge on this city. There should be a mass clearing."

"Sure," Nick said, "But then where would these people go? Round them up and put them into camps?"

"Careful what you joke about," Hsu said, still focused on his work, "My wife's grandparents were Japanese internees."

Nick made a mental note in his file about the mysterious case of Hsu's spouse.

"Not a joke. Same principle. These people threaten your idea of 'organized society' just like Japanese-Americans threatened people's idea of security. I'm saying both are examples of the wrong way to deal with a problem."

Hsu crawled out of the tent, having found nothing of merit.

"Not so. Those camps were for citizens who had done nothing wrong. The streets are full of addicts, prostitutes, and insane people who should be in care facilities."

"Or they're people who are just down on their luck."

Hsu pulled his mask off. "Where is this coming from? A minute ago, you were ready to threaten the entire block with a night in lock-up. Now you're defending their right to sleep on the streets?"

"I'm just saying that some stories are complicated."

"That you have right," Hsu said. "Veli is a dead end unless we can find this Sketch guy. If he exists. I say we go back at him and see what other stories he has to tell."

Hsu headed back to the car. Nick looked down the highway. DC was warning another shanty resident about eviction, helping him unload his possessions before the next round of demolitions began.

The sun had moved the shadow out from under the overpass. The smell of urine cooking on the concrete hit his nose. He couldn't remember the last time he'd breathed fresh air. At that moment, he hated everything about Los Angeles.

11

Imani's bus ride from Vermont to Adams was more nausea-inducing than usual. She didn't have enough for the return trip, but she figured it was better than walking both ways. Also, they didn't sell prenatal vitamins at the corner store. And even if they did, if she bought something like that in the neighborhood, word would get to her mom. Or worse, to Darius. She predicted his method of birth control was beating on her belly until she bled out. At least if she died, her mom would leave Darius. Then Byron would be safe.

The Ralphs supermarket was bright and clean. When her mom used to be home more, they shopped there all the time. She missed those days. When it was just her, her mom, and Byron. They were good together. Even when her mom had other boyfriends, they didn't dare touch her. She'd become a woman around Darius. And he'd showed her he'd noticed.

Her eyes scanned the vitamin aisle. There were so many. Calcium. Magnesium. Alpha-Lipolic Acid. Something gross called St. John's Wort. She wondered why anyone would want to take wart pills. The bottle said they helped with depression. Imani thought she should just give up on finding prenatal vitamins and get her mom some of that wart stuff. Maybe then she'd feel better about herself. Realize she was too good for Darius. But then she'd be mad about getting warts. If her mom was covered in warts, Darius would leave. Probably not. He'd just turn his attention toward Imani more, and that was the last thing she wanted.

Imani didn't know why she was even bothering. She didn't want to have the baby. All she wanted was to graduate high school and go to LACC and get a good job so her mom wouldn't have to rely on lazy, perverted men. But she knew she couldn't afford to get rid of it. So, if she had to have the thing, she might as well take care of it. Make sure when she gives it up for adoption that it's not all messed up and someone will actually want it.

Her stomach grumbled as she gazed at the candy bars lining the checkout counter. Celebrity beach bodies mocked her from the small magazine rack and she silently cursed them for not having actual problems.

For now, she was doing an okay job of hiding the growing bump with baggy sweatshirts. Teachers hadn't questioned her frequent bathroom breaks. Not yet. She'd have to get some new clothes. And she wouldn't be able to hide this in her gym sweats much longer. What was she going to tell her mom? Who was she going to blame it on? Could she tell her it was Darius? Would that get him kicked out of the house, or would her mom take his side? She could tell her mom it was a boy from the neighborhood, but her mom would want a name. Maybe she could tell her it was a USC student. That she didn't get his name, she just met him at a party. But then her mom would go on a rampage. Start a whole scandal. Get the paper involved. All Imani wanted was to remain invisible for the next few months. Disappear and then make the baby disappear. Was that even possible?

She wished there was a way she could hold the shopping bag so it didn't make any noise, but with every step she took, the big jar of vitamins shook with it. All she could feel were the eyes on her as she exited the store and made her way through the parking lot.

Shake. Whore. *Shake.* Cock hound. *Shake.* Slut.

Once she was out of the sea of white faces and back in familiar territory, she stopped on the raised steps of a nearby house and collapsed into her hands. Nobody told her about all this other stuff in Sex-Ed. Sure, she learned what happens when the sperm meets the egg, but then they get all technical and skip the real life stuff. Baby takes nine months to develop, then they show you that gross birthing video that's supposed to keep you from having sex.

Why do they skip the important part? How it feels to grow a life inside you that you didn't want put there? How you're supposed to make sure you're doing everything right? How it feels to have your organs shoved around by some demon inside your belly? She didn't dare go get one of those pregnancy books from the library. First, she'd have to go get a library card. There was no way she was going to check a book like that out from the school library. Would they even have something like that in her middle school? Or if they did, would it be something written in this decade?

All the thoughts rushed to her head and she could feel the veins at her temples throbbing with boiling blood. She put her head between her legs and tried to keep from hyperventilating.

Was this hurting the baby? Who cares? Wait, she didn't mean that. It's not the baby's fault how it came to be. She shouldn't punish it. Or should she? Maybe if she passes out and goes to the hospital, they'll just take it from her because she's too young. That's possible, right? Maybe she needed to watch more of those doctor shows on TV.

"You all right, girl?" a deep voice cracked out at her.

"Hmm?" she raised her head, ready to shoo off another strange man hitting on her.

"Dropped these," the man said, holding out the bottle of vitamins. She would've been embarrassed that she'd let the bag drop and the bottle roll away, but she was trying not to stare at the man standing in front of her.

He had kind brown eyes and smooth caramel skin. Wisps of a beard traced his boxed chin and he had chunky, bleached yellow hair. The bottle looked huge in his hands, though they were normal size. His arm, the one not holding the bottle, would've nearly reached the ground, if it weren't holding a single Tiny Tim crutch to keep him balanced. His torso was squat and his legs short. He wasn't a midget, even though Imani knew that was the incorrect way to say it. *Little person was what they liked to be called. But he wasn't that either. Was it a dwarf? Not like the Lord of the Rings dwarves.* She had so many questions, but didn't want to ask them.

"You look a little young to be expecting," the man said. "For your mom?"

She snatched the bottle out of his hands and nodded. She made a point of wiping the tears from her eyes with the bottom of her sweatshirt to keep from making eye contact or staring.

"Guess I was wrong, huh?"

"What?" Imani said, now openly gazing at the strange-looking man in front of her.

He took a step back, maneuvering the crutch with the deft skill of someone who used it daily.

"Noticed the bump when you pulled up your shirt. Ain't gonna judge, though. Glad to see you want to take care of it."

Imani shoved the bottle back into the thin plastic shopping bag with a shake. She looked for the shaming judgement in the man's eyes. It wasn't there. Still nothing there but kindness.

"Dunno if I'll even take 'em."

Imani stood up. She had yet to grow into her full height, but towered over him. From this perspective, she could see he was shorter than Byron.

"The daddy not around?"

"None of your business."

"Didn't mean nothing by it. But if you decide not to take 'em, well let's just say I just know someone who could take care of it for you. Free-of-charge."

"Ain't nothin' free."

He smiled, "Girl, ain't nothin' get by you, huh?"

"You don't know me."

"No, that's for sho, but I known a lot like you. We all need friends."

"I got plenty of friends," Imani said. She didn't know why she hadn't turned around and walked away. Maybe it was his eyes. Maybe it was the crutch. Or that he had scanned her face and belly, but she hadn't caught him glancing at her chest. There didn't seem to be a threat there. Unlike most of the men in her neighborhood.

"Not like me," he smiled, "Name's Burke."

"That your first name or last name?"

"It's what people call me. What people call you?"

She hesitated. Before the mantra at school was "Violence Is Not The Answer," it was, "Don't Talk to Strangers." But she had enough to fear from the people she was familiar with. What more could a stranger do?

"Imani."

"You like that, or you wish you was called something else? Like with a secret identity and shit?"

Imani laughed despite herself.

"What kind of name is Burke? Your secret identity?"

"Something like that."

"I gotta go," Imani said. She had been gone long enough and it would take her another twenty minutes to get home. If she didn't check in soon, Darius would notice she was gone.

"All right, Imani," he said her name deliberately, "But if you decide you want your little problem taken care of, you find me, okay?"

"Yeah, you just hanging around like Rumplestiltskin granting wishes?"

She blanched, her eyes going wide. He had been nothing but nice to her.

"Nope," Burke laughed. The comment didn't seem to phase him. "You'll see my truck around. Just moved into the neighborhood."

Burke gestured across the street to the white box truck. It had seen better days and had been tagged several times over, the spray paint overlaid in no particular pattern.

"Or you just want to talk or need a new outfit or make-up or something. I got lots of girls I take care of."

"What, you like a fairy godfather?" she asked.

"Sure. Something like that." Burke turned and hobbled off the curb into the street. "You take care of that little one, now."

Imani stood and watched him open the door to the box truck and toss his crutch in. There was a pull handle on the door, and he used his muscular arms to heft his body up into the driver's seat. He waved at her as he closed the door and started the truck up.

As he drove away, she pondered how his feet could reach the pedals. And also what he meant by having lots of girls he took care of. She may have been young, but she'd lived in this harsh world for a long time. She may not have known what do about this pesky baby growing inside her, but she knew exactly what Burke did for his money.

”Asthma attack.”

“What?” Nick asked, taking the file folder from Jerry Nimmo, the medical examiner.

A few days had passed without new information. Nick and Hsu had tried their best to get someone to give them a lead out on the streets, but no one had heard of Sketch, Applebox, or Ayida Weddo — or if they did, they weren't saying so. Forno had been cooperative, so they'd decided not to hold him on the possession charge. Veli got smart and lawyered up. Even the over-worked court-appointed attorney could see they had nothing to hold him on. He was gone too. His alibi had come through that morning. He'd slept on Alvarado on the edge of MacArthur park. In full view of an ATM camera. How convenient.

Nick had spent most of the previous day looking into honey guys online. Hsu thought the farmer's market angle was the wrong direction to take, but with no other reliable witnesses feeding them something about Sketch or his whereabouts, Nick figured looking into the honey guy was as good a tactic as any. He was still waiting on a call back from the farmer's market association. Apparently, artisan candle makers were a higher priority than murder investigations. He'd made a joke to Hsu about their business practices being none of his beeswax. He got no response.

Both of the detectives hoped whatever was revealed in the autopsy would give them another direction to take. It was their first case together and in only a few days, they had yet to reach the point of even agreeing on what to have for lunch. At least Willie Grant enjoyed trying new restaurants. But she was working with Marconi in Narco now. And Marconi had probably gotten to try that new ramen place Willie talked about going to. If only Nick had held off one more week before accusing her of corruption and having his teeth bashed in by a psychopath, he'd be enjoying a bowl of miso and pork belly instead of watching a medical examiner eat a sandwich three feet from a corpse locker.

"Cause of death. Asthma attack. The strangulation bruises were a day or two old. Abdomen mutilation was post-mortem," Jerry said.

"So, the girl died of panic and shock once they started cutting into her?" Hsu asked.

"No, I'm saying she died before anything happened to her. Someone wanted this to look like a brutal murder, but it's not that at all. Blood spatter patterns from the tent aren't consistent with a stab victim struggling. It looks like someone had it on their hands and flicked it off their fingers."

Nick scanned the papers in front of him.

"Really?"

"Trauma might have caused the asthma attack, but not trauma of such severity. Enough time passed between her death and mutilation to give us a decent picture of the stress put on her pulmonary system."

"Any reason someone would take an accidental death and make it look like first-degree murder? Sounds counterintuitive, doesn't it?" Nick asked no one in particular.

He flipped up another page of the medical examiner's report. He'd seen enough jargon on reports to get the gist of things, but most of the time he needed the language explained to him. Hsu sat on the edge of the desk.

"Also, the pregnancy was late term. What we could piece together of her uterine walls, hormone levels, and amniotic fluid — the mother was around 37 weeks. Assuming it wasn't already stillborn or stabbed, it may have survived, but according to forensics, there were no signs of it in the tent," Jerry said.

"One of those Caesarian kidnappers would know preemie survival rates, right?" Nick turned to Hsu. "You said they do heavy internet research before something like this."

"True," Hsu said, "But a psychotic break that would induce this sort of behavior wouldn't prevent something like this from happening."

Jerry took another bite of sandwich. "Why do you think this was a possible Caesarian kidnapping?"

"It was one theory Hsu came up with," Nick said. "Jane Doe is stalked by a wannabe baby momma and snatched off the street. The anxiety of a kidnapping causes our victim to have an asthma attack and in a panic, the kidnapper goes at her abdomen with the closest sharp object, hoping to save the fetus after the mother dies."

"It would explain the severity of the wounds, but wouldn't explain why the tent should have looked like an abattoir, but didn't," Hsu said.

"That today's word of the day?" Nick asked, not really wanting the answer.

"No. Today it was *Garrulous*. Full of trivial conversation."

"Let's avoid using that one in a sentence today, shall we?"

"I believe we're doing it at the moment," Hsu said.

Nick rolled his eyes. Jerry put his sandwich down on his desk and wiped the crumbs away from his hands.

"I don't think that's what happened," the medical examiner said.

"Why not?" Hsu asked.

"Maybe the baby had nothing to do with this," Jerry said.

"Then why remove it at all?" Nick asked.

"The only thing I can think of is to cover up something else. What if the girl was never supposed to die? What if her death was an accident and who she was with didn't want to be caught with a body? Dumping the body and cutting it open like that might lead you down the wrong path, right? Away from an illegal abortion operation?" Jerry said. "No one in their right mind would request or supply an abortion at 37 weeks, but stranger things have happened."

"I suppose," Hsu said.

"There were some signs of vaginal trauma, but nothing consistent with rape. Not sodomized. And there was no presence of labor-inducing prostaglandins. However, if the child was removed prior to her death, it may explain the vaginal trauma if they were trying to remove the child vaginally and it wasn't working."

"Any chance at all this is a late-term abortion?" Hsu asked.

"Doubtful. At 37 weeks, a baby is almost to term. It can survive out of the womb on its own without an incubator. She was severely mutilated, so I can't be absolutely certain, but the amniotic sac could have ruptured and they tried to do an emergency Caesarian to save the baby and botched the hell out of it. I didn't see any evidence of staples or sutures, but her abdomen was in bad shape. Evidence of a recently closed incision could have been destroyed. If that's the theory you're going with, Caesarian is right, but kidnapping may not be."

"Jane Doe has an asthma attack during a back alley delivery. To cover their tracks and keep from being exposed, whoever was at her bedside moves the body to a brothel tent they know is muddled with scores of DNA and cuts her up to obscure any procedure," Nick said.

"Without evidence of the little one, Caesarian kidnapping could still be on the table," Jerry said. "But there is no way of knowing if the delivery was forced or voluntary."

"What sort of blade are we looking at here?" Hsu asked.

"A few," Jerry said, "Cuts were clean. Nothing serrated."

"Butterfly?" Nick asked.

"Could be?" the medical examiner shrugged.

"If we assume this guy, Sketch, did the carving in the tent, what's one step backwards? If he's helping someone remove the baby, removing it in a tent in a public place doesn't seem like a smart move. There would have been a hell of a lot of noise coming from our Jane Doe. Was she doped?"

"There was fentanyl in her system," Jerry said. "Fentanyl could be used in a pinch as a general anesthetic as there was no evidence of an epidural or other common delivery pain meds. Or she could have just been high on a street batch, but it wasn't enough to O.D. on. I ran a test for misoprostol. It's used to dilate the cervix in late terms or miscarriages. If that comes back positive, she wasn't trying to keep the baby. But an amateur might not bother with it and, like I said, this wasn't a cervical extraction."

"None of the witnesses said they'd seen her prior to the night of her death. Nor did they see anyone going in and out of the tent," Hsu said.

"The girl didn't die in the tent, but she didn't just magically appear there," Nick said.

"She wasn't moved far. There wasn't a lot of time for her blood to settle in the back of her body. It couldn't have been more than a fifteen or twenty-minute drive," Jerry said.

"Time of death?" Hsu said.

"Based on core body temperature alone, between 3 and 4 a.m."

"At that time, that close to the highway, we're looking at a lot of city to cover," Nick said. "Thanks, Jerry. We'll let you know if we need anything else."

Nick and Hsu left the medical examiner's office and got into the elevator.

"Next move?" Hsu asked.

"Let's find Sketch," Nick said. "If Jerry's theory is what we're looking at, I want to know what spooked him to such a severe reaction."

"People do strange things when they think they could go to prison."

"Not this strange."

Nick's phone buzzed when they were between floors. It was Jenkins. He answered it.

"Archer."

"Arch—got—found—sus—," the call was breaking up. Cell service in the elevator had always been shit.

"What?"

"What?"

Nick hung up and waited for the elevator to let them out into the lobby. Once he had a signal again, he redialed.

"Did you hang up on me?" Lt. Jenkins asked.

"Sor—can't—you—," Nick said, faking that the call was breaking up to return the favor.

"Cut the shit, Archer. We found the suspect you were looking for. Boyd Ballantine."

"Who the fuck is Boyd Ballantine?"

"African-American. Hands covered in scars?"

Sketch wasn't a ghost after all.

"You holding him there?" Nick asked.

"Some early morning hikers found him at the Old Zoo. Hanging by his ankles in one of the enclosures."

"Dead?"

"Might as well be. Whoever went after him wanted to make sure he never talked to anyone ever again," Jenkins said. "He's at Glendale Adventist. Hollywood Division will meet you at the scene."

"Son of a bitch," Nick said. "Put out an alert on Yusuf Veli."

"Already done," Jenkins said, and ended the call.

"Another body?" Hsu asked.

"Apparently Sketch's real name is Boyd Ballantine. And someone thought us finding Ballantine in proper working order was a bad idea."

13

"C'mon. Just a little tit. Ain't often we get privacy."

Boom-Boom Rappaport's knockwurst-fingered hands groped at Sweets' thighs, the calluses running a trail of gooseflesh underneath her tights into the dark and wet he hoped to discover.

She shoved his hands away, playful but forceful.

"This is what you call privacy?" she nodded at the patient on the bed next to them.

The new arrival was asleep. The edges of his sparse beard singed and black. His right hand was wrapped in a thick bandage, a combination of the wooden cabinet slicing through his palm and the heat of the metal siding giving him second-degree burns. The skin around his mouth and neck was stained blue from toilet water.

"You and I both know you've made it with more company," Boom-Boom said, giving up his beaver hunt for a lighter touch at the nape of her neck.

"What?"

Sweets shoved his barreled chest and stood up. She swatted at his shoulders and face with frustrated strength, one of her long fingernails catching him under the chin and cutting a small trail of blood. He took the beating without fighting back, hanging his head like a puppy that had pissed on the rug. He knew what she was, and she knew what she was — or rather, what she had been — but that didn't mean bringing it up made it right.

Boom-Boom tugged on the lobe of his cauliflower ear, but didn't apologize. She threw on her goose-down jacket and left the comfort of the warm cabin. She was going to go find *him*. Listen to *him* spew some more bullshit while she gave *him* the googly eyes. And there wasn't anything Boom-Boom could do about it but wait for her to come back. His fists had always been better at solving problems than his brain.

Anyone who followed amateur Mixed Martial Arts might have picked up news of Boom-Boom's rise through the lower divisions of the big show. He got his nickname from the lethal jab combo that had become his finishing move.

Boom, right jab. *Boom*, left jab. His opponents were lucky if they got out of the fight with only a severe concussion and didn't have to drink all their meals through a straw for six months.

Challengers trained and trained, but there was no way for them to use their advantages to take him out. Boom-Boom once crippled an opponent by grabbing his foot in a roundhouse kick, squeezing hard and shattering all the bones. As the guy hobbled to the edge of the octagon, *Boom*, his head went into the fence, *Boom*, he went down.

The muscles in his neck were so thick that even if someone got him into a choke hold, he would relax into it, push off of them and drive his whiskey-barrel body so hard into theirs, both fighters' ribs would snap. But Boom-Boom's secret was always pushing through the pain. Push through the pain until the bell rang.

No promoter wanted to put their fighters in the ring with him. He was a mad-man. Insane. With no marketable skills, he soon lost what meager possessions he'd gained while fighting. All he had was a small house in Panorama City and a shabby economy car. He couldn't even get a job as a trainer because his method had been all rage and no technique. That's when he'd gone underground.

Without his previous contacts in the fighting world, he'd fallen in with a seedier element. Fights with street thugs who didn't care about rules. It didn't matter how much it hurt. He didn't care. He'd nearly lost a kidney during the fight where he'd met Sweets.

She was the ring girl. Or what sufficed as a ring girl in a makeshift boxing ring of used tires. Boom-Boom was getting the life kicked out of him by his opponent, who'd taped broken glass to his knuckles. Both of the hustlers who had put up money for the fight didn't give a shit. Fighters were nothing but meat for the grinder.

It didn't matter, though. All he could see was her. He didn't care about the fight. He didn't care about the hundreds of tiny cuts on his face and chest. Or that he may have ruptured his left testicle and would piss blood for a month. All he cared about was talking to the girl. The quickest way from Point A to Point B. Point A being that moment, Point B being the moment he could get her to shoot that smile at him up close.

Boom-Boom grabbed a rusted bumper and made a beeline for Glass Hands. The other fighter put up his arms to defend his face, but the chrome shattered both of his forearms. When he brought them down from his face, the metal dented his skull. The crowd stopped to watch blood and grey matter ooze out of the wound. The scene was a silent vacuum. What broke it was Boom-Boom's backer claiming victory.

The prize: $500 and the ring girl.

Glass Hands' backer griped that weapons weren't part of the deal. The gun was out and fired before anyone knew what happened. Boom-Boom barely heard the sound. One of his eardrums had ruptured months before, causing a permanent tinnitus in his cauliflower ear. All he knew was the crowd had scattered and there was another man bleeding out in the dirt.

Boom-Boom smiled at the girl through bloody and broken teeth. If he could've heard anything but the ringing in his ears, a slow Righteous Brothers melody would've echoed through his head.

"Hi," Boom-Boom said, a dead-eyed grin on his face.

His backer grabbed the girl by the wrist, claiming his prize. Too hard.

Then there were three dead men.

"You okay?" Boom-Boom asked her.

"I should ask you," she said. The girl was quivering in shock. Her mind had yet to catch up with watching three men murdered before her eyes in a matter of minutes.

"Your hands okay?"

"I've had much worse," Boom-Boom said.

She smiled. And that was all Boom-Boom wanted. That smile. Crooked with some yellowed teeth. An uneven gap on either side of her canines. But it didn't matter.

To Boom-Boom, it was perfect.

With that flash of teeth, he knew he never wanted to be apart from her ever again.

Sweets' real name was Erica. Erica Newhall. She grew up in a home with restrictive sugar rules. So when she hopped on a Greyhound before graduating high school, that meant as much candy as she could get her hands on. When her pimp had recruited her, a sniveling dope fiend who called himself Q-Mug, her skin was horrible from consuming nothing but processed sugar and the occasional value meal.

Q-Mug gave her a black eye shortly after he'd made a show of buying her a steak and she'd pushed it away like an obstinate child. He didn't do it in the restaurant, of course. He told the waiter they would be right back, excusing himself politely, asking her to talk outside. All he did was tell the valet to turn around. With the tone he'd issued, the valet didn't ask why, he just did what he was told. And *POP!* The muscle surrounding her ocular bone swelled immediately. He handed her a handkerchief to wipe her tears away. Then he took her back inside and watched her eat every bite of that steak, even cut the meat into small pieces for her, like a loving parent, just to ensure she didn't choke on it through the sobs. He told the waiter to add another steak to his bill. This one out of the freezer. When they left the restaurant, Sweets had to keep one porterhouse in her stomach and the other pressed to her swelling eye.

"See? Don't that feel better?" he asked her. Then he got into the car the valet had brought around and left her on the sidewalk, not waiting for her answer. She waited until his car had turned the corner to puke up her fine steak dinner into the gutter. She kept the other steak pressed to her eye as she walked back to her tent, even though the smell of the thawing meat continued to make her nauseous.

This was the same guy who had provided her as a bounty for the illegal street fight, sold her for a cut of the take. It was all the story that Boom-Boom needed to hear. Both of them were living on the streets, nowhere to go but the dirty hovels they had constructed for themselves. As they wandered the streets, hand in hand, blood-stained star-crossed lovers, Boom-Boom wanted to know everything about her. And that was when she'd told her story.

It was getting cold and the only thing keeping him from losing consciousness was that he didn't know if the angelic beauty guiding him through the abandoned Los Angeles streets would still be around when he came back to the land of the living. What he needed was an address from her. A transient hotel off of Western and Santa Monica.

"Knock on the door." That's all Boom-Boom said. "Just knock."

She did.

And then they had a place to stay.

Q-Mug's cash kept his body on ice in the bathtub, until the end of the month when rent came due. It was the sort of place where the faint rot of decay would go unnoticed. But after a couple of weeks, it didn't make a difference. Bloated flies made their way out of the rough seal they'd created under the bathroom door and they were sick of shitting in the kitchen sink. They left before the month was out. No one came looking for them.

After that, Boom-Boom and Sweets were inseparable. The only time they'd been apart was when the threat came of the two of them becoming three. Each of them fantasized about what it would be like to have a family, but they had both experienced firsthand what it was like to grow up in an environment where never having enough made everyone's life an ongoing nightmare. So Sweets disappeared for a few days. Boom-Boom woke up one day and she was gone.

Days of unending despair. Nothing he ate had any taste. He'd gotten into a street fight, just to feel something. He was arrested, but nothing came of it.

When he was released, there she was. Back to him like nothing had happened. He didn't ask where she'd been or what she'd done because he didn't want to know. Simple answers. There was a problem. She solved it. Details would just complicate things.

But that separation opened Boom-Boom's eyes. He knew there was nothing in the world for him but Sweets. So, about a month after that, when they'd seemed to settle back into a routine of street living, he didn't question her when she suggested taking some time away from the city. Getting out of Los Angeles where their problems and past seemed to stew around them. A trip to the mountains. To a place Boom-Boom never imagined he would finally feel free. Never in a million years. A forest utopia.

Now he was a glorified babysitter. There was something disturbing about the guy on the bed beside him. Pulled from some fire and making people uncomfortable. Boom-Boom didn't understand what the big deal was. In his sleep, the burned up guy whined like an injured kitten. *What made this guy special? What was so scary about his Russian-looking tattoo?* Unlike most things that Boom-Boom questioned, he was sure this one didn't have a simple answer. He was told he wasn't supposed to talk to him, just watch him to make sure he didn't leave. Report when he woke up.

But the guy's presence had spooked Sweets out of giving him some private fuck time. And that he couldn't stand. Boom-Boom never was good at following directions.

"Hey," Boom-Boom nudged the sleeping man's shoulder. He moaned, but didn't awaken.

"What'd you do, eh? How come you get the princely treatment?"

The man's eyes fluttered, and he blinked at the low light of the room. He did a poor job of hiding his disdain for the mashed and distorted face hovering over him.

"Awake, I see."

Boom-Boom nearly knocked the chair from beneath him as he stood up and swung around. He had never been afraid of anyone. Not even his father when he'd beat him within an inch of his life. But this man he was afraid of. Boom-Boom had seen the games he played with people. They never ended well.

"Was just about to get you," Boom-Boom said. There was a low-shake to his voice.

"I can take it from here," Reggie said. "Wait outside."

Boom-Boom stood up and shuffled to the door. From behind him, he heard Reggie say, "Now, Cobb, you ready to see what all the fuss is about?"

He closed the door, happy that it was this Cobb guy stuck alone in a room with Reggie and not him.

14

Wealthy mining magnate, Griffith J. Griffith, envisioned a space in central Los Angeles that would rival New York's Central Park. Griffith Park was no stranger to crime. Fitting, given that Griffith tried to murder his wife in 1903 and served two years in prison for assault with a deadly weapon. There's a statue of him on Los Feliz Boulevard. Los Angeles has a short memory.

The Old Zoo was abandoned in 1965, the animals moved a few miles north. A maze of stone enclosures that were once large fenced-in exhibits. Hikers can wander through the places that once held lions and tigers. It had become one of the more inviting tourist attractions in the park.

Nick and Hsu turned off Los Feliz Boulevard up Crystal Springs Drive. The dry brush throughout the park gave no hint that Los Angeles had a wet winter.

"Park here," Hsu said. He pointed at the lot that was well below the site of the Old Zoo, but was already abuzz with activity. Nick pulled the car in and they got out. There was a team surrounding a black Porsche Cayenne, dusting it for fingerprints and taking blood samples from the back seat. The detectives made their way around the Merry-Go-Round. It didn't open until the summer, but Hollywood Division had called the caretaker to pull up the shutters. The red and white striped dome shaded the painted metal faces of the horses. The frozen figures stared back at them from the shadows, and the last of the late winter leaves swirled around the base in a cool breeze. Like most things built for children, there was an eerie silence to it once the lights were off and the smiling faces had gone home to bed.

Ballantine was found by a couple of hikers looking to do some early morning exploring. The cement animal enclosures had two paths running at the bottom and top. Access to the enclosures from the lower path was easy and ready for photo opportunities. The upper path was fenced off, but it was merely for show. There was a gate with a rusted chain and padlock on it, but the chain and lock held the gate together with a broken wire easily pushed apart. Either side of the poles of the gate had dirt trails, so if someone didn't want to make the minimal effort of pushing open the "locked" gate, they could just walk around it. What was easy for people to sneak through made it hard for vehicles. It would explain why the Porsche sat in the parking lot. From what Nick could see, there was no blood trail numbered by forensics, so the real beating probably began at the crime scene.

Chain-link fence ran along the top of the enclosures, but holes were cut in it at strategic points to allow entry. The breaks in the fence were clean and not jagged, the metal pulled to the side like a curtain. The park rangers did their due diligence by stringing caution tape across the openings every few months, but no one paid attention to it and the broken yellow strips alerted people where the holes in the fence were rather than deterring them from entering. Steep staircases dipped down into the lion's den, every inch of faux boulder covered in graffiti tags.

At the top of the hill, there was a shack marking the edge of the exhibits. It had a corrugated tin roof and loose plywood sides. The fencing outside was a tangle of rust. Based on the size of the shack and the cages outside, it was initially a space for small primates or an aviary. It had been painted a dull beige several times over the years to cover up decades of spray paint. The inside was a different story.

It was an explosion of color. Every surface was sprayed with bright blues, greens, and yellows. The floor was littered with cans of spray paint, crumpled up balls of paper, and empty bottles of Modelo Especial beer. Someone had brought up a 1000 piece puzzle and jigsaw pieces were scattered everywhere. Had the space not been crawling with photographers and crime scene techs, Nick would have thought the place was an art installation. Whoever brought Ballantine up here and beat him within an inch of his life wanted him to be found.

Detective Cass Quevedo of the Hollywood Division met them at the entrance of the building. She was severe and all business. The type of person for whom smiles were probably painful.

"David," she said. The greeting she gave Hsu wasn't exactly cold, but it wasn't warm either. The two of them had been partners before Hsu took his leave of absence. Nick might have suspected a deeper story there if she didn't seem to treat everyone she interacted with as if they were trying to sell her something.

"What do we have here, Cassandra?" Hsu asked. Nick thought putting these two together in a room must be what watching a cicada grow into adulthood felt like.

"African-American Male. Approximately fifty years old. Trussed and strung up. Severe wounds sustained to the face, neck, and chest coupled with the pooling of blood in the brain from prolonged inversion," Cass said.

Nick had heard of the singularity between robots and humans encroaching on civilization. Meeting Cassandra Quevedo, he feared the machines had taken over long ago.

"Did your on-board computer scan his DNA to identify him?" Nick asked. RHD detectives had a reputation for talking down to detectives from other divisions and Nick didn't like to play into that stereotype, but it was just too easy to fuck with Quevedo.

"He was naked to the waist and his wallet was found in the detritus. Must have dropped out when he was strung up," Cass said, holding out the evidence bag to them and refusing to react to Nick's comment.

"How badly was he beaten?" Hsu asked.

"He's in surgery now to relieve the bleeding in his brain, but was barely breathing when he was discovered. Another couple of hours and he likely would have died of exposure," Cass said. She waved over a photographer and had him scroll through the pictures of Ballantine before they cut him down.

What was left of his face wasn't human. His nose was mashed flat and purple. Eyes swollen into thin slits. Cuts open on his jaw and chin ran up his face, striping him like a candy cane.

"You're sure it's him?" Hsu asked.

"Tattoo on his forearm confirms it," Cass said.

"Tattoo?" Nick asked. His racing heart made him wonder if it was the same tattoo found on Victor Mochulyak and Yuri Karsenov. The tattoo that translated to "Property of The Bear." A link back to Ray Cobb.

The photographer clicked through the digital photos on the back of the camera. Ballantine's hands were carved with small scars, like Yusuf Veli had said. Hundreds of them. It looked like Boyd Ballantine took 10,000 hours of practice to heart, and his mitts had paid the price.

The tattoo read: *Aelan*.

"It was on his rap sheet. We called in the wallet as soon as we discovered it. Mr. Ballantine was an unpleasant person."

"Unpleasant, like he didn't take his shoes off on freshly vacuumed carpet?" Nick asked.

"His last conviction was for human trafficking. Women shipped in cargo containers from Southeast Asia fifty at a time with one bucket between them. They left those who died of dysentery with the rest until egress at the Port of Los Angeles."

"That would match with our Jane Doe," Nick said.

"Sounds like he should be spending some alone time at Pelican Bay," Hsu said.

"Plea deal for early parole. Used to work for Pretty Boy D'Arby. He was inside when his boss got killed. Spilled on the operation once he found out the big man wouldn't be around to take vengeance on him. Served four years on a twenty-five. My guess is he made a few enemies," Cass said.

"Anyone in D'Arby's former organization we should look into?" Nick said.

"D'Arby?" Hsu said the name like it burnt his tongue. "Good luck."

Hsu shot a snarl at Cass that Nick would have to ask about later.

"Ballantine up to his old tricks since his parole?" Nick asked.

"Not since being released. On paper, he was keeping his nose clean."

Nick wagged the wallet in his hand. "Was this catalogued?"

"Nothing out of the ordinary. Driver's license. Cash is still in it, so this wasn't a robbery. Car in the parking lot by the Merry-Go-Round. Seat set to a point that it looked like Ballantine was driving, or reset anyway. Fob was in his pocket."

"We saw it coming in."

"Could have been knocked unconscious and brought here," Cass said.

"Big guy," Hsu said

"It couldn't have been a one-man job," Cass said.

"It could have," Nick corrected. "It just isn't likely." He didn't need to say it. He just enjoyed annoying someone more boring than Hsu.

"True."

"Did he have a butterfly knife on him?"

"Also found in the vicinity. It's already bagged and on the way to the lab for DNA to see if it matches your case," Cass said.

Matches our case, Nick thought. He had no problem messing with Cassandra Quevedo for being an emotionless robot, or joking about the death of a knife-wielding pimp who may have gotten what he deserved, but he couldn't stop from being emotionally drawn to the pregnant young girl who'd been torn apart. Usually, he could keep his distance. He'd seen people mutilated before. Hell, he'd found the severed penis of Low Seward under a milk crate. But the fright frozen on the girl's face bothered him. The struggle she must have had to find any gasp of air. He was having trouble categorizing this one in his mind as just another case.

"I suspect Mr. Ballantine doubled down on his old business," Cass said. "We contacted his parole officer and the last time he'd checked in, he was unemployed."

"Didn't know unemployment checks covered the lease on a Porsche," Nick said.

"No way he gets a lease on a parolee's credit. Scrubbed VIN."

"A parole officer would notice that ride and ask questions, so he was good at hiding it, or that car isn't his," Hsu added.

Nick chewed on the inside of his lower lip. They were missing something. And someone was right there to snatch the next floorboard from underneath them at every step.

He scanned the shed, stepped outside, and looked down at the vista of Griffith Park. People walked this path every day. At Halloween, they ran the haunted hayride through the Old Zoo. It was a strategic location. He went back inside.

"There are plenty of places up here where he could have been beaten to death and not discovered for weeks. He was placed here. Why leave him alive?" Nick asked.

"We need to question one of our suspects again. We release him, then the person of interest he flagged for us turns up here the next day," Hsu said.

"Veli didn't give us the impression he was capable of something like this," Nick said.

"Not all the best actors in this town spend four hours in the Dolby Theatre every March," Cass said.

"He was scared," Nick said. "We thought it was of Ballantine, who he called Sketch, but maybe he was scared of someone else."

"The pictures don't do Ballantine's beating justice," Cass said. "If you'd seen what I did this morning, you'd be scared too."

"Has anyone gone to the address on his driver's license yet?" Hsu asked.

"Figured you would want to run with that one. I've got my hands full here," Cass said.

"Let us know if you find anything else. Ballantine was placed here for a reason," Nick said. "We just have to figure out what that reason was."

15

Ray's skin was ready to leap off his body. The worst burns were on his hands, but he had also singed one of his calves. Whoever had wrapped his wounds had done the job of a medical professional, but if he didn't change the bandages every few days, he risked an infection.

Reggie told him they were keeping him stocked with antibiotics and had already administered some while he'd rested. Ray guessed they had given him something else. Each movement of his head and limbs seemed slower. He'd wanted to struggle when the guy built like a bourbon barrel lifted him from the bed to the wheelchair, but he couldn't. He shoved a pair of used Sorels onto Ray's feet without tying them. Neither of them helped him with the used polyester-down coat they threw into his lap before opening the door to the cold.

The gauze rubbed against his burns with every bump along the shoveled path. Reggie and his crew had brought Ray to a camp in the woods. Several cabins, each of them billowing smoke from wood-burning stoves, were arranged in a semi-circle around a central area marked by a bare flagpole. The place had probably been a summer camp at one time.

Shoveled paths criss-crossed the camp. Heavy snow was heaped into snow banks, creating a mini wall around the cabins. The paths were smoothed and packed to create sidewalk-like surfaces. The wheelchair didn't glide along the paths, but didn't get stuck in ruts either. Ray didn't think it would've been necessary if it weren't for whatever sedatives they'd given him. He was certain his legs worked perfectly fine, but he couldn't get his brain to send the correct signals to get them up and moving. He chose instead to focus on what he could. Focus on the people. Look for familiar faces.

A dozen people in the camp, maybe. There was a bustle about the grounds that was disturbing. An urgency to every moment. As though everyone had a task to perform and had to get busy doing that very thing, lest they suffer consequences of not finishing. But there wasn't an oppressive or dour mood to the workers. They seemed happy in their work. Preparing for something larger than themselves. Whatever it was, Ray knew it couldn't be good.

He didn't recognize anyone from Los Angeles. There weren't even people he had seen down on the streets of Big Bear. Everyone was content to stay in the little commune and do what they had to do. It wasn't what Ray had expected to find when he began this journey. Now there were more questions for him to answer.

What did this place have to do with kidnapping girls to manufacture drugs? What did it have to do with framing him for murder?

And why was he still alive?

That was the big question that had been nagging at him since he woke up. If these were the people who had barricaded him in the trailer, then set it on fire, why did they bother reviving and patching him up? Wouldn't they be better off leaving him for dead?

Reggie said nothing after getting him into the wheelchair and pushing him down the path. He was humming the chorus of *Wild Horses* by The Rolling Stones repeatedly. Ray wanted to tell him to shut the fuck up, but it took too much concentration and energy.

A brisk wind shocked Ray into a shiver and he could feel the drugs loosening their grip on his mind. Even if he flipped the chair over and made a break for it, the entire camp would be on him in an instant. He didn't see anyone carrying a weapon, but with the heavy jackets and layers, anyone could've been packing. Not to mention that he didn't know what was waiting for him beyond the tree line. If he chose the wrong direction, he could wander into the mountains and freeze to death.

Why the fuck didn't he just stay home, go to prison, and live with the goddamn tattoo?

"What's this place?" Ray asked. The words were heavy and slurred. His mouth and mind weren't communicating yet, either.

"Home," was all Reggie said.

"Great."

Reggie pulled the wheelchair to a halt at the end of the flattened path. There was another trail headed into the woods that wasn't manicured, but the snow was well-worn by footprints. Boots had brought up mud and grass and it was an odd brown stream in the white calm. Reggie let go of the handles and started down the path. About ten yards away, he turned back to look at Ray.

"Well? C'mon."

Ray didn't move at first. It was a combination of his trepidation and pain. In order for Ray to get out of the chair, he would have to push up on the armrests with his bandaged hands and hope his legs stayed underneath him. He had dealt with worse pains. His hesitance was based on other factors.

From what Ray had seen in the bar, the fire, and now the path at the edge of the woods — Reggie liked to play games. The expectant smile on his face as he stared back in Ray's direction told Ray he reveled in it. Reggie knew it would be painful for Ray to get out of the chair without help. Counted on it. He also knew he hadn't given Ray many other choices.

Ray didn't like being played with. If he ever figured out what the hell was going on, he was going to make sure Reggie never toyed with anyone ever again.

"You've come this far, Cobb," Reggie said. "Don't you want to meet the man you've come all this way for?"

If anything were to get Ray up, it was that. He pressed his sore hands into the hard plastic of the armrests and pushed up. The healing skin shifted under the bandages and Ray could feel warm blood and cool pus flow into the gauze. His knees shook, but he held his standing position as he pulled his hands away, palms already stained deep brown.

The first step was painful and labored, the burns on his calf rubbing against the cloth of his pants, but it didn't rub any skin away as far as he could tell. He found his gait quicker than he imagined he would've, but kept his movements slow. There was no reason to let Reggie know he was more able-bodied than he let on.

There was still the small lump at the bottom of his sock he had been smuggling around for a month. They hadn't found that and confiscated it.

Once it was apparent Ray wouldn't collapse into a snowdrift, Reggie headed down the path into the woods and turned out of sight of the clearing. Ray glanced behind him at the bustle of the camp. No one seemed to pay him any mind. But he had no way of knowing what was waiting for him out in the woods. There could've been a dozen pairs of eyes on him, waiting in the bush for his next move. Beyond the tree line, Reggie waited for him, leaning up against a wide oak, bald of leaves. In the distance, he could hear the rhyming thunk of a pileated woodpecker searching for grubs in a dead tree.

They walked for nearly twenty minutes, most of the time on an uphill slope. Sweat beaded on Ray's forehead, not just from the exhaustion, but also from the pain in his hands, which were alternately burning and freezing, depending on the moment.

Going to all the trouble to keep him alive, only to bury him in a shallow grave in the woods, would've been anti-climactic. Then again, Ray knew when he tried to predict what someone with loose morals and unhinged psychosis was about to do next, he found himself in a lot of trouble.

And then he heard it. Distinct and piercing through the trees creaking in the wind.

Laughter.

It wasn't raucous. It was collective. A group laughing in agreement rather than at an outright joke. The type of laughter heard in board meetings and self-help seminars. The laughter of groupthink.

Except for one distinctive sound. A laugh Ray had grown accustomed to.

The piercing cackle was Deuce's laugh.

Had Deuce been part of Reggie's game all along? He reflected on the circumstances. It was easy to gain Deuce's confidence. Easy to get Deuce to let him crash with him. Deuce asked him no questions about his life before arriving in Big Bear.

The whole time Ray thought he'd been using Deuce's weaknesses against him, it was he was the one getting played.

Reggie was perched on the long trunk of a fallen tree. He had brushed off the snow and lit what smelled like a blueberry cigarillo. Of course, a piece of shit like Reggie would smoke tobacco sticks that even high schoolers had abandoned for vape pens.

The edges of Ray's mind ran calculations about how stupid he could've been. Ray stopped and leaned on the tree trunk, looking down at the group at the base of the other side of the hill.

"That cigar smells like shit," Ray said.

"I know," Reggie said, "But nobody ever asks to bum one."

Ray braced his legs for the downhill walk.

He caught bits and pieces of what was being said, but the speaker at the center of the circle was being intimate with his audience. Deuce looked up the hill, made eye contact with Ray, then shifted his attention back to the subject at hand, ignoring his former roommate.

Upon reaching the edge of the circle, they didn't ask Ray to join in or sit down, even though there was a free stone polished by a hundred summer camp rumps. The fire pit in the center was clear of snow and pine needles, but wasn't blazing. Another few residents of the camp were listening with rapt attention to the man at the top of the circle.

He wore a solid grey flannel shirt and thick work jeans. Sawdust speckled the laces of his work boots. He wore gloves, but his thinning blonde hair whipped in the breeze. His ears were red from the cold, but it didn't seem to bother him. There was a perpetual smile on his face as he addressed his acolytes. Purely based on this man's charisma, Ray could only assume he was Malkin.

"It isn't a matter of if, it's a matter of when. Whether we are attacked by a foreign power with an EMP bomb or a hacker gains access to our power grid, we have become far too reliant on modern technology. What we are building here represents the exception to the rule. We are people who don't have to be taught how to survive a disconnected world. We are the disconnected. When the world plunges into darkness, it will need leaders. People to step into the roles previously held by the government. We are not here to end the world. We are here to save it."

Smiles and nods encouraged Malkin's rhetoric. Ray stood at the edge of the circle, his face holding skepticism. Outside of Deuce's passing glance, no one had acknowledged he or Reggie had arrived.

"Do you know why people like you die in the streets? Because society can afford to lose you. But I see your value. When their society is gone, they will see your value, too."

All of it was too familiar, like Ray had heard it before.

Bred in the brain of a schizophrenic albino and coming out of the mouth of a charismatic leader. Crazy was crazy.

And Ray knew it was impossible to reason with crazy.

16

The address on Ballantine's driver's license was a Department of Corrections reentry facility on 6th and Alvarado. Several of the residents could come and go as they pleased. Some had GPS tracking devices, but most wandered on an honor system. Because Ballantine had served out the full term of his reduced sentence and didn't take advantage of the release program, he didn't have an anklet. It would've made tracking his movements the night before a lot easier, but Nick realized nothing about this case was going to be easy.

The halfway house administrator let Nick into Ballantine's room. It was bare. No personals. Bed made. It looked like the facility was waiting to fill the spot.

"Am I missing something?" Nick asked.

"Ballantine slept here because he had to as part of his parole. And that's all he did. Was always in five minutes before curfew. Showered and out the door when we unlocked the gates in the morning."

"Ever see him driving a Porsche crossover around?"

The administrator snorted a laugh. "Most of these fools barely have enough change for the vending machines. And those who have jobs aren't making more than minimum."

"No clue where he spent his days?"

"He wasn't tagged. We had no cause to monitor him. Other residents are on a 180 day rehab program and are essentially still in the prison system. Those are the boys we keep a close eye on. As long as he was back by curfew and wasn't picked up on something else, he could come and go as he pleased."

"Never saw him with a knife?" The administrator gave Nick a look that told him to stop asking stupid questions. "Any enemies here?"

"Place like this, it's easy to make enemies, but he wasn't here enough. Kept his head down."

Nick sensed the bad cologne of apathy and impatience wafting off the administrator. With Ballantine in the hospital indefinitely, it was one less head he had to count.

"Mind if I talk to your other residents?"

"Be my guest. Can't say any of them will talk to you, though." The administrator walked off, leaving Nick in the room. If that dickhole had been his landlord, Nick wouldn't spend a lot of time at his apartment either.

The whole place could smell cop on him. Nobody wanted to give him information. They didn't want to disappear off the halfway house radar like Ballantine did, only to have another resident snitch on them.

Nick made his way outside to call Hsu, hoping Veli admitted to everything and they could move on to something else.

"Got a cigarette?" a rumpled resident asked Nick. He had a bandage on his face and the medical tape buckled and came loose when he talked. Nick saw he had a deep slash sealed with a couple dozen stitches.

"What happened?" Nick asked.

"Nothin'," he said, pressing the tape back on his face.

"Someone cut you?"

"I fell."

Nick raised an eyebrow.

"On a running lawnmower?"

The resident chuckled, the laugh cut short with a jolt of pain.

"You looking for Ballantine?"

"I know exactly where he is. Someone nearly beat him to death last night."

"Good."

"Why do you say that?"

"Fifty bucks."

"For what? If snitches get stitches, you've already got that covered," Nick said.

"You a cop or a comedian?"

"I moonlight."

"Fifty bucks and I tell you where he goes every day."

"Twenty."

"Twenty don't get me shit," Stitches huffed.

"Then you're shopping on the wrong corners."

"Thought you were supposed to keep us off the junk?"

"Not my department," Nick shrugged.

"Forty bucks," Stitches said, "I know you got a couple twenties, if you're willing to give me one."

Nick reached into his back pocket and pulled out his wallet. He fanned up the twenty and the five he had in the back flap. He found keeping all of his cash in the same place was a bad idea when he went digging for information.

"How about you find a cash machine?"

"I'm with a credit union. Anything around here and I'm hit with fees," Nick said. "How about you take the twenty-five or nothing?"

"Fine," Stitches said. He walked back toward the door.

Fuck. Nick didn't expect the called bluff. The guy's clothes were hanging off him and he couldn't afford a vending machine Cup O' Noodles. But Nick knew there was a high price for squealing. He dug into the watch pocket in his jeans where he kept his informant stash and pulled out another twenty.

"Okay. Forty," Nick stopped him.

Stitches turned around, his left side up in a smirk.

"Your math is off," he said. "I see forty-five."

Nick held up the three bills, but didn't hand them over.

"What you've got better be worth forty-five."

"What I've got wasn't worth this," he pointed at his face.

"So it was Ballantine?"

"Motherfucker did his best to keep cool. Kept that knife hid. Didn't dress flashy. Didn't fill his room with shit. But he wasn't as smart as he thought he was. Shoes gave him away. I start to thinkin', if he's got money to be a sneaker pimp, he's got other money somewhere. Followed him."

"Where?"

"He's got this little place over on San Pedro. Hell of a walk. Goes in. Changes clothes. Locks up. Heads over a few blocks to a parking garage and gets in this car. One of them kinda not quite SUVs."

"Porsche? Black?"

"Yeah. Black. Didn't see the logo, but it weren't no Chevy and not so flashy as no Escalade neither."

"And he caught you breaking into his place?"

"Not saying nothing about that. But if I were to do that, I wouldn'ta done it that day. Not that stupid. I followed him a few times. Same place. Same routine. But he musta gone back there to change every day because he always came back here dressed in thrift shop shit. Except for his shoes."

"When did he cut you?"

"Few days ago. Usually, he wasn't paying attention. But he was looking over his shoulder a lot, like he was expecting someone to be on his ass. Didn't expect it to be me. I caught a glimpse in his window. Dude liked doodling. Walls were covered in little drawings and pictures. He caught me and gave me this for my trouble. Said if I told anybody, I'd be dead, but I heard he's not doing much of anything soon, so fuck him."

Nick handed over one of the twenties. "Where is this place?"

"It's gone."

"What do you mean, gone?"

"It wasn't like an apartment. It was like a shanty. Had a lock on it. A roof. City took it away."

"Like a tiny house?" Nick asked.

"You've seen 'em, then?"

"Yeah," Nick said, letting out a deep breath, "I've seen them."

17

When Malkin finished speaking, the group got up, each shook his hand, then went back up the hill toward the camp. Deuce passed by Ray without a nod. Ray watched them go, Reggie pulling up the rear of the group as they disappeared into the woods and snow. He and Malkin were alone.

Neither man moved. Ray remained on the edge of the circle and Malkin on his worn stone seat.

"My name is Xavier Malkin. But I suppose you surmised that already. I expect you have a lot of questions."

Ray noted Malkin's accent. The first hint of a Ukrainian connection in the camp. Though it wasn't quite as low and intimidating as The Bear's had been. It was warmer. Slick. Practiced.

"Only one," Ray said, saliva caught in his throat. "Why me?"

"Right to it. That's what I like about you, Ray."

"You don't know me and I don't know you. Don't pretend otherwise."

"That's where you're wrong. Your presence here isn't an accident."

"If you're trying to tell me you orchestrated everything that led me up here, then that shit you just fed those people around your little kumbaya circle isn't the biggest load of garbage I've heard today."

Malkin chuckled, "You're right. I'll be honest with you. I didn't know you were involved in my business until Osip Kosbur told me he'd framed you for Yuri Karsenov's murder."

"Who the fuck is Osip Kosbur?" Ray asked.

"The man you killed in the bathhouse."

"I didn't kill him," Ray said, quick. He hadn't been there when Kosbur had taken his final breath and he was certain Kosbur was the one who had tried to burn him alive.

"If you say so," Malkin said. The potential death of the Ukrainian drug lord didn't seem to phase him in the least. "I'm building something up here. Something special. And I want you to be part of it."

"Funny way of asking."

Malkin stood, pushing down on his thighs and giving a little groan. The smile never left his face.

"If you mean the tattoo, I'm sorry about that. Not my idea."

"You don't seem like a person who lets things happen without his permission," Ray said.

"It was my fault for thinking I could delegate some authority. The man you killed—"

"I didn't kill him. He probably drowned." Ray shut his eyes tight and held his mind from flashing to the thrashing water. Hands grasping at nothing but seaweed. Sand in his mouth and eyes, mixing with the tears. He shook the images away.

Malkin nodded and smiled. Ray could tell he didn't buy the narrative and was pushing hard to convince Ray that he'd caused Kosbur's supposed death.

"He was my first recruit. Wanted to help me shape the new world."

"By running drugs and women out of a greenhouse in Pasadena? Noble."

"The tattoos were his idea. A way to identify the chosen. Something I should have stopped as soon as he tattooed himself, but you can't buy that kind of devotion. The fortunate thing about such an identifying mark is that it won't get traced back to me. Those in the factions under him thought he was the top of the pyramid. Few of them were as smart as you."

"I'm supposed to believe that you're grateful I took down your little purple powder operation?"

"You helped me remove a gangrenous limb," his tone darkened, "which is why you're being offered a choice."

There it was. Malice underneath the pleasantries. The threat of death that had been hanging over everything. But Malkin could threaten Ray all he wanted. Ray knew he was still alive for a reason. Malkin wouldn't sacrifice whatever game he was playing, waiting for the first refusal of indoctrination.

"All this for an apocalypse cult, huh?"

"Between you and me, if the fall of society never happens, I'll be the happiest man on Earth. But I've seen too much to know that it is inevitable."

"I've seen Camp Doomsday. It doesn't really seem like my crowd," Ray said. "How about we make a deal? I forget about the involuntary tattoo. You leave me alone. Sound fair?"

"And you return to Los Angeles, take blame for the bodies attached to you, and mention nothing about this place?" Malkin asked.

"If it means not getting set on fire again, sure, why not?" Ray lied.

"May I offer another scenario?"

"Considering you had your man pump me full of something to slow me down, I'm not running away soon. I'll bite."

Malkin stood and walked toward Ray. He beckoned him to follow up the hill, but kept his distance lest Ray lunge at him.

"What became affectionately known as Shadow Dance was nothing but a failed experiment. Methamphetamine is losing its shine. A backwoods drug visibly tearing its users apart. Opiates are the impending danger. You wouldn't know it with money flowing in from the ski tourism, but opioid addiction is a big problem here in Big Bear. As it is in most small communities. So we put something new out into the market. Field testing. Market research. And, alas, it failed. Clinical trials fail. But it failed early, and it failed quick. A full operation wasn't in place yet, but it was only one of many endeavors. The casualties were few. For the next, it may be many, or it may be none. Diversification makes business grow. Watching the market trends and capitalizing. Business 101."

"Yeah, and what's the business that's working?" Ray asked. Malkin had given this speech before. Crafted in a way to cajole and soothe. He'd given it to every other person involved in the failed Shadow Dance operation. Those who were still alive.

"Each person here is like you. Plucked from the streets. Chosen for their skills and instincts for survival. To the outside world, including the local sheriff, we are an artist's commune, plying our trinkets to flea markets and craft fairs, catering to the disposable incomes of SoCal Millennials. We're kitschy and homemade. Pewter figurines, hand-poured candles, and artisan jams to them. But for us, we're learning useful skills for after the fall of man. Metallurgy and scavenging. People only see what they wish to see. You say you're just another homeless man, Mr. Cobb, but I've seen the things you've accomplished. You are far from ordinary."

Malkin was strolling at Ray's pace, happy to pontificate about a subject he had cultivated for years. Ray was listening and taking it all in, curious what part he had to play in all of this.

"Sounds like a trumped up summer camp," Ray said.

"I chose this place because it provides possibilities. When the grid goes down, we will use hydroelectric power from the mountain run-off or repurpose the wind turbines in the high desert valley. It also provides a tactical advantage. Venturing into high altitude isn't typically the primary focus of urban scavengers. Our choice was never an arbitrary one."

They had reached the end of the tree line and Ray could see the faces turn toward Malkin like he was the rising sun. These people trusted him and relied on him. Whatever drug empire he had tried to build and failed was nothing to this. Money could buy only so much power. But faith? Faith bred unlimited control.

A bell chimed. The group stopped their respective tasks and made their way to the long cabin Ray guessed was the mess hall.

"Hungry?" Malkin asked and followed the group.

Ray stood in the snow. Malkin made no move to stop or beckon Ray to join him. He disappeared into the open door with the rest of the campers.

If he didn't know better, Ray could have turned around and walked back down the mountain away from the craziness. Then he saw the man-sized paperweight who had been guarding him in the infirmary. The only time he seemed to draw his attention away from Ray was when this malnourished blonde walked past him into the cafeteria. She was swimming in a calf-length down coat and looked like a twig wrapped in marshmallows. But from the look the meathead had on his face, Ray could tell she was the only woman in the world for him. When Ray advanced toward the door, the man moved with him. They met at the entrance.

"What are you? My bodyguard?" Ray asked.

"Supposed to watch you. Name's Boom-Boom."

"Baby names are getting stranger every day," Ray said.

"That's not my real name," Boom-Boom said, missing the joke.

"You don't say? And what's your end of the world craft? Taffy pulling."

Boom-Boom snorted out a dry laugh. His oft-broken nose whistled a tune with the expelled air.

"Should we get to know each other better, or are you going to kill me in the woods after dinner?"

"Dunno. Did you do something I should kill you for?" Boom-Boom asked, and held the door open.

Ray couldn't figure out where he stood. The group of Ukrainian drug dealers who had gotten him into this mess had been nothing but a footnote in Malkin's grand plan. But what was his grand plan? The way he spoke to his campers, it was as though they were planning for the fall of society. Banding together to use their skills as artisans to stay alive in a cruel new post-apocalyptic world with no electricity and no modern amenities. But as soon as Ray sat down in the communal dining room to share a meal with this ragtag crew of doomsday preppers, he knew that they were nothing but a group of sheep following a charismatic leader.

Sure, they knew how to make candles out of beeswax, but in the harsh snow of the mountains, they didn't butcher the fresh meat from their own livestock. There wasn't a chicken coop providing poultry and eggs. He'd spotted a small greenhouse attached to one of the cabins — much like the one that had caged kidnapped girls in Edgar's backyard. But they weren't eating fresh-cut vegetables from a winter garden. The shit was store bought. Ray had eaten enough food he'd foraged or scraped out of cans to know the difference.

Malkin handed Ray a tray of food and beckoned for him to sit down. He did as he was told, sandwiched between his nemesis and his new musclebound friend. Once everyone was eating, Malkin stood.

"Excuse me, everyone," he said. The room stopped what they were doing and turned to face him. If these had all been people who had recently lived on the streets, it would've taken a lot more than a quick word to turn their attention. Ray's initial assessment had been right. Whatever feral instincts these people had once had were now domesticated out of them.

"As I'm sure you all have been buzzing about today, there is a new face in camp. Now I won't go through the rigamarole of asking you all to make him feel welcome or showing him how things work around here. None of those things will be necessary. Welcome him into the fold, as I have welcomed you."

Malkin raised a glass of pink goo and drank. The rest of the room followed suit.

They clung to the prophecy. Hung on his every word.

Loyalty was easy to shatter, but blind faith was unbreakable.

In that moment, Ray realized how much trouble he was in.

He wasn't trying to get out from under the thumb of a drug kingpin.

He was trying to escape the influence of a Messiah.

<h1 style="text-align:center">18</h1>

"I own you. Fuck who I want you to fuck and you do it smiling, or I sell your organs by the pound. You wanted a choice? You got one."

Burke didn't like hitting the girls. He enjoyed it, but he didn't like it. The bruises made them less appealing, no matter where they were on their body. A tender purple boo-boo on a girl's thigh didn't change a man's mind once her panties were off, but a crooked nose or a burst blood vessel in one of her eyes deterred repeat customers.

Establish control and reap the benefits. The girls who didn't take to beatings, he drugged. Those who weren't keen on the needle, he got his crew to rape into submission. Once he'd broken the horses, he loved them or starved them. One thing Burke made sure of, his girls never got comfortable. Some boys liked to make one of their girls their bottom bitch; the lady who collects for them and even runs the girls. He could see the strategy behind it. Wanting to keep the girls at a distance. But Burke was a hands-on man. Distance gave girls the thought that a little more distance could let them disappear. And he sure as shit didn't need that. He needed to know that they could be controlled, even when he wasn't around.

"Get your nappy ass outta here. You're short this week and I'll get it from you one way or the other," Burke said. The thick girl leapt off the back of the truck and wandered into the neighborhood at a quick pace. She knew not to run. That would get her in more trouble.

Leaning his crutch against the bumper, he lifted the loading ramp from the blacktop by its fabric straps and heaved it into place with his powerful forearms, the greased ball bearings rattling as the metal locked into place. He unhooked the long string he'd attached to the door from the side of the truck and pulled down, ready to move his business elsewhere just in case the bitch got bold. That happened every once in a while. Bitch would get out of line and convince whatever man she was with that he could have the next pump on the house if he went and paid Burke a visit. The girl and the man usually got a rude awakening from that one. Girls are lying if they say size doesn't matter. But Burke knew that being small had its advantages. Lower expectations. Last man who a girl convinced to get bold got a butter knife shoved in the soft spot between his crotch and leg. Burke kept the tip of it sharp enough that it would go through cheap denim, but the blade dull enough that when he pulled the knife up and out it yanked at the flesh and made the insides one hell of a mess. Word got around.

He was about to get into the cab of the truck and find a new spot to camp when he saw the fine young thing running down the sidewalk toward him. Didn't matter how big a sweater she wore, that ass and those tits showed through. Legs were still skinny, but the right amount of swollen to entice men into the thicket hiding just inside the micro-mini he could provide. He didn't think he'd see her again so soon, but he had a way to read certain girls. He could tell this one didn't have options.

Burke climbed into the cab of the truck like he hadn't noticed her and started the engine. Of course, he had no intention of pulling away and leaving her crying on the sidewalk without providing some help, but he didn't want it to look like he was waiting for her. He opened the cooler he kept in the well of the passenger seat, pulled out a bottle of apple juice and an ice pack, and wrapped it in a clean towel. Nothing reduced swelling like ice and sugar.

"Wait," the girl said. He saw her reach out toward him in the long side mirror. He tried not to smile, just in case she saw him, and put on a concerned look. What was her name again? Wouldn't matter soon enough, but it would if he wanted to get her in his good graces.

Illrissa? Naw. *Imandra?*

Imani. That's it.

"You all right, girl?" Burke leaned out the open window of the truck.

Tears were streaming down the girl's face and there were two small lines of blood coming out of each of her nostrils. She had wiped it away with the edge of her baggy sweater and it streaked on her cheeks.

"What would I hafta do?" she said through the tears.

Burke opened the door and lowered himself onto the running board, attempting to make it look difficult, even though he'd done it a million times and could make it up and down easily. If his janky legs gave out on him one day, he could be like one of those circus freaks who walked around on his hands. Didn't matter the day, he could give the pull-up boys in the park a run for their money. Not that he ever worked out there in the light of day. Better not to show what you can do until you have to.

He handed her the ice pack. She put it to her nose without a thank you. He uncapped the juice and held it until he was sure she was ready for it. The towel was quickly soaking through with blood and snot.

"Want some juice?"

She shook her head no. Burke put the cap back on and set it on the running board of the truck. He leaned hard on his crutch to make it look like an effort to shift to the side, and guided her to sit with his other hand. Calm and concerned. A man ready to listen. Something she didn't have at home. She didn't know it yet, but she was already on the hook. And Burke had all the time in the world to reel her in.

"You told the daddy, huh?" Burke asked.

"Not exactly."

"He saw the bump, I expect?"

She nodded.

Burke knew how the rest of it went. The man was in denial. It was her fault, even though most men in this hood wouldn't know a condom from a concrete block. He called her a little whore. A fucking slut. Told her he wouldn't help for shit. That she could get the real daddy to pony up. At least that was the story he'd heard over and over. But this girl was different. She was young. Too young. Either the man who gave her that child was barely a man himself or he was too much of a man to be dealing with a girl her age, no matter how filled out she was. From how swollen and crooked her nose was, Burke guessed it was the latter. Only a grown man's fist could do so much damage.

"You want me to make him disappear?" Burke asked. He had no intention of going after whoever had polluted this little girl's innocence. Hell, he'd love to find the man and shake his hand for breaking her in for him. But he had to ask. Had to make it look like he could do it. If she said yes, and they sometimes do, he'd offer an alternative solution. The solution that he was going to offer eventually, anyway.

Imani was thinking about it. Staring into the ground. He knew that look. Fantasies of the man busted up. Begging for mercy. Maybe even dead. But they were fantasies. Products of confusion and rage. All he had to do was let the movie in her head play out until she got to the part with the consequences. Then she'd ask—

"No. How about the other thing?"

There it was.

"You sure? I ain't no doctor, but you pretty far along," Burke said, tinged with a tone of concern. The guy he used, pretty sure it didn't matter how far along you were.

"Is it too late?" Imani asked, the tears flowing again.

She was almost his. He took a step toward her, but didn't touch her. That wasn't what she needed right now. She just needed one more gesture to put her over the edge. He offered her the bottle of juice again. She took it from him and raised it to her lips, careful not to let the edge of the lip touch the underside of her tender broken nose.

"Never too late to ask for help," Burke said. He watched her drink. Tentative at first, then in big gulps. There wasn't much laced in there. Mild dose of ketamine. Enough to make her pliable, but not enough to knock her out. Enough to keep her from changing her mind.

"I know what you do," she said. It was blunt and curious. A statement that reminded him under that bust line, he was still dealing with a child. But he knew plenty of clients who liked them young. He needed more product to cycle through. Because in his business, the young ones grew up real fast.

"Do you now?" Burke smiled.

"You're a pimp."

"I'm a businessman. I don't force no one to do nothing."

"How'm I supposed to trust you if you can't even admit you're a pimp?" she asked him.

Burke smiled.

"All right, then. I run girls. But that ain't all I do. I'm diversified. So, yeah, what I offer ain't free, but that don't mean you got to pay with your pussy," then, to reassure her, he added, "you too young anyhow."

"I'm old enough," she said, defending her age before she knew whether it was a good idea to do so.

"Your growing belly proves that much," Burke said. "My guess is from your busted nose you didn't ask for the fucking that got you here."

She bent her head and looked up at him through darkening eyelids. Whoever had hit her didn't give a fuck what she would look like afterwards. Burke could use that to his advantage. Which is why he'd given her the drugged juice instead of telling her to keep moving on down the road.

"Tell you what? What we're gonna do, we can't do until tomorrow night. That'll give you some time to think about it," Burke said.

"I can't go home," Imani said, tears welling in her swollen eyes.

There it was. The girl feared one of two things. Either she had a vindictive momma or daddy waiting for her at home, or it was daddy or a brother who got her in a family way. Either scenario was one that Burke could exploit. Just how he liked it.

She had slumped against the side of the truck and was leaning on the running board. The drugs were chipping away at her resistances bit by bit.

"Okay," Burke said. He scrunched his brow and limped toward her. She didn't slide away when he took a seat next to her. Nor did she recoil when he touched her thigh. Little tests Burke had developed.

"Here's what we'll do," he said. "I got a motel I operate out of sometimes. I'll get you a room tonight. Then tomorrow, we take care of your problem."

She scanned his face. Her eyelids had drooped. When she moved her head, it was dreamy and deliberate. He watched her eyes go to his ripped arms, then to his withered legs, and finally up to his face. An empathetic look offered solace. *I'm your friend.*

"I ain't gonna fuck you," Imani said. The way the curse slurred from her lips made her sound like a child practicing to be an adult.

"No offense. I don't get turned on by little girls. Besides, you want to know a secret?" He leaned in with a dirty lie, soaked in convincing honesty. "My legs aren't the only part of me that don't work right. Couldn't if I wanted to."

It was the sort of admission that was rare and raw and designed to create an instant connection.

"My momma's boyfriend, he did this." She pointed to her face. "And this." She lifted her sweatshirt to show the distended round belly button pushed from an innie to an outie from the pressure.

He opened the door to the truck, and she climbed up, crawling over to the passenger side. He threw in his crutches and hefted himself up after her.

"Let's solve this problem first. Then we'll see what happens next."

Burke turned the key, checked his mirrors and pulled into the street. He glanced over to where Imani had placed her head against the curved glass of the passenger side window and stared out at the houses they passed. The corner of his mouth went up in a slight smile.

Gathering girls was almost too easy.

As soon as he left the halfway house, Nick looked up DC Cretu's non-profit on his phone. It was an address in Highland Park, the part of the neighborhood hipsters hadn't invaded yet. Bars on the windows were a common sight, and there were more taquerias with a "C" health rating in the window than places serving gourmet sausages and prohibition-era cocktails.

The thought and care DC put into making huts for the homeless didn't extend to his own house. The yard was a scrabble of dirt and patches of yellow grass. Chipped paint covered an exterior that even in the dark testified to its dry rot. The side yard was a mess of plywood, roofing, siding and paint. Based on the condition of the house and the part of town it was in, DC was renting at a dirt cheap rate, or he'd inherited the house from a relative who'd bought it when property values in the area didn't reflect the rising tide of real estate in L.A.

Nick was about to get out of the car when he saw DC come out with a heavy duffel bag. In his other hand, he had a two handed bolt cutter. Instead of his tie and vest hipster gear, he was in a dark grey jumpsuit. He'd washed and combed the pomade out of his hair, giving it a frazzled, floppy look. Aside from the gear he was bringing with him, what made

Nick suspicious was he had removed all of his ear hardware, including the gauges. Nick couldn't be sure from a distance, but the stretched out lobes weren't hanging low without the mahogany circles holding them down. DC had closed them somehow. Tape or spirit gum.

Nick ducked down in his front seat when he saw DC scan the area. He opened the fence to the driveway and hooked up an empty flatbed trailer to a rusty Chevy truck. Wherever DC was going, it wasn't to drop off another house. It was to pick something up. If what he'd said earlier was true, that he custom built the houses for his tenants, DC would know Boyd Ballantine and maybe who might want him dead.

Yusef Veli was gone. With no evidence, they couldn't hold him without charging him. He was the only other connection to Ballantine. There was no way for them to know if he was genuinely afraid of Ballantine in the interrogation or if he was putting on a show. If he wasn't Ballantine's attacker, he might fear additional retribution from whoever had tried to silence him. If Nick promised him some protection, he might flip on D'Arby's former organization.

While Nick was staking out DC, Hsu had to check in with the black and white assigned to keep an eye on Veli's tent. Nick should have called Hsu for backup, but during the last interaction they'd had with DC, Hsu had done a monumental job pissing him off. Hsu had gone home for the day anyway, back to the mysterious wife he never talked about. Nick had nowhere special to be.

Nick followed DC up Figueroa and west on the 134. He kept his distance, but even with the large trailer clanking behind him, DC was going at a fair clip up the highway. Nick assumed he was going into Griffith Park toward the crime scene from that morning. Instead, he exited San Fernando Boulevard into an industrial district between the railroad tracks. It was the only place in the city where the Los Angeles River actually looked like a river. DC drove past the frontage road and turned the bend toward ReCyPeeps. Only in Southern California would a company need to hipster-ize recycling and eWaste reclamation to make it sound like a pop-up restaurant.

Nick turned off his headlights and parked once they'd passed the turnoff. There was a dead end straight ahead and DC would notice any other cars coming down the small cul-de-sac.

Razor wire and fencing surrounded the recycling center. Corrugated tin lined the fence to prevent anyone from clipping through it, grabbing loads of copper wire, and selling the scrap metal back to them. DC probably purchased his building materials from the recycling center at a deep discount, but the place appeared to be closed. Nick's finger flicked the button on his radio, but he hesitated calling in a robbery-in-progress. If DC was his only connection to whatever Ballantine was involved in, Nick wanted to make sure DC was actually doing something illegal before he spooked him and turned any chance of cooperation sour.

Nick was also curious what DC's next move was. There were signs posted declaring 24-hour video surveillance with armed security personnel monitoring the feed. Bright halogens shined from every corner into the yard. The 134 freeway also ran right over the place. Every car driving toward Glendale and Pasadena could look over the edge of the highway into the sprawling, brightly lit dump.

DC parked the truck on the street and got out. He pulled the duffel bag out of the flatbed. Instead of making his way to the recycling center, he turned toward the offices of a small dairy distributor next door. Stopping at the closest electric pole, he used the bolt cutters to snap the lock and access the junction box. It was a smart move. The security wasn't as intense across the alley, as the demand for stealing gourmet cheese wasn't that high.

He pulled out a small tablet and connected it to the box with a couple of alligator clips. The lights in the driveway went out, shrouding DC in darkness except for the glow of the tablet. DC placed the tablet face down in the grass, extinguishing even that light.

Nick couldn't see where DC had gone. Getting out of his car was stupid; he knew it, but he didn't want to lose eyes on the suspect. Nick snuck around the corner. There was just enough light coming off the halogens of the construction dump.

He kept his distance, but he was close enough to peer over DC's shoulder as he worked. Another tablet came out of the duffel bag as DC tapped into the next electric pole attached to the office building. There was a precision to the way he carefully moved between each step. Planned movements. On the tablet, Nick could see DC had tapped into the security camera feed. Shutting down the video feed would be a bad idea. That would immediately alert anyone who was paying attention that something had gone wrong. But DC had done this before. He didn't shut the video feed down. He set it on a loop. So when he made his next move, the only people who would notice were speeding by on the highway overhead at a 70 mph.

The halogens went out. But not all of them. Just the ones directly overhead. It was a calculated and surgical strike. Anyone in the area would notice if the large scrap yard experienced a full blackout, but if a small section went out, it was a faulty light. And in the exacting darkness, it didn't matter how many cars passed by overhead. Shrouded in black, DC could take whatever he wanted.

As DC moved further down the driveway, Nick slipped into the fence, following the same path. He was deep in it now. If he turned back and went to the car for backup, he would blow the whole thing. Whatever DC was taking out of there, he would need to come back to the truck.

Staggered and held together with thick nylon straps, a set of long flatbed trailers sat stacked right next to the corrugated metal fence. The owners of the scrapyard probably never thought that someone would use them as a ladder. The top of the stack was in full view of the security cameras and usually bathed in bright light. But in the blackout, that's exactly what DC did. A pile of rubble on the other side kept him from falling twenty feet into the debris, and he disappeared from sight.

Nick grabbed one of the nylon straps and hoisted himself. He took his time moving up the flatbed ladder, careful not to alert DC someone was following him. When he reached the top, he kept low and peered over the fence.

At first, he saw nothing. Concrete and drywall dust covered everything, making the whole yard look frosted. Rusted metal tangled in piles of busted bricks. Stacked pallets separated sections. It was a scene out of an apocalyptic wasteland. Images of first-responders digging through the rubble of the twin towers flashed through his mind. It was what he imagined downtown Los Angeles would look like once the big earthquake finally hit. In the low light, he saw DC move along the edge of the darkness, scanning the piles.

Nick had to move. If DC progressed to a different section and changed the light pattern, Nick would be a sitting duck. He took a step over the fence and did his best to find his footing. His foot slipped. The concrete shifted beneath him. He scraped the skin off his calf where his jeans rode up, but didn't draw blood. It still hurt like a mother.

He pressed his back against the crumbled sheetrock, construction dust drying his mouth out. He was certain DC had heard that, but now Nick's only move was forward. His feet slipping was the first thing that reminded him of how impetuous he was being. When he filled out the report later, he could say he was pursuing DC on a robbery-in-progress, or at the very least, breaking and entering, but it didn't excuse why he hadn't called it in. It would be a paperwork nightmare. He had no choice now, he had to continue pursuing DC and arrest him, or he was trespassing without probable cause.

The wait seemed infinite. But when DC hadn't backtracked with a gun drawn, Nick slipped carefully down the pile of junk onto the solid ground. He pulled his service weapon before turning the corner around the pile, not knowing what was waiting for him there. Lack of light and a maze of blind corners didn't make Nick excited to continue into the scrapyard, waiting for DC to come at him with a rusty pipe or nail-ridden 2x4.

The burglar was hefting broken sheetrock and other scrap off of the plywood siding he'd put together months before. The city had taken the time to separate the small houses into easily moveable pieces. In the temporary blackout, it would be easy for DC to heft them onto his shoulder and carry them back the way he came. Nick could still make out the bright paint of the houses, even if they were a little scuffed or dusted from their brief stay in the scrapyard. He crept up and placed the cold metal of his gun barrel against the base of DC's neck.

"That wouldn't be Boyd Ballantine's house, would it?"

DC jumped at the sound of Nick's voice, perhaps thinking initially that the gun against his head was a stray piece of scrap metal. He spun on Nick and let out a little shriek when he saw the weapon.

"Jesus! Fuck!"

"Out for an evening stroll?" Nick asked.

"The owners, they let me in," DC said. He must have thought that Nick was a private security guard and didn't recognize him.

"Uh-huh. LAPD," Nick said, not bothering to reach for his badge.

"Bullshit," DC shot back at him. "What? You come here to protect what you stole from me?"

"I could arrest you right now, take you in for breaking and entering, but I think you can help me."

"I've seen what you fucking fascists do to people who help you."

"Fine," Nick said. He pulled his cuffs from the holder at the back of his belt. "Turn around."

"See? Fucking pricks. All of you."

Nick cuffed him and sat him down in the dirt.

"I spooked you and you're emotional, so you get another chance to help me. Do you recognize the name Boyd Ballantine?"

DC strained his eyes to get a good look at Nick's face.

"I remember you. From the 110. Your gook partner here too?"

"That's not nice."

"What? You going to beat on me until you get what you want? Fucking police state," DC grumbled the last bit under his breath.

Nick picked up a handful of dirt from the ground.

"No. But my guess is there are some things in here that would easily cut your retinas if I blew it in your face," Nick said.

DC paused. He wasn't ready for that. Nick had no intention of hurting the little racist hipster. It would be easy for his uppity little ass to get litigious.

"What do I get if I give you Ballantine?" DC asked.

"So, you do know him?"

"Don't turn my words on me and give me that crap. I'm happy to keep my mouth shut until we're in a more comfortable environment."

"If you want to do that, we can. But you'll go through processing and I've got probable cause for following you in here. You'll have some trouble helping the homeless from prison," Nick pulled out his phone. "Say the word and I'll call for backup."

"You're a real asshole."

"An asshole wouldn't give you a choice. I think it's good what you're doing. Giving people a place to live out of the elements. Can't say I like how you get your building materials, but I can see your side of it."

"Glad you approve."

"Ballantine. Tell me about him. If I like what I hear, we both walk out of here like this never happened and you never do this again."

DC took in a deep breath and coughed out some construction dust.

"Met him a few months ago. Built him a house."

"A few more details, please. This isn't a Hemingway story."

"Haven't seen him. Didn't get to warn him before you pricks cleared him out."

"What made you build a house for him? Out of all the people you meet out on the street?"

"I was scared of him, all right?" DC spit out. "His hands. All scarred up. Looked like he'd seen some shit. But then I heard his story."

"About how he used to ship girls from Asia and pimp them out for pennies?" Nick asked.

DC gaped at him. "What? No. Who told you that?"

"His arrest record."

"He was an artist. Drawing. Woodcarving. That's how he sliced up his hands."

"He fed you a load of shit."

"You don't believe me? Look at his house, or what's left of it," DC said, nodding to the pile of scrap wood.

"Which one is it?"

"Bright orange."

Nick turned around and squinted at the pile. He couldn't make out distinct colors, but could tell the red tones from the purples. He shoved over a few panels to get at the ones underneath.

"See?"

Nick could see what DC and the guy from the halfway house had been talking about. What had been plain plywood for most of the scrap was a tangle of drawings and doodles. Whatever talent Ballantine lacked in cutting people open, he made up for in artistic finesse. Nick tapped the flashlight on his cell phone and the tangle of drawings lit up in the darkness.

"If you wanted to keep this interrogation under the radar, this isn't the way to do it."

"Shut up," Nick said.

Among the drawings was information. Whether Ballantine drew around it to hide it, or if he was a natural doodler and used the surface of his walls as a notepad, Nick would never know. In the tangle of flowing lines, there was a portrait in the mess. A woman.

Curves and angles in all the right places. Dark eyes. It looked like a portrait of the Virgin Mary. Sketched by a blue-balled Joseph. Love and care were in every stroke of the Sharpie. Tenderness there as though he didn't want to forget any detail, but there was also a longing. Deep-seated passion where her delicate fingers brushed at the nape of her lithe neck, perched to trace a trail down to the cleavage below her soft collarbone.

It was her. The girl from the tent.

The first evidence she existed outside of the Jane Doe file in RHD.

Nick snapped a photo of the panel and even though they didn't seem to contain pertinent information other than doodles and tags, he took pictures of each of the other panels too, hoping there was something else there he would see when he wasn't in the darkness of a scrapyard.

"Somebody overhead saw those flashes," DC said, his voice panicked. "If you want to keep this under your hat, we have to get out of here, and quick."

As much as Nick hated to admit it, DC was right. A deal was a deal, and he'd promised to let the little shit go. Richard Cretu had made some bad choices coming in to steal his houses back, but ultimately he was doing more good for the world out of prison.

Nick removed DC's handcuffs, ready to follow him out of the scrapyard. He had the information he needed and had done his good deed for the day.

Crack! What little light Nick had went temporarily black. Bright specks of light flashed in and out of his vision. He was back on his ass in the dirt and it took him a moment to register that the crown of DC's forehead had bashed into the bridge of his nose. He was gone at a full sprint before Nick could get to his feet and run after him.

DC was scrambling up the pile of rubble at the edge of the fence line. He turned around to see Nick had shaken the blow off and was pursuing him. He picked up a large piece of cement and heaved it down. Even while he was trying to get his bearings back, Nick easily dodged the projectile.

Problem was, heaving the rock at his pursuer caused DC to lose his balance and then his footing. The pile crumbled underneath him. Instead of stumbling back onto the concrete, he tried to catch himself and fell forward.

Nick skidded to a halt in the dust. All movement stopped. The only sound he could hear were the tires above him rolling along the cracked blacktop.

He didn't see what had happened until he was right on top of DC. A stray piece of rebar, sharpened and bent at the wrong angle, had broken his fall. It had impaled him through the back of his neck, killing him instantly. There was a shocked glaze in his eyes, the life stolen away from him before his mind could process what had happened.

Nick stood stark still over the body. He had pursued DC onto private property without calling for backup. He had held him without placing him under arrest. Nick had made a deal with someone committing a crime to get information. DC had died while Nick pursued him.

Accident or not, Nick was in a lot of trouble.

And he didn't know what to do next.

<h1 style="text-align:center">20</h1>

After Ray's initial introduction to the group, they left him to explore the camp and settle in. It made him nervous. He had come up to the mountains for some epic confrontation with the people who had indentured him against his will and met with no resistance at all. They gave him a choice. Stay or go.

But he knew it wasn't a true choice. He could disappear. Leave everything he knew over the past few years and find a new life in a new place. It wasn't like he hadn't done it before when everything had fallen apart. The first time, it left him with emotional scars that never faded. Memories that influenced every choice he made. This time, it would leave him with physical scars. The tattoo would remind him he was being hunted. Wanted for murder by the LAPD. A target of whoever Osip Kosbur had deigned to protect him from. And even though Malkin pretended to not care about the tattoo and what it meant, there had been too much effort put into keeping him in the mountains.

A fire that was never meant to kill him, instead merely injure him enough to understand he was vulnerable. The hulking bodyguard who never seemed to disappear. The illusion of choice. Ray came up to the mountains to be free of the bonds the tattoo represented. If he walked down the mountain, uncovered Low Seward's Audi and drove off to some unknown destination, he would always have a target on his back.

He took a few days to stay in his cabin and recover from his wounds. When he finally emerged out into the snow, the burns scabbing over, he needed to find out what was really going on. Whenever he approached someone busy at a task, they would make small talk with him and give him a knowing smile, but the conversations never deepened past the surface subject. They had offered him an apprenticeship in several vocations, but he refused every one, telling them he wanted to get a larger assessment of what was missing from the group and see how he could input his own unique skills.

From what Ray could see of the group, they were adept at creating the sort of artisan crafts that hipsters at flea markets flocked to, but he couldn't see how they translated into practical survival skills. Malkin pitched him that each of the tasks were a mask for something else, like Mr. Miyagi teaching Daniel-san to paint the fence when he was really teaching him how to block a punch, but Ray had yet to see how knitting potholders would provide much beyond having a stockpile of afghan blankets when the world of men collapsed. Small cliques formed when groups took breaks. The rhetoric spread by Malkin bled into the conversations of those who followed him:

"When the world falls, we will be the shining beacon of light on the mountaintop."

"Syria, Mexico, El Salvador. These are governments overshadowed by gang control. More than organized crime. Organized chaos. And what's the result? Crumbling structures, mass migrations, civil wars? We don't want these things."

"And yet your worst days, the most destitute and shameful minutes of your existence, pale in comparison to how those cities controlled by ISIS or The Cartel survive. You can still find running water. You can

defecate in a fountain knowing you won't have to turn around and drink the same water."

These people had given their lives over to the possibility of the downfall of society. One man raving on a street corner was amusing. A group of people spreading it as gospel was a frightening prospect.

But Ray didn't believe it. The words coming out of Malkin's mouth didn't jibe with what Ray saw.

In the dark of the woods, generators weren't running the lights. There were no solar panels wiped free of snow on the outside of the cabins. The camp was connected to the grid that Malkin claimed to fear. These people weren't being trained to live off the grid. He was training them for something else. He was training them to be docile. Pliable.

There didn't appear to be a stockpile of chemical toilets or a system for distilling snow and rainwater. Everything was still flushing and coming out of the taps. Perhaps Malkin was employing a "use it before you lose it" philosophy with the campers, but they still seemed ill-prepared for the dark days he was predicting.

Each group's task had a purpose. The creation of some piece of a larger puzzle. Ray did his best to keep track of all of it in his mind, but he was also being careful of what food and drink they gave him after his initial drugging. After years spent scraping by for every meal, he tried not to get indoctrinated into Malkin's three-meals-a-day regimen, but he was weak and depriving himself of calories would take its toll.

Malkin had said that everyone in the camp had come from the streets, hand-picked because they'd learned to survive on their own. But if the Ukrainian savior had been running this scam for as long as it looked like, most of these people had forgotten how to live on the streets. How to depend on themselves. Being able to find the best canned goods in a dumpster behind a supermarket didn't give you the skills to can your own food when the supermarket didn't exist. He had sold these people a lie. If Ray had known that Malkin's empire was based on horse shit, he wouldn't have even bothered to make the trip. He would've just lived with the ugly tattoo. But several things didn't sit right with him.

Ray thought that maybe instead of banking on the money-making operation of Shadow Dance, perhaps Malkin was taking in all the profits from items sold at the craft fairs and flea markets, telling the sheep he was using the profits to build up their infrastructure for when the end came, but was really pocketing the profits.

That wasn't a likely scenario, either. Two or three people each working on their given talent at a relaxed pace, buying materials, plus booth rental at flea markets and transportation costs — Ray didn't know exact figures, but basic deduction told him those enterprises were probably losing money or breaking even.

Malkin claimed he didn't know about the details of Osip Kosbur's goings-on in Los Angeles, but that was a lie, too. The game was too tight. The network too connected. A fledgling group of drug-dealers peddling a new designer drug would've started on the ground floor with the junkies and club kids and worked their way up the food chain. The Shadow Dance cartel didn't do that.

Ray had kept up with the details of the investigation, reading newspapers and hitting the public library for any details of the operation he'd helped take down as he looked for Malkin in the woods. The Shadow Dancers started at the top. A couple of movie stars. And they'd used a high-level agency assistant as their dealer. No one with a business school degree on track to become an agent at one of the biggest talent pools in Hollywood would decide that a drug dealing side business that was merely "testing the market" was a good idea. Whoever had recruited the kid responsible for killing Low

Seward, there was no way they were working without Malkin's go-ahead. The way Malkin had been moving Ray around like a pawn on a chessboard had been carefully calculated. Too smart. Ray was still trying to figure out what Malkin's end game was, but there was one thing he had figured out for certain — Malkin left nothing to chance.

And now Ray was in it. Apart from being physically unable to fight his way out of the new situation, he had Boom-Boom watching his every move. Whatever trap Malkin had set for Ray, he'd walked right into it. And Malkin made Ray want to find him. Stayed at arm's length just long enough.

Ray was tired of making the right moves in the wrong direction.

It was late. Some campers had already turned in for the night. But Ray was staying up. He hadn't seen Deuce for a few days and was waiting for the light in his cabin to flick on.

The kid had been avoiding eye contact since the gathering around the fire pit. Every time Ray had made a move toward him, Deuce magically found somewhere else to be.

Then Deuce was gone. The only other person in camp with a Bear tattoo had vanished. Maybe they gave Deuce the same choice, and he had chosen wrong.

Someone grabbed him by the scruff of his coat. Ray swung around to see his bodyguard and his waif of a girlfriend standing behind him. They had become his constant companions. Ray had to stay in Boom-Boom's line of sight and Boom-Boom never wanted to be over ten feet from his girlfriend, so Ray had become a de facto third wheel. The lack of sex was building up and Boom-Boom was becoming more frustrated with Ray's presence with each passing day.

"You found somethin' you like doing yet?" Sweets asked. When she talked, she giggled at the end of every sentence. At first, Ray found it annoying that he was being followed around by the human equivalent of an anime schoolgirl, but eventually concluded that Sweets wasn't all there. He thought her happy-go-lucky attitude resulted from a slow stream of opioids, which Malkin lamented as being a problem on the streets of Big Bear, but then he realized she had a slight mental disability. It almost made him feel sympathy for the D-Battery who was holding him by the neck like a lost puppy.

"Haven't quite found my calling," Ray said. He wriggled out of Boom-Boom's grasp.

"I help with the flowers," Sweet said.

"Yeah, I know," Ray said. Since realizing she was a little slow, he'd tuned the sarcasm out of his responses when talking to her. "Figured I might apprentice with your boyfriend."

She giggled again.

"He doesn't do nothin' except keep me company," she said, oblivious.

"Haven't been able to since you showed up," Boom-Boom growled at Ray.

"I'm talking about your other skill set," Ray said.

"What, like tongue stuff?" Sweets asked.

"Shut up," Boom-Boom scoffed at her.

"What? You do good tongue stuff."

Ray smiled and got an idea.

"Maybe I'll work on my tongue stuff," Ray said, and turned to the silent camp.

He scanned his brain for the craziness he'd buried there years ago. Things in a dense manifesto that led him to a treasure in the Hollywood Hills. The mad rants of a murderous conspiracy theorist he once thought was his friend.

"Zealots and thieves have overtaken our government!" He yelled to no one. "I've watched them squander their resources to line the pockets of their corporate overlords while those of us trying to improve our lives scrounge on the edges of death. They rigged the system so that you're better off having nothing than having a little. They want you to fight for your tiny piece of the pie. Hoping that your scuffle for crumbs will keep you from seeing that they've already cleared the table!"

Doors opened and groggy faces stared at him. A crowd didn't gather. Instead, they gave the raving, bandaged man his space. Boom-Boom didn't know how to deal with Ray in this state. Ray could see Boom-Boom vacillating between what to do next. If he grabbed him and put his hand over Ray's mouth, he would validate everything Ray had been saying. If he clomped him across the back of the head and knocked him unconscious, the other residents might fear he would do the same to them if they continued to follow the rhetoric. So he did what Ray didn't expect.

"Yeah!" Boom-Boom added. When Ray looked back at him, he gestured at Ray to shut up, but Ray was never good at following directions.

"Leaders think they have the answer to the problems we face. But when they oust the previous leaders from power, all they do is follow their own agendas. We aren't doing enough here. When the power goes off and you will actually have to find your food, what will you eat? The bark from the trees?"

Sweets giggled, but stopped when she saw Reggie approaching. Ray turned to face him. Malkin's flock perked up, focused on what was going to happen next.

"Have they given you the weapons to defend yourself?" Ray said, directing his diatribe at Reggie. "Physical weapons and mental ones? Have they given you resilience for resistance or have they taken away your drive in pursuit of meaningless tasks?"

Reggie stopped a few feet from Ray, a lazy smile on his face. "What?" Ray confronted.

"Oh, don't let me stop you," Reggie said to Ray, gesturing for him to continue. Then he turned to Boom-Boom. "Go take a break with your girl. I got this."

The big man didn't have to be told twice. He grabbed Sweets by the hand and dragged her off to the cabin to get the alone time he'd been craving.

"Are you going to set me on fire again if I don't stop?"

Reggie shrugged and lit another one of his stinking cigars. The rest of the group seemed to take their cue from him and went back to their bunks.

"Malkin was really hoping this would work out, but you're just as stubborn as I pegged you."

"What did he want me to do? Roll over and help lead these people into the promised land?" Ray said, no longer yelling.

"You have a flair for rousing speeches," Reggie said.

"Used to listen to someone spout that exact crap on the streets of Los Feliz. Funny how the same words coming out of a respectable mouthpiece can make all the difference."

"Good to know I'm not the only one who doesn't believe Malkin's bullshit hook, line, and sinker."

"So, what? You're my buddy now?" Ray asked.

Reggie stepped in closer and lowered his voice. Ray's first instinct was to jump away, but he didn't want to give Reggie the satisfaction of showing weakness.

"May not seem like it now, but I'm the only friend you got up here. I've got another proposal for you."

"Why? This could be a chance to be a part of something meaningful," Ray smiled. "I know there's more going on here than you let on. I'm not stupid. But fighting has gotten me nowhere. Maybe it's time I gave in."

"Come with me," Reggie said. He started toward a cabin at the top of the hill, the one attached to the greenhouse. Ray didn't move.

"This is between you and me now. Alone," Reggie said with his back to Ray. "If you want to kill me, this is your big chance."

21

All the stress from the past month of devastation came pouring back with one night of sweat and anxiety. The steam of the shower rushed over his body and Nick could feel the panic welling up from his gut. It started as a tingle, a vine of ivy snaking around his intestines before winding tightly around his stomach. The fear doubled him to his knees as the shampoo stung his eyes. When the threads of the attack reached his lungs, he gasped for breath, then coughed as he inhaled water and soap. Tears streamed down his face, his eyes burning. He turned the taps off as he crouched in this standing shower, head pressed against the hard plastic where black mildew had formed. Suds ran between his shaking fingers as he closed his eyes.

Flashes came at him quick in the darkness.

Bernard's face exploded in slow-motion behind his eyelids.

Nick's eyes shot open as he vomited into the shower drain. Bile and chunks of the fast food he'd eaten in the car outside DC's house splattered the yellowing plastic.

He turned on the water again and held his mouth open to wash the taste away, eyes closed to the spray.

DC gurgled in his mind's eye. He could smell the iron from the scavenger's blood mixing with the rust of the rebar sticking out of his throat.

Nick sputtered at the water and lost control again.

On his hands and knees, he did his best to regulate his breathing as the basin covered his wrists and knee caps with watered down puke, remnants of fries and burger clogging the drain.

Once the panic passed, Nick turned off the water and slid the door to the shower open. He used his fingernails to scoop the larger pieces out of the drain and flung them into the toilet.

As clean as he was going to get it, he stood up, lathered, and rinsed clean.

Out of the shower, he blew his nose to get the last bits that had retreated into his nasal cavity and opened his medicine cabinet, looking for mouthwash.

A bottle of Xanax the police psych had prescribed after the incident in West Hollywood stared back at him.

He hadn't taken them.

The sheer fear of becoming a cliché held him back.

He also hadn't thrown them away.

The mouthwash burned his throat as he swished, the taste of sick mixing with antiseptic alcohol.

Hollow eyes stared back at him as he closed the medicine cabinet. The anti-anxiety medication stayed where it was for the moment. A fix he knew he needed, but didn't want.

He slumped onto the toilet, cataloguing all the evidence he'd left behind.

Did he bleed when DC hit him? The image staring back at him showed a slight bruise on the bridge of his nose. No black eyes, beyond the lack of sleep he'd collected over the past month.

Was there skin from where he scraped his shin? Did it snake down his pant leg and settle next to the body?

He rubbed his face and tried to shake off the speculation of the pile of DNA he might have left at the scene. What he knew he couldn't cover up were the footprints. Drywall dust covered everything. Even an amateur sleuth would take one look at the scene and see that DC hadn't been alone.

The bile rose in his throat once more.

And then he heard it.

Thunder.

The elusive rain that only visited L.A. in the winter months had one last gift to grant Nick in his rising panic.

He ran to his living room and shoved open the curtains.

It came down in sheets. A torrent of forgiveness. A glimmer of hope.

Nick collapsed in front of his window and wept.

All the hurt and pain and suffering he had been keeping inside for the past month broke forth from inside him. The rain telling him it was okay to feel. To mourn the loss of his mother. To embrace the post-traumatic stress of the Low Seward case.

You panicked. You ran away. A gut reaction. Nothing more.

The sobs subsided and Nick sat up, the back of his head pressed into the cushions of his couch.

With a few deep breaths, he stood and went to the kitchen, cracked some ice into a glass, and filled it from the tap.

Clutching the cold to his forehead, he heard his mother's voice echo through his temples. Nagging him to do the right thing. Every instinct told him to listen to his mother, but like every stubborn child, he knew it was the last thing he wanted to do.

22

Reggie's cabin was designed to reflect the tastes of a man who wished to live a life of simplicity. It was one room, save the bathroom. In the corner was a wood burning potbelly stove. It was larger than what the cabin needed to stay warm and was blasting heat. Ray thought it might have doubled as a kiln for one of the camp's artisans. One of the few indications that part of the camp was actually off the grid.

There were several wood sculptures of wildlife scattered throughout, but the ones that were the most accurate were the bears. On the wall there were several large glass octagons. The contents were moving. Upon closer inspection, Ray could see Reggie had filled them with bees. Thousands of bees.

"There are little tubes where they filter into the greenhouse one at a time. Pollinate the plants and bring the nectar back to make some of the sweetest honey you've ever had."

"Out of all the shit going on here, wouldn't have pegged you as a honey guy," Ray said.

"What would you have thought?" Reggie asked.

"Seamstress."

Reggie chuckled and went to his wet bar. He made himself two versions of his disgusting drink and offered one to Ray. Ray didn't reach for it, so Reggie kept it.

"What are you going to do when society falls and they stop making that crap?" Ray asked.

"I'll figure something out," Reggie took a sip. "You want to tell me why you came looking for us instead of trying to disappear?"

"You want to tell me why you didn't kill me when you had the chance?" Ray asked.

"I could kill you now if that would make you feel better," Reggie said.

"I don't think you will," Ray said, tired of the meaningless bluffs.

"We have a good thing going up here. Or had, until you got in the way."

"I didn't ask to be involved."

"But you are now," Reggie's tone changed. "Tell me what you want."

"I want out," Ray said. All the light banter had vanished from his voice. "Whatever this is. Whatever it means. I want no part of it."

Reggie looked at Ray and smiled. It was a look of pity for someone too ignorant to understand simple concepts.

"And what do you think it means?" Reggie said, eyes going to the tattoo under Ray's coat.

"Somebody told me it says 'Property of The Bear.'"

"Not what it says. What it means."

Ray's instinct was to leap up and shove his fist toward the back of Reggie's head one punch at a time. Unfortunately, he was still weak from his burns and Reggie would easily best him in a man to man fight. He'd have to bide his time.

"Cut the semantic bullshit."

"I'm serious," Reggie said. "When you came up here, what were you planning on doing? To be free of us, or whoever you thought was holding the puppet strings?"

Ray opened his mouth to speak, but realized he had no answer. Tattooed against his will, indentured to a master for no specific purpose, he'd let blind rage take over. He wanted nothing more than to bulldoze any obstacle in his path. But he didn't stop to think what that path was. Or why it was so important for it to be clear.

"I take it from your lack of answer that you don't really know," Reggie said.

"I just wanted to be left alone, all right. That's all I've ever fucking wanted, but everybody on the planet seems to have other plans for me."

"You really don't see it, do you?"

Ray's anger was bubbling high. He was worried he might snap his molars from clenching his jaw. His breath was coming out hot and heavy from his nostrils like a horse after a throttled gallop. His eyes were searching the room for any weapon he could use to cut the smile from Reggie's smug face, but there was nothing within reach.

"That tattoo enslaved you, yeah. But the moment you killed Osip Kosbur, it became a death sentence."

The hairs on the back of Ray's neck stood up and his body awaited the death blow.

"Kosbur wasn't lying when he said he wanted to protect you. If you hadn't been such a hothead, who knows, you could have had money, power, whatever you'd have liked."

"I don't want any of that."

"So I've learned. Care to tell me why?"

Ray looked through him with angry eyes. "No."

"Fine. It doesn't matter why you're doing it, it seems to be what you want. Unfortunately, you've cost us a hell of a lot of money and we don't live in a world where you get something for nothing."

Here it comes, Ray thought.

"Whatever Kosbur was planning on doing with you was his business. And his business was merely one division of what we're trying to accomplish."

"Yeah? And can I ask what that is?"

Reggie returned Ray's look from earlier. "No."

"If I don't do what you want?"

"You go back to your life in L.A."

Ray snorted out a laugh. His life. Wanted in connection with a murder. All evidence pointing in his direction. His life in L.A. would be short-lived.

"I assume you laugh because you think as soon as you show your face in the city, the LAPD will pick you up. But, here's the rub. You've got bigger problems than me or Malkin or the police. You may not mind living on the street. God fucking knows why. You may even enjoy the freedom of it enough to reject the conventions and conveniences of normal living. But you don't want to go to prison. And you like breathing. You don't have a death wish. You aren't suicidal."

"How do you know?"

"You escaped the fire."

"Panic."

"I also know you're good at gaining people's trust. Only took you one night to get Deuce to let you stay with him."

"Pretty sure you put him up to that."

"I told him to befriend you. The rest of it was all you."

"Don't take offense if I have a hard time trusting anything you say."

Reggie ignored him.

"You're clever and resourceful. You can think on your feet and use whatever is around to get the job done."

"Was that what that garbage at the bar was all about? Now that I've gone through my three trials of valor, can I have the Holy Grail?"

"We'll let you go. Forget all about you. Plant some evidence taking the heat off of you for the Mochulyak murder. Even pay to have your tattoo removed. But I need you to do something for me first."

Ray stared through him. Whatever he was going to ask, it wouldn't be fun. Or legal.

"If our connection were as easy as laser tattoo removal, I wouldn't be sitting here," Ray said.

"I wasn't being facetious when I said that tattoo is now a death sentence. It is. There are people out there, the people Kosbur was protecting you from, who weren't pleased when Kosbur took over some of Pretty Boy D'Arby's business interests. We did our best to cover it up when you killed—"

"Drugged."

"—*drugged* Kosbur, but in your haste to get away, you left witnesses. Have you seen anyone here other than Deuce with one of those tattoos? Do you remember how many people you saw who had one? Think about it."

Ray paused and made a mental map. Edgar didn't have one. Neither did Crowley.

Deuce. The dead guy in the car. Mochulyak. Osip Kosbur. And Kosbur's lackey at the bathhouse. How many had there been?

Towel attendant. Changing room guard.

No. Wait. He hadn't seen a tattoo on the guards. He only assumed they had them. Only the towel attendant.

"Six, including me."

"Ten. That we know of," Reggie said. "And opposing forces are mounting to destroy anyone and everyone involved in Kosbur's operation."

"You mean *your* operation?"

"No. Those tattoos were never our idea. They were his. Loyalty oaths he brought with him from his mother country. We thought they were a bad idea because they would be an easily identifiable mark for law enforcement. Now, we're seeing that they are an easy mark for criminals too. The tattooed are going to be hunted by our enemies. One was Kosbur's bodyguard."

Reggie pulled out an old flip phone and pushed it in Ray's face. The picture was grainy on the ancient cellphone, but it was the guard from outside the bathhouse the night Ray was there. A bullet hole at his temple.

"Kosbur was gone. Which means whoever took Kosbur with them took care of the guards. Answers would probably start with this guy."

Reggie sorted through some papers and handed a file to Ray.

"What's this? Your tax return?"

Ray opened the file.

Inside was a picture of a man who was red-faced from too much booze or dancing or both. He was in the middle of a laugh or a cough. It was a really shitty picture of the towel attendant from the bathhouse. The one who Mr. Crowley warned about his dying dog.

The one who had let Ray walk away.

Ray sat with the photo for a moment, then looked up at Reggie.

"If you don't know what happened to Kosbur, how did you know I drugged him?"

"The guy in that photo cut the security footage shortly after you left."

"Which means you have footage of me and Kosbur," Ray let out a frustrated snort. "I wasn't as free to leave as you implied."

Reggie lit another cigar and slow-clapped.

"This isn't a choice at all," Ray said.

"That guy and the other two tattoos are in the wind. What I want is for you to find them before they get taken out by whoever cleaned up your mess and bring them back here so I can protect them."

"How do you know I didn't kill the guard?"

Reggie smiled. "I'd have put a bullet in your brain as soon as you crossed the city limits. You may have killed people, Ray, but you're not a murderer."

"If people with the tattoo are being hunted, that means me too, huh?"

"See?" Reggie finished his drink. "Clever."

"But I'm safe here. Aren't I? Why would I go back to L.A. and put myself at risk?"

"Because as much as Malkin thinks he can bring you into the fold, I don't want you here. You've shown that you want no part of this place and the better tomorrow we're trying to build. We can't trust you. And if I send you out into the world, you can't walk away from this. You'll always be looking over your shoulder for death to come knocking. Waiting for that footage to make its way to the LAPD. If there's one thing we know about you, Ray, it's that you want to live and you want to do it on your terms."

"Let me get this straight? I become a bounty hunter for the price of my freedom or I walk away right now and spend the rest of my life hoping I don't get killed or arrested."

Reggie nodded.

Ray weighed his options. He'd been manipulated and lied to on too many occasions to take Reggie at his word. There was another game he was playing.

Reggie leaned against the desk across from him, arms crossed, a benevolent smile never leaving his face. He'd honed the pitch. Practiced. Like he'd given it before.

They had led him into a maze with nothing but dead ends. Ray sighed and leaned back in his chair. "Where do I start?"

"According to the LAPD, you're still the only connection to those tattoos," Reggie said. "If law enforcement finds any more bodies, fancy a guess who their first suspect is going to be? If you end up in police custody, no one wins."

"What if that's exactly what I want?" Ray said.

Reggie shot him a condescending look. They both knew that wasn't true.

"Like it or not, you're in this. The only question is how do you want to get out of it?"

"And what are you proposing?" Ray asked.

"I heard you're good at solving mysteries. Here's a chance to put your skills to use. Other than that guy in the picture, there are two more surviving members of Kosbur's crew. This guy is a piece of shit. A worthless coward. But he's our only connect to the other two. And those two have skills we can use. Find him, get some answers."

"Still don't get why you need me?"

"Kosbur's death likely spooked them. Won't trust anyone without one of those tattoos. Once you've made contact and sent them our way, you're free."

"Pardon me for not trusting a goddamn thing you say."

"Your pride got you here. You're not righteous or puritanical. I saw what you're capable of. You tore the street mystic apart to get what you needed. Attacked Kosbur. You're a survivor. All I ask is for you to hone your natural skills."

"And if I told you to go fuck yourself?"

"Then I know exactly how you'll die. And I won't have to lift a finger."

"If I let this 'hunter' keep coming, he'll make his way to you," Ray said.

"True. But you'll already be dead," Reggie said. "You don't have many choices here. Either help me hunt down Bear tattoos or become a victim yourself."

"Or third option: I could kill you right now and wait and see if I can make a deal with our mysterious hunter."

"You and I both know this is your only way to get free. Having one of those tattoos makes you an endangered species."

There was another story here, but staying in the camp where Reggie could control the variables was a bad idea. If the story was true, it indentured the three people with Bear tattoos. Maybe he could recruit them and take Malkin down for good.

"These are my options? Hunter or prey?" Ray asked.

Reggie nodded.

Ray pretended he was contemplating his options, but he'd already decided. After a month in Big Bear, he'd found the man he was searching for and instead of enacting his revenge, he was voluntarily heading back to Los Angeles. There was something else going on, but he wouldn't figure it out under Malkin's thumb and Reggie's horse shit.

"I'm gonna need a car."

23

"Hope you didn't spend all night in the rain staking out that address in Highland Park," Hsu said.

Nick pretended like he was sorting through files, but he was staring through the desk a thousand yards away. He'd forgotten that Hsu knew about Ballantine's tiny house. And that he had registered with the department that he was staying on-shift to tail DC. Nick didn't know how to respond. The truth would damn him, but Hsu was adept at dealing with liars. Even his own colleagues.

"Why?" Nick asked.

Hsu handed over a sheet of paper, still warm from the printer. Nick scanned what turned out to be the morning briefing sheet from the Glendale Police Department. They'd found DC's body.

"Attempted robbery," Hsu said. Nick looked over the report, but it was light on details. He was trying to remain steady and professional, but Hsu was no idiot. He could probably tell that Nick hadn't slept a wink the night before.

"I went to his house," Nick said, sticking to stating facts.

"And that's the reason you didn't find him there."

Hsu probably assumed that Nick had staked out the place all night with no results. That was why his eyes were puffy and bloodshot. Not because Nick had committed involuntary manslaughter and fled the scene. Hsu didn't ask for any follow-up and Nick knew better than to offer without prompting.

"What happened?" Nick asked.

I killed him.

"I called the lead in Glendale as soon as I saw it this morning. Still preliminary, but looks like Richard Cretu tried to break into ReCyPeeps to get his building materials back, slipped and found himself on the business end of some rebar embedded in a piece of concrete. It severed his spine, so if he didn't die right away, he didn't feel much."

The image had played itself over and over in Nick's mind for the past twelve hours. The blood gushing out of DC's neck. The hollow, shocked eyes peering back at him. Accusing him of murder.

It wasn't my fault.

It was an accident.

"Accidental death," Nick said. Not a question. Statement.

It wasn't an accident.

It was my fault.

"That's how they've ruled it," Hsu said. Nick could see he was happy to review what he'd gleaned from Glendale this morning. Nick rubbed his hand over his mouth in a sign he was pondering what could have happened. In reality, he was wiping the thin line of sweat from his lip.

"If he was going after the house material, it must have been important to him. Maybe there was something out there at the scene we could use," Nick said.

If the two of them could go down to the scene, Nick could see what everything looked like in the light of day. Security footage DC hadn't accounted for. Evidence Nick had left behind. Any witnesses. But really, Nick was looking for anything that might justify why he ran as far as he could from the junkyard the night before. Running from the consequences of his own impetuous stupidity. Instead of calling it in. Instead of doing his job and facing the music.

"Sounds like he had an elaborate set-up and had stolen from them before," Hsu said. "Sad irony of it was that DC died for nothing."

I know.

"What do you mean?"

"Well, not nothing, I suppose. If he'd been more sure-footed, he would've gotten away clean with his materials, ready to use them to build another house. However, they were the first things pulped this morning. Destroyed them before the morning crew stumbled upon the body."

Nick let that sink in. The drawing. It was on Nick's phone. And he couldn't tell anyone why or how he'd gotten it. The only lead on a suspect in his case gained by ill-gotten means.

"Do you think we should look into it?" Nick asked. Maybe they hadn't destroyed all the evidence. Maybe there was something that he could use to justify digging into what he'd taken pictures of the night before. Ensure Nick's involvement with DC's death was worth something more. Show that no matter what Nick had done, DC would've had his accident. Anything.

"I say we have enough to do here. Let Glendale do their jobs. If we hear anything that makes it look like foul play, we shift our focus." Hsu put the fax on one of the many messy piles on his desk. "Why? Did you see something at his place last night that made you think he was involved in the attack on Ballantine?"

Maybe.

"Nope."

Nick forced a smile.

"Any sight of Veli?" Nick asked, trying to change the subject.

"Nothing to report, though it's a good thing we searched his tent when we did. Not much of a homeless code. The uniform on patrol reported that people were in and out of it all night picking it clean. If we want to catalog what's left, we'd better get there this morning before it's gone."

"The car is still posted?"

"Until the tent gets stolen or Veli shows his face. But with a patrol permanently staked out, residents will keep a low profile." He gave Nick a once over. "You okay?"

"Mmm-hmm. Tired."

"Snap out of it or take a nap. I've become accustomed to your sarcasm and without it, I admit, I feel lost."

"I'll head to Coffee Bean. Want anything?" Nick asked.

"I'm good," Hsu said. "I can cover you for a few hours, let you get some shut-eye?"

Nick waved him off. Hsu went back to his desk and Nick let out a long breath. Just as his partner was giving hints he might be worth working with, Nick had jeopardized their entire investigation with one impulse decision. But he knew there would be no way to bring the pregnant girl's killer to justice if he was being investigated in a suspicious death. He knew he had done nothing wrong aside from breaking protocol.

Right?

Would DC have slipped anyway? Or was it his fault?

When he reached the street, he stopped and leaned against the granite wall. He didn't know how criminals did it. How they could be surrounded by people whose job it was to find out if they were lying, then have the confidence they'll get away with it. The entire time he was at his desk, Nick felt like there were dozens of eyes on him, watching his every move, certain he was guilty of something, even if they didn't know exactly what.

It was pure paranoia, of course. Nick knew that. The only person who could remotely connect him with DC's death was Hsu. All Nick had to do was make sure Hsu didn't get suspicious or curious. And the best way to do that would be closing the case before things got more complicated.

Instead of going to get a cup of coffee, Nick wandered over to a bus bench and sat down. He knew he had to delete the pictures. Remove them from the cloud. Scrap every trail. But how? They were key pieces of evidence connecting Ballantine to the girl.

Nick took in a few deep breaths to steady himself. Put his hands to his chest to stop them from shaking. And that's when he felt it.

The burner phone. The one the redhead had slipped to him in the cemetery.

Standing, Nick glanced around. He was too close to the station. There were too many eyes.

He pulled his phone out and dialed Hsu.

"You still there? Can you get me a muffin?" Hsu said instead of 'hello'.

"Did you ever hear from the farmer's market guys?"

"Alas, no. But I can call them again."

"This Ballantine thing has me antsy. How about you head over to the Farmer's Market Association and see if they'll talk to the police in-person? I'm going to go to the hospital and see if Ballantine is talking," Nick stood.

"Sounds like a waste of time, Archer. He's on a breathing tube."

"Wouldn't be the first time I got info out of an incapacitated patient."

"Any tips you have on getting through to them I could use?" Hsu asked.

"You interviewing a lot of vegetables?" Nick tried to joke.

"Well, I am going to the farmer's market."

Nick snorted a laugh despite himself. Yet another solid partnership he was on the road to fucking up.

"Talk soon."

He ended the call and headed toward his car. The burner phone bounced against his ribs as he moved.

The weeks he had spent with that phone, waiting for it to ring. Hoping somehow he would run into the redhead again with an update on what Ray Cobb had been up to. He had spent too much time chasing a ghost.

It was time to create one.

24

The red-faced man in the picture mocked him. Whatever he was laughing at didn't matter. Ray could hear the coughing howls through the picture. The disdain.

"Now what?" Boom-Boom asked.

He glowered on the bench in the corner. When he had curved the Jeep onto the 101, bypassing the downtown exits, Ray didn't say a word. The beer barrel sneered the whole two hours through the desolate wasteland of desert sprawl back to Los Angeles, never communicating more than a grunt, occasionally checking his phone for text messages. Glances at the phone constantly cut Ray's attempts at small talk short, punctuated with a scarred fist slamming into the hard plastic of the dashboard. If it had been a late model car built by another company, Boom-Boom probably would have put his hand through the electronic steering column, but the car took the beating like a champ. Ray guessed Boom-Boom's opponents in the MMA ring weren't as resilient.

Ray pretended not to listen when Reggie gave Boom-Boom his assignment to monitor the man still recovering from his burns. Boom-Boom had protested, asking if his girlfriend could come along. Reggie put a gentle hand on the beast's shoulder and assured him that Sweets would be safe and waiting for him when he got back. No chance for him to say goodbye or tell her where they were going.

In the camp, Boom-Boom played the good little soldier and did what he was told. But Ray guessed he wasn't getting a return on the text messages. Between that and their abrupt departure, Boom-Boom was redirecting too much of that fury at Ray and he wondered if Reggie's protection order was more of a guideline than a rule.

It was strange for Ray to be in the bathhouse again. The last time he was there, he was in a death match tussle with a huge naked Ukrainian. Ray didn't really know who he was fighting, but the man he later learned was Osip Kosbur wanted Ray dead. After years of trying to keep him alive, the fat man had finally snapped and wanted to be rid of the homeless nuisance once and for all. But Ray had other plans. When he left the bathhouse, Kosbur was floating face down in a pool of water, blood, and vomit. The man in the picture saw what Ray had done. He'd given the ruddy man the choice to save his boss' life. For Ray, that was where the story ended.

Reggie seemed to be sure Kosbur was dead. Or that's what he wanted Ray to think. While Ray had been in Big Bear, someone had scrubbed the bathhouse clean. No sign of Kosbur. Stranger yet, no sign of Ray to feed to the murder investigation. They had shut it down. Boarded it up.

Without the sweat of steam cleaning the walls, the body odor of countless Eastern European bathers seeped out of the grout between the puke green tiles. Ray imagined it was what riding a full bus through Crimea in August smelled like. The only light in the room highlighted a small square on the edge of the empty bath. Dust motes danced in the spotlight.

The sound of Boom-Boom biting his nails and spitting them onto the floor echoed around him.

What had the towel attendant done when Ray walked away? Where had he gone?

Reggie wouldn't have just sent Ray to L.A. with nothing but a moron ex-MMA fighter to keep him company without an ulterior motive. Malkin seemed to have everything planned down to the most minute detail. There was something he was missing.

Ray stood up and walked over to Boom-Boom, who was checking his phone for the umpteenth time in the last minute.

"She call?" Ray asked, knowing the answer.

"Service sucks in here. You done yet?"

Ray held the photo out to Boom-Boom.

"Any reason Reggie would only give us this? No name. No address. Nothing?" Ray asked.

Boom-Boom didn't take the picture. He shrugged and stood up, pushing past Ray for the door. "You gonna look for anything else in here or can we go? This place is making my nose run."

"Yeah."

Ray shimmied between the plywood used to cover the front door. His eyes watered from the immediate change in lighting, but he took in deep breaths to cleanse his nose of the wet claustrophobia of the bathhouse.

Boom-Boom held his phone in the air and then shook it like a magic eight ball, hoping that a missed call or voicemail would magically appear on his screen. He was out of luck. He mashed his sausage fingers into the touchpad. Before he hit the "call" button, he double-checked the number to make sure it was correct, then held the phone to his ear.

Ray could hear it ringing on the other end and watched the fury rising as Boom-Boom's canines ground against each other and hot breaths wheezed out of his deviated septum. When he got the voicemail prompt again, his tone didn't match his anger.

"Hey Sweets. Me again. Anythin' you want while we're here? Want me to go to the candy shop for you or somethin'? Get you some gummies? Call me so I know what shapes to get."

He ended the call and shook with rage.

"Sooner we get this done, sooner you can get back to her," Ray said.

Fury-filled eyes rose slowly from the face of the silent phone. In all his time on the streets, Ray had looked death in the face more times than most. He knew what it looked like. It was staring at him right now.

Move.

His brain didn't signal his feet fast enough, and Boom-Boom closed the distance between them before Ray had the chance to turn and run.

Boom-Boom's giant hand wrapped around the back of Ray's coat and dug into the thick muscle at the base of his neck. If Boom-Boom hadn't just chewed all of his fingernails off in the bathhouse, they would have clawed a pound of flesh out of Ray's shoulder. With a monstrous paw around his neck, Ray could feel his eyes bulging out of his sockets. Boom-Boom snatched the picture out of Ray's hand and held the crumpled thing in his face.

"Something could be wrong with my girl! She could be sick or dead, but all you fucking give a fucking shit about is some asshole getting drunk in the fucking SOLVIZT CLUB!" Boom-Boom squeezed harder.

Ray could feel the consciousness slipping out of him and the blood vessels straining to burst in one of his eyes.

What did he just say?

Boom-Boom was in a rage fugue. There was no way he would listen to reason. This was a man who had taken every kind of beating imaginable and gotten up and walked away. How was David supposed to slay Goliath?

Using the last bit of energy available to him, Ray shoved his index and middle finger into Boom-Boom's nostrils like a Brit telling someone to piss off. He shoved up and didn't stop. Boom-Boom's eyes watered and blood seeped down his philtrum, but he didn't let go. Ray's fingers dug in further, his sharp fingernails digging into the soft cartilage, digits threatening to meet each other under the badly healed bones. It was all Ray had left.

"AHHHH-CHOOO!"

The sneeze involuntarily consumed Boom-Boom's entire body, and he flung Ray onto the cracked concrete.

"CHOO! CHOO!"

They came violently, sending a spray of snot and blood all over the dumpster and speckling the bottom of Ray's pants.

When the sneezing fit subsided, Boom-Boom shook his head and sucked some rogue snot back into his head. He peered over at Ray with a dumbfounded look, his mouth agape, and let out a small, throaty laugh.

"That's a new one," he said, his voice stuffed like he had a head cold.

A coughing fit hit Ray, which scraped the edges of his throat. It felt like his larynx had cracked and he gripped his forehead to make sure one if his eyes wasn't hanging down his face, dangling by the optic nerve.

"What did you say?" Ray scratched out.

"Never had someone pick my nose before."

If Ray had any energy left, he would have launched back at Boom-Boom in a fury. But then he really would be dead.

"Before that. Solvizt Club."

"What did I say?" Boom-Boom was back to slack jawed and confused.

Ray struggled to his knees and crawled over to the ripped and crumpled picture of the towel attendant. He held it up to

Boom-Boom between the snot and blood-stained fingers that had just been up the fighter's nose.

"Uh," Boom-Boom took it and crooked his head like a dog hearing a strange noise, "that there."

His meaty digit pointed to the bathroom in the background.

"Went there for a fight meeting once. Had to ask which one was the men's room, cuz it was in Russian or somethin'. Forgot 'til just now. Didn't even realize I remembered."

Ray collapsed, his face against the sour milk smell of a dumpster caster.

"You remember where it is?"

"Pacoima."

"Great. Before we go, I'm gonna need some water."

"How come?" Boom-Boom asked, innocent, as though the last ten minutes had disappeared from his short-term memory like a fart in the wind.

25

"Any luck?"

Detective Quevedo raised an eyebrow at Nick and looked back at Boyd Ballantine through the glass of the ICU isolation room.

"What part of that set-up makes you think he's talking to anyone?" Cass asked.

Three of Ballantine's limbs were in suspended casts. A wrap of gauze rounded his skull from the emergency surgery. Both of his eyes had swollen shut, the rest of his face covered in a ventilator. Beneath the sheets, a catheter was helping him piss. Even if he wasn't in a coma, the feeding tube snaking down his throat and resting in his stomach would prevent any conversation.

"I mean outside this quaint little room," Nick said.

"Old Zoo is like your tent crime scene. Found plenty of DNA. What's useful? Likely nothing," Cass said. "We found a couple of fiber samples. Looks like the assailants prepped. Wore protective gear. Lycra. The only reason we had some is a stray string snagged on his coat zipper. Anything at the halfway house?"

Nick and Hsu hadn't found any Lycra in Veli's tent. It didn't mean he wasn't involved, but Veli didn't seem to have the resources for the Lululemon Stealth Collection. Or, like everyone else, he was lying. Nick tried to focus on the task in front of him.

"Ballantine was smart enough not to keep any belongings in his dwelling. Porsche was paid for in cash," Nick said. "Best bet is to find out where that money came from."

"Oh, I know where the money came from," Cass said.

Nick turned to her, his eyes showing he wanted her to finish her thought.

"Just can't prove it," Cass chewed on the inside of her bottom lip.

"Mind letting me in on your hunch?"

"I follow evidence, not speculation. That path will get you into a lot of trouble."

The look she gave him told him to drop it. Nick's guess was a young, headstrong Cass once followed the speculative path, and it didn't end well for her.

"Can we go in there or is he immunocompromised?" Nick asked.

"What are you looking for? Maybe I can save you the time getting into a PPE suit."

"The tattoo. Was it on his broken arm?"

Nick knew it wasn't. It was on his right arm. But he didn't want Cass to know he paid that close attention.

"I thought it wasn't the tattoo you were looking for. We've got pictures of it."

Nick played dumb, "Remind me of his arrest record."

"Picked up on some minor stuff over the years. Nothing stuck. Then we caught him on a technicality. Conspiracy to commit fraud. Had nothing to pin on him for making the documents, otherwise it would have been federal and he'd have gone away for a long time. Few years, early parole."

"I thought you said he just got out?"

"He did. Parole violation. Low risk. Did a few months, and then shuffled to the halfway house. He wasn't a flight risk according to the courts, so no anklet. His P.O. got regular meetings and reports. Nothing out of the ordinary."

"But you think there was," Nick said.

"Again. Speculation."

"Right."

"What's your interest in that tattoo?"

"I'd hate to tell you," Nick said. "Speculation."

Robot Cass Quevedo didn't react to the phrasing being thrown back in her face.

"Go ahead and look, Archer. One thing that might help with that tattoo is that he didn't have it when he went in. The first time."

"So, he got it when?"

"Just over eight months ago."

Nick didn't know how that was useful, but he was stalling. Giving Quevedo the appearance of due diligence.

"Wanna come in with me? Do some puppeteering?" Nick smiled.

"Wasting my time here. I'm going to head back to Hollywood. Let me know if you discover anything."

"Will do." Nick saluted her and watched her go.

The suit of personal protective equipment was just what he needed. If he'd slipped into Ballantine's room and pulled out some rubber gloves, it might have aroused suspicion. But now there was no way he was contaminating the evidence. If any of the nurses or the uniform outside the door popped in, they would see Nick gently pulling Ballantine's free arm up from beneath the sheets and turning it over to get a closer look at the meaningless tattoo.

They wouldn't see the phone that Nick pressed into Ballantine's hand. It was ashy and dry from disuse, but there was still enough natural oil for a couple of smudged thumbprints. A pulse oximeter covered the index finger, but Nick got a decent imprint of the rest of the digits. If he did this right, he'd only need one clean print, anyway. The rest was for insurance.

Blocking the window with his body, he slipped the phone out of Ballantine's hand and into his pocket.

Manslaughter and now evidence tampering.

It was a slippery fucking slope.

Nick turned around as he could feel the sweat soaking through his protective covering and ran into a nurse who had just entered the room, nearly knocking her over.

"Oh, sorry."

"Are you quite through with him? I don't care what he did. We have to keep him alive. Constant exposure to people coming in and out at all hours isn't helping," the nurse said.

Panicked from being caught, Nick nearly pushed past her without asking for a follow-up.

"Wait. What do you mean?"

The nurse checked Ballantine's vitals and made notes on the chart.

"He isn't talking soon. His trachea went through severe trauma and he's in an induced coma. Do you possess telepathy?"

Nick was speechless. Which the nurse took as an admonition. She sighed and softened her tone.

"Sorry. Long night. Between the officers and his personal physician, I'm sick of the questions."

"Personal physician?"

"Dr. Solish. The attending wasn't happy to see him either."

"Why?"

The nurse slid the chart back into its spot and put her hands up in supplication.

"You should talk to the attending doctor. I've already spoken out of turn. Check the nurse's station to see if he's still on shift."

"Solish? You're sure about that name?"

"That's what he said."

Nick left the room and got to the nurse's station to page the attending physician. He had to wait for the doctor to finish up with another patient. By that time, Nick had checked the visitors log and didn't see the name Solish on anything.

The attending physician let out a conciliatory sigh as he approached the nurse's station.

"What can I do for you, Detective?"

"Were you the attending physician to Boyd Ballantine in Room 703 last night?"

"Attending for the entire floor, so yeah, probably."

"Do personal physicians often come to visit ICU patients and offer consults?"

"Not unless they're friends. We can get medical records electronically. Usually they figure we know what we're doing up here."

"You didn't find it unusual that Ballantine's personal physician came in last night?"

"Nobody visited him last night, as far as I'm aware. LAPD posted the guard at his door. Authorized personnel only, right?"

"But the nurse—"

Nick stopped himself, put his mask back on, and went into Ballantine's room.

He took the chart from the wall and looked at the vital stats.

No notes from twenty minutes before.

She had only pretended to write Ballantine's vitals.

And with all the PPE, she would be nearly impossible to identify.

His hand went to the pocket where he'd put the phone with Ballantine's prints on it.

It was gone.

Nick slammed his hand into the alarm button.

26

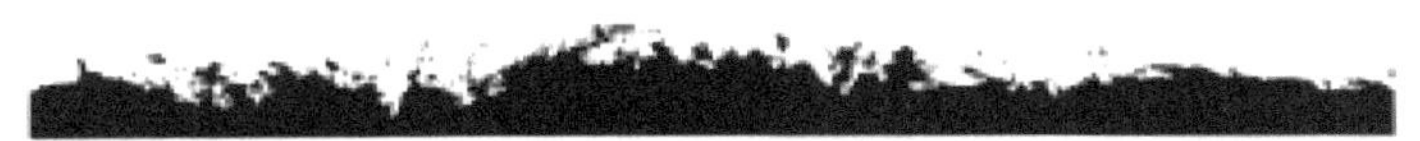

Borscht dribbled down the old man's chin. It curved a dark line around the crag of wrinkles, shifting when it hit the Band-Aid covering the scab of a removed melanoma. It dripped off a spot the old man had missed shaving, highlighting the white prickles with reddish-brown broth. It splotched his crisp white shirt. The man hardly noticed.

When the body of the towel attendant crashed through the wood paneling of the bathroom, it shocked Ray as much as the old man who was sitting in direct eye line of the hole in the drywall. Boom-Boom hadn't built to the grand finale, instead he'd asked one question and then burst.

"Where's the rest of 'em?"

"Excuse me?"

That was all the towel attendant said. *Excuse me?*

There was no malice in the "Excuse me?" No accusation. For all Ray could tell, he hadn't heard correctly. Boom-Boom likely meant to bash the guy against the wall, jog his memory before he could get his fly up, but there was too much of a windup. The Solizt Club was in a seedy area of Pacoima and it looked like it was built when most of the surrounding area was still lemon groves. A private drinking club at night, by day they served lunch to the underpaid immigrant populations who didn't have family connections, organized crime or otherwise.

Termites and water damage had eaten the walls away. Ray was no physics professor, but the sheer amount of force Boom-Boom had to exert to get a full grown man through an intact wall was impressive.

Boom-Boom walked around the corner and through the wooden door, rather than navigating through the tangle of plaster and plumbing he'd just sent the pissing man through. He dragged the towel attendant through the emergency exit; the alarm sounding. He didn't wait for Ray, nor did he ask him to follow. He just continued the path of devastation toward the Jeep, picked the towel attendant up by his throat and crotch and tossed him in between the roll bars. If Ray hadn't calculated quickly that the few patrons of the club had seen the two of them stroll in together, he would've waited for Boom-Boom to leave, then wandered off to find his own way. But he had to run behind the steamroller of a man and hop in the passenger seat of the Jeep before it tore out of the parking lot.

"Who are you peop—," he recognized Ray. "You."

"Shut the fuck up," Boom-Boom growled out. From the frantic look on his face, Boom-Boom clearly had thought none of this through, nor did he have a plan for what to do next. After he'd thrown the guy through the wall, the only thing his lizard brain could process was that he had to flee, even if that meant not taking the man he'd sworn to watch with him.

"Turn on Oxnard. Here," Ray said. He had to raise his voice above the towel attendant's sobbing and didn't mean it to come out as demanding as it did, but it was effective as Boom-Boom yanked the wheel, the tires screeching as they pulled around the corner at the yellow light.

"And slow down. We don't know how much everybody saw and speeding won't help," Ray said.

If the police got wind of the two of them, Ray knew he was still the prime suspect in the murder of Victor Mochulyak, and the man he'd recently learned was Osip Kosbur. What was more worrisome was whoever ran the Solizt Club might seek renumeration for the improvised remodel. Whatever the endgame of this mission was, whether it was to find the tattooed crew, or some other purpose that Malkin had been planning since the beginning, Ray had no intention of ending up in a cell. Malkin had been too good at controlling all the variables up to this point. Ray had no way of knowing just how far his reach stretched.

"We need to get this thing off the road. I'm not as familiar with the valley. Any suggestions?" Ray asked. When he made eye contact with the towel attendant rolling around in the back of the Jeep, there was wild-eyed fear in his gaze. Not at the man who had just pounded him like a drywall nail, but at Ray.

"Yeah," Boom-Boom said under his breath. "Tits."

They pulled into the driveway of an auto shop that hadn't opened yet. Boom-Boom shut off the engine and kicked out of the driver's seat, leaving Ray alone with the man he hadn't seen in a month.

"He's like a child who doesn't know his own strength," Ray shrugged. It was a good thing the towel attendant had been evacuating when attacked, otherwise Ray was sure there would be a pungent puddle in the back of the Jeep when they got out.

Boom-Boom grabbed a blue tarpaulin, pulled it through a hole in the chain-link fence, and tossed it over the top of the Jeep without waiting for Ray to get out. He pulled the towel attendant out from under the crinkling plastic and dragged him across the street into the parking lot of the Pink Panda. Ray trotted after them.

The neon sign of a panda in a fluorescent pink g-string was probably a strange beacon glowing in the night, advertising that it was open 24-hours. When shut off in the early afternoon sun, it was nothing but a testament to the sadness surrounding it. The parking lot was full of discarded beer cans, cigarette butts, and matted hair extensions. A couple of used condoms. Ray figured it was the sort of place where the girls didn't make all of their money on lap dances. When they pushed into the dark room out of the sunlight, it greeted them with what Ray had expected.

Tired cocktail waitresses didn't bother to get off their phones. A handful of patrons who looked like they never left nor had a single dollar bill to rub up against a lotion-fresh leg peppered the joint. Each of them a calculated space apart from each other so they could jerk off under the tiny cocktail tables in peace. The girl dancing on the stage was about as attractive as what one would expect from a Tuesday after lunch, as were the girls who were waiting their turns to pounce on the newcomers to see if they wanted a private dance.

"Three waters," Ray said to the waitress before she opened her mouth.

"Two-drink minimum," she said back.

Boom-Boom reached into the towel attendant's jacket pocket and the frightened man gave a little squeak as Boom-Boom pulled out his wallet. He yanked out the first credit card he could find and handed it over.

"Whatever your cheapest beer is, bring six," Boom-Boom grunted.

"And put twenty percent on for yourself," Ray added, doing his best to wipe his water comment from her memory.

She turned from them without a smile and went back to her phone after placing the order with the bartender.

"Think we can get a cash advance on that card?" Boom-Boom squeezed the back of the towel attendant's neck. "You look like you need to loosen up."

"Please, just—"

"What's your name?" Ray asked, sick of thinking of the guy as "the towel attendant."

"Dimitri Chayka," he shivered.

"Okay, Dim," Ray yelled over the music, "tell me a story."

Dimitri shook his head like a child refusing a fork full of broccoli.

Boom-Boom squeezed the back of his neck and he shrieked. Ray realized if he didn't step in soon, Boom-Boom would break Dimitri's vertebrae and they would be no closer to the information they were looking for.

"Although this wouldn't have been my first choice of venue, it allows for a certain anonymity," Ray explained. "Say my companion wants to break your ribs one by one, *The Stroke* will cover up your pained screams and you could cry through most of *Pour Some Sugar on Me* with none of the ladies in here taking much notice. I would recommend you talk so he can get back to his girlfriend. I'm sure being here is reminding him of what he's missing."

The waitress brought their drinks, all six of them, and set them down on the table. They were in plastic cups. Glass was too classy. She didn't give one shit what was happening at the table. None of the other girls had made their way over, either. She'd probably warned the dancers to avoid them.

Dimitri reached for the closest beer and chugged half of it. Neither Ray nor Boom-Boom made a move to stop him. When he put the cup down, Ray grabbed his sleeve and yanked the jacket up. The lines of the tattoo on his forearm were red and scarred. Telltale signs of laser removal.

"I have money."

Ray could see from the look on Boom-Boom's face that his patience had run out.

"Maybe you didn't hear me," Ray lowered his voice under the music instead of trying to yell over it. "He really misses his girlfriend. And every second you waste is an extra second he's not with her. I don't know who you are, I don't know what kind of nasty shit you're involved in, but if you don't point us toward the other people with those tattoos, and right now, I'll just say it. You're fucked."

Boom-Boom grabbed the hand holding the empty plastic cup and squeezed. Ray didn't know if it was the crack of the plastic, or the crack of every bone in Dimitri's hand, but *Toxic* didn't do a great job covering the scream that came from his throat.

"Now we are on everybody's radar and you're making me mad," Ray threatened. "You don't want to know what we can do to you."

It was a hollow threat, but it worked. Dimitri had seen what pain Ray had inflicted on Osip Kosbur. He knew what Ray was capable of.

Some of the more adventurous strippers were peering over at their table. Pickings were slim. They were going to take any chance at making twenty bucks. It was a shift where fortune favored the bold.

"We have to use the bathroom."

Ray sidled out of the booth and beckoned for Dimitri to follow. He didn't move, but Boom-Boom did.

"No. Stay here. Get a table dance. The less suspicious we look, the better," Ray said.

"Not supposed to—"

Ray knew the next words were, "let you out of my sight," but he had to keep Dimitri afraid and interrupted.

"There are no windows in that John. Guarantee it." He hoped that Boom-Boom didn't miss the subtext. "He's not going anywhere."

Boom-Boom got the message and stayed put. He wrapped his giant hands around one of the beers, but didn't drink.

The bathroom was empty and disgusting. There were paper towels strewn all over the floor and each stall Ray checked was more spattered and fucked up than the next. Whoever was the janitor in the place either was terrible at their job, or knew that this was how the place ended up nightly and wanted to save all the putrid nonsense to be cleaned out in one fell swoop.

"Pick a stall," Ray said.

"What? Why?"

"You don't answer my questions, that's the one I watch you lick clean."

Dimitri picked the middle stall. It was the only one that was just covered in piss instead of shit, like the other two.

Ray grabbed him by the hair and shoved him into the furthest stall. The one that looked sprayed with chili and pea soup. Dimitri dry heaved as soon as his face hit the bowl. Ray was doing his best to stay tough, but he felt a familiar tickle in the back of his throat. He figured his tough-guy image would take a ding if he lost his lunch on the back of Dimitri's head.

"That night. What happened to The Bear?" Ray asked.

"I can't—"

Ray shoved Dimitri's face down into the vomit-filled bowl. When Ray yanked the man's face out of the putrid water, he was coughing and retching up the meager contents of his stomach. The sewage soaked through the bandages over Ray's burnt hand. For as much time as he'd spent in his own filth on the street, he suddenly wanted to dunk his entire arm in a vat of disinfectant.

"If you had called Malkin or saved Kosbur's life, neither of us would be here right now," Ray hissed. "I would've been dead in the snow weeks ago. So, you tell me why we're both alive, or I get my associate and he makes sure your life extension ends now."

"D'Arby."

The name slapped Ray across the face. The slave trader whose death left a vacuum in the Los Angeles underworld. When Osip Kosbur had kidnapped Ray and framed him for murder, he'd claimed that he'd been protecting Ray from the people who had filled the void in Pretty Boy D'Arby's absence. It seemed like a load of horseshit. But now that The Bear was dead, Ray realized that Malkin may have been the least of his worries.

"D'Arby's dead," Ray scowled.

Dimitri had lodged himself between the toilet and the stall door, shaking. Tears ran down his face as he pressed his forehead into the empty toilet paper dispenser.

"I didn't know what to do. You said it yourself. I had to choose. I didn't know."

Ray could see he was tumbling into a state of panic and shock. He'd seen it on the street; reality slipping away as it became too much to deal with. Ray stamped down on Dimitri's foot, hoping the pain would bring him back. It worked.

"What did you choose?" Ray asked.

Dimitri sputtered out his answer between sobs, "He turned over, out of the water. I watched him. I pulled him out, but the look in his eyes, he stared through me, started laughing. Mocking me. I remembered what he put me through. Knew I would need protection. I pushed him down. Beneath the water. This," he tapped his arm, "I did not ask for it. It is a brand for my sins. Like you said, my chance to be free."

If that was true, then it wasn't Kosbur who had lit the trailer on fire in the woods. If not him, who?

"Tell me about D'Arby and what happened after I left," Ray asked.

"I called. He came. Now I'm his. Sold myself from one slaver to another. As did we all."

"All?"

"What do they call it in police shows? Immunity? Safe passage?"

"Who else?" Ray asked.

Crying into the graffiti on the stall, Dimitri sputtered nonsense, "I knew I should have gone. When he missed his last pickup. Should have known."

"You better start talking in complete thoughts," Ray threatened, doing his best not to breathe in the collective fumes rising from the puddle surrounding Dimitri.

"Elias Culp."

"That name supposed to mean something to me?" Ray asked.

"They make videos. I don't know where they film. It's somewhere in the Valley. That's all the boys know. Culp. He has one. The tattoo."

"Who else?"

"That's all I know, please."

"Culp. How do I find him?"

"We've never—"

"I'm going to give you one more chance to tell me any detail that could point us in the right direction, otherwise your insides are going to be your outsides."

"A van comes to St. Germaine Cousin every Thursday night. Brings the boys back Friday mornings. They make sure I don't know too much. To them, I am just a pervert."

"All the more reason for me to call in my partner and see if he can throw you through another bathroom wall."

"I'm strictly cyber. Never touched a child. But it's not cheap. I collect kids with terrible home lives and help them make money."

"By getting naked on the Internet?"

"It started with pick-pocketing. Malls. Theme Parks."

"How?"

"I'm a youth pastor."

Ray didn't even know where to begin with hating this man huddled beneath a strip club toilet. He wished he were a different person. The guy who would have no problem putting a bullet in the back of the crying man's head. He didn't even have the low moral character to call Boom-Boom into the bathroom and do the job for him. When his thoughts drifted to Boom-Boom, he realized his proverbial partner was probably panicking and would make his way to the restroom soon enough. Ray needed to think like one of these lowlife assholes.

"Who's the crown jewel? The kid who doesn't ask questions."

"Um, Manuel Raphelo. Manny. He coordinates the pickups. There's supposed to be one tonight, but Culp didn't show last week."

Boom-Boom picked that moment to come into the bathroom to find Ray standing over the cowering man in the stall.

"See, no window," Ray said.

"You get something?"

"A start."

"Good," he turned to Dimitri. "Bite the bowl."

"What?"

Boom-Boom grabbed the man by the back of the head and slammed his mouth into the curb of dirty porcelain, cracking all of his front teeth.

"Bite." *Wham.* "The." *Wham.* "Bowl!"

When he let go of the sniveling pedophile, all of his teeth were broken or gone. There was so much blood surrounding his mouth he looked like a zombie that had just devoured a pile of raw entrails. He'd passed out from the pain.

"What the fuck?" Ray yelled. "I thought we were collecting them! Bringing them back to the mountain."

"You heard wrong. Take out for pickup," Boom-Boom said. He had gone to the sink and was gently scrubbing the blood and chipped teeth from his hands as though he had done it hundreds of times before.

"Why?"

"I don't ask."

If what Dimitri said was true, the other tattooed crew was working for whoever was running D'Arby's business. This wasn't a collection, it was a culling.

Ray tried to think about who he was protecting. If he found all the traitors and let Boom-Boom take care of them, what was to prevent Boom-Boom from turning on him next? A pedophile and a kiddie porn producer. Ray didn't want to know what madness the third person was involved in. No matter who they were working for, these scumbags had to be taken off the streets.

"We've got a name and a location. Elias Culp, St. Germaine Cousin church. Tonight."

"What about the third?" Boom-Boom asked.

"You want to ask him?"

Dimitri was face down in the puddle of toilet water and regurgitated cabbage rolls. Blood and saliva drained out of his slacked mouth. Small chunks of teeth flowed out like krill escaping a whale.

"Don't call Reggie," Ray said.

"I don't take orders from you. He said he wanted them back," Boom-Boom said.

"You said he wanted them found," Ray said. The paper towel dispenser was empty, so Ray had to grab one of the used ones off the floor. He picked up one that he hoped was only damp with water and dug into Dimitri's pocket for his phone.

"I don't know much about this asshole, but he's clearly stupid, and he's got a compulsion for—"

There was nothing in Dimitri's camera roll, but it didn't take much searching in his phone's files to find what he was looking for. It made him cringe.

"Did you know you could text 911?" Ray said as he sent the picture.

"What did you do?" Boom-Boom asked.

Ray flashed Boom-Boom the picture he'd found, and even his thick mind knew enough to recoil from it. Ray made it Dimitri's home screen and then called 911 and set the phone at his feet to ring.

"You don't want that guy up in the mountains with you sharing a bunk," Ray said. "It's time to leave."

Back at the Jeep, Ray couldn't get the smell of the strip club bathroom out of his nose. It was amazing how a couple of weeks back to regular hygiene could change one's sense of smell.

"There's another problem," Ray said. "I think I found out who's causing all the problems for Malkin. But he's not hunting tattoos. He's recruiting them."

"Who?"

"Dimitri was talking about a gangster named D'Arby. But that's impossible. D'Arby was killed years ago."

"You know something I don't?" Boom-Boom started the Jeep. "D'Arby ain't dead."

"Pretty Boy D'Arby is real dead," Ray said.

"I ain't talking about him. Talking about his brother," Boom-Boom said. "Callum D'Arby is real alive."

"Feel better?" Hsu asked as he handed Nick a coffee.

Anyone on the force who had spent any time on the streets was familiar with the department shrink. But everyone who paid a visit to the LAPD psychologist never really let loose everything that was bothering them. There was an unspoken code to unload just enough personal information and emotional vulnerability to be reassigned to active duty. Anything deeper meant a report to superiors and further visits until the patient wised up to playing the game. Nick was sure to describe the dreams he'd been having. Nighttime visitations of his deceased mother. Gruesome visions of an entertainment assistant's head exploding. The cycling faces of the important women in his life accusing him of betrayal. Reminders of everything he had gone through in the Low Seward case.

He would grab the tissues and talk about his father enough to pass his psych eval and get back to work. But he didn't tell the doctor about the man he watched die a few days ago. The guilt of pretending he wasn't there. The constant anxiety of potential discovery. Or that the only reason he was in the hospital in the first place was because he was evidence tampering. And least of all, that he felt like he was losing who he was and everything he thought he stood for.

After his panic at the hospital, slamming his hand into the code alarm and causing the entire medical staff to flood into Boyd Ballantine's room, he had to give the psychologist something to justify his paranoia. He confessed to his lack of sleep and admitted he hadn't touched his prescribed anti-anxiety meds, but made it sound like his resistance was out of strength rather than fear. He broke down about the horrors he had seen in the city and confided he was only human. The appointment was just a check-in, suggested by Nick when the situation in the hospital hadn't turned up any justifiable leads. Proactive assurance to his colleagues and the brass that he was taking care of himself.

No one had seen the unknown nurse he was talking about. There were no staff or visitors out of the ordinary. The guard at the door couldn't identify if the person in question was any different from the nurses and CNAs that moved in and out of each room of the ICU. The hospital had done a full markup on Ballantine after Nick pressed them to do so, fearing that the man's life was in danger. Everything came back negative.

The only viable explanation, and the reason his pockets were empty at the end of the interaction, was because she was there for him. If that were the case, and removing the phone from his possession was her plan all along, then someone had eyes on him for a long time. And had likely seen him at the junkyard. It was also the only reason he didn't mention the doctor's name in his report.

Solish.

If it was fake, nothing more than misdirection on her part. If it was real, the mention was intentional and for Nick's ears only.

So, no, Hsu. He didn't feel better.

"I suppose that really isn't the point, huh?" Nick raised the paper cup in a gesture of thanks.

"That's why I employ a personal therapist. Takes a chunk out of the take-home, but beats the alternative," Hsu said.

"Anything you need to tell me?" Nick asked.

"No. Unless you've noticed a lapse in my judgement lately."

Nick paused for a moment, holding back the tic in his eyelid. *Was Hsu implying something? What did he know?*

"If I do, I'll let you know," Nick smiled and looked across the woods in front of him, averting his eyes from the possibility of Hsu's searching gaze. "So, honey guy?"

"Farmer's market association works with several honey companies. Many of them are subsidiaries of larger conglomerates. No surprise that the farmer's market isn't exactly all small businesses. But this one raised a flag. This is the registered address for the booth application, but there are no other registries. No small business filing, no articles of incorporation, no trademarks."

"What were you looking for?"

Hsu handed Nick a copy of the farmer's market application. Reginald D. White.

That name sounded familiar, but he couldn't place it.

"We've got this Topanga Canyon address, but as you can see from our current environs, no corporation. No evidence of the brand outside of the farmer's market," Hsu said. "Which means the proprietor is a lazy hippie accidentally committing tax fraud or something else is going on here."

Nick gestured Hsu toward the front door of the address on the application, showing he should take the lead.

Trinkets and tchotchkes scattered the front porch of the small house. Dreamcatchers galore. The standard package for a hill house in Topanga Canyon. Probably bought for some skunk weed and a B.J. in the '70s and now worth over a million dollars.

A small, thin woman answered the door. Gardening clothes, light makeup. More mall walking retiree than elderly Janis Joplin doppelgänger. They flashed their badges.

"Hello, miss. Does Mr. White live here?"

"No, I'm sorry, you have the wrong house," she sighed and brushed a wisp of grey hair from her sweaty forehead with the back of her hand. "I have some of his mail, though, if you'd like that."

Nick and Hsu exchanged a look of shock at their luck.

"Um, actually. Yes. Yes, we would," Hsu smiled.

She bent down and pushed a small wicker basket full of junk mail over the doorjamb.

"Used to mark it return to sender, but the post office seemed to ignore that. Now I collect it, cut out the plastic windows and use it for compost."

Nick bent down and dug through the pile. Everything addressed to White had to do with the application he'd filled out for the farmer's market association. Hive advertisements, invoices, invites to mixers.

"Do you sell honey?" Nick asked and handed her the farmer's market application.

"I do. Just in small batches, mind you. Nothing serious. Mostly to friends. Just enough to fund my small apiary. Two small hives don't produce much. All anybody wants anymore is that Manuka stuff from New Zealand now, anyway."

She took out a pair of reading glasses and scanned the application.

"You've got the right address. Explains why you came knocking at my door, but this isn't me. Come on in. You can look at my production facilities if you don't believe me."

She guided them into the house. It was quaint and modestly decorated. There were random statues dedicated to Hindu deities, placed aesthetically rather than for any point of worship. Records on a shelf above an ancient Hi-Fi. Books scattered on every surface in stacks, all of them appeared to be secondhand. Cooking smells clung to the old wallpaper and the lingering cumin smelled like B.O. Without them asking for I.D. she fingered through a pile of paperwork in a wall sleeve and slid a passport across the counter. The name next to the forced smile was Eve Hennepin.

"Put that right back. I'm headed to a silent retreat in Bali tomorrow and if that goes missing, you're going to have one angry pacifist on your hands," Eve called behind her.

Nick snapped a photo of the passport on his phone and put it back. With the confidence they were going to let her leave the country, Eve either had nothing to hide or she was getting out of town before everything became unraveled.

The French doors leading to the back patio were already open. She walked the detectives through a well-manicured lawn, past a line of trees, and pointed down into a small valley.

"There you go. Any closer and I'd recommend a suit. But I only have the one, so we'd have to share."

Nick peered down into the valley where two white boxes sat in the sun. A small haze of honey bees buzzed out into the forest behind and another slew returned full of nectar ready to fill their combs.

"Do you know of any reasons Mr. White would use your address for his operations?"

"After the umpteenth invite from the farmer's market association garden parties, I assumed he knew I had a couple of hives and put it out there if anyone came snooping. Some of these guys slap a certified organic sticker on their bottles and then go buy a jug of crap from a wholesaler and sell it as their own. People in this town will pay beaucoup bucks for something with the right marketing behind it."

"And you're certain you've never heard the name before?"

"Oh, I've heard it before. I'm sure you have, too."

"Ma'am?" Hsu said, confused.

"Thought it was a joke when the mail first started coming," she put her thumb to a piece of junk mail Nick was holding, "Reginald D. White?"

Nick stared at the envelope confused, but after a moment, Hsu started chuckling and palmed his forehead in a mock "well done idiot" gesture.

"Now I'm embarrassed I didn't notice this before," Hsu chuckled.

"Yeah, you should be," Nick said. "Notice what?"

Regret washed over Nick as Hsu turned to him with a knowing smile. The breath he took in reminded Nick of every other time Hsu broke into professor mode and pontificated about a subject for an hour.

"Reginald D. White on its own has no significant meaning, but could break down in several ways. One, that the pseudonym 'John Smith' is overused, so why not adjust it to something just as milquetoast like 'Reg White'? Two, perhaps the nom de guerre has been lengthened rather than shortened and our Apoidean imposter was a fan of the Super-Bowl-winning Green Bay Packers in the '90s and their defensive juggernaut, Reggie White. But no, I believe that the most clever and heinous combination is our target. Reginald D. White? Reginald... Dwight?" Hsu's eyebrows went up, expecting Nick to finish the thought.

Nick's mind searched for the answer like a drunk during a pub quiz.

"Elton John," Eve jumped in. "It's his real name."

"Precisely," Hsu said.

"Great," Nick shrugged. "Time to put out an APB on Rocketman. Case closed."

"If we run out of leads, we can pay a visit to Beverly Hills, but perhaps this gives us more than we think. If our honey guy is not so creative with his false names, he may use other celebrity nom de plumes, and we may track him that way." Hsu turned to Eve. "Has anyone named Dave B. Owie or Shock A. Khan bought honey from you?"

She chuckled, "No, but I can put a list together if you'd like. Might be the wrong tree you're barking up, but gotta check every angle, right? C'mon in. I think my sun tea is ready."

"You mind if I stay out here for a bit, walk the property? Sir Elton might have just picked your address out of a hat, but there might be something else," Nick said.

"Would you mind if I used your facilities? Long drive from downtown," Hsu asked.

"Be my guest," Eve said. Hsu waddled up the hill back to the house.

"When you hit the birch trees, that's where my back neighbor's land starts," Eve said as she turned to follow him.

"And what is her name? Joan E. Mitchell?"

Eve laughed, "Nope, plain old name, I'm sorry to say. Uses the property for one of those home share websites. Weddings and weed tourists mostly, different people coming and going, so haven't seen him in a bit. Alex Solish."

The back of Nick's neck went hot.

Eve didn't seem to notice Nick go flush and called up the hill to the house behind Hsu. "Second door in the hall!"

Nick waited for her to disappear through the patio door and took a leisurely stroll down the hill, giving the bees a wide swath. He ducked under some branches into the woods. Once beyond the tree line, he bolted through the underbrush, his eyes searching for the line of birch trees.

Solish. That name. Had Solish actually gone to visit Boyd Ballantine in the hospital? Did the nurse feed him the name to throw him off the trail? Or had she given him the name to put him on the right track?

Nick reached the edge of the property line. One step over and he would officially trespass and conduct an illegal search.

He had already broken too many laws, and he had no probable cause outside of a name whispered by a ghost.

Solish's house was set forward on the property far enough that Nick could only get an outline from the trees, but there was no fence or demarcation of any kind that would prevent Solish from sneaking through the property in the middle of the night, grabbing some honey and then going back to his house with Eve none the wiser. But what the hell did stealing honey have to do with a woman torn apart in a tent by the highway? The medical examiner had said it was an accidental death made to look like a crime. And the body had been moved. What was the connection between Jane Doe and Solish?

Nick pulled out his phone. The canyon had shitty service, but he still had one bar. He typed the name into Google. After a moment of loading, it came up.

Dr. Alex Solish. Cosmetic surgery.

And he had a clinic in Koreatown.

Until Nick had some hard evidence to connect Solish, he wouldn't mention it to Hsu. His partner would ask too many questions.

Find some evidence, then search Solish's property. Legally.

Nick turned and made his way back up the hill. If he was going to pay a late-night visit to Solish's clinic without his partner, he was going to need the caffeine in that sun tea.

28

She watched the little girl fidget in the passenger seat. Biting her nails. Waiting for the tiny pimp to come out of the clinic. She had watched a lot of girls come in and out of this place. Seen the relief and the sadness. Known that she could have given them another option. Take care of them. Care for the baby inside them.

The little girl rolled down the window of the truck and spit out her fingernails. Her face was starting to fill out from the tiny life growing inside her. There were dark circles under her eyes from lack of sleep.

She wouldn't make the same mistakes with this one.

There had been so much blood in the tent. The girl torn apart. The baby gone, too. All the time she'd spent watching from a distance, wasted. She'd waited too long for her moment. It happened so fast.

Here. Now. A second chance.

She would be more careful with this one. Get to her early. Make sure she could protect the life inside her.

"You want gel?"

She pulled her feet out of the massaging bath and smiled at the nail tech. Her sunglasses stayed on. To them, she would be just another forgettable bitch. But the nail salon was the perfect place to watch the clinic. Watch for the mothers.

"Yes, thank you."

The small man limped out of the clinic toward the truck. She watched the little girl's spine go rigid. Rubbing her sweaty hands on her pants below the dashboard. Trying to seem older than she was.

"Careful, please."

The nail tech hadn't done anything wrong. The foot massage actually felt nice after the stressful weeks she'd had. But she had to sell the rich bitch attitude. Sound like she was a regular at the Line Hotel bar.

She knew how to play it. Be nice, but not too nice. Tip, but don't under or over tip. Never be memorable. Blend. Disappear.

The girl rolled the window down. He looked up at her, flashing that fake, dirty smile.

She saw him mouth the word, "Tonight."

He tucked a crutch into his armpit and held his hand up to her through the open window. She put her arm out, he took her hand, and gave it a reassuring squeeze.

It made her sick. She wanted to jump up from the plush chair, throw down the fashion magazine, and waddle over to him with toe spreaders flying. Slam his head in the truck's door. Grab her and take her someplace safe. Give her a different choice.

But she'd made the rash move before. And everything came crumbling down.

"Tonight," she whispered under her breath.

The truck drove away and she scanned the parking lot for the best place to wait.

Tonight.

29

Sweets missed Boom-Boom, but not as much as she knew he missed her. He was a good guy and took care of her, but whenever they got a free moment, all he wanted to do was fuck. He wasn't bad at it and did his best to make sure she got off, even if most of the time she was pretending. If there was one thing having sex for money taught her to do, it was to get good at faking it. The better she pretended, the more likely she was to have a repeat customer. Repeat customers were better than a bunch of randos. At least with the repeaters, she knew what to expect. The repeaters had specific needs she could cater to. The repeaters cared about her. Like she was a part of their sad little lives. It was the one-timers she had to worry about. The ones who appeared out of nowhere with their faces covered. Asked if she was an undercover cop more than a few times. Then they got rough if she didn't suck their dick just right.

She loved Boom-Boom. She just didn't want to have sex with him anymore. There were girls she met, some of Q-Mug's other girls, who used to talk about the difference between fucking and making love. Like they could separate themselves from it when they were just doing the job. They said doing it with Q-Mug was different sometimes. Almost tender because he was taking care of them. But Sweets never saw it that way. She always remembered that first day. The mixture of blood from the medium rare steak and the taste of iron from her split lip. She'd always remember how it tasted coming back up. Retching the chunks of half-digested meat into the street. She didn't even want to think about cows after being force fed by a man who threatened to slice her from collar to cunt.

For her, sex was like that steak. Didn't matter the intent behind it anymore. Or that no one was forcing it on her. It changed. Brought back memories of every other time she did it without wanting to. She wished she had a brain that would seal up those memories. Put them in a little compartment at the back of her skull and forget about them, but she couldn't.

When Boom-Boom left, she tried to pretend that it was hard for her to watch him go. But she was happy for the break. Happy for the moments she would have alone. Take the time to see what she could do up on the mountain.

Ever since they'd gotten to Big Bear, she had listened to Xavier talk, and everything made sense. He had such power. Such caring eyes. When she slept, she imagined him touching her and it wasn't the touch she wanted to put away in a box. Or a thing to be forgotten. She had always dreamed of that. It wasn't sexual, though sometimes she would wake herself up, realizing that she had come in her sleep. It was the idea of him touching her and holding her. Boom-Boom tried to touch her like that, tried to be tender, but his hands didn't work that way. They were blunt objects never designed to be gentle.

No one got close to Xavier the way she wanted to. There were no favorites among them, save Reggie. But Reggie was different. He bent to Xavier's will, but wasn't part of the group. Reggie bridged the world between the mountain and real life. He kept the trappings of society. His gadgets. His television. His candy.

It was the candy that she'd noticed. He would come to the group meals with the rest of them. Share the same tables and conversation. He never drank his smoothie, which Sweets always found to be the highlight of the meal. Instead, he got snacks. Everyone noticed he had them, but nobody said anything. Nobody complained. They weren't being held captive in the camp, but with no shopping allowance beyond what they took into town to provide for the group, there was no extra for little treats. It was a part of the deal that Sweets didn't understand. If they were preparing for the end of civilization and a world where surviving with the bare minimum was going to be the norm, shouldn't they get to have comforts before they disappear? That made more sense to her.

She knew Reggie kept a stash of snacks in his cabin. Boom-Boom seemed scared of Reggie. She knew that whatever Boom-Boom was afraid of, she should be afraid of too, but she had different ways to wiggle out of situations than he did. If Reggie caught her in his cabin, she could say that she was waiting for him. Waiting for the opportunity to get him alone with Boom-Boom finally off the mountain. If he rejected her, then she lost nothing. If he accepted, then she would close her eyes and imagine it was Xavier's hands on her body. Xavier kissing her. Xavier inside her.

The cabin was unlocked, as she expected. There was no reason for locks on anything. If anyone came up from town and got a little curious, he sent them packing. Sweets knew the group didn't have an armory, but there were enough weapons scattered around for the group to protect themselves after the fall. A couple of people made it their business that everyone knew how to use the guns for hunting and protection. But never for attack. That was one thing she liked about Xavier. His message was never, "Take from others," it was always, "Protect what's yours." She wanted to be his. His to protect.

She shook off the fantasy and focused. There was something different about Reggie's cabin, a place she'd never been inside. She'd asked Boom-Boom what it was like when he was called in for meetings, but Boom-Boom never mentioned details. Except for the bees. He always came back from a meeting trying to shake the hum of their buzz out of his head. Boom-Boom was allergic. Said even one sting would kill him and he couldn't afford the fancy antidote stick-pen thingy. She didn't know if that was why he was always a little jumpy around Reggie or if it was something else.

She knew they were in there. Everyone did, but she didn't know how he kept them from stinging everybody. They supplied the honey Reggie sold at farmer's markets and the kitchen used to flavor desserts. It was the only thing they had in camp that even came close to refined sugar. Sweets figured even if she didn't find the candy stash, she could grab one of the honey jars that wasn't boxed up and squirrel it under her bunk. The hardest part would be finding moments to sneak a spoonful when Boom-Boom wasn't around. He was such a light sleeper, she wouldn't even be able to do it in the middle of the night. The smell would probably wake him up like Captain Hook hearing the crocodile. She would have to take advantage of the only alone time she ever had and store what she found in the ladies' privy.

Her boots slipped off and the slush dripped onto the rubber mat. It was strange being in an unfamiliar space alone. There wasn't the constant noise of other campers working around her. No sound of Boom-Boom breathing through his deviated septum, that constant high whistle he stopped noticing a long time ago, but which aggravated her to no end. Instead, there was nothing but the light tap of insect bodies against glass as dozens of them crawled over the honey combs, creating delicious natural sugar.

The tiny hairs on their front legs rubbed against their mouths. They mesmerized her, watching them work. Sweets didn't know how so few bees could produce so much honey. The amazing work of nature. Imagine being able to make your own sugar whenever you wanted instead of sneaking around like a scavenger.

She'd hoped there would be a candy jar sitting open on the desk within arm's reach of Reggie while he was doing work, but she knew she wouldn't be that lucky. The desk was unlocked, but yielded nothing aside from papers and office supplies. She found the wrapper of an Abba-Zaba in one of the bottom drawers, so knew she was at least on the right trail in the forbidden place.

She rolled the desk chair back to get a look at the pencil drawer, and the castors snagged the threadbare rug underneath. There was a seam in the wood and a metal handle worn shiny from constant gripping. The design of the camp was such that it wasn't prone to secret hideaways and passages, but it had been there long enough that underground dry storage wasn't strange. Reggie's cabin was close to the kitchens. The greenhouse attached to it was a recent addition, built specially for the group, so the chance that it could have been used to store supplies at some point wasn't too odd a thought.

She had to scoot the desk aside to gain access to the trapdoor, but it was heavier than she'd expected and she had to place her feet against the wall and push. Her wool-stockinged feet slipped against the polished wood and kicked one of the glass panels holding the bees. It didn't crack or break, but she could hear the small bodies bashing up against the glass increase in frequency. It would be a bad thing if the panel opened up and filled the room with irritated honey bees.

She stopped and giggled at herself. If Reggie walked in on her now, he'd see a scrawny girl stretched over the gap between the desk and wall, her toes gripping at anything to push the desk away all for a chance to score some candy bars. There was something comforting about doing something so stupid. Everything didn't have horrible consequences after all.

She dropped to the floor and poked her head into the hole. There was a small stairway and enough light coming from the cabin to see to the bottom. A bare lightbulb hung from the ceiling with a string dangling below to turn it on. Boxes filled with honey jars, both full and empty, lined the walls. It was dry storage, just as she had suspected, and she could see from the top that there was one box that didn't look like the others.

Sweets giggled to herself with the uncontrollable tic she'd always had. She knew there was nothing magical about the place. No buried treasure to be found. But there was something exciting in the forbidden. Something different to break her out of the day to day. She hadn't felt that way since the first day they had arrived in the mountains, expectant yet unaware of what awaited them next. Even if there was nothing of interest in the box, or if she didn't find the candy stash she was looking for, she would know one of Reggie's secrets. And secrets were power. She would have one less reason to be afraid. And that was reason enough to open it and see what was inside.

It looked like a hope chest. Something she never had in her tiny house growing up, but had seen on TV, on those fixer-upper shows. There was a latch and a keyhole, but it was loose. The lock was ornamental to make the chest look like it was full of pirate's booty or prized mementos. She flipped the latch and there her prize was, in all its glory.

"Looking for something?"

Sweets slammed the lid of the box down and spun around. Reggie was leaning against the wall at the base of the stairway. One hand was in his pocket and the other clutched a couple of Twizzlers from his stash.

"I—," she didn't know what to say next. Being this far into her mission, she knew she couldn't use the seduction defense.

"It's all right," he said, pushing off from the wall. He took one of the licorice whips into his mouth, where it sagged like a sad cigar, and offered her the other one. She hesitated, then took it with a shaking hand.

"Was lookin' for your candy," she bit into the sweet strawberry goo and smiled with pieces stuck in her teeth.

Reggie lifted his foot, and she flinched, thinking he was going to throttle her jaw, but he used the toe of his boot to open the lid of the chest once more.

"And you found some."

Sweets turned around and stared back into the contents of the chest. Piles and piles of small baggies, each containing the bright purple sugar she had seen in tubes in candy stores. Sweet and tart flavors she remembered dumping into her mouth from paper sticks. Grape flavoring that stained her tongue when she dipped the bland white sugar stick into Fun Dip packets for hours on end.

"What is it?" she asked, embarrassed she couldn't hold back another involuntary giggle.

"Just like you said, it's candy," Reggie smiled. "And you can have as much as you'd like."

A low moan echoed through the vents. Female. Pained, but clinging to consciousness. The beam of his flashlight only illuminated whatever was staring down the barrel of his service weapon. The muzzle of the gun pushed the door open, and Nick followed. No power. Emergency lights lit the room, casting ghosts against the white paint.

He swung his light into the room and jumped back with an involuntary twitch before he realized the face across the room was a poster. A dowdy woman next to the mirror image of her smiling self once she'd invested in cryo-sculpting. Chairs worn, but clean. Magazines expired and dog-eared. It was a waiting room. Any waiting room from any clinic in the country.

Double vestibule doors kept the faint odor from permeating the clinic, but once past the set of doors to the basement, his stomach turned. Rotting meat was the base layer. Then chemicals. He imagined it was what a Civil War battlefield smelled like after the bodies had been baking in the Georgia sun for several days.

Nick wouldn't like what he found. Even if it was Dr. Solish sitting at his desk doing paperwork, unmoved by the stench.

When Nick had pulled his car into the parking lot of the vacant strip mall, there were no other vehicles in sight. The vestibule of the clinic was dark, but there was a glow of utility light in the room beyond. The front door was unlocked, even though the hours showed the clinic was closed. It would be the second time he'd entered somewhere without a warrant in the last twenty-four hours, but when he opened the door he realized the emergency lights were on and only powering essential equipment.

He'd have to explain how he'd picked the doorstep of this clinic to investigate out of the hundreds in the city. The clinic was nowhere near his commute home. Power failure was enough for him to justify entry with probable cause, as it only seemed to affect the clinic and not the whole complex.

He wanted to leave the door open behind him for a quick exit if needed, but knew closing it would be the smart play. If there was someone waiting behind one of the blind corners, they could easily slip out of an open door and onto the street, leaving Nick alone with whatever was waiting beyond the double doors. He pushed the door shut until the knob clicked and listened for movement in the inner office.

Nothing.

The darkness continued inside as he slow-stepped forward. A voice at the back of his skull hammered, *Call for Backup*, but he knew he couldn't. He'd gone too far already. Gotten in too deep. Whatever he found, he had to face alone.

Down the stairs to a door. A padlock left open in haste.

The smell. Metallic and visceral. Flesh and blood.

Whatever this place was, whatever he was about to find, it was bigger than his job. His pension. His reputation. He'd make up an excuse for the illegal search. Face the consequences for DC's death.

Nick turned out the door, his movement through the air lumbered and viscous, his radio miles away.

He heard the scream and stopped.

Female.

Young.

Pained.

He was back inside the double doors before he knew what he was doing. Head on a swivel. Left, then right. Gun followed eyes. He tried to keep his breathing shallow, the smell growing, the sound drowning out anything but the hum of flickering lights above. Nick harkened back to every horror movie he'd ever seen.

This is where you should leave. Get out. End the horror before it begins.

He never was very smart.

Standing at the center of the hallway was getting him nowhere, so he swung right and hoped he'd chosen the correct path.

He didn't. Instead, he discovered the smell. Or the worst of it.

Organs, stacked in neat rows, packaged in a long meat locker. Red biohazard bags lined the freezer. Full. Someone had shoved it over to block the back exit. Hearts, kidneys and livers scattered in the bags of their own juices. With the lid open and the power off, the contents were quickly spoiling. These were the nightmare images Nick was worried about. Until he saw the eyes.

Jars of eyes, corneas removed and stored in separate containers.

He'd seen some crazy shit during his time with the force. A severed penis. Someone's face blown off two feet from him. But there was something about the eyes he couldn't take. The haunting cloudy stares.

He tried his damnedest not to contaminate the crime scene. Everything in his training told him to keep it together.

Then he saw something else. Empty bags strewn on the floor, crusted with fluid.

Their contents improperly disposed of.

Down the garbage disposal.

Moans echoed. The girl. An injured animal. Straining to keep breathing.

Drained, Nick raised his gun again. He took every open doorway with military precision. Focusing on the task at hand. Anything to keep his thoughts from wandering.

Exam room after exam room. Empty.

Then the moan came again, this time from the end of the hall.

Nick forced his breath out, refusing to take another in. If the madman who made this place was beyond that door, he wouldn't live long. Nick would make sure of it. DC's death was an accident. This wouldn't be.

"Freeze," Nick squeaked out.

A woman stared at him, tears running down her cheeks. The woman with red hair.

The one from the cemetery.

Ray's redhead.

In her hands she held bundles of gauze, shining with wet crimson. Her face streaked with dried blood. Her front soaked through.

There was a young black girl on the gurney. The source of the sounds of draining life. She couldn't have been older than thirteen.

Nothing seemed to stop the river flowing out between her stirrup-spread legs.

"Please," the redhead said, "Help us."

31

"There's gotta be something wrong," Boom-Boom huffed. "She never takes this long."

The way he was squeezing his phone, Ray thought it would have been a pile of plastic and microchips by now. But it was still intact, which let him know that deep down there was some restraint inside the body of the hulking galoot, a tiny voice inside his tiny brain telling him that the phone was the only connection he had to his girlfriend in the mountains and that destroying it would be a stupid move.

"In my experience, ladies like a little hard to get. Maybe she's sick of you pestering her," Ray said. Boom-Boom turned on him. Whatever restraint he was holding off on the phone wouldn't apply to his comrade. Ray shrugged and shut up.

After switching out the plates, they parked the Jeep outside the church and found an out-of-the-way spot to watch and wait. Between the attack at the Solizt Club and the bloody mess they'd left at the strip joint, Ray assumed that the grounds of the church would be swarming with police, windbreakers tearing apart the rectory, unplugging and confiscating the computers, and starting a list of boys Youth Pastor Fuckface had befriended. But nothing happened.

It was Ray's idea to park the Jeep close to the church so they would have access to it when the van came to pick up the boys.

He also wanted to see if the patrons at the Solizt Club or the Pink Panda had called in a description of the assailants' car. If so, it would entice the wandering eyes of law enforcement. Again, nothing.

Ray's mind started working out plausible scenarios. If Dimitri had been found in the bathroom unconscious with the damning evidence in front of him, the FBI would be out in droves. If Dimitri had been found and somehow, the evidence had been overlooked, there would still be a scene at the church. They'd been waiting long enough that news of the youth pastor's attack would have filtered down to the parishioners. But that hadn't happened either. A couple of black and whites had driven down the block. Not one of them had bothered to even slow past the Jeep. With all that time to contemplate "What if's?" Ray had drawn one conclusion: Dimitri was gone and Callum D'Arby had made him disappear.

He had now spent nearly two full days with the lump of meat hunkered in the bushes next to him and had gotten little more than grunts and requisite words out of him. But the hours weren't slipping by with the speed he'd hoped, so he did the last thing in the world he wanted to do. Ray decided to get to know his captor.

"How'd you two meet?" Ray asked as Boom-Boom once again scoffed at his phone screen.

"What do you mean?"

Ray choked back his sarcastic remark.

"Your girl."

"You care?"

"It's just... you seem to hate being apart from her. She must be special. How come?"

"Her smile," Boom-Boom said. He was staring at the wall of the alley opposite, as if he was imagining her there right in front of him.

Ray had seen that smile. It could break mirrors. Best described as "Buscemi-esque."

"She smiles at me and it all goes away. The world. The pain. It disappears when she looks at me. Like I'm the only guy in the world."

"I know what you mean," Ray said.

"You got a girl, too?" Boom-Boom asked. It was the first time he'd asked Ray a personal question.

"I know that smile," Ray said, his own memories bubbling to the surface. "When it's suddenly not around, you feel empty, right?"

"I only want to know she's okay. "

Ray knew exactly what he meant. There were some people who needed to be protected, and when we let them down, the consequences can be dire. Ray swallowed the lump in his throat.

"I mean, I ain't the smartest guy around, but she don't always make the best choices," Boom-Boom continued. "She's, like, slower. She don't think things through before she does 'em. That's how we ended up with Malkin."

"You don't have one of these," Ray lifted his sleeve.

"Hell, no. I knocked her up and she didn't want to have it. I woulda liked it. Having something that was the two of us in one mushed up person, but she was afraid it would come out retarded because of, well, I don't know, but she was sure it would be. She went and got rid of it and when she came back, she had this idea about the mountains."

"You don't believe the mumbo-jumbo about the end of civilization, huh?"

"It's not mumbo-jumbo. Malkin knows stuff we don't know, so I believe him. And even if he don't, life was shit before we went up there."

Boom-Boom swung his moods like a kettlebell. He and Sweets had found kindred spirits in one another, but Ray realized if they didn't have the structure of the Big Bear compound, they'd both either be dead or institutionalized. Malkin was providing them with the semblance of organization in their lives. A stability that they wouldn't have been able to buy on their own. Structure, rules, and indoctrination. In a few brief moments, Ray did exactly what he'd hoped to avoid. He empathized with his enemy.

"Has Malkin made you kill people?" Ray asked.

"I killed people, but not after getting into The Bear. He says plenty of people will die without our help. He wants to teach us how to live."

"The skills he teaches, eh?"

"I wanted to learn how to make blankets. Like with yarn and stuff, but my fingers don't work good sometimes. He said my job was most important anyway. That I have to keep the other people doing their jobs."

"That's what he told you about me? That you have to keep me doing my job?"

"You is, ain't ya?"

Ray let out a laugh with his breath.

"Guess I am."

Whatever Malkin's grand plan was, having enforcers like Reggie and Boom-Boom were essential to maintaining power, but also kept his hands from getting too dirty. In the few days that Ray had spent in the mountains, he hadn't seen what Sweets' job was. Or why she'd been recruited to join the exclusive community.

"What does Sweets do for Malkin?"

"Dunno," Boom-Boom shrugged. "Every time I ask, she tells me it's flowers, but I ain't seen a lot of flowers come out of that greenhouse. I tell her all my secrets. She only got one skill I know about. And if she's doin' that, we can go back right now so I can kill him myself."

Ray wanted to delve into the conversation further, but in the darkness, a group of boys had gathered in the parking lot of St. Germaine Cousin. They were all giving each other shit, showing videos on their phones, and fucking around like pre-teens do. One kid stood off to the side, not taking part in the shenanigans. From what Ray could see, he was hovering on the edge of puberty. Tall, but with boyish features. There was an innocence missing from his eyes that sex work stole from even the most resilient victims. His soft, androgynous features probably made him a prime download.

As Ray watched the group, he wondered if they knew what they were doing. What they were getting into. Raping kids and forcing them into child pornography wasn't what was happening here. Culp was making them willing participants. It echoed what Malkin was doing in the woods. Entice with the promise of cash, power, glory, then make them do increasingly horrible shit until they don't realize it's wrong anymore. Ray guessed that Culp probably went through kids quick. Except for Manny, with that broken, distant look. Simple tasks with substantial reward.

Now, let's try the picture with your shirt off.

He shook off the thoughts, knowing that the imagined abuse would disturb him as much as the real thing. If these were the sort of people that Malkin wanted to collect for the end of the world, Ray would rather die with the rest of humanity.

Forty-five minutes had gone by and most of the boys had gotten impatient. Manny had convinced a few of them to stay, but most of them succumbed to the distractions of youth and had gone home. The last two kids stayed for another ten minutes, pestering Manny the whole time until he gave in to his own impulses and grabbed one of them.

"Quit your fucking whining or go home," he hissed. Even at a distance, Ray could tell his voice hadn't dropped.

"Fuck you, it ain't worth it," the kid said, wriggling out of Manny's grip. The two of them ran off, and Manny cursed after them.

"He ain't comin'," Boom-Boom whispered and made a move to get to his feet.

Ray grabbed his arm without thinking about it. There was nothing he could do to keep Boom-Boom from putting him through the brick wall behind them, but Boom-Boom followed Ray's lead. It was the second hint Ray had gotten that Boom-Boom may have been a powerhouse enforcer, but he easily defaulted to authority. Between that knowledge and his blinding affection for the too-skinny girl still in the woods, Ray knew there had to be some way to turn Boom-Boom to his advantage, if not to his side.

Manny started pacing back and forth in the parking lot, cursing to himself. There was probably some extra incentive in gathering the boys and getting them to their destination unaware, and he'd lost every single one of them.

The kid stopped pacing and pulled out his phone. After five minutes, a car pulled up. Nothing suspicious looking. A plain old Hyundai Elantra.

"We gotta go," Boom-Boom said, this time not halting at Ray's hand.

"We don't know who that is. Get the fuck down, he'll see you," Ray whispered.

"It's an Uber, dumb shit. Didn't you see the sticker?" Boom-Boom said, "He walked here. He ain't goin' home. He's going to Culp."

32

Nick called the ambulance before he knew what he was doing. His instincts had taken over and he went into cop mode, trying to help the redhead stop the bleeding. The girl was hemorrhaging so much, Nick didn't realize the human body could hold so much blood.

The RA Unit came in and hauled the girl away to the closest hospital. The firemen surrounded the redhead and checked her for injuries. Once she had the all clear, she was questioned by the arriving officers. There was no time for Nick to talk to her or to corroborate stories. No time for him to come up with a reason for breaking and entering. No reason for being here and discovering what was behind those doors. He was about to be in deep shit.

"You want to explain to me what we just found?" Lieutenant Jenkins asked. With the body parts found in the kitchen sink, along with the cooler full of harvested organs, RHD was called in to handle the case. At such a large scale, Jenkins wanted to oversee the investigation personally. Instead of assigning individual detectives to this one, it would be a full department investigation. And if they didn't solve it quick, the FBI would be involved soon enough.

What Jenkins didn't realize when he made the trek down was that one of their own was already there.

"I don't know what this place is," Nick said. "Just be glad you weren't the one who found it."

"I'm going to give you the benefit of the doubt here and assume this had something to do with our Jane Doe in the tent?"

Nick nodded. He didn't have to come up with a story yet. Which was good. Any lie he told, he'd have to back up with a chain of investigation of what led him to this doorstep. Otherwise, whoever perpetrated this horror show would go free on a technicality. And Nick would face a manslaughter charge for DC. It wasn't a scenario anyone in the department would tolerate. Nick had fucked up hard.

"I think this is where she died. Then someone moved her to the tent."

"You think?"

"We won't know for sure until we catalog everything here," Nick said, hoping that documenting the crime scene would buy him the time he needed to come up with a valid story, maybe even a DNA match with the body and some of those organs.

"And that woman told you this?" Jenkins asked.

Nick tried not to react. He had no way of knowing what she had told the other officers. But whatever it was, Nick could see that Jenkins was suspicious. Because of the way he was talking, Nick was no longer an investigating detective. He was a suspect.

"When we received the autopsy results from the medical examiner, Hsu and I had a theory that it was a back alley abortion gone bad. We didn't know it would lead to something like this."

"And the woman led you here? To this clinic?"

"Did she give you the story of what went down?" Nick asked. He was doing his best not to tip Jenkins off that this was more than a normal cop to boss conversation.

"She gave us *a* story. Don't know if it's *the* story."

"Why wouldn't you believe her?"

"She called you down here and you discovered the scene. Is that correct?" Jenkins asked.

It was a trap. Nick knew it. He just didn't know what part of the question the trap was under.

"One of our interviews early this week gave me the name Solish." It wasn't a lie. "I looked it up and was on my way here, anyway."

"And this woman called you to the same scene? What? By coincidence?"

Nick didn't answer. His shrug wouldn't be admissible in court.

News vans and reporters were everywhere. Both of them knew they had to be careful about what they said out on the street. Jenkins nodded toward his unmarked.

"Join me in my office."

Nick did what he was told. Jenkins was playing everything too close to the vest and that worried him. The guy didn't make lieutenant because of political moves. He had worked his way up. He got there by being a damn good detective. Much better than Nick would ever be. And both of them knew it.

Inside the car, Jenkins turned the key and brought it to life. It was warmer in there than the parking lot of the strip mall, even though the air conditioning had been blasting and the radio blared the chorus of The Clash's *Police and Thieves* before he turned them both down to a reasonable level. Jenkins had the driver's seat pushed back as far as it could go, but the bottom of the steering wheel still pressed a crescent into his bulbous stomach. The car smelled faintly of Wendy's Baconators and Nick knew he'd never be able to smell one again without feeling nauseous.

"Look, Archer. I don't know how you ended up here, but you better figure out a reason and quick. I also don't know who this Lauren Ashmore is —," Nick finally had a name, "but both of your stories are shit."

It seemed like an honest man-to-man plea for the truth, but Nick had worked for Jenkins for almost four years. He'd never spoken to Nick without wanting to rip him a new asshole. It was a ploy.

"Maybe, but it's the truth."

"Yeah?" Jenkins asked, reaching into his coat pocket. "Then how do you explain this?"

He pulled out an evidence baggy and handed it to Nick. Inside was a business card. The white paper had yellowed and was bent from being handled over time, but the writing on it was clear as day. The inlaid black print said *Detective Nick Archer*. And there was no reason for it to be in an evidence bag.

"Looks like something that would come in handy if you wanted to call a detective," Nick said.

"You gave her this card recently?"

"You know how many of those I handed out in Skid Row when Willie and I were looking into Low Seward? Hundreds. Or she could've picked it up in the street."

It was a boldfaced lie. It was his old business card. The one he had when he was working on cold cases. It had his old extension on it. He knew where she'd gotten it. He'd given it to Ray Cobb before he'd dropped him off on Beverly Boulevard all those years ago. His mother was still alive and Nick was making better choices. Prior to Ray being a murder suspect. Before he had sent Lauren Ashmore to Nick with a cryptic voicemail on a burner phone.

"That's what she says. She had this card from when you were looking into the Low Seward case and she saved it for a rainy day. I guess the rainy day came today. Where's your partner?"

Nick had been on the other side of this. Too many times to count. You get a suspect to weave themselves further into their own lies until they are so tangled they don't know where the thread began. He wouldn't let that happen.

"I didn't call him."

"Why not?"

"It's late."

"How courteous of you. I called him."

"Yeah?"

"Yep."

"Is he on his way?"

"He'll be here shortly. Funny, he didn't mention you finding anything out about this place in your investigation."

Caught in a lie already. And it was a small one. One he didn't plan.

"Okay, Lieutenant, I know how this works. You keep boxing me in until you get the information you're looking for. Why don't you just come out and tell me why you think my shit stinks?"

Jenkins took in a deep breath and blew it out of his mouth. Nick caught the faint smell of spicy chicharrones.

"When you and Grant found it was me that leaked the Seward crime scene to the press, albeit accidentally, neither of you said a word. I appreciated that. I didn't ask for you to cover for me, but I appreciated it. We all fuck up in this job. It happens. It's part of being human. Problem is, when we fuck up, we don't get a lot of second chances. You know how the world is with law enforcement these days, Archer. The public looks at us like the enemy. We have to watch every fucking move we make. We have to be better."

That was Nick's usual cue for a snappy comeback. He didn't take the bait. He gave a slight nod.

"This? Here?" Jenkins said, pointing at the clinic through the flashing lights. "Do you know how long organs survive outside the body before they're worthless? 9 hours. 12, tops.

Which means those were all harvested recently and there's someone out there waiting for them. If it was all eyeballs and kidneys, then some folks lost a bet and had a bad day. Hearts? Livers? People don't keep moving around after those are gone. Do you know how complicated a heart transplant is? This isn't some backwater operation. There is infrastructure. Think about that."

"I know," Nick said, soft and solemn.

"This guy? Solish? If he's our guy and you being here without a warrant lets him walk? That I can't forgive."

"He won't."

"Then I'll tell you what. I'll give you all my unanswered questions and leave it at that. You come up with some answers before we get this guy? Great. We move on. I owe you that. You don't? You are chum for the sharks, boy-o, and I will lead the crusade to get you prosecuted. Hear me?"

Nick did what all smart suspects did when they didn't want to incriminate themselves. He stayed quiet.

"First off, who is this Lauren Ashmore? How is she connected to this? Giving her a reason to be in this place without being my primary suspect would be a gigantic step toward earning my trust. And I'll tell you, you better get me something before that other girl is stable, because if your story and that little girl's story don't match up, I'm going with the little girl's version and calling IAD on your ass."

Nick gave a slight nod.

"I need a trail to this doorstep and probable cause for you walking through the doors without a warrant when the business is clearly not open. A trail that you can back up with witnesses and paperwork."

"Is this the part where you ask for my gun and my badge?"

"Fuck you, what is this, a movie? No. You're going to need those to do this right. If you're standing at my desk and you hand me that shit, you hand me that shit forever, you hear me? We don't do idle threats in my department."

"Anything else?" Nick asked.

"Yeah," Jenkins said, his tone slipped out of interrogation mode. "I want to know if you want to keep working for me. Because if this is shit you're going to pull, or if you're not satisfied with upholding the law by following it, I don't want you anywhere near the rest of my crew. You could take your new partner down with you. Do you want that? Do you want to compromise the integrity of a department that is already balancing on a razor's edge? I want you to really think on that. The right answer may not be the one I want to hear. All right?"

"Gotcha."

"Now get the fuck out of my car," Jenkins said. He wasn't joking.

Nick slammed the door and walked off. He knew Jenkins wasn't leaving the scene soon. He was giving Nick time to get out of his sight. Given the history those two had with one another, it was in Nick's best interest to disappear. He headed for the EMTs.

"Where can I find Ms. Ashmore?" Nick asked the EMT, who was closing the doors to the back of his ambulance. There was no need for them there any more. The forensics van was going to be there for the rest of the night, though.

"Your boss interviewed her after we checked her out, then he let her go."

Jenkins thought he was doing Nick a favor by releasing her out into the world instead of bringing her back for an interview. He probably figured Nick would rendezvous with her away from the chaos so they could get their stories straight. But Nick's job would've been a lot easier if they'd taken her into custody.

Jenkins was already bending the rules for him. Nick could see how taking one small step outside the law could snowball into something beyond your control.

The last place he should show his face was at the bedside of the girl who he'd found hemorrhaging in the clinic. There would already be someone else from RHD assigned to interviewing her when she stabilized. But right now, that girl was the only connection to Lauren Ashmore. A name Nick knew was fake the minute Jenkins said it.

He was good and rightly fucked. There was only one place he could go next.

33

Ahead of them, the Uber turned up Saticoy toward Panorama City. Boom-Boom was right. Manny led them to where he'd taken the van a dozen times before. If he didn't show up with the group, at least he'd be there waiting when Culp showed up. His loyalty wouldn't be in jeopardy.

The Hyundai pulled up to a ranch-style house. Perfectly suburban with a well-manicured lawn. A standing light in the front yard illuminated the path up to the stained glass front door. The kid got out of the car and it pulled away. Boom-Boom shut off the headlights and they stopped a few houses down while Manny trotted up the front steps.

"Should we grab him?" Boom-Boom asked. His pull toward authority was stronger than Ray had imagined. All of Boom-Boom's life he had probably defaulted to the most intelligent person in the room. Now, it was the guy he was supposed to be babysitting.

"Hold on," Ray whispered. He watched the kid trot up to the house and ring the doorbell. He peered through the stained glass windows and then rapped on the door. No one responded. No one came out. He disappeared around the side of the house and Boom-Boom made a move to leave the car.

"Wait," Ray said again.

"You wanna lose him?" Boom-Boom argued.

"How much time did you spend out on the streets before you took up with Malkin?"

"Enough."

"Not long enough to pay attention to your environment," Ray said. "Look at this neighborhood. Nice, but not too nice. Houses punctuated with apartment buildings. Comfortable."

Boom-Boom peered through the windshield of the Jeep again, looking for any sign of Manny emerging from around the house. The kid's disappearance didn't bother Ray in the slightest.

"If what Dmitri said was true, neighbors are going to notice a group of kids piling out of a van into a house regularly and then piling back out. If there was any indication of what really happened in there, I'm sure there would be someone nosey enough to raise a red flag. Look at that place. Simple and inviting. Which means—"

Manny came around the opposite side of the house that he'd gone around. He stood on the lawn for another moment, hoping to see movement inside, then shrugged and pulled out his phone again. Moments later, another car arrived, picked him up, and drove away.

Boom-Boom made a movement to start the Jeep. Ray stopped him again.

"We're where we need to be."

Ray got out of the car and walked toward the house, Boom-Boom trailing behind.

"What were you saying about the house? What does it mean?"

Ray stopped short and ducked into the yard of the apartment complex next door. It wasn't as well lit and would give them access to the back of the house.

"It means," Ray pointed to the small square window at the base of the house, "it's one of the few houses in the neighborhood with a basement."

They crept into the darkened yard and peered through the window. Below them was a finished basement, complete with a pool table and a flat screen.

"We used to call that the rumpus room when I was growing up," Ray said. "Neighbors will know he has it and if he's involved with the church, holding a youth group meeting won't look out of place."

"How the fuck did you know that shit?" Boom-Boom asked.

"I used to know a lot of people who spent too much energy trying to look normal. Me included," Ray said.

"I don't know what the fuck that means either," Boom-Boom said.

"Neither did I until I tried to escape it," Ray said.

Opening up about his former life with Boom-Boom was strangely easy. It was as though the MMA fighter was an amnesiac therapist who didn't offer ways to solve his problems.

He got up and went to the back door of the house. The kitchen light was on. Either the lights were on a timer or someone had left hastily. No one was home.

He tried the knob. It jiggled more than it should have, but was locked.

"Any chance you're an expert lock pick?" Ray asked.

"No, but I ain't the first one to try," Boom-Boom said, pointing at the door. Ray hadn't noticed it, but there were several marks in the doorjamb made with some kind of pry bar. And from there, he could see there were paint chips and splinters on the concrete steps. Fresh.

"Whoever did it loosened the lock," Ray said.

"The kid?"

"Not enough time."

Boom-Boom wrapped his ping-pong paddle palm around the door handle and turned it hard as he put his shoulder into the wood. It gave a slight crack and more wood splintered onto the ground, but they were inside.

They closed the door behind them and Ray nodded to the stairs by the pantry that led to the basement.

"You don't wanna check out the rest of the place?" Boom-Boom whispered.

"If whoever got here before us is still here, they avoided that bay window. Only one place to do that."

Ray went for the knife block and Boom-Boom stopped him.

"You really want to go down there without a weapon?"

"Who said anything about me goin' down there without a weapon?"

He pulled a taser out of his pocket and showed it to Ray. All this time, Ray had assumed it was Boom-Boom's fists that were supposed to keep him in line.

Ray held his hands up. "You first."

Boom-Boom headed for the stairs without question. The first step creaked. He peered back at Ray.

"Ah, the element of surprise," Ray said.

Boom-Boom continued down the stairs as Ray slid a cast-iron skillet out of the dish rack and hid it behind his back. It was a little *Looney Tunes*, but anything in a pinch.

They reached the basement and found the same calm scene they'd seen through the window. Boom-Boom turned around to Ray and nodded to the only closed door. Ray nodded back. If Boom-Boom had seen Ray's weapon, he didn't mention it.

Playing out the scene of every action movie he'd ever seen, Boom-Boom kicked in the door and then swept aside, waiting for a hail of gunfire.

It didn't come. But there was a smell both of them were more familiar with than they'd like to admit.

Fresh blood.

Boom-Boom went into the dark room, followed by Ray.

A lone laptop computer sat on a simple desk. The flatscreen monitor showed a frame by frame layout of film editing software displaying a scene that Ray tried not to take too close a look at. The far end of the room was spare, except for a double bed and a few props that made it look like the room of a pre-teen. Theatrical lighting hung from the ceiling, and the cord from a DSLR camera ran from the tripod directly into an external hard drive. Culp was on the bed.

He didn't look like what Ray had expected. There was no v-neck t-shirt that exposed a tangle of chest hair beneath a gold chain. No ponytail clinging to the dregs of a balding scalp. He was clean cut. Jeans and a golf shirt. The only things that kept him from looking like he was about to go to a PTA meeting were the Bear tattoo on his forearm and the gash across his neck.

"Guess we're too late," Ray said.

"He could still be here," Boom-Boom said, ready to search the house.

"Left and locked the back door behind him. He's gone."

"Who do you think 'he' is?" Boom-Boom asked. He'd turned his attention to the computer. From the look on his face, Ray could see the scene disgusted him.

Ray stayed in the shadows of the room, keeping his weapon concealed, but the crime scene made him nervous. The killer had used a straight razor and placed it delicately on the bed next to the body.

Just like Osip Kosbur had with Victor Mochulyak.

The realization hit him in a flood that took his breath away.

The Bear was still alive.

Dimitri had lied.

Which meant either Malkin didn't know or, more likely, he had sent them on a wild goose chase and Boom-Boom was going to take him out as soon as they found the third tattoo.

He swung the skillet back and cracked it across the back of Boom-Boom's head. It made a resounding clang, but he didn't go down. He stood up slowly and turned around.

"Oops," Ray shrugged. The prongs of the taser hit his chest. He was still in a fit of convulsions when Boom-Boom grabbed the laptop and swung it across Ray's face, halting his consciousness.

The guard at the gate let Nick into Holy Cross Cemetery after hours, just as he had every Sunday for the past month. He didn't seem to notice that it was Wednesday and didn't ask about the change in routine. The sheer magnitude of stress Nick had gone through over the past few hours must have read like grief. As a cemetery guard, the man would have known to never be too cheery anyway, just the right amount of pleasant. Grieving cops got special privileges.

Nick wound his car around the paved curves carved through the peaceful grass. Save for a few monuments, all of the stones were set in the ground. A well-manicured lawn on the edge of a field. Fertilized with the loved ones of Los Angeles.

Crickets chirped in the grass as he scuffed his shoes across the dew. He usually brought out the lawn chair he kept in his trunk for these visits, but tonight he was too keyed up. Too antsy. When he reached his mother's grave, he stood slightly off to the side, as he always did. Not that he believed any part of her soul was interred there, but it felt disrespectful to set up a lawn chair where her remains sat six feet below, even though the calculating scientific part of him knew that nature was already doing much worse to her than the divots of a chair in the grass.

He stared at the smooth marble for a while, breathing in the crisp air. The temperatures during the day had already crept back up to Southern California normal, but the nights held their desert frostiness and he could see his breath if he really focused.

"I messed up, Ma," he said, his voice low.

"Thing is... I don't know if I would've thought so if I didn't get caught."

Nick had joined the force because his mother had gotten sick. He'd always liked the idea of fighting crime, but wanted to do it on his own terms, like those guys on TV. When he got a job with a stable paycheck so he could help with his mother's upside-down mortgage, he never figured she would live a decade past her diagnosis. It was a morbid decision to make and one he wasn't really conscious of until she kept on living. He remembered the day he'd realized it. The day he wondered how he'd gotten so deep into the LAPD. Then, the guilt over lamenting why he'd taken the job.

"After Dad left, do you remember how you said you felt guilty? Guilty that you knew he loved you more than you loved him. Guilty you couldn't return his affection in the way he wanted you to, so he found someone who could? I blamed you for that for a long time and never told you. Like, because you couldn't love him enough, he couldn't love me enough, so he left. Even though I knew you loved me enough for both of you."

He rubbed his face with his hands and exhaled up into the darkness tainted by light pollution.

"I think that's where I'm at with the job. I'm good at it. I know. It loves me a hell of a lot more than I love it, and now I'm acting out. Pushing it away. And it's making me stupid. Taking chances that could let some bad people get away with some bad things. I think it all started here. I deleted that fucking—sorry—voicemail. And I think I understand both of you now. The job feels rejected like Dad did, so it's lashing out at me. And I feel like you. Like I want to be the perfect partner and do everything right, but it's not in me and I ended up a cynical mess. I don't know. I'm confused. That was confusing."

"I'm confused just listening to you."

Nick hoped she'd be there. But he didn't know who he was dealing with. Someone with no problem lying to the police and, by proxy, the FBI. She'd snuck up on him instead of approaching from the front. For all he knew, she was working with Solish and had a gun on his back right now, ready to find a fresh grave that only needed a foot of displaced dirt to make him disappear forever.

"I thought you'd be more careful. I smelled your shampoo," Nick said.

"I had to wash the blood out of my hair," she said. It came out flat and weary.

"Suppose I took the 'married to my job' metaphor a little too far. But I meant it, whatever I meant." He still hadn't turned around. "If it makes a difference."

"Really? Because it sounded like the performance of someone trying to convince me they're on my side."

"And what side is that?" Nick asked.

"The side that finds Solish and brings him to justice."

Nick pulled his hands out of his coat pockets and turned around. She didn't have a weapon. She'd changed out of the bloodstained clothes. The breeze blew wisps of her hair into her face, but she didn't brush it away. She wasn't the strong, confident woman he'd met in the same cemetery a month before, delivering a cryptic message from an old friend. And she wasn't the panicked, frail victim who was interviewed and released by the police. She was a mixture now. Confident in her stance, eye contact unwavering, but clutching herself against the slight cold, showing him her vulnerability even if she didn't realize it. Nick could read her body language right away. He was feeling the same thing at that moment. Both of them wondered if they'd made the right choice to come back to the cemetery that night. Both of them hoped the person standing across the grass was someone they could trust.

"What do you mean by 'justice'?" he asked.

She didn't answer him. Her look told him all he needed. It was his choice. Which path to take? Whatever information this woman had for him would get him closer to justifying his presence in the clinic, but joining forces with her would mean he would likely enter a world of unknowns.

"Why did you lie for me?" he asked. He took a few steps closer to her. She didn't make a move to run, but closing the distance between them put her on the alert.

"That girl was thirteen years old and was over four months pregnant. You saw what he did to her."

"Yeah," he whispered, "I know."

"Have you identified the other girl yet?" she asked.

"Which one?"

"You know which one," she sighed.

Nick didn't like this. The cryptic back and forth. It was a game of chicken where neither wanted to be the first to turn away. He knew when that happened, it usually led to a crash.

"What did Cobb tell you about me?" Nick asked. He figured a different angle might get them out of the battle of words.

"Three years ago? That I could trust you. A month ago? Nothing. Deliver a phone. That's it."

"Don't think you can trust me now?"

"He told me you were good police. Sort of guy who would listen instead of assuming. But being a good detective means following procedure. I know you didn't find that place by doing normal police work."

"What makes you say that?"

She pulled the phone out of her pocket, but made no gesture to hand it over. Nick's breath caught in his throat. He knew she noticed.

"Whatever you were planning on doing with this would've gotten you into a lot of trouble."

"I thought you were shorter in the hospital," Nick said.

"You were so nervous, you couldn't have picked me out of a lineup if I'd belly-danced into that room."

Looking at her now, the wind blowing her hair around her lithe neck, Nick highly doubted that assessment.

"I tracked it," she said, sliding the back panel off the phone and pulling out a small chip. "You've been busy."

Nick tried not to show his surprise. She had been watching him. Keeping tabs. She could place him at the junkyard the night of DC's death. No wonder she stole the phone. Leverage. He covered his concern by going on the offensive.

"So, *Lauren*, how are you caught up in this?"

"That's not my name," she said.

"Figured. What should I call you?"

"Lauren is fine. For now."

"Well?"

"The woman you found on Juanita. Her name was Aelan Kham. She had no passport. No address. No visa. You won't find her on any official record."

"How did you know her?"

"She traveled here in a shipping container with twenty other girls. Four of whom didn't make it through the full trip. Sold to a pimp by the name of Burke, then sold to Sketch. Getting all this so far?"

Nick nodded.

"She might not even be on record in Laos. Maybe a birth certificate, if you're lucky."

"Beyond you, there's no one to I.D. her?"

"Me or Ballantine. Based on what happened to him, doubt if he'll ever talk again. If I say I knew her, then I'll get asked questions I don't want your bosses to know I know the answers to," she said.

"The tattoo. Aelan is on Ballantine's arm. Name is rare enough that's not a coincidence."

"But how did you get the name?" she asked.

Nick thought about it. There had to be someone out there who knew why a pimp would tattoo one of his girls on his arm. Until he found that connection, Aelan would remain Jane Doe.

"What about this guy, Applebox? Ever heard of him?" Nick asked.

She snorted out a laugh.

"Applebox? You floated that name around?"

"Here and there. What's so funny?"

"Got that from Zeke, huh?" she smiled.

Nick saw the mocking in her look. He'd been chasing ghosts for days.

"Lemme guess, you're Ayida Weddo?"

"He's got a little nickname for everybody. Calls me that because he thinks I'm some sort of vigilante fertility goddess come to save the souls of damned women."

"Okay. So, who's Applebox?"

She put her hands in her pockets to shield herself from the cold, "Apple boxes are used to make things higher on film sets. Or make short actors taller. Burke is a little person."

"Therefore, Applebox," Nick stared at the ground, feeling like a rookie again.

"Jackpot. Burke gets you an I.D. on your victim. He was the one who brought that little girl into Solish's clinic, so likely he brought Aelan in there as well. He might have a lead on where Solish ended up."

"We find Burke, bring him in for trafficking a minor, get him to rat on Solish, problem solved?" Nick asked.

"Not quite. You still have to tell your superiors how you ended up in the clinic," she said. "I make a statement and the timeline unravels."

"We have to find Solish on our own," Nick realized. "Any chance you know where to find Burke?"

"Drives a box truck covered in graffiti. Operates out of that. Finding him isn't the hard part. Solish is. I thought the illegal abortions were his only gig."

"The organs make him connected to something bigger," Nick thought out loud.

There was a lot of information coming at Nick at once. If Lauren knew what happened to Aelan, she was holding it back. She was already his alibi for the clinic. She wouldn't be his alibi to place him at Solish's house. It was too convenient for Jenkins to overlook.

"If Solish is arrested before we can get to him, a talented lawyer will have him out the door by the afternoon," Nick said.

"Then we find him first."

He didn't know what to do next. His police brain told him he needed to start from zero. Look for the box truck. Find Burke. Find Solish. Fill in the gaps between those steps. But he knew he couldn't put out a call on the radio for Burke's box truck, not without getting questions he didn't have the answer to when he filed his report. If some uniforms got to Burke before he did and ended up arresting him on the suspicion of another crime, Nick couldn't get the information out of Burke he needed before the diminutive pimp took a plea deal. Which meant no justice for Aelan, no jail time for Solish, and no job for Nick.

He still wasn't sure who this woman was. Was she the sobbing girl in the clinic, the noir fantasy woman who had approached him in the cemetery after his mother's death, or the mysterious vigilante who stood before him? She was a chameleon, and that made her dangerous. There could be layers of identities that she had presented to him. Was she the cooperative partner? The concerned matron? A determined rogue? All of it could be lies. But to what end?

He had to admit that his thirst for curiosity about her had gone beyond what he should have allowed. He should have thrown himself to the mercy of his fellow detectives. Asked their advice on how to handle this situation. It would have been ignorant for him to assume he was the first detective to gather damning evidence on a suspect without using proper procedure. As far as Nick knew, it was happening every day. The problem was, what Nick had uncovered was so sinister and now, so public, there would be no way for him to put the genie back into the bottle. Jenkins had implied as much. But being with this woman, who was still an unknown variable, he knew he was beyond his depth. Still, there was something nagging him in the back of his brain. Her connection to Aelan, Solish, and Cobb.

But he was out of allies and needed someone's help.

"I have a lead on where Solish might be holed up, or someplace we could find something on him," Nick said, "but there's no way I get to that doorstep logically. The mortgage is under a corporate trust, and I can't get a subpoena for those records without evidence."

"How'd you get it?"

"Nosy neighbor. But the source is out of the country. If we wait until we can reach her or until she can see the media blitz, he'll be gone."

"We need to connect you to Solish," she said and tossed him the phone. "Don't lose that again."

He opened the back to check that she'd removed the tracking chip and looked up at her, holding her gaze.

"I didn't kill the kid in the junkyard," he said.

The words hung there in the air between them.

"I know," she said. "Accidents happen."

She walked past him, heading for his car.

"Does that mean you've decided to trust me?" he asked.

"No. Have you decided to trust me?" she asked without turning back.

"No."

"Good," she said over her shoulder. "Let's get to work."

Butterflies rose in his stomach.

He didn't know if they were out of elation or fear.

But he dreaded them both.

35

"Kosbur is still alive," Ray coughed out.

Boom-Boom had thrown him in the back of the Jeep, but hadn't bothered to restrain him.

"Dimitri lied," Ray said.

"Shut the fuck up."

Ray couldn't believe it. If Malkin had known that Kosbur was still alive, why would he send Ray to go collect the other tattooed conscripts?

Maybe Malkin didn't know that Kosbur was still alive. That Callum D'Arby had taken over his business in exchange for letting him live.

Either way, the other piece of the puzzle was the last of the tattooed criminals. They had to find him to either uncover Kosbur or get some answers about Callum D'Arby. But Boom-Boom had already steered the Jeep onto the 10, halfway to San Bernadino.

"We have to get the last guy," Ray said. "Turn around."

"I gotta get back to Sweets," Boom-Boom said. "And I need permission to kill you for hitting me with that pan."

"You and Sweets have to get out from under Malkin's grip," Ray said. The pain in his body hadn't subsided, but he had to figure out a way to get Boom-Boom to turn around.

"Shut the fuck up or I'll zap you again," Boom-Boom said.

Ray stopped talking, but he knew there was something he would have to say to get Boom-Boom to turn around. The blood wasn't dry on Culp, which meant if Kosbur hadn't already gotten to the next guy, he was heading there next. Without him, Ray had nothing.

"If we don't finish this, Malkin is going to send us back out, which means more time away from your girlfriend."

"If that's what Malkin wants. That's what Malkin wants," Boom-Boom said.

Ray didn't think that Boom-Boom had become as indoctrinated by Malkin's words as he put on. In fact, Sweets always seemed like the doting worshipper and Boom-Boom was the puppy nipping at her heels, sniffing whichever way the wind between her legs was blowing. Boom-Boom didn't give a shit about Malkin's cult. Sweets was his true north.

Ray knew he couldn't physically overpower him, so he would have to hit Boom-Boom where he knew it could hurt him.

"I saw the way she looked at him," Ray said.

The Jeep swerved hard into the right lane as Boom-Boom's fist swung around to bash Ray's brains against the backseat of the Jeep. He didn't seem to notice that he'd nearly sideswiped a Cadillac and was grasping for Ray in the backseat like a cat's paw through a mouse hole.

Ray had backed his body up to the lift gate and was just out of Boom-Boom's reach. He would have to be careful with what he said next. Boom-Boom wasn't one for multitasking and would be happy to pull the car into oncoming traffic if it meant he had a better chance of taking a significant chunk out of the homeless man in the back seat.

"Are you going to keep following orders of someone who's got an eye on your girl?"

This time, Boom-Boom didn't bother swinging for him, but still wrenched the wheel hard to the right, crossing several lanes of screeching traffic. The car stopped. He was out before Ray knew what was happening. A fist tore through the flimsy plastic and was grabbing for him.

"Fuck Malkin. I'll kill you myself."

Ray scrambled to the driver's side, scraping his back on the gearshift and tumbling out onto the gravel. Boom-Boom ambled toward him with murder in his eyes.

"Hold on. Listen. I can get you out. I can—"

Boom-Boom lunged for him. Either he couldn't hear Ray with the traffic speeding past, or the anger filled his head with blood and had closed his Eustachian tubes. Ray dodged at the last minute, then jumped back onto the shoulder after being nearly flattened by a Semi. Saving his own life turned out to be a mistake. Boom-Boom had him in a bear hug. He could feel all the air being squeezed out of his lungs.

"We can save her," Ray squeaked out, "But we can't do it with them watching."

Boom-Boom's grip tightened, the pressure pushing the last air out of Ray's lungs. All that remained was for Ray's consciousness to leave him. But that didn't happen. The end didn't come. Instead, the grip slackened enough for Ray to take shallow breaths. And against his back, he felt the heaving chest of his captor and his shirt becoming wet with muffled sobs.

It took Ray a moment to realize what was happening. He thought about how ridiculous it must look to the traffic speeding by to see a grown man being held backwards by a large man who was weeping uncontrollably.

Ray didn't speak. He let Boom-Boom get out the emotions he had been holding in. He also didn't know how to deliver on what he was promising. With any luck, the promise itself would get Ray the answers he needed. And fulfilling it would resolve itself by Malkin ending up dead or in prison.

After an uncomfortable amount of time, Boom-Boom set Ray down on the gravel. Ray turned around and looked at the bubbles of translucent snot popping out of Boom-Boom's nostrils.

The beast wiped his nose with his forearm, tangling his arm hair with mucus, and gestured for Ray to get back into the Jeep. When it seemed like Boom-Boom wouldn't renew his attack, Ray complied. Boom-Boom started the Jeep, pulled back into traffic, and at the next exit, turned around and headed back toward the city.

"So," Ray finally broke the silence, "any ideas?"

Without looking at him, Boom-Boom reached down into the footwell of the passenger seat. Ray lunged away, thinking he was about to have his kneecap dislocated, but Boom-Boom popped back up with the laptop he'd taken from Culp's basement. It had a streak of Ray's dried blood on the bottom. He tossed it in Ray's lap.

"Figured there was something on there Malkin would want," he said. "Maybe we want it too."

Ray opened it up and creaked a little. It would be just their luck that his skull had damaged the hard drive. He hit the power button. It didn't turn on. Figured.

"You didn't grab a power cord, did you?" Ray asked.

Boom-Boom's look told him what he needed to know. Also that he shouldn't talk any more on their way back to Los Angeles.

36

Burke saw her out of the corner of his eye from the line at the donut shop. By the time he'd hobbled over to his seat with his coffee and Boston Cream, she was in plain sight. He took a bite of his treat and a little custard squeezed out onto his fingers. He licked them clean and watched her through the windows. An exhibit in an urban zoo.

If she was a working girl, she was out too early in the afternoon. The sun was on its way down, but this wasn't the sort of neighborhood where men went prowling after work before they went home to their wives. Wasn't enough time to wash the stink of street pussy off and blame the delay on traffic. Burke knew for damn sure you couldn't cover it up with cologne. You needed to Lava Bar that shit. Scrub your business like you just finished tarring a roof with it.

She was wandering the block with no purpose. A window shopper would've gone into one of the little boutiques if only to get out of the sun for fifteen minutes. She sat on the bus bench under the shelter for a while, but when an overweight cleaning lady sat down, the look she gave the girl made her get up and lean against the glass ad sheet. She periodically rummaged through the oversized purse she had on her. The one that looked like she was carrying her whole life in it. Twice she came up empty, then found what she was looking for. A piece of gum stuck in some receipt paper. The girl peeled it apart carefully and scraped the crusty old piece of gum into her mouth with her front teeth. Burke could see that it took a bit for her to work the crunch out of it, but eventually her jaw did the work and sated her oral fixation.

Burke didn't like running girls near his home base. It was bad for business to mix the two. But the raid on Solish's clinic took the little girl off of his roster. Pissed him off to lose such fresh, innocent meat, but he counted his blessings that he planned to pick her up after the procedure rather than wait around. It was the closest he'd come to being pinched in a long time. Might as well try to recoup some losses.

He pulled out his phone and dialed. A cough answered.

"You got Baby Brim, who dis?"

"Brim, it's Burke."

"What you want, Skee Lo?"

"You running a girl off Beverly by the B.K.?"

"Where on Beverly?"

"In the Bello."

"Why the fuck you care? That ain't your block," Baby Brim said over the phone. Burke could sense his hackles were up.

"I know it ain't. I see something I like and be askin' a courtesy. You got a girl here or not?"

"Little too Eastside for me, but if I were around, it'd be my girl."

"So is it?" Burke asked, sick of the back and forth.

"Is her feet pretty?"

"How the fuck I know?"

"Cuz you low to the ground muthafucka, you notice that shit."

"Her feet nasty, a'ight," Burke lied. "She your girl?"

There was a pause on the other end. Burke could tell that Brim was deciding whether to gamble.

"Nah, man. Ain't mine. Do your thing."

"Thank you. How's your moms?"

Baby Brim laughed on the other end, "Muthafucka, go get yo dick wet. Askin' bout my moms like you give a fuck. Shit."

Burke ended the call and finished his donut. He checked his face for frosting and left his half-full coffee cup on the table. He didn't want her to see him coming, so he hobbled down to the corner and waited for the light. He knew he had to be careful with the antsy ones. Approach them slow like a lion on a gazelle. Wait and see what chemicals they like. Then give 'em too much of something else. Tricks almost made it too easy.

"Hey girl."

She nearly leapt out of her skin as she swung on him. Her dark hair came out of the loose twist she had it in and hung ragged at her shoulders. There were edges of an old bruise around her left eye. He didn't see any grab bruises on the forearms she had crossed over her belly, accentuating a pair of titties that were more than a handful. Whoever she worked with hadn't beat on her on the regular. Good sign she was a free agent.

"Get the fuck away from me," she said, her voice graveled, but shaking.

"Just wondering if you wanted some gum," he said, a pack of Extra held out to her.

"You get that at the chocolate factory you work at?" she said without smiling.

"Trying to be nice," Burke said, hiding his rage. He'd make her pay for that one. Later.

The girl bit the skin on the inside of her lower lip, still giving him the stink eye, then spit the hard piece of gum she was chewing out into the street. She took a piece of gum and popped it in her mouth, then flicked the wrapper from her middle finger and thumb into the lap of the cleaning lady at the bus stop.

"Thanks," she gnawed loud on the gum and turned away from him.

"You need somethin'?" he asked. She didn't answer him. Just kept looking across the street. But she hadn't left. And that was all Burke needed.

A bus pulled to a halt in front of the shelter and the cleaning lady got on. The girl made no move to get on and gave the bus driver a slight nod "no" when he asked if she was coming. The bus pulled away, and the girl shuffled around Burke to take a seat on the bench. Burke turned around on his crutches, but didn't make a move to sit down next to her.

"Damn sure you ain't got nothin' I need," she said, almost a whisper.

"Looks can be deceiving," Burke smiled.

"Yeah? What you got?" she asked, shifting in her seat.

"Like I said, what you need?"

"You a cop?"

Burke let out a guffaw.

"Holy shit, damn girl. That's fuckin' funny. Can honestly say I ain't ever been asked that."

"Well, are ya?"

"No. You?"

She snorted out a laugh and scratched her arm.

"That ain't no answer, neither," Burke smiled.

"If I was, I'd have a car to get away from your tiny ass."

"There you go with the insults again," Burke said. He wondered if he would crack a tooth the way he was clenching his teeth. This girl was damn fine looking under all the bullshit. He hoped her cooze was dipped in rainbow sprinkles and tasted like strawberry jam for the shit she was giving him.

Her time on the bench was short-lived. She got up again and dug through her purse, not looking for anything in particular, then did a lap around the bus shelter.

"Sorry about the—," she started, "thanks for the gum."

"No problem, girl," he smiled. "You look like you could use some taking care of."

She shot him a suspicious look. He rarely went in for the kill so quick, but he needed to know where he stood before he wasted any more of his time. It took a moment for her to respond.

"Well," she breathed out through her nose and snapped her gum, "I wouldn't say no to a Whopper."

Burke laughed and glanced over his shoulder at the Burger King.

"If you's hungry, I can take care of that, but I can also get you something to stop your jitters."

"I ain't gonna fuck you," she said.

"Who says I want to?" he shrugged.

"Everything's got a price," she said.

"Okay," he conceded. "How 'bout we say this one is a kindness and another taste will cost you, if you're willing to pay. That's how this usually works, right? I'm being open with you."

She stared at him for what seemed like forever. But she wasn't still. She was trying to be. Trying to hold back the inevitable fidgeting that came with opiates leaving her system. Sweating in the cool breeze. He could tell she had it bad. Someone as far gone as her might as well be a Parkinson's patient trying to steady their hand. She couldn't play tough much longer. Now that she knew what she might pass up. But he knew if she tried to keep playing with him, anything other than an affirmative answer out of her mouth and he'd walk away to enjoy the rest of his day.

"A kindness?" she finally said, more to herself than him.

He nodded.

She swiped her forearm under her nose, chewed on the inside of her lower lip, her eyes doing all of her thinking for her, and finally gave him a small series of nods.

The right side of his mouth went up in a smile and he hitched his crutches back under his armpits. He knew he would have one more hurdle to get over, but the simple part was over. In her mind, she already had the drugs in hand. Once she saw the box truck, it wouldn't be enough of a hinderance to keep the triggers in her brain from thinking that the high was already on the way.

There was no way to place the truck completely out of sight. The neighborhood was a jungle of strip malls and buildings no taller than three stories. He'd parked the truck in an alley that got little traffic except for when there were late night deliveries. Even the smattering of tags on the truck wasn't enough to draw attention. The two of them could sit in there all day if they wanted, letting the drugs take hold, her letting him do things to her she would never allow in broad daylight, or in the right state of mind. He might even beat on her a little for the mouth she was giving him. That is, if he couldn't find a new use for that mouth quick enough.

She stopped a few yards from the box truck as he approached the padlock on the back lift gate.

"In there?" she asked. He could sense fear, but she was doing a decent job of hiding it.

"We ain't gonna snort this shit in the donut shop."

She looked up and down the alley, her eyes squinting against the sunlight, then walked up and stood at his side as he slipped his key into the lock.

The door made an echoing rattle as it went up and Burke barely glimpsed feet before the collar of his shirt hefted him up into the dark of the box truck.

"What the fu—"

"Shhh," the girl said, still standing on the ground. He was ready to raise holy hell, but she had the blade he kept in his boot fixed on his dick. She'd pulled it out in one fluid motion at the same time that the asshole in the truck had yanked him inside. How the fuck did she know where he kept his knife?

"You just made a big mistake, bitch."

"Talk nice to the lady," the man said, clutching the back of his shirt like it was a puppy's scruff. He was wearing a ski-mask and had something disguising his voice.

"Walk away before you jack the wrong man."

"Keep talking and you won't be jacking anything ever again," she said, pressing the blade into the pit between his crotch and leg. He tried not to move. He knew how sharp it was.

"Considering how conspicuous this vehicle is, you'd think you'd be better at hiding your stash," the man said.

"Smart people know not to fuck with me."

"You calling us dumb?" she asked. He noticed her hand was steady. The shakes gone. Her voice had changed, too. Her eyes were piercing now. Forceful. This wasn't a couple of junkies ripping him off. This was something else.

"No," he said, his voice quieter, "I want to know what this is."

She took the keys out of his hand and tossed them to her partner, who jumped out of the truck and grabbed the nylon strap to close the back.

The door slammed down. They were alone in the dark briefly, then the lights flicked on. Her partner had been in the truck long enough to know where the lights were, along with his stash. Burke knew he had a problem.

"You're good at pretending to be sweet," she said. "How good are you at pretending to be stupid?"

37

"Ask her," Boom-Boom pointed to the meek girl with an iced coffee bigger than her head, tapping away at the keyboard of a black laptop.

Ray held the gunmetal grey laptop up in front of Boom-Boom's face and pointed at the power cord port, "Wrong company."

"How'm I supposed to know?"

Even though Ray had forced both of them into the coffee shop bathroom to clean up a bit, they were still a sorry sight. There was a crust of blood under Ray's hairline where the laptop met his face and Boom-Boom hadn't gotten all the snot out of his stubble. Dust covered both of them from their tussle on the side of the desert highway. To make matters worse, if they managed to find power for the dented device they were carrying around, the thing could boot up to some grotesque sounds and images that would draw unnecessary attention.

All the aspiring screenwriters passing the time with free Wi-Fi and expensive coffee weren't likely to give the motley pair the time of day, let alone their power cords. Ray gestured to Boom-Boom for some cash and went up to the counter.

"Hi, welcome to Pourover Paradise. What can I start for you today?" the too-cheery barista asked.

"Um, can I just get a drip coffee?" Ray asked, squinting at the board for the cheapest thing on the menu.

"Here at Pourover Paradise, we only used ethically sourced, locally roasted beans poured through with ionized distilled water. The process takes about five to ten minutes depending on your selection, but the slow-filtering is worth the wait," the barista recited the script as second nature.

"Okay, uh, small one of whatever that is then," Ray forced a smile.

"Un Petit Café. Are you a rewards member? All it takes is an email and a phone number to sign up."

Ray could feel Boom-Boom's hot breath behind him, ready to pour the barista into the display of sandwiches.

"No, just the coffee." Ray handed over a ten and received a lot less change than he was expecting for a small coffee.

"Name for the order."

"Leo."

"Okey-dokey, Leo, we'll call you when it's ready," the barista said. Ray looked behind the counter to see the 'we' he was talking about. There was no one else there.

"Thanks, oh, by the way. Do you have a Lost and Found? I was in here a few days ago and I think I left my charger cord behind." Ray held up the computer.

"I've got the same one. Happens pretty often. Let me check the back."

The barista disappeared into the back office. Boom-Boom glanced around to see who was watching and then shoved some organic 95% cacao dark chocolate bars into his pocket.

"Those won't taste like you think they will," Ray whispered.

"They're for Sweets. And his fucking smile is pissing me off."

The barista emerged holding a long white charger cord.

"Is this it?" he held it up like it might have any distinguishing features at all.

Ray reached out for the connecting end of the cord and compared it to the laptop.

"That's the one. You're a lifesaver," Ray said, putting his meager change into the tip jar.

"Enjoy your day in paradise!" the barista said. When he turned his back to grab the Ethiopian beans for grinding, Boom-Boom grabbed some more candy out of spite.

There was a table in the corner where the display would only be visible to anyone coming out of the bathroom. Given the amount of faces buried in screens, Ray wasn't worried about nosy neighbors.

"Here goes nothing." Ray plugged it in and waited for it to boot-up. If there was any damage to it, they were back to square one. No way they were taking it to get repaired and reported to the FBI.

The computer made a loud startup noise that caused anyone not wearing headphones to swing around and look at them. Boom-Boom's sausage fingers went for the volume control on the keyboard and he ended up hitting more keys that made even more noise. Ray pushed his hands away and hit the mute button.

"Go sit over there. You're making me nervous," Ray whispered as the rest of the patrons went back to their work.

"You pull any shit and I'll hit you with this thing again. Info or no info."

Boom-Boom sat down in the chair opposite and unwrapped one of the bitter chocolate bars. He took a big bite and cringed. Ray glared at him over the loading screen.

"Don't you fucking dare spit that out," Ray hissed under his breath.

The hulking mass chewed the chocolate, the whole time with the face of a toddler forced to eat broccoli. His eyes watering, he pulled at the contents of his pockets, dumping out the rest of the pilfered candy bars and various pieces of crumpled paper. He found an old napkin and scraped his tongue with it. Brown saliva goo and the rest of the stolen candy went into the trash.

The laptop was password protected. Of course it was. Why should anything be easy?

"Any guesses?" Ray swung the computer around at Boom-Boom as he sat back down.

Boom-Boom tapped on the keyboard, taking special care to only tap one key at a time. He shrugged and turned it back around to Ray.

"What did you try?" Ray asked.

"Password."

"Password?"

"Yeah, Password. That's my password," Boom-Boom said. He started unwrapping and playing with all the other pieces of paper from his pockets, separating them into piles.

Ray clenched his teeth and looked over at the barista, who was measuring whatever the fuck 'ionized water' was in a beaker on a kitchen scale.

His limited access to computers over the last decade told him that whoever was hiding illegal pornography on their laptop probably used nothing easily guessed. For the hell of it, he tried *PropertyoftheBear* and *CallumD'Arby*. Neither worked, of course, and he didn't want to risk being locked out.

Boom-Boom had folded a small paper plane out of a post-it note and was having a lot of trouble getting it to take flight.

"Any other bright ideas?" Ray sighed.

"How about this?" Boom-Boom unfolded the post-it and handed it over. "Found it taped under his desk while I was trying to decide to kill you. Thought it might be important for Malkin."

"You didn't think about it before trying 'Password'?" Ray asked.

"Nope. Thought it was a code only Malkin would know."

Ray typed in the long string of letters and numbers, getting it wrong once when he thought a "7" was a "1", but it worked. Luckily for them, the home screen content was benign. When everything loaded to the desktop, a calendar notification popped up in the upper right-hand corner.

Today. Your booking with House-Tel.

There was nothing bookmarked in the browser, and all the email clients required another password. Ray tried the same one from the post-it, but came up with nothing.

"What's House-Tel?" Ray asked the air more than Boom-Boom.

Boom-Boom was watching the barista pour boiling water over a small brown filter, tiny dribbles of coffee materializing in a glass container below.

"Uh, I think one of those places where people rent their houses to strangers. Saw an ad on a bus one time."

Ray clicked on the notification. It opened up the calendar. It was full. Including the delivery dates and times of the boys from the night before coded as _Youth Group_. Ray clicked on the note for that day. It was an automatic invite from an email.

An address in Topanga Canyon. The entry repeated going back a month. It was always only a one-day stay. The bookings started the day after Ray attacked Kosbur in the bathhouse.

Culp was contacting someone up there regularly. He was supposed to have another that night. Whether it would be the last tattooed stray, Callum D'Arby, or Osip Kosbur himself was a roll of the dice.

"I don't know what we're walking into, but I've got a lead. Let's go." Ray unplugged the computer and wrapped the cord around it. Boom-Boom stood and followed without asking questions.

As they pushed out the glass doors, the faint sound of "Un Petit Café for Leo" echoed behind them.

38

"I told you. The girl came to me asking me if I knew any doctors," Burke sighed, sick of the repeated questions.

"And you didn't know this girl?" Hsu asked.

"Had seen her around the neighborhood. That baby bump growing."

"And out of everyone in her life, she chose you to confide in. Out of the blue?"

"Yep. Like I said," Burke shifted in his chair. "Again."

Hsu leaned back. There was something about the man's attitude that rubbed him the wrong way. He was too sure. Too confident in the sequence of events. Hsu had been running the scenario in circles for a couple of hours. Asking the same questions in slightly different ways. Looking for holes in the story. Problem was, there were no holes. It was an air-tight narrative. And that was the problem. Tell the truth and things vary; sequence, things said. After the same questions over and over, a suspect will summarize. Develop an internal shorthand. But the pimp was giving him the same story verbatim. He acted innocent, even a little stupid. But he'd rehearsed it. The little man was no Olivier.

"I'm trying to get the timeline right here. So, you see the girl in the neighborhood. Enough for a nod when she walks back and forth to the local store. Then, when she decides, from your cordial interactions, that she can confide her biggest secret in the world to you, you send her to this doctor?"

"Dr. Solish," Burke corrected for the twentieth time as if by rote. "Could I get some more soda?"

Hsu nodded to the camera in the corner.

"Do you know the girl's parents?"

"No. Like I said. Just saw the girl around."

"But you don't live in the neighborhood?"

"Who says?"

Hsu was waiting to see if he needed to throw in this new information, along with Burke's snack.

"Do you live there, or don't you?"

"I live out of my truck, so I live in all neighborhoods."

"DMV has you at an address in Montebello. That's where it's registered."

"Ain't lived there for months."

"If we got a search warrant, we wouldn't find anything of yours there?"

"Go ahead, you'd be buggin' the hell out of whoever lives there now." Burke fidgeted with the foam rubber on his crutches. He was getting antsy. Right where Hsu wanted him.

"You're living on the streets and decide to be a Good Samaritan? Right?" Hsu's tone remained measured.

"The girl was in trouble. I helped. Why is that so hard to understand?"

"We live in a world where altruism is suspicious. Especially given your arrest record. You still run girls out of your truck?"

He didn't take the bait. "I never did. If that's in your little file, it's wrong."

"Might have heard about you from time to time, in passing," Hsu said.

Burke ignored the attempt to stroke his ego.

"Look. The girl was in trouble. I sent her to this doctor I heard about. She didn't come back. I got worried and called my girl Lauren to look into it. That's what happened. It ain't changing."

"Why call Ms. Ashmore? Why not call the police directly?"

"If I need to explain that, you stupid," Burke said. Hsu could see he was getting aggravated at the repetition. Angry people make mistakes.

"Assume I'm stupid."

"Like I ain't done that already."

Hsu didn't react.

"Little black girl goes missing, you ain't putting out no Amber Alert. Besides, I was coverin' my ass."

"Did you think she was in danger when you took her to Solish?"

"Danger, no. He mighta done stuff that wasn't exactly legal, but I don't know nothin' about what goes on between doctor and patient."

"You admit it was illegal, but sent her anyway? That's endangering a minor."

"He's a legit doctor. I sent her there for a check-up."

"Cosmetic surgeons aren't obstetricians," Hsu said.

"I look like I know the difference? Where I'm from, a doctor is a doctor," Burke raised his voice.

"Okay. How do you know Lauren Ashmore again?" Hsu asked.

"I'm thinking you're hard of hearing," Burke said. "We almost done?"

"Almost. Tell me again."

Burke rubbed his eyes from exhaustion. Hsu had all the information he needed. It was a solid sequence of events. Imani Johnson got to Dr. Solish's clinic because of Burke. Burke got worried when she didn't come home and called Lauren Ashmore. Lauren went to go see if Imani was at Solish's clinic. When she suspected foul play, she called Detective Nick Archer. Everyone's story fit. Timeline established. Alibis verified.

Hsu knew he shouldn't have all that information. Burke was a pimp. His entire case jacket spelled it out, even if he hadn't been picked up for that specific crime. Anyone who worked Vice knew the pattern of citations and arrests that surround the black hole in someone's record that spelled out Pimping and Pandering. Felonies avoided and fines on misdemeanors paid by a bevy of helpful "companions." He could easily charge Burke with contributing to the delinquency of a minor, but the evidence was weak, and the fine was small. What was keeping Hsu in the room was that Burke had walked into the station and asked to make a statement. Pimps don't do that. Even the ones who think they're bulletproof. He also hadn't asked for a lawyer. Didn't even hint at it. Someone with his history and arrest record always found a lawyer before questions got too intense.

"Lauren is like this fairy godmother. She comes in to these communities and gives away food and stuff. Helps people. Drives old ladies to the grocery store. Most people ain't too sure of her at first, but she's a good person."

"And you know her from passing her on the street, too?"

"Yeah."

"People in the neighborhood would know her too if we started asking around?"

"I dunno. Maybe. They might not know her name. But I saw her help those people I told you about."

"That was a handy list," Hsu said. It was the first thing that had made him suspicious of Burke's motivations. The three name list was too ready. Too prepared. Too in alphabetical order.

"Find them. They'll tell you," Burke said.

"And if I just started asking around in the neighborhood?"

"Can't guarantee people would know her. Most people mind their own 'round that block."

"Except you," Hsu dug in.

"This is why people don't trust cops. You try to do something good for someone, help the people around you and you get shit."

"I want to know why your story is so clean."

"Because sometimes that's how things work! Now, if you don't have other questions to ask me, I'd like to leave."

"You're free to go whenever you'd like," Hsu said.

Burke grabbed his crutches and pushed away from the table. As he limped toward the door, Hsu had one more thing to say.

"Sorry I doubted your motives. If you'd ever met Detective Archer, you'd know I have no reason to doubt him. Have you ever met Detective Archer?"

A flash of panic crossed Burke's eyes. Hsu could tell whoever fed him his story hadn't covered this bit. Burke focused on the floor like he was watching where he placed his crutches.

"Lauren knew him. Never met him."

"If I asked him, he would say the same?"

"Can't say. I'm pretty memorable. Guess you'd have to ask him," Burke pulled open the door to the interview room and didn't say another word.

Hsu let him leave, but watched him the whole time. He limped down the hallway to the elevator. When Burke turned around to glimpse whether he was being watched, his look told Hsu something stunk.

Burke hobbled down the steps over to his van. He climbed in, started it, and pulled out of the lot. After a few winding turns, he was certain that the cop he'd interviewed with hadn't followed him. He turned onto the 10 freeway, glancing at the address scribbled on the piece of paper he was told to open once he'd spun his story.

Parked in front of the house, he double checked the address. Then, he pulled out a cheap disposable lighter and lit the paper on fire.

When he rapped on the painted security door, the dog next door started barking. The inner door opened. A large man in a stained tank top and coveralls tied at the waist stood behind the wire mesh. He had a bottle in one hand and something Burke couldn't see in the other. Burke could smell the booze through the door, but couldn't check the address again. This had to be the wrong place.

"What you want?"

"You Darius?" Burke asked.

"Who askin'?"

Burke swallowed hard, ready to bolt, but he had heard the stories. The Queen of Lindberg Park took people's balls. There was nowhere to hide. She found you. He had to follow her instructions to the letter.

"Friend of Imani's," Burke answered.

The security door kicked open, knocking Burke backward. He didn't have enough time to cuss a response before he saw the .38. The bullet through his forehead locked the look of fear on his face.

Darius swung the gun wildly as he kicked Burke's body down the stairs and stumbled onto the sidewalk.

"What happen?! Bitch tell the whole block? Come get me! Can't do no worse than how they do kid rapists in lock up! You know where to find me! I'll wait!"

He swayed back up to the porch and plopped down in a rocking chair, flecks of peeled paint scattering on the warped floorboards.

Tears streamed down his face as he took another swig of whiskey and put the pistol under his chin.

The pop echoed off the metal door.

No neighbors came running.

No sirens sounded.

The dog kept barking.

39

Boom-Boom parked the Jeep down the hill and the two of them walked up. Ray didn't like that he was making a habit of venturing into the wilderness with people he couldn't completely trust. He still didn't know how he was going take down Malkin and his whole fucked up operation. All Ray knew was that this was the path he was on. Whether he was being manipulated to carry out some megalomaniac's grand scheme, or if it was just a plan to get Ray out of the way while they figured out the best way to kill him, finding the last man with a Bear tattoo seemed like the best course of action. Either he could recruit this guy to help him take down the Bear or he could reason with whoever was taking out the tattooed criminals and get them to redirect their homicidal efforts.

From the street, Solish's house was tucked into the hill overlooking a copse of trees that blocked the vista to Topanga Canyon. There was a bridge over a small ditch built for rain run-off to prevent mudslides in the rainy winter months. The house looked like an English country cottage, complete with ivy and moss growing on the weathered shingles. Bright blue flowers in the boxes under the crisscrossed window panes were an unlikely accent of color in the conservative brown and cream of the outside. It didn't look like the place someone would use for a secret hideout. It actually looked like a septet of dwarves would emerge from the front door at any moment and no one would blink an eye.

"You want to knock, or should I?" Ray asked.

Boom-Boom shrugged and headed around to the side of the house. After his emotional breakdown on the side of the highway, he kept asking how Ray was going to get Sweets away from her charismatic guru, but had grown surly when Ray couldn't give him a straight answer. Ray thought the beast was regretting his decision not to kill his companion and was behaving like a cranky child.

Ray waved Boom-Boom back to where they were going to jump over the fence. The back screen door was open. Not surprising given the seclusion of the backyard, but still unusual. And after what they'd found in the basement of Culp's house, they had to be cautious.

Drawing back the curtains, Ray cursed the universe.

The entire living room was destroyed. Furniture turned over. Glass broken. Streaks of blood covered the walls and droplets speckled the upholstery.

A shuffle of movement came from somewhere else in the house.

They weren't alone.

Ray and Boom-Boom each went in search of something that could be a weapon. There were no tools to stoke the gas fireplace. No heavy bronze statues that could cause blunt force trauma. Ray grabbed an overturned table lamp. The bulb had busted and the remaining glass could do some damage if he caught someone by surprise. He yanked the cord out and placed it softly on the torn couch cushions. Boom-Boom wrapped a throw blanket around his hand and forearm, then picked up a shard of glass from a bashed picture frame. If they were about to face a gun, they'd both look like idiots. But if a bullet had caused the wound that had painted the living room, there wouldn't have been as much of a struggle. With a nod, both of them knew their best weapon was surprise.

Ray placed his back against the wall and took a few shallow breaths. Nothing but a mid-century modern lamp between him and a psychopath who hated the tattoo on his arm. He stuck his head around the corner and pulled it back quick. Nothing.

Before he stepped into the hallway leading toward the front of the house, he waved Boom-Boom in behind him. He put his hand up to halt his partner at the next open doorway. He'd seen enough cop movies to know this was how they swept a house. Clear one room at a time.

There was no sign of the movement they'd heard earlier. Whoever had made it was gone or was waiting for them to make a mistake. Ray assumed it was the latter.

Boom-Boom stood next to Ray, then swung into the next room. Whatever he saw made him drop to the ground and scurry for cover down the hall.

BLAM! BLAM! BLAM!

Gunfire splintered the doorjamb and the drywall across the hall. Ray sprinted for the living room and leapt over the upturned couch, looking for cover. His face pressed into the broken glass of the coffee table, but he focused on keeping as low to the ground and out of sight as possible.

"Come the fuck out!"

The voice had a slight Middle Eastern accent and was shaking. Ray didn't dare peer over the couch to see where the gunman was. The back patio door was still open and Ray's only hope was that the gunman would assume they'd made a break for the backyard. If the neighbors hadn't heard the scuffle earlier, the open patio door would have echoed the gunshots throughout the canyon, cacophony of leaf blowers or not.

He still had the lamp, but from his prone position, there was nothing he could do to gain leverage. He might as well have been clutching a baby blanket. He only hoped that his attacker went for the patio door and ignored the back of the couch.

"Turn over. Slow."

Why would Ray think he should be so lucky?

He raised his hands over the powder burnt polyester to show he had no weapons on him except for the broken lamp, which was now out of reach. The sound of fear in the shooter's voice told Ray that he was better off risking a few fingers than getting an extra hole in his head.

"How many of you motherfuckers are they going to send?"

The gun in his hand went off and sent up a splinter of hardwood next to Ray's head. After what seemed like an eternity of waiting for the kill shot, Ray pulled his arms away from his head and uncurled himself from the fetal position.

Boom-Boom's hand palmed Solish's head like a basketball. The force of the shove sent a blood spatter up the wall that looked like the top of a pineapple. Boom-Boom gave the man's head one more slam into the wall for good measure, checked his pulse, then pulled the .45 out of Solish's limp hand.

"Thanks," Ray gasped out. He checked to see if he'd shit himself. To his surprise, he hadn't.

"Something you should see," Boom-Boom said and walked back toward the hallway, not waiting for Ray to follow.

"Shouldn't we—?" Ray called after him, gesturing to Solish.

"He's not gonna go anywhere."

"I wasn't worried about that. I'm not sure he's going to stay breathing."

Boom-Boom shrugged and turned the corner. His nonchalance about the whole thing made Ray wonder why he'd returned to the bedroom and not to the car. Then he recognized the defensive wounds on Solish's forearms and the long cut along his torso that was blossoming red into his button-down shirt. He'd asked Ray how many people were being sent after him. Which meant he'd bested another attacker before Boom-Boom and Ray had showed up.

He found Boom-Boom in the hallway, staring into the doorway where Solish had fired at them.

"Wanna explain this?" he gestured with Solish's gun. It looked like a pea-shooter in his meaty hand.

Ray looked into the room.

On the floor, a waterfall of blood gushing from his jugular, was Deuce.

There was a straight razor held loose in his hand. He kept raising it in a half-assed threat. Continuing to defend himself. But the fright in his eyes and his greying skin told Ray that the movement was the involuntary tic of a man grasping at life.

Ray made a step into the room, reaching for a bed sheet to stop the bleeding, but Deuce used the last of his energy to swipe at the air in front of him with the razor. Speckles of blood flew from the end in an arc and hit the cuffs of Ray's pants.

"I'm trying to help."

"Don't you fucking touch—," Deuce coughed up through the growl. "Fuck you."

"What did I—"

"O... sip... Kos... bur," Deuce managed.

"He did this?" Ray asked. His suspicions were right. The Bear was still alive.

Deuce's head lolled left, then right. He lifted his hand and pointed at his chest with the razor, almost stabbing himself in the sternum.

"Osip... Kosbur," he gurgled, "Junior."

With his last gasp, he spit a spray of blood at Ray with such furious disdain that Ray realized why Deuce used his final breaths to hurl vitriol in his direction.

Osip Kosbur Jr.

Osip Kosbur, the Second.

Deuce.

In the time he'd lived with the kid, no one had ever called him anything but Deuce. He'd never seen a driver's license. Never saw his wallet. He'd assumed Deuce brought it into the bathroom with him when he showered out of paranoia. Now Ray knew the truth.

Reggie didn't send Ray to find the other tattooed men.

He sent him to be the last victim and trail his presence through each crime scene.

"Why would he send us out here if Deuce was already taking care of the job?" Boom-Boom asked.

Ray couldn't believe he'd been so stupid. He regretted looking down at the sheeple he thought were willingly going to slaughter up in the mountains. When you want something bad enough, you stop thinking rationally.

"It was a play out of Kosbur's book. Every place someone with a tattoo showed up dead, a witness would point me out or my DNA would show up. The perfect patsy."

Deuce helping Malkin clean up his father's mess.

"Ray," Boom-Boom cracked out of a dry throat.

"Hmm?" Ray said, not turning around.

"You keep turning up like a bad penny."

That was when Ray turned around. The voice wasn't Boom-Boom's.

Detective Nick Archer had his Glock pressed to the base of Boom-Boom's skull.

"Oh," Ray said, "Hey."

"Hey? Really? Living room. Now."

As he stood up, Ray saw another unexpected face in the hallway.

"The rest of the rooms are clear?" Nick asked the woman Ray only knew as The Queen.

"Something you should see," she said, and walked into one of the other bedrooms without waiting.

Nick kicked the gun Boom-Boom had been holding into the room away from the body and motioned for them both to follow.

In a room that seemed untouched by the chaos of the rest of the house, The Queen nodded over to the dresser.

There, in the top drawer, was a small newborn. It was sleeping soundly, wearing the tiniest pair of noise-cancelling headphones Ray had ever seen.

40

They all stared down at the drawer. An extended struggle and spray of gunfire, the house destroyed and the Ukrainian mob heir dead in the next room. Through it all, the child slept peacefully. In another life, one of them would leave a glowing review on Amazon for those headphones.

Then, as babies do for no reason, it shifted in the wrong way and wailed.

Boom-Boom backed away like it was an IED. The Queen and Nick exchanged a look. But Ray didn't hesitate. He picked up the child and put it to his shoulder, patting it on the back. He swayed back and forth, jiggling her bottom ever so slightly. With deft fingers, he unsnapped the base of the onesie at the leg and checked the diaper.

"She's wet," he said, as though he dealt with the issue daily. Then his movement stopped. The swaying, the patting. The child was screaming in his ear so loud, he could have used the headphones himself, but it was as though there was no sound in the room at all. He was staring off into nothing.

Everyone noticed him stop, like they knew before he did. Ray took a step toward the dresser, placed the baby back in her drawer, and backed out of the room.

"She's wet.... She's wet..."

He wouldn't stop repeating it. He held his baby to his chest, rocking her back and forth. The towel and blanket covering her were gritty with wet sand. Thick tentacles of her hair tangled in his fingers and dried to his neck as he pulled her closer.

"Sir, please," the sound of the paramedic's voice was strained through an echo chamber. Tears burned his eyes as he squeezed them shut, trying to banish the blue of her skin and the sound her sternum made as they violently attempted to push the water out of her lungs.

"No. She's wet. She's cold, please, no... no... please... no," he cried into the top of her head. A faint smell of shampoo mixed with the dank fishy smell of the lake. If he pressed into her hard enough, he might find some warmth there. Some life. Something.

He didn't know how long he sat on the beach. How long did the medics let him sit there? The crowd dispersed except for a few stragglers waiting for the ambulance to leave so they could move their cars, their only care in the world was that they beat traffic in time to give their families a story over dinner. The sun ducked to the horizon and disappeared.

Her skin never went pruny the way it did after being in the bath too long. It stayed taut and slick, then as the minutes passed, it went cold before her body stiffened in his arms. He knew that if he didn't let her go, she would be stuck in rigor mortis in an awkward sitting position, the limbs in the tangle he clutched to his chest.

He had only looked away for a second. Just a second.

Why didn't he slow down?

Trying to be the cool dad. Every other weekend. Had to make the most of it.

The life vest shed as the sunscreen went on.

Rent a boat. Tahoe is beautiful. She's becoming too much of a city kid.

If he had been high or drunk or even just fucking around, he would have had an excuse.

No excuse.

All he did was look away.

A moment. A distraction. The wrong wake in his path.

Bad timing.

The autopsy determined that the fall killed her, not the water.

But all he remembered was the empty life vest bobbing on the surface.

The struggle to get his own vest off as he dove for her.

A second.

And then nothing.

His ex-wife had sued for negligence, but the courts threw it out before it went to trial. A mother's grief is no substitute for evidence. He gave her what she wanted and more in an unnecessary settlement. She didn't want it either. All she wanted was her daughter back, same as him. She still took everything he had.

Nothing mattered anymore. Work days he didn't take off when she had a cold. Recitals missed for late meetings that could have been emails. Time wasted when he didn't know how limited time was. Nothing would bring her back. Not rent or bills or heat or shelter. He wished he was the sort who could end it all, but he wasn't.

Ray didn't know if that was a testament to his strength or cowardice.

It didn't happen all at once. Things just fell away. Work. Friends. House. His only family was in an urn in a house they would never let him into. His invitation to the celebration of life never arrived.

He said goodbye by saying goodbye to everything else.

Slept on the street one night.

That turned into a week. Turned into a month. Turned into forever.

Then one day he saw an albino being attacked on a street corner.

He had always helped people. He couldn't help himself, but when he saw people having a hard time, he couldn't walk away.

She got that from him. She always helped.

It only took a second.

He decided not to look away.

One.

Second.

"Hey, you okay?" The Queen asked. She'd followed him to where he had slumped onto the back porch steps.

Ray swung around, wiping his eyes, "Yeah, it's, yeah." He swallowed the knot in his throat.

"Archer found some diapers. Don't know if he'll be able to put them on though," she said. He knew that tone. Don't spook the frightened animal.

"He'll figure it out. He's a big boy."

"I didn't know."

"Didn't know what?" he asked, jaw clenched.

"I never would have brought you to Holy Cross all those years ago if I'd—"

"It was just sex, no promises, remember? And if you are going to pull a big reveal on the outcome of that tryst, save it. I don't want to know. If there's a kid, it's better off without me around."

She sat down next to him. Just sat with him. Waiting for him to speak. It wasn't right away, but didn't take long.

"Bring me up to speed. How the hell did you end up here with Archer, of all people?" Ray asked.

"I screwed up. Got cocky," she said, holding the horizon in her gaze like he was. "A girl came to me. It wasn't my usual. She was already pregnant. Hiding from the father. Undocumented. Lots of pitfalls. But I didn't care. I went rogue. My team didn't agree to it and me being me, I thought I could do it on my own. I was on my own for a long time before I put together my group, didn't realize how rusty I was."

She paused, waiting for Ray to ask a follow-up question. He didn't.

"Her pimp was in prison. She wanted to disappear while he was inside. I couldn't put her through my regular channels without getting immigration involved. Trafficked in, but had been in the country long enough that INS wouldn't give a shit. I had to find another way." She ran her fingers through her hair and took a deep breath. "But I took too long. He got out early. Good behavior. She went back to him."

"Can't win 'em all," Ray said, barely audible and without looking at her.

"She ended up dead. I assumed it was the pimp, but it was more complicated than that. I needed help and believe it or not, I don't trust many people. Your boy was the only one who came to mind."

"What about your people?" Ray asked.

"I lost them. Slowly. The crusade wasn't enough for them. Altruism has a half-life. It may have seemed like I had control over everyone in my employ, but when people get murdered, they scatter," The Queen sighed.

"Solish killed this girl?" Ray asked, finally giving her his full attention.

"I thought so. I was just as surprised to see that baby as you were."

Nick came out to the porch, the tiny diaper in his hand.

"I'm lost in here, could you—?"

Ray didn't move. The Queen gave him a moment to volunteer, then stood up and took the diaper out of Nick's hand before disappearing back into the house.

"Did you decide my partner in there isn't a threat?" Ray asked.

"He's keeping watch over Solish, waiting for him to wake up. Keeps checking his phone like he's waiting for a call," Nick said. He leaned against the doorway and Ray was glad he didn't make a move to sit down next to him.

"So?" Ray asked.

He turned around and could see from the way Nick's eyes dodged to meet his own that his former ally still didn't know whose side he was on.

"So, what?" Nick asked, his voice low and steady.

"Any idea how to free ourselves of this shit show?"

"You're asking the wrong question."

Ray's eyebrow went up.

"I know what I want out of this," Nick said. "Find the person responsible and bring him down. Legally. Make sure he stays in prison for a long time."

"From what I've seen today, you're pretty far off that path," Ray said.

"But I know what I'm working toward. How about you? What's your endgame in all this? No one had a bead on you. You could've just disappeared. Started over. But you leapt right back into it. I can't figure you out, man."

Ray leaned on the planter framing Solish's porch. He picked at the small azalea leaves and let them flutter out between his fingers onto the power-washed patio bricks. He took a deep breath and let it go between his teeth. His eyes didn't meet Nick's. They bore a hole a thousand yards away, deep underground, settling on some far away memory deep within the mantle of the Earth.

"The goal was never to get off the street. Buy a house. Get a steady job. Pay taxes. Walk a damn dog. I did that once. It knocked me on my ass."

He pulled a flower from its stem and spun it between his fingers, his focus on the perfect mathematical spiral of the petals.

"The job, the house... it didn't save me. The street didn't save me either."

He turned his arm over and pushed up his sleeve. Nick recognized it immediately, and Ray could tell he was trying to process what it meant.

"You're trapped," Nick offered.

Ray shook his head. Nick didn't get it.

"You want to know what being trapped really is? A man who was told if he followed the right steps in his life that everything would be perfect. Make a life for the sake of your family, then have it all taken away."

"I think that's bullshit," Nick said.

Ray let out a snorting laugh in disbelief.

"You think because you took this 'Vow of Poverty' or whatever the fuck you've been doing for the last decade, that your life is going to be better? That you're going to change? Give me a fucking break."

Ray stood up, angry. "Thanks for listening, asshole."

Nick closed the distance between them, his finger in Ray's face.

"I looked you up. When you were in the hospital. Your guts sewn together, a bullet taken for a dead man. Don't you fucking tell me you don't care and that you're just a loner trying to survive. Fuck that. I know what you lost."

Ray shoved Nick hard enough to put him on his ass.

"Yeah? And I'm sure your research project gave you all the details. Every moment of pain. Now that you've read the dossier, you know me? You want to tell me I'm putting up blocks? Running away from confronting my feelings? Fuck you, Archer. You can read all the shit you want. You don't have a fucking clue."

Nick didn't move to stand.

"All of this, the whole reason I, we, are in this is because I wanted to stay gone," Ray spit the words out. "The moment that they tied me to Mochulyak's murder, I had two choices. Turn myself in, take the rap for something I didn't do, or try to clear my name. It was never about a fucking tattoo. This is just fucking ink."

Ray stopped, trying to hold back the shake in his voice, forced to finally confront what he'd been doing out on the street all this time.

"For those people I hurt and left behind, I was dead, disappeared, out of their lives. Now that I'm missing, on the lam, where do you think your detectives went to investigate first? They didn't deserve what I did to them before I gave up on my life. Every time they saw me, they saw her gone. My presence was pain. They don't deserve to have it brought back up to them. And worse yet, what if, just what if, there is a small, perfect world in which they have found it in their hearts to forgive me only to have me laid at their feet, the murderer they pictured me as. When I was talking about being free, Archer, that's what I meant. I'll never be free of the pain and the memories. It doesn't matter how much I give up or self-flagellate, that will always live as part of me. But those people don't have to live with me as part of their lives anymore. I let them be free of me when I left."

Nick relaxed the tension in his jaw and gave Ray a sympathetic look.

"I get it. You think life is supposed to go one way, and it doesn't. So, you make a different choice. And then that doesn't work out. And then another. Pretty soon you look at all these fucking decisions and you're no better off than if you had just stayed put doing what you were doing."

"Don't give me that regurgitated therapist bullshit," Ray shot back at him.

Nick stood up and wiped the dust off his pants.

"Both of us have to admit eventually that life isn't just happening to us, we're making it happen. This house here, this was supposed to be the end of this case for me. Lauren, or whatever the fuck her real name is, was supposed to give me probable cause that led me to this doorstep. I wasn't expecting gunshots, yet another fucking tattooed body, and I sure as shit was not expecting to find you." Nick took a deep breath and softened his tone. "I'm out of my depth here and unless you've made some miraculous discovery in that house, so are you. You want to quit cracking fucking wise and come up with a solution here?"

He knew if he said something else, tried to hide from the truth Nick was spouting, he'd end up with a fist in his guts. It was time for Ray to stop being a lone wolf. If they were going to end this, he was going to need the entire team on the same page.

"You're right," Ray said. "We've got a couple of missing pieces before we get in over our heads. Let's get some answers, shall we?"

41

"You good?" Boom-Boom asked Ray as he pushed back into the house, "We've got a problem."

Blood had soaked through the towel that Boom-Boom was holding to Solish's gut. The Queen came out of the bedroom awkwardly holding the shrieking baby; the diaper hanging onto her waist for dear life.

"Oh shit, would someone," she moved to hand the baby off to Ray, who hesitated, then moved to Nick.

"Someone just fucking hold her so I can keep this guy from bleeding out," she said.

Nick reached for the baby, but Ray pulled her to his chest and moved over to the couch. He pulled up the onesie and attached the diaper properly. The Queen grabbed more towels and pushed them into Solish's stomach.

Kneeling to get a better look at the wound, Nick whipped off his belt and wrapped it around Solish's middle, trying to increase pressure on the makeshift bandage. He wasn't pumping out, but he would need better medical care, and fast.

"Call 9-1-1," Nick said to whoever was listening.

"No," Ray had placed the baby stomach down on his forearm, cradling her neck with his palm and swinging her back and forth.

"He's going to die," Nick said. "In case you forgot, I'm not in the letting people die business."

"Who are you people?" Solish coughed out as he regained consciousness.

The Queen stepped forward.

"First, a story," she crouched in front of him, rage in her eyes.

"No," Nick said, not intimidated by her gaze, "first, a medic."

"Give me your phone," Ray said to Boom-Boom.

Boom-Boom hesitated. Ray could tell he was still figuring out his place in the new group. But all the eyes on him made him uncomfortable, so he tossed it over.

Nick glanced over his shoulder at Ray. "Thank you."

Ray glanced at The Queen, shrugged and opened the phone. Soon it was playing a sweet lullaby for the baby, who was already asleep.

"Are you kidding m—," Nick wanted to leap for Ray, but right now he was the only thing keeping Solish's blood in his body.

"Shh," Ray said, "You'll wake her."

"Please," Solish gasped.

"How did you get her?" The Queen nodded to the sleeping child.

"Promised," Solish whispered.

"He's going to bleed out," Nick said.

The Queen tightened the tourniquet, causing him to wrench in pain.

"How?" she asked, eyes boring through him.

"He came to me. To get rid of it."

"Ballantine?"

He nodded, his breathing labored as cold sweat popped on his brow. Ray didn't like how Solish was losing color. It worried him that Archer hadn't stepped in to this little interrogation. How loose had his morals gotten?

"She begged him to keep it. Don't know why, he said yes. I got paid for nothing, didn't see her again for months. Found out he had gone upstate."

"Meanwhile, you were harvesting organs, going about your business?" Nick chimed in. There was the anger Ray was waiting for.

"Harvesting is—" Solish's head lolled like he was going to pass out. The Queen flicked his forehead, "—not the word I'd use."

She grabbed his ear and tried to focus him out of the blood loss and concussion. "The girl."

"About to pop. She didn't want to get rid of it. Didn't want him to have it. Made me promise. Keep it from him. She was too small. Had to do an emergency C-section."

"All the sudden, you grew a heart of gold."

"Paid me. Must've taken the money from him. Fear in her I've never seen." He met Nick's eyes. "And I've seen some fear."

Whatever Nick caught in those eyes, he was the first to break the gaze.

"She was... recovering..." They were going to lose him soon. "Came back... he was there... blade out. I told him... the baby died. He didn't believe. She was scared. Gasping for... like she was... water. He wouldn't let me near..."

"Drowning. Asthma attack," Nick said.

Solish nodded, "She was gone. I couldn't... didn't believe... he cut her open... searching... grieving. Looking for the child. He took her away... that's the last..." he passed out.

The Queen stood up. "It was Ballantine after all."

"She died before he cut her up, but not much before. He scared her to death. Not murder, but not far off," Nick said, lost in his own thoughts.

Having sat through all of this in silence, Boom-Boom finally chimed in, "Hospital or not?"

Nick pulled out his phone.

"Hold on. Before you do that, you need to know this guy isn't at the top of the pyramid," Ray said. "He was selling organs? We might know the buyer."

"Who's pulling his strings?" Nick said, ready to dial.

"Thought it was the guy who tattooed me, guy by the name of Xavier Malkin."

The Queen twitched at the name, stopped breathing for a second, and slumped to the couch.

"You okay?" Nick asked.

"Yeah... just... it's... yeah," she said, focusing on the floor.

"If it isn't Malkin—" Nick asked. She flinched again. There was something there, but it wasn't something Ray could focus on. Solish was losing too much blood.

"—then, who is it?" Nick finished.

"Callum D'Arby," Ray said.

Ray could see Nick was doing math in his head. There was something keeping him from being a Boy Scout and calling 9-1-1. That made Ray nervous. Nick's cop mind never turned off. Ray could almost watch the switch as he put the sleeping newborn to his shoulder.

Nick typed something into his phone and pointed at Boom-Boom.

"Find some cleaning gloves, grab a quilt, wrap him up and dump him at the closest ER. Kaiser past Ventura," Nick said. "Sidewalk, don't drive all the way to the drop-off. Avoid the security feeds."

He turned to The Queen, "You have a next of kin on Aelan?"

"No one," she said, refocusing her attention on the conversation. Ray could see something had definitely changed.

"You're going to Tarzana," he flashed his phone at The Queen. "Different hospital. Safe Surrender site. They'll give you a bracelet that will match the baby for people who change their minds. I don't know our next move, but I know it can't be done with a newborn. If you want to get her later, you can."

"You want to let the rest of us know what you're thinking?" Ray asked.

"No time. You're coming with me," Nick said to Ray.

"Still don't trust me?" Ray asked.

"Should I?"

Ray shrugged with his eyebrows and gently passed the baby to The Queen. He stroked his thumb across the wisps of black hair on her forehead.

"You're better off without us, sweetie."

"And the body in the back?" Boom-Boom asked.

"Leave it," Nick said. "We've tainted this crime scene enough."

"What about you?" The Queen asked Nick.

"I've got to go get some answers on D'Arby. Then figure out how to make it look like we were never here," Nick sighed.

Boom-Boom found some yellow gloves under the sink and dumped the limp Solish into a comforter.

"Welcome to my world, Archer," Ray smirked.

"Fuck you, Cobb."

42

The last place Nick expected to end up was at a convalescent home in Pomona, but it was where Hsu told him to meet him when he called.

He sat in the car, engine idling.

What the fuck was he doing?

Ray had told him everything in the car. Osip Kosbur, Viktor Mochulyak, Shadow Dance, Malkin, the commune in the woods, and how it tied to the tattoos and Callum D'Arby. Sounded like they were smack dab in the middle of a territorial war between two organized crime syndicates. Nick had seen enough movies to know the cops in those stories always end up dead.

Now he was going to interrogate his partner about a sensitive subject. Whatever disdain Hsu had for D'Arby, it may have led directly to his transfer out of Vice.

The home was eerily similar to the facility where his mother had spent her last breathing months. There was more anxiety spreading in his chest at walking through those doors than figuring out how to dump a murder suspect at a hospital.

He had officially gone off the deep end.

Nick shut off the car.

"You okay in there?"

"If you're going to drop me off at the Hollywood Station, we're not friends anymore," Ray said through the backseat. Nick couldn't risk someone spying him in the passenger seat of his car, but he didn't want to lose track of him again. He could have left him in his condo when they went to change clothes, but if this plan was going to work, he needed Ray to stay put.

Nick walked up the drive of the facility and rapped on the door. It took a moment for a CNA in purple scrubs to pop her head into the lobby. She looked at him through the glass, pointed at the watch on her wrist, and wagged a finger at him. He pressed his badge to the glass and saw her make an exasperated walk to the front desk to buzz him in.

"After hours," she said. "Residents are asleep."

"I'm looking for David Hsu," he said.

"He shouldn't be here either," she scowled at him.

Hsu emerged from the kitchen of the facility. His tie was loose, shirtsleeves rolled to his elbows. He glanced up at the lobby from the yogurt he was stirring.

"Let him back, Alma," Hsu said. His voice was low as to not awaken the rest of the residents who were letting snores drift into the hallway.

"You both have to go soon," she shot back at him, but let Nick pass.

The whirr of machinery and groans of fitful sleep brought Nick back a month earlier, when he spent all of his free nights giving his dying mother as many creature comforts as she could stand. Whoever Hsu was visiting here, he'd have to recommend the Garden Commons. The facility wasn't as nice, but the staff sure as hell was.

Nick took his time entering the room Hsu had disappeared into, unsure of what to expect. Hsu sat on the edge of a bed. He gestured to Nick to take the chair in the corner as he put a spoonful of yogurt into his mouth.

"See?" he said with his mouth full. The woman in the bed clutched the blankets up above her mouth and was shaking her head. Disheveled hair from fitful sleep framed the dark circles under her eyes. Nick recognized her immediately from the pictures on Hsu's desk.

"Okay," he said and put the uneaten yogurt on her bedside table. "Try going back to sleep."

"Hi," she said in a small voice in Nick's direction.

"Hey," he rasped, his throat dry.

"Jen, this is my new partner, Nick," Hsu said.

"Potty mouth," she said.

Hsu laughed, "That's the one."

"Hi," she repeated.

"Okay. We're going to go," Hsu said, standing.

Jen turned over in the bed, dropping the covers. She was as pretty as she was in the photographs, even without the benefit of sunshine or makeup. She grabbed something off the other table that was covered with various cards and figurines.

Hsu ripped a page off the top of the desktop calendar and placed it gently in a drawer. He read from the top page.

"Effrontery. Shameless boldness. Insolence."

"Use it in a sentence," she said, "Effrontery."

"David could not believe the *effrontery* of his partner showing up at his wife's bedside."

"Thanks, Effrontery," she said, using the word as if it was Hsu's name. She turned off her light and pulled the covers over her head, leaving the two men in the dark quiet. Hsu grabbed his coat and gestured for Nick to follow him into the lobby.

"The Word of the Day calendar is how I reset her every day to remember me. Used to be a morning ritual with us, and it solidified itself on her brain. She's got a calendar on her bedside table and the word becomes a code, so she knows it's me. I know it's annoying, but with everything else going on and the investigations and getting back to work, the only way I can remember the word every day is by repeating it."

"How come you never told me?" Nick asked.

"You never asked. And I'm not a big one for ostentation," Hsu caught himself. "Sorry. Sometimes I forget I'm doing it."

"Can I ask what happened?"

"Car accident. Someone on their phone ran a red light. She came through it relatively unscathed, but slammed her head into the driver's side window. Trapped her between the car where the other driver had died and a concrete wall. By the time they got to her, the swelling in her brain had done irreparable damage."

"I'm sorry, this could've waited," Nick said and turned to go. Hsu stopped him.

"No, you said it was urgent on the phone. And avoiding things is why it took us this long to talk about it. I think it's why Jenkins paired us up in the first place, after what happened to your mom. Thought we'd be kindred spirits in grief. I bet he never surmised that each of us would be too stoic to reveal the details of our personal lives."

"I still feel like a shit," Nick said.

"You should," Hsu smiled. "Now, what do you need?"

"What can you tell me about Callum D'Arby?" Nick asked.

The color left Hsu's face. He slumped into the closest chair.

"You swear you didn't know about this?" Hsu pointed back at his wife's room.

"No," Nick sat down opposite. "Why?"

Hsu let out an exhausted breath and rubbed his face.

"The last six months I was in Vice, I was trying to build a case against D'Arby, convinced he had taken over his brother's business after Pretty Boy died. But the son of a bitch stayed clean. Couldn't find anything that would stick. I'd get a lead on something, then either a witness would clam up or a trail would go dead. I'll admit, it became something of an obsession."

Nick nodded. If there was anyone who could understand going further than you wanted to in a case, he was feeling it right at that moment.

"Finally, I get a call from an informant. The first domino. It's late. Jen is sick of hearing about Callum D'Arby. Sick of the dead ends and the late nights. Big fight. I leave. She decides she needs to get out of the house."

"No shit? That night?" Nick asked, breathless.

"The tip was garbage. By the time I found out what happened to her, it was — put myself on administrative leave to take care of her. Asked for a transfer. Chasing the white whale cost me everything."

"I didn't know. Seriously. None. If I'd have known—"

"What do you want with D'Arby?" Hsu asked. Nick could tell that he was playing at weariness, but there was a tension in his question. A hope that Nick had broken through the barrier to bring D'Arby down.

"It might be nothing, but I've got a lead on something he might be involved in."

"Is D'Arby involved in that clinic?" Hsu perked up like an addict offered a free fix.

"Jenkins told you to keep clear of me for a few days, right?"

"Whatever you're doing, if it means putting D'Arby away, I want in."

"No," Nick said, firm. "This is something else."

"I can help."

"Best you don't. If I'm wrong, or I fuck this up... not being a cop anymore will be the least of my troubles. Get me?"

Hsu narrowed his eyes at Nick.

"If you find something on that asshole, you take him down. For me. For Jen."

"Any idea where I can find him?"

"He's easy to find. But that won't do you any good," Hsu said. "You need to get at him another way."

"What do you mean?"

"The D'Arby boys have a weakness for gambling."

"He was skimming a casino?"

"No. We could've caught him at that easy. Something harder to track," Hsu said. "Underground boxing."

"Any hints at venues?" Nick asked.

"No. They rotate. We only got dips into the aftermath of most matches. Brutal scenes."

"Didn't pick anybody up on those hoping to connect them to D'Arby?"

"Sure. But they're scared of him. Just like people were of his brother. Maybe even more-so. I don't know what that says about the fear Callum commands. He's not missing half his face."

"Nothing you know that wouldn't be in the official investigation report?"

"Effrontery?" Jen screamed from her room, "Effrontery?"

Hsu stood up quick, "Damn it, she knows I'm still here."

The nurse's assistant rushed past them to answer her call light.

"Effrontery?"

"She won't calm down unless I say goodbye," Hsu said. "Most leads I can provide will have you chasing your tail. I wish there was something else."

"No, it's okay," Nick said. "I've got some ideas."

"Good luck," Hsu said and disappeared into his wife's room.

Nick pushed open the door of the facility and stepped into the cool air of early spring. He knew he had a way in with D'Arby. The problem was convincing Ray's bodyguard to go along with it.

43

Unfamiliar didn't seem like enough to describe what was happening. Smells came from every corner. Old motor oil. Ball sweat. Rotting flowers. Vindaloo. Description and rational comparison went out of Nick's head.

It was Jabba's Palace in an abandoned K-Mart. Scum and villainy abound. To say he had to be cautious was the understatement of the year.

Ray was scraping up garbage from the ground with the side of his foot into a small pile. Bits of broken glass, screws, nails, gravel—anything sharp stayed, anything round, plastic or dainty got picked out and tossed to the side. Crouching like a kid building a sand castle, Ray scooped the handful of tetanus and sprinkled it over the double-sided tape surrounding Boom-Boom's knuckles.

"Sure you don't want me to go to the methadone clinic and grab some discarded needles?" Nick asked.

Ray and Boom-Boom gave him a look that told him not to be ridiculous.

Nick cracked the door of the manager's office they were using as a staging room and watched the current bout.

A woman shaped like a bundt cake bit into the cheek of a girl who was missing various fingers, bandaged with dirty gauze, the blood poisoning already creeping up her forearms. If Bundt Cake didn't kill her tonight, the infection would.

She shrieked as Bundt Cake wrapped her hand in the bedraggled curls. Leverage brought Blood Poisoning's head down into the blacktop and Bundt Cake spun her like she was an Olympian doing the hammer throw.

Blood Poisoning's eyelid tore off and one of Bundt Cake's fingernails punctured the vitreous humor of her left eye. Nick regretted not looking away a moment sooner.

"Hey. Breathe."

Nick looked up. He didn't even feel Ray's hands on his shoulders to steady him.

Ray held his gaze. "You need to blend. Can you do this?"

"He's gonna pass out," Boom-Boom laughed.

"Shut up," Ray hissed back. Boom-Boom knew crazy when it reared up. And he knew not to mess with crazy. He did as he was told and went back to wrapping his hands.

"He's still not here," Nick said, gulping in breaths.

"He's here," Ray said. "Likely through a proxy. But he's here. That's why we need you. You don't have to watch what's happening, probably best if you don't. You just need to listen. Track the bets."

Nick steadied his breathing and nodded.

"Someone will bet big when the fight turns. Don't bite on that. Counter bets will come in slow. Boom-Boom will get the fight to where it seems even. It won't last long. That's the bet. Follow that bet."

"You should do this. I'll fuck it up." Nick wiped his sweaty palms on his jeans.

"I've got something else to do. She'll be tracking it, too. Just trust she'll push the bet in the right direction."

As if on cue, the crowd exploded in a series of whoops and whistles.

Their entry fee.

She hadn't altered her looks much from when they had accosted Burke. Same dark hair and scarring. The black eye was back. But now she was wearing a handkerchief as a shirt. Low-rise jeans that exposed her butt dimples, cut off just above the knee to show off tattooed calves, muscles taut from the eight-inch heels. Lauren or The Queen or whatever-the-fuck-her-name-was didn't half-ass her characters, that was for damn sure.

She worked the crowd, wiggling her side boob at the least disgusting spectators, which was a thin distinction. Wads of bills passed around. Men drooled at her like dogs at raw meat. Even with all the carefully curated flaws, the devils could tell there was an angel among them they couldn't wait to get filthy.

"You're on," Ray said.

Boom-Boom stood up and delicately hiked up the makeshift cup he'd placed over his nuts.

"This is where we say goodbye," Ray said to Nick.

"How will I know this works?" Nick asked.

"Wait for the phone to ring."

"And if it doesn't?"

"Then we lost," Boom-Boom chimed in.

Nick stayed deliberately ignorant of the details after he played his part. He was already deep enough in lies and had yet to get any sign that Boom-Boom's hospital drop off had been identified as Solish.

"Good luck. Don't die," Nick said. He climbed up a stack of flimsy boxes and wriggled out the small window.

Legs dangling out over the alley below, he realized he could have planned this better. There was a dumpster a few feet to his left. He swung his legs and managed to catch the edge with his toe.

He heard the fight promoter open the office door and he knew he had to disappear. The awning window slammed down on his fingertips and he dropped. His nuts split the edge of the dumpster and he slid onto the pavement in pain.

"Oh, fuck," he groaned out, scrambling to his feet. Sweat dumped into his eyes. Retiring in disgrace from the police force didn't look so bad after all.

He sprinted around to the warehouse entrance and supplied the bouncer with the password. He was tearing up from the pain in his groin and the bouncer paused a moment before letting him in.

Wishing for an ice pack, Nick navigated past abandoned shelving. Advertisements for aging supermodels' lingerie lines and last attempts at Blue Light Specials were stacked in the corner. Someone had been using cast off inventory as a bed. He shuffled to the edge of the crowd, already humming from the fight in progress.

Boom-Boom's hands were around his opponent's neck. The blood vessels in the smaller man's eyes bulged from trying to keep the orbs in his head and his tongue lolled out the side of his mouth like a paralyzed dog's.

"Fifty on the little guy!" Nick spit out as he pushed into the circle, hoisting a wad of dirty ones in the air.

There was a collective pause as the crowd turned to the struggling man, his legs kicking out in futility like he was dangling at the end of a noose.

The group's collective head swung back in Nick's direction.

"Yeah, right, sucker," he heard someone say. No one was taking the bait. Everyone who had bet the long shot already knew they were going to lose. Why make it worse?

Blood gushed from Boom-Boom's thumb as his opponent bit into his knuckle, the lubricant loosening his grip just enough for the other guy's toe to catch him in the groin.

A frayed belt whipped at Boom-Boom's Adam's Apple. There was a crack as the metal buckle hit the fragile bones in his voice box and he fell down to his knees.

Eyes went wide all around and the betting resumed.

Crumpled bills made their way through the crowd in chaos. There was a central bookie somewhere handling the odds and the action, but Nick couldn't place him. There was too much randomness to it. Too many failsafes, so nobody knew who to roll at the end of the night. But that wasn't Nick's job. He was just supposed to be the catalyst.

It looked like Boom-Boom wasn't ready for what was happening. The scrawny fight club reject had the upper hand. He converted the belt whip into a garrote and now Boom-Boom's eyes were fighting the same battle his opponent's had been a moment before.

The money was going to stop flowing again unless he turned it around. But Nick knew better than to intervene. He glanced over to where The Queen was being groped by the master of ceremonies. Their eyes met briefly and he could tell she had lost track of the handoffs. The money was moving fast. She didn't know where it would end up. They were about to lose their shot. And based on the purple in Boom-Boom's face, about to lose an ally as well.

Someone rammed into Nick's back, trying to get closer to the action. He nearly stumbled into the fight.

He swung around.

"Watch your fuckin' ass!" Nick snarled.

"Kiss my dick, tourist," the toothless spectator hissed at him, flashing a blade from under his coat.

Nick smirked and broke the guy's nose with a headbutt.

Scrambling to his feet, blinded by blood, the spectator lunged and Nick dodged his telegraphed movement, kicking him in the tailbone to give him momentum.

The blade slid into the skinny fighter's kidney and he released his grip, hands grasping at his back.

Nick slipped into the crowd as "security" grabbed the spectator and dragged him into the darkness.

Nobody noticed. They were too busy watching a man get suffocated by dirt.

With a wheezing breath, Boom-Boom grabbed the man by the hair and yanked him to the ground. To make sure he stayed still, he cupped his hands together and brought the powerful fists down on the base of his opponent's skull. The body started involuntarily twitching as the man lost the ability to lift his face from the ground and gasped in dust and debris.

He hoped The Queen found her mark because the money had stopped.

Nick didn't know what to do now. He was told to slip out in the excitement after the fight. His brain told him the fight was over. But the hyenas were waiting for the lion to walk away from the downed prey.

Bets started moving again as to whether the downed man would live or die. The man's sick gurgle slowed and Boom-Boom rolled off.

The MC's hands went up and with it, the cheer of the crowd, who then filled the gap in the circle ready to collect their winnings from the decentralized proxy. It was like watching a human blockchain at work.

As intrigued by the situation as he was, Nick had to have more willpower than Lot's wife. He needed to keep his head down and disappear into the dark. Last thing he wanted was—

"Where you goin'?"

They weren't talking to him, right?

"Stop walkin' or start bleedin'."

He turned around, slow.

"Yeah? What?" Nick said, trying not to be intimidated. He didn't know the man by face, but Boom-Boom had described him. The other fighter's promoter. The one they offered The Queen to in order to get Boom-Boom into the fight.

"You're new," the promoter smiled, exposing his black gums.

"First time for everything," Nick said, doing his best to smooth the shake in his voice.

"I saw what you did to my fighter."

"What do you mean?"

The smile disappeared, and the promoter sighed, "Why is it that no one can ever own their shit, even when they know lying will get them nowhere?"

The security team took one step toward Nick before their heads slammed together and they crumpled in a pile at Nick's feet. A lithe hand slipped around the promoter's neck as a straight razor deftly cut the crotch out of his suit pants and pressed up against his hanging commando balls.

"I might cut you for fun. Walk away," The Queen whispered in his ear.

Eyes wide, he nodded ever so slightly. She swiped the blade up, cutting a thin line of blood from somewhere Nick didn't want details on. The promoter clutched his jewels and ran off.

Nick stood stock still, as though she would attack him next. He never realized how dangerous she actually was.

"Snap out of it," she said. "He needs patching."

That was when Nick noticed Boom-Boom, who had apparently used the last of his strength to do away with security. There was no way calling an ambulance would get them out of there before the promoter called reinforcements. He didn't know if the two of them were strong enough to get their fighter to the Jeep.

"Did you get it?" Nick asked, wrapping Boom-Boom's arm around his shoulder and straining to a standing position.

"Only one way to find out," she said, grabbing Boom-Boom's other side.

The sun was coming up as the bagman pocketed the cash into his Kevlar lined coat made to look like something pulled from a donation bin at the Midnight Mission. Both fighters headed toward the ER meant he had his work cut out for him for the week. Blasting Adderall for the last few days kept him alert, but he took a few Oxy so he could sleep after the drop. He would have to take them at just the right time so he didn't run his busted Datsun through the guardrail on Mulholland.

When he saw who was waiting for him at the truck, he was glad the uppers still juiced him.

"I know someone who's looking for you," the bagman said.

"Throw a rock, you could hit someone looking for me," Ray said. "I need one-on-one with—"

"You don't need to say it. I know who you mean." He shook out his keys. "Get in."

Ray looked him up and down, then headed toward the passenger side.

The bagman got in the truck, leaned over the seat, and pulled the knob to release the manual lock. Ray hefted himself onto the faded upholstery.

"You want me to stop for breakfast somewhere before you die?"

"Not hungry."

He put the car into gear.

"Torture is probably better on an empty stomach, anyway."

The bagman checked for oncoming traffic and pulled the car out, ready to deliver an unexpected delight to his boss.

44

The battered truck idled in the fire lane in an old strip mall in Upland. After holding open the passenger door like a chauffeur and scanning the parking lot, the bagman patted Ray down for weapons. He came up with the burner phone Ray was supposed to call the cavalry on and slipped it into his pocket.

"Can I get that back? I prepaid and still have thirty-seven minutes left."

The bagman pulled the phone out of his pocket.

"Sure."

He slipped the back cover off the phone, checked it for a chip, then removed the SIM card and battery and whipped them into oncoming traffic. He snapped the phone in half at the hinge and dumped it at Ray's feet.

"Here you go," the bagman smiled.

Ray looked down at the phone. Thank God for back-up plans.

"Based on where we are, I can either go get some SR-22 insurance, a payday loan, or get fitted for some new bifocals," Ray said. "Sounds like a hell of a day."

"There," the bagman said, nodding to the store across the parking lot. Ray read the sign.

"World of Stats Collectables and Cards? Open a little early aren't they? Sure you don't want to go get some breakfast first, tell me all your hopes and dreams?"

The bagman pulled the stuffed envelope of cash out of his coat and tossed it onto the faded fabric between them.

"Go buy a Pokémon card. Ask to buy the Test Print Blastoise."

"Wouldn't you rather just shoot me?" Ray asked.

"He won't have it. But he'll tell you he'll put it on hold for a deposit."

Ray picked up the envelope. "Deposit?"

"You're smart. No wonder you survived this long." The sarcasm was thick as banana pudding.

"Then what?"

"Browse a little. You might see something you like."

Ray shoved open the door to the Datsun and got out. Before his feet could touch the ground, the truck was gone. Either the bagman didn't want to be around for what happened next or Ray already had enough eyes on him that the guy didn't have to worry about him taking the money and running.

The bell above the door gave a little "ding" as Ray stepped in. It was like going back in time. Ray used to collect baseball and football cards when he was a kid. Like every kid did. As a child of the 1980s, he always heard that rumor of someone's grandmother throwing out their dad's mint collection. If the rumors were to be believed, every kid in America once possessed a Mickey Mantle rookie card that got tossed into the trash.

Between all the grubby fingers trading to get a Bo Jackson or Robin Yount to complete their set, anything they held onto for long would have been nowhere near mint condition. By the time they grew up to the point of anything really having any value, it had been enjoyed the way it was supposed to be;

stuck in a book to mark your place or strapped into your bike spokes to make it sound like a motorcycle.

The store smelled of stale cardboard and expired bubblegum.

"Can I help you?"

The clerk looked trapped in time as well. Untucked flannel over a faded Def Leppard t-shirt, the only thing the years hadn't stolen from him was his hairline. He looked like Ed O'Neill with hair.

Ray looked around. He didn't see any Pokémon cards. That was probably the point.

"Yeah, could I look at your test print blast waist?"

"Don't know what that is."

"One of those, fuck," in one ear and out the other, "Pokeyman."

"Test Print Blastoise? Pretty rare card to just hope to find."

"For my kid."

"You always just try to buy your kid a $350,000 Pokémon card?"

Ray tried not to choke on his own saliva. "Little shit was trying to pull one over on me."

The clerk went back to his inventory.

"Sorry to waste your time," Ray said, turning to leave.

"If you wanted to put down a deposit, I could keep an eye out," the clerk said, not raising his eyes from the computer.

"Little too pricey for me. Even with 10% down," Ray said, continuing toward the door.

"I'll make an exception, Cobb."

Ray stopped in his tracks and turned on his heels.

"Lock the door."

Ray flipped the deadbolt and walked back to the counter. He didn't see it the first time. The almond-shaped eyes, the blonde mixed with the grey, the ear shape. Hard to make out the family resemblance when the person to compare it to was missing his face.

"There is a lot of absorbent merchandise in here. I would prefer not to blow your brains out without laying down some plastic first. Put the deposit on the glass case and we'll chat."

Ray did as he was told, but was still trying to process how he was going to transition from a tarp of blood to business partners.

"I'll tell you, this isn't what I was expecting from a crime kingpin who built up the meager beginnings of his brother's slave trade."

"Hollywood killed the car wash and the laundromat as fronts. Easy to tell the IRS you bought a Michael Jordan rookie card for cash, then sold the same thing for profit later that day. I can put just about anything on the ledger I want, within reason. Art and diamonds are the obvious commodities. People will pay obscene amounts for collectibles. Not because they're hiding their money from the government. Mostly just sad husbands trying to keep the bank statement arguments from their wives. Been in business for almost 25 years. Never audited once. I don't even go to trade shows anymore. Estate sale and storage pickers find me."

"The hobo fights are just a hobby, then?"

Callum D'Arby laughed through his teeth.

"They said you were funny."

"Thank 'them' for me."

"It really is too bad, you know. My brother was a piece of shit. Sure, there were plenty of things that I was happy to take over once he was gone, but the slavery thing always rubbed me the wrong way."

"Rubbed you the wrong way? What an adamant dismissal."

"You know how in *The Godfather*, Vito Corleone was fine with gambling and prostitution, but wanted to stay away from the drugs? We all have our limits."

"If I'm not mistaken, that got him shot in the back."

D'Arby's smile dropped. "Then his family killed everyone who had crossed him."

"What if I told you killing me now would be bad for business?"

"I would say you got used to having someone protecting you and don't know what I have to do to you to save face. You lost me several streams of income this week. Word gets around."

"One, that wasn't me. I was set-up and apparently it worked. Two, you're still going to kill me. We'll make sure of that. But you're going to take care of something else that has been bugging you in the process."

"Osip Kosbur is dead. I absorbed his business. Didn't even have to pay for it. What else you got?"

"Kosbur may be dead, but The Bear isn't."

D'Arby leaned back in his chair. "Spill."

"I'm going to take off my shoe. You good with that."

"You've been homeless for a decade. I don't think anyone would be good with you removing your shoe in an area that isn't well-ventilated."

"Plug your nose. It's worth it."

D'Arby unhooked the latches holding the sawed-off shotgun from beneath the counter.

"You fuck with me and I'm staining some inventory."

"Fair."

He nodded with the end of the barrel for Ray to go ahead.

Ray slipped off his right shoe and both of their noses involuntarily puckered from the smell. He dug in the toe for the package he'd been smuggling around in his sock for the past month. Once he slipped his shoe back on, the smell lingered. There was no putting that genie back into the bottle.

Ray tossed the warm packet of purple powder onto the glass case in front of D'Arby's cash register.

"Yeah? So?"

"Same stuff you've been trying to copy for a month."

"Who says I've been trying to copy it?"

"I thought you absorbed all of Kosbur's business. No chemist, no product."

D'Arby shook his head with a chuckle. "Okay, hotshot. So what if it is? We've got that recipe. It's too jazzed, needs to be softened. People find out this shit is frying their brains and they're going to stay away. Why you think bath salts never became a thing?"

Ray smiled. "This is the new and improved version. You want it? I can get it to you."

"How?"

"I know where they've stashed their chemist," Ray lied. "A bit further out than Pasadena. But they're moving out in the morning. This is a now or never situation."

D'Arby cocked the shotgun. "Or I could end this stupid quest that 'honor' has put me on for the last few years and go get a sandwich."

Ray didn't think that apathy was going to have a horse in this race, but there they were. "Just so we're clear. All this vendetta crap between you, me, and The Bear? It doesn't matter to you at all? Never did?"

"Nope." The shotgun didn't move.

"So all I have to do to get you off my back is die?"

"Yep."

"You let me live today and I make sure I die so that people think you made it rough on me. And you get to take out your competition."

"I could blow off your kneecaps right now and send a team instead. In case you haven't heard, I like the incognito boss part of this gig."

"Don't tell me there isn't a part of you that hates how Kosbur capitalized on your brother's death for all those years. Your underlings have seen Kosbur's bosses keep you at bay, even after you claimed his assets as your own," Ray rolled up his sleeve to show off the tattoo. "If you make a show of taking me out, any whispers behind your back will be silenced. You kill me here? Nobody knows. I'm still a fugitive from justice, like before. A liability. And you'd have to scrap this location. I'm a bleeder."

D'Arby snorted a laugh and stared at Ray. All Ray had to do was hold the slight smile. Hold it and force the sweat to pour down the back of his neck instead of his forehead.

The shotgun *cha-chucked* in slow-motion and Ray was certain he was about to be leaking from a lot of tiny holes. But the barrel pulled up, the ejected shell resting in D'Arby's palm.

"If there were more cash businesses nowadays, I wouldn't give it a second thought, but between the clinic and the porn den, I can't afford to lose any more real estate," D'Arby sighed, "All I have to do is kill you? Publicly?"

Ray shook out his pant leg slightly and checked the floor for a puddle to make sure he hadn't pissed himself.

"Relatively publicly. Before you do, you need to send a team to scrub a scene like you did with Kosbur in the bathhouse."

"Who said that was me?"

Ray ignored his dodge. "Solish's Topanga Hideaway, where Culp was making the drops. Your tattooed recruits had a rough week. Better send a clean-up crew there tonight. The place isn't on the cops' radar yet, but it won't be for long. You'll find Kosbur's next-of-kin. He didn't like that you'd recruited his people. Sooner you take care of it, sooner that can of worms is closed."

D'Arby kicked his heels up onto the glass case and leaned back in his chair.

"Alright, Mr. Big Stuff. You've got a deal," D'Arby smiled. "How do you want to die?"

45

Nick paced his condo. He wanted to open up a six-pack of craft brew and wash down the Valium in his medicine cabinet, but he knew he had to stay alert.

Lauren — calling her The Queen felt fucking stupid — had scrubbed the burner phone of any evidence of him and had passed it off to Cobb before she went to be the ring girl. He knew that she and Boom-Boom were going to head up to Big Bear to rescue his girlfriend before the carnage started. Meanwhile, all he had to do was wait.

He hated waiting.

Not to mention all the things that could have gone wrong. D'Arby had probably searched Ray for the phone and smashed it. Which meant that Nick wouldn't have any way to justify calling the sheriff to intervene in the confrontation between D'Arby and the Bear. Which meant Boom-Boom and The Queen were heading toward certain doom.

The phone buzzed in his pocket. Finally. He pulled it out slowly to avoid answering it. Ray needed to leave the voicemail they'd scripted for him.

But it wasn't Ray.

It was Jenkins.

"Yeah," Nick answered with a dry throat.

"Where are you?" Jenkins asked.

"Home," Nick said. At least he didn't have to lie about that.

"Solish showed up," Jenkins said.

Fuck. They had identified him fast. He hadn't thought about what to do once Solish regained consciousness and identified everyone who had found him. Without a straight story and that tattoo on Solish's arm, a quick cross-examination would quickly identify Ray Cobb, Lauren Ashmore, and Nick Archer.

"Dead," Jenkins continued.

"What?" Nick gasped. He didn't know if it was fear or relief.

"Found him dumped at Las Virgenes. Wrapped in a comforter, doused in bleach and lit on fire. Luckily, the polyester blend took the brunt of the flames and we could identify the body right away."

Fuck. Boom-Boom went off script and got creative.

"Burned alive?" Nick asked. He was having a lot of trouble finding more than one syllable.

"Nope. Multiple stab wounds. Head injury. Guts slashed open with a straight razor. He was dead before the flames got him. Whoever tried to make him disappear did a piss-poor job."

No. No. No. Fuck.

"Now what?" Nick asked.

"Feds will take over searching for his buyer," Jenkins said. "Your involvement here is still suspect, but we've got a trail that gets you to Solish's door. That's all I asked for. Jane Doe may still be part of this, but she gets a back seat for now."

"Hsu is aiding?"

"As best as he can. Your witness on Solish and the clinic went back to South Central and ended up on the front end of a bullet. There's a lot more bodies here than make me comfortable."

Boom-Boom didn't save Solish.
Burke wasn't supposed to die.
Something was wrong.

Nick tried to get his saliva flowing again before he spoke.

"What do you need from me?"

"A few days off. Show up on Monday. You're parked at a desk until I can figure out what's next."

"Okay."

Jenkins ended the call with nothing to add. Based on his tone, Nick could tell that he didn't believe any of the crafted narrative, but didn't have any evidence to point him in another direction.

If Boom-Boom made sure Solish was dead before ditching him, then he was planning something other than what they'd agreed to.

Ray should have called by now. Or The Queen should have sent the text. There must have been something that went south.

Nick checked his phone. No missed calls. No new texts.

He checked his weather app. Severe storm warning for the mountains. Service would be garbage.

Ray and The Queen were running right into a trap.

He grabbed his keys and hoped his shitbox of a car wouldn't need snow tires.

In the time it would take to get to Big Bear, they could all be dead already.

46

Sweets jolted awake as Malkin banged around the room, searching for a boot. He was chugging a smoothie and ranting.

"Yes, why didn't I see it before? Of course... we have to move.. today... we have to show them... show them all!"

"Baby, why don't you—"

He leapt onto the bed and stood over her, the ceiling fan whirling behind his head, creating a mad halo of light and sound.

"We've waited too long. Become too soft. We must act. Nothing can get in our way."

Sweets let out an involuntary giggle, even though he was scaring her a little. But this was what she loved about him. His passion and his charisma. His abs were pretty nice, too.

"Can we at least have breakfast first?"

"Here," he dropped to his knees, straddling her on the bed and put the smoothie to her lips, "Drink."

She was thinking about pancakes and bacon, but the way Malkin talked about the future, she figured she would have to get used to his smoothies. She took a sip and liked how sweet it was, but he didn't take it away and the sweet pink glop dribbled down her chin and onto her chest where the sheets had fallen down.

Sweets smacked his wrist, harshly reminded of being force fed steak. Malkin didn't take offense, but smiled and began licking the remnants from her neck and chest. This time, she didn't push him away.

At first it was tender, just how she liked it, then even as she knew all the smoothie had to be gone, he pushed his face into her skin harder, nibbling, then biting at her, the pleasure soon becoming pain.

"X, you're hurtin' me!" she pushed on his shoulders, but it didn't deter him, so she grabbed the hair on the back of his head and yanked. When he came up for air, she could see there was something different in his eyes. Something vacant and wild.

She snuck away from underneath him and scuffled away from the bed, snatching her panties off the floor. As she bent over to put her feet through the lace, she felt funny. She knew that feeling. The same as Reggie's candy.

"I don't feel so..." she glanced over at the smoothie just as Malkin picked it up and chugged the rest of it.

"You feel uneasy? Different? That today the world will change?"

Sweets stumbled across the room and pulled on some leggings and a t-shirt, her head too fuzzy to deal with the mechanics of a bra.

"What's in that?" she grabbed the empty cup from him.

"Life. Nutrients. Nothing false."

"You sure about that?"

"What do you—?"

There was a crack in the distance. Malkin's head swung toward the window.

He had worked with wood enough to know the sound of a branch breaking from the weight of snow. This wasn't it.

Another crack. This time closer.

"What was that?" Sweets said, boots in hand, ready to bolt.

Malkin smiled. Snow swirled in the wind outside. The late in the season dusting would be a welcome invitation to the residual snow bunnies on the mountain.

The cracks changed to pops. There was no mistaking the sound for anything but gunfire.

In the courtyard of cabins, he watched a couple of his acolytes running for cover. Then another pop. Someone dropped into the snow, a bloom of red spreading around them.

"We have broadcast my thoughts to the world and the forces of evil wish to stop us from taking our rightful place at the helm of humanity."

Sweets knew there was something in that smoothie, but she couldn't focus her mind. There was enough of her aware to know she was in trouble. But she just couldn't motivate her feet to move.

"I want Boom-Boom," she squeaked out as she dropped to the floor.

"No time for that now, love. The war has started."

Malkin pulled the case out from under his bed, ignoring the few screams from outside, still not sure where the gunfire was coming from. He opened it and pulled out the carving chainsaw. It roared to life in his hand as he pulled the chain.

A hellish chuckle escaped his lips. He grabbed Sweets by the neck with his other hand and kicked open the door.

47

They had both dressed for the cold, but didn't have the footwear for the heavy snow. Even though Boom-Boom wanted to put the Jeep into four-wheel drive and crank it right into the center of camp in his search for Sweets, she'd convinced him otherwise. Which meant a trek through the unplowed woods where nary a cross-country skier dared to tread. The hiking boots she'd found prepping for the mountains were filling with snow. It was halfway up her calves and rising quickly.

Boom-Boom hadn't changed his footwear since he and Ray had come down through the high desert a few days before. He pushed through the trees at a pace that The Queen couldn't keep. She didn't know how close to the camp they were, so didn't want to yell out his name to get him to slow down.

Once Ray was in D'Arby's clutches, he wouldn't get much alone time. She was certain that D'Arby would have searched him and confiscated the phone, so she brought another one along for backup. But Ray was supposed to alert Nick before the fighting started, when D'Arby's crew was on their way. If she sent the text and Ray didn't convince D'Arby this was the best course of action, then Nick would have suspicions back on him for alerting the sheriff's department without a warrant. If she didn't send the text until the fighting started, it would be too late to save anyone.

She bent down and picked up the heftiest pine cone she could whip through the trees. Even though he was a shadow through the storm, she could still see Boom-Boom's lumbering form. Hoping that the wind wouldn't take it off course, she wound up and whipped it at his head.

He stopped and swung around at her. Through the snow, she couldn't see what she imagined was fury on his face. She waved her hands wildly for him to stop and made her way to him.

"What the fuck?" he growled.

"I have no clue where we are. You disappear, I can't back you up," she hissed.

He grunted out a laugh. Mr. MMA had no idea she could drop him easily. They wouldn't find him until the snow thawed.

"There," he said and waved her to the tree line.

They made their way to the edge of the hill and peered down into the small valley where the sleepy camp rested under the snowfall. A couple of Malkin's crew were futilely shoveling the paths. They may as well have been seagulls carrying grains of sand for eternity.

"Which cabin is she in?" The Queen asked.

"Middle left. It was ours. Least I think she's there, she might be—"

One shoveler dropped a split second before the sound of the gunshot caught up. The second shoveler made a break for it, but dropped in the center of the cabins, body draped around the base of the flagpole.

"No!" Boom-Boom was to his feet and scrambling for the embankment.

The Queen grabbed him by his belt, but it was taking all of her strength. Her boots didn't provide enough grip on the ice.

"Lemme go!"

"You don't know where she is. You go down there now, you're as dead as them."

Others had piled out of the cabins with small arms and melee weapons, but the gunman took out a few more of them before they knew what direction the shots were coming from. If D'Arby had sent a small army to deal with Malkin's camp, the massacre would be heard for miles and bring the authorities. The small strike team made the assault sound like firing range practice.

Boom-Boom's energy focused below, his eyes scanning for Sweets, but he had stopped struggling enough that she could move in front of his field of vision.

"We go in quiet, slip into the back of the cabin and get her out of there before they send in the advanced infantry. Got it?"

Before Boom-Boom could answer, his eyes went wide, and he charged forward. She had enough wherewithal to use his body weight as leverage and flipped him onto his back, where she put him in a sleeper hold headlock.

Tears streamed down his face as he frantically pointed down.

A shirtless man in bare feet and unbuckled jeans emerged from his cabin. He wielded a small chainsaw in one hand and a dazed blonde in the other.

Raising his chainsaw above his head, he screamed out "THE FALL HAS BEGUN!"

Doors opened around the camp. Pistols and shotguns fired at the trees, hoping to wound the invaders. D'Arby's surgical attack plan was blown and the blonde man gave no sign he feared law enforcement showing up.

"Got her... Mal... kin...."

She had dropped much bigger men with this move in much less time. He wasn't going down.

He grasped back at her, wrapped his arm around her knee, then yanked forward. It wrenched the wrong way, dislocated. She screamed in pain and let go of him. He charged down the hill into the fray without giving her a second thought.

Clutching at her twisted knee, The Queen crawled to stop him, but it was too late.

She looked down at the blonde and the man she was with.

"Wait," she gritted her teeth through the tears, struggling to stand, "that's not Malkin."

48

Once he had called all of his followers to arms, he knew he had to lie low. Malkin skirted the woodpile and ducked down into the fluffy snow.

"How are you holding up my dear?" Malkin took Sweets' confused face into his hands.

Shots rang out. Someone was holding their guts in, trying to make it to the mess hall.

"Somebody's makin' popcorn," she cried.

Malkin's frenzied eyes took in the camp's devastation. Their attackers had killed almost everyone, but not before taking some stragglers with them first. He scanned the bodies for signs of Reggie, but couldn't see his telltale jacket through the haze of the snow.

Petra, the woman who ran the canteen, huddled behind the latrine, clutching a hunting rifle that looked too big in her hands. She looked over to where Malkin was crouched. The wood around his head splintered up and cut his face. He barely took notice of it and raised the running chainsaw above his head, showing that Petra should leave her place of cover. Blindly obeying, she leapt into the action, firing wildly. She hit two gunmen who had moved their firing line up before the top of her head burst and took out a window behind her.

Malkin looked down at Sweets, who was trying to make a doll out of tree bark as though nothing was happening around them. He spied Reggie's cabin and bolted for the glass greenhouse. It was pocked with bullet holes, but if they stayed low, they might survive. If nothing else, he could use the girl as a shield. As he closed the door behind him, he heard a low pitched screaming charge.

Boom-Boom kicked open the door to the greenhouse pushing Malkin back from barricading the door.

"Give her back," Boom-Boom growled. He was drenched in sweat and melting snow.

Malkin had Sweets by the hair. She was looking up at him like he glowed.

"She's free to go with you whenever she pleases. I command no one here," Malkin smiled, his eyes wild. Whatever he had given to Sweets, it looked like he had taken a double dose.

"Gods and monsters and misters and men, you are none of them," she giggled out, not realizing she had rhymed. Then, without breaking eye contact, she lathered up Malkin's neck with her tongue.

"Sweets, c'mon. It's me," Boom-Boom begged, tears filling his eyes.

"You can be together, but this is hardly the time," Malkin chuckled out.

"Who do you think brought them here?" Boom-Boom was sick of talking, but the grumbling chainsaw in Malkin's hand kept him at bay.

The smiling veneer cracked.

"You jealous moron. Do you know what you've done? You've drawn the lambs to slaughter before they were ready for the coming end!"

"If the world really is ending, I want her with me."

"Like I said, you can have her," Malkin sneered, "but you're going to have to pay for your betrayal."

He threw Sweets to the ground and charged. Boom-Boom wasn't used to dodging onslaughts, but timed his punch not to uppercut Malkin's jaw, but his wrist. It threw Malkin off-balance. The chainsaw went into the wall, slicing into the frame of the glass beehives.

"Baby, no, watch the buzzin'," Sweets said softly from under the table. She wasn't talking to Malkin.

The honeybees, agitated from their home being disturbed, were marching out of the hole single-file, looking for someone to be the focus of their aggression.

One of them landed on Malkin's neck, sinking in its stinger. It pulled away, the little apian drone not knowing that this single attack meant certain death. There were enough drugs in Malkin's system, it didn't register. But he could see the panic in Boom-Boom's eyes as he backed toward the door, trying to watch each of the escaping insects.

Malkin raised the chainsaw and shaved the rest of the enclosure off the wall, exposing the teeming hive. Boom-Boom backed up past Sweets to the door, trying to cover every bit of exposed skin with his coat.

Wham! Wham! Wham!

Malkin slammed his fist against the wall to break the bees from their comb. They swirled around him, looking for enemies to attack and defend their home.

"Get outta here, baby, go," Sweets pleaded with the threadbare coat burrito.

"Not without you," he said, muffled under the polyester down.

Sweets stood to go with him, trying to keep from being distracted by the buzzing.

"Ungh!" she was yanked back, the running chainsaw close to her neck.

"Come get her," Malkin smiled. He was getting stung constantly now, but didn't seem to mind.

Boom-Boom's hand reached for the knob, but he couldn't grip it wrapped in his sleeve. It would just be a second. He reached his fingers out and—

He barely felt it. But he saw the slight bump there. He knew what came next.

"You need more motivation," Malkin said and pressed the chainsaw into Sweet's neck, silencing her screams. Flesh sliced away as blood gushed down her throat. "Now will you stay and play?"

Every bit of hatred Boom-Boom had ever experienced channelled through him. He bellowed as he charged Malkin, the coat dropping and exposing his skin.

Bees stung Boom-Boom's face as his fists whirled in a fury. His wails of anguish and rage became a muted mishmash as his face swelled and his throat closed up.

He dropped to his knees and dragged himself over to where Sweets was still gurgling. He could hardly see out of his swollen eyelids and couldn't wheeze in enough air to keep from going into full anaphylactic shock.

"Gonna be... okay... gonna fix..."

His tongue stopped working. Engorged pustules blinded him, ready to burst.

She was losing blood fast, but reached up and stroked the cheek of his puffy face, insects dancing in his hairline.

With her last breath, she gave him what he always wanted from her. When it came down to it, all their time, the sex, the fights; he only ever wanted one thing.

Before she knew he could no longer see her, she looked up at him and smiled.

That smile.

It was still on her face as her eyes went dark.

Boom-Boom held her to him, staring at her face, trying to will his renegade facial muscles to return that smile.

"Not.. wit... ow... you..."

He collapsed in her arms on the warm floor of the greenhouse.

Malkin, out of breath, his bare chest covered in bee stings, gave them a slight two-fingered salute.

"For never was a story of more woe than this of... shit... I forgot your names."

He let out a sardonic laugh, revved up the chainsaw, and whipped open the door. The swarming honey bees flew out into the night, dropping in the snow as the cold froze their wings.

49

Nothing was going to plan. The shoulder Ray had dislocated years ago was out of its socket and screaming with pain. His pinky finger bent the wrong way. He had swallowed a lot of blood from his broken teeth, and was having a lot of trouble breathing through his shattered nose. Rusty snot had crusted over his nostrils and he had to snort the clots up to get anything through them. D'Arby's lackeys had gone at him while the crime boss sat sipping a West Coast IPA. He was certain that they were going to tear both of his ACLs and slice through his Achilles to cripple him. Dump him in front of Malkin in a wheelbarrow.

The long drive up to the mountains gave him a long time to contemplate his fate. Every time he shifted from the pain, the thick painter's plastic covering the backseat crinkled, reminding him that all they had to do was blow a hole in his head, dump him with the rest of the bodies in the woods and be home for a late dinner.

He needed water. During the drive through the desert, D'Arby sat in the front seat of his SUV, chugging a large iced coffee, the condensation dripping onto D'Arby's moisture-wicking pants.

While they had been in the collectibles shop, D'Arby had made a couple of hushed phone calls, then had him go over the details of Malkin's compound several times. When the doorbell of the store rang, D'Arby had walked around the counter, grabbed him by the neck and slammed his face into the display case, cracking the glass and his nose.

"Have to make it look real," D'Arby had crouched down, smiling at him. "Just business."

It was only the beginning of "just business." While his crew indulged in an interrogation, D'Arby kept asking the same questions Ray had already answered.

Callum D'Arby was as unpredictable as his brother. Ray was sure that the plan to fake his death was gone. This game was very real.

Everyone except Ray looked dressed to go for a ski weekend. How D'Arby got his team to find several SUVs already equipped with clam shell ski racks was beyond him. They had the right props for anyone who might ask questions, but hidden compartments were filled with an arsenal. As though a mountain massacre was on D'Arby's to-do list and he had been planning it for months.

When they had loaded Ray into the back of the car, he could barely see the faces of the rest of the crew. The quick organization of the job was frightening. D'Arby never wrote anything down. Didn't bring a cell phone. Didn't touch a weapon. If something went south, they wouldn't find his fingerprints on anything.

Now they waited. D'Arby had the passenger side window cracked and was listening out the window at the sporadic gunfire, counting bodies on his fingers.

This little piggie had roast beef. This little piggie died screaming.

He was calm. Docile. Waiting for his turn.

"Okay," D'Arby said to the quiet man who was keeping Ray hostage in the back seat. He got out of the car and zipped up his Patagonia fleece. The quiet man gestured with the tip of his shotgun for Ray to follow. Ray nodded and wiped his bloody nose. It hurt his broken hand, but he reached over and pulled the handle, sure to leave a clean bloody fingerprint on the inside of the car. The quiet man was so focused on his boss, he didn't see Ray grab the headrest of the passenger seat under the plastic for leverage, leaving behind a smeared handprint. They would likely clean away all evidence once they made their way back to the car without him, but he had to try.

Ray led the way into the camp. The quiet man held the shotgun at the base of his neck. D'Arby followed, whistling the theme to *The Andy Griffith Show*. For him, this was a leisurely stroll down to the fishing hole.

"Boss," the quiet man whispered. There was a shake in his voice, and Ray could see why.

Malkin's doomsday cult had put up a hell of a fight. In the time that Ray had spent up in the mountain camp, all he had seen were a bunch of formerly homeless placated with a few meaningless skills. But Reggie must have sent Ray on his mission before Malkin could show him what was really happening. He indeed had been building an army for the end of the world. And they were ready for what was coming.

The city folk's arrogance had gotten the better of them. No one was left standing.

D'Arby stopped whistling.

There was an eerie quiet. No wounded begging for medical attention. Just the wind blowing through the tunnels created by the cabins. The weight of the heavy snow cracking the tree branches.

"Doesn't appear this was as one-sided as you thought," D'Arby said, his tone still light. "How about we find this Malkin so we can finish this?"

Snow covered most of the bodies, but Ray was going to postpone finding Malkin as long as he could. There still might be a way to negotiate out of his fate. D'Arby was expecting a lot more witnesses to Ray's sacrifice. Maybe there was something he could leverage out of that.

"Start flipping bodies," D'Arby said. "Don't get any ideas about discarded weapons either."

His shoulder and ribs were on fire, but Ray did as he was told and dropped to his knees in the snow.

He heard the chainsaw before he saw it.

Charging at them, shirtless and covered in welts, Malkin wielded the chainsaw wildly in front of him, screaming in rage. Ray was his intended target. He didn't seem to notice the men with him.

If Ray hadn't dropped to the ground like Indiana Jones facing the trials of the grail, he would have lost his head.

Instead, the chainsaw ground into the barrel of the quiet man's shotgun before it went off into the snow. Malkin brought the whirring menace back in an arcing swing, slicing through the quiet man's torso. Goose down and guts sprayed into the air.

Ray was trying to army crawl away, but he couldn't lift his arm and buried himself in the snow. The pain in his shoulder went away as the chainsaw dug through the leather and rubber in his boot and sliced into the flesh below his right calf.

"You're not running away again!" Malkin yelled above the grinding chain.

Ray was sure he was going to pass out from the pain when there was another gunshot.

It struck Malkin in the shoulder and spun him around. The saw pulled free from Ray's boot.

D'Arby had scrambled in the snow to grab the closest weapon and was popping away at Malkin's chest with a .22 rifle. It was meant for squirrel hunting, not taking out a Leatherface impersonator. Malkin was bleeding from each of the small wounds, but he was taking the hits as though they were from a Nerf gun. He leapt toward his attacker as D'Arby brought the .22 up for one last shot.

It was a winner.

A small lead projectile went up Malkin's nose and into his brain. His body went limp in midair, but not before the chainsaw served its purpose.

Right down the center of Callum D'Arby's face, the chainsaw whirred through flesh and bone, creating a deep cavern between D'Arby's eyes from the bridge of his nose down to his mouth. When Malkin's finger slipped loose of the chainsaw's trigger, D'Arby's head slumped to the side, his dead eyes staring at Ray.

"Family resemblance," Ray coughed out before collapsing in the snow.

50

Reggie lifted the trapdoor beneath his desk once the sound of gunfire and the chainsaw had ceased. Purple powder spilled out of his backpack, but he was leaving the rest of his life behind. Just as he had done dozens of times before. He glanced out the window of his cabin, searching for movement. After a moment of nothing stirring in the snow, he emerged from the doorway of his cabin.

"Figured you would hide until the fighting was over."

Reggie spun on his heels to see The Queen step out from the tree line with a limp. He let out a sighing laugh and glanced down at his feet. It took him a moment to speak.

"Looks like you've got a little hitch in your giddy-up," Reggie finally said.

She did her best to stabilize her stance and act through the pain. "You can drop the character. Everyone who bought it is dead."

The corner of Reggie's mouth went up in a slight snarl as the hump in his posture disappeared. When he spoke, his voice shed the Ratso Rizzo rhythm, and he reverted to a smooth playfulness in his tone.

"Who're you with? Not these?" Reggie said, pointing at the sprawl of corpses. "No. Has to be Cobb. He around here somewhere? Bleeding out?"

"No hello? No apology?" she asked.

"Should I be glad you're alive or sad that you survived with the trauma all these years?" he smirked.

"I've always wondered if you knew what was about to happen when you sold me to those men," she said. "There was a small part of me that hoped you didn't know. Hoped you were ignorant of the inevitable outcome. I should have known better."

"I never heard from law enforcement about those jobs we'd pulled together, so assumed you were dead," he said. "Thanks for not snitching."

"I had other things on my mind," she said.

"Are you going to shoot me or do you want to get a coffee and catch up?" Reggie asked.

The Queen pulled the strap on the automatic rifle she'd scavenged from one of the fallen and swung it around to her hands.

"I take it you're more of a tea drinker now?" he smiled.

"You don't care at all, do you? About anything?" she snarled at him.

"When I found you and taught you, you had this grand illusion that I was going to replace your father. You had no idea you were merely replacing the last assistant I had to throw to the wolves. But you aren't stupid. I never gave you any impression that our relationship was more than business."

"I was fourteen! I loved you," The Queen said.

"And I loved you. In a way. You were the best I'd ever seen. But we both know it would've only been a matter of time before you realized you were better than me. And you would've betrayed me when you realized you didn't need me anymore."

"That's what you thought of me?"

"That's what you were," he said. He had his hands up, but he was moving toward her slowly. "That girl would have shot me in the back when she first saw me up here. But whatever you've survived through all this time... it changed you. Maybe you should thank me."

She pulled the trigger and let loose a spray of gunfire at his feet. He stopped moving.

"See? You do love me. I'm ten feet away," he shrugged.

"A bullet is too good for you."

He burst out laughing, "Oh my God! Really? That's... wow... have you spent the passing years writing revenge movies? Jesus, if you're going to throw cheese ball lines like that at me, you might as well shoot me. Put me out of my misery."

"This isn't a joke!" she lifted the rifle to her shoulder.

"Of course it is. All of this. Life. It's all a joke. I would've already walked away from this prayer circle if it weren't for Cobb throwing a wrench in the works. I had the recipe for that magic drug all figured out. Even leaked it to Low Seward through a mutual friend, so Malkin thought that his competition was coming from another source. I've been micro-dosing this entire camp for months, waiting for my out. But, you, my dear, presented me with the Gunfight at the O.K. Corral. Saved me so much trouble. Don't you see? It's all a game and if you're not having fun, you're not doing it right."

"You wanted him to get caught," The Queen shook her head. "You knew there was an outstanding warrant on the Xavier Malkin alias somewhere."

"Had to ditch the comic book guises a long time ago because of the heat. Well, that, and all the goddamn superhero movies. Switched to classic rock. I'm thinking books are next. Care to join me again? You could be... ah... Daisy... Carraway. Gatz is a bit too on the nose."

The Queen stared through him.

"You're a psychopath."

"More of a narcissist, but I wear both badges with honor," Reggie held his hands out, giving her a free target. "Go ahead, then. Kill your father."

"You are not my father!" she screamed. He could feel that he'd broken her calm. After all these years still so easy to manipulate.

"Might as well have been," he shrugged.

She choked back the tears. "I want you to suffer like I suffered. Understand what I went through."

"That doesn't sound like fun at all."

Reggie pulled the 9mm Winchester Magnum from the back of his waistband and fired. When the bullet clipped her shoulder, the spray from the end of her rifle splintered wood from the tree he'd jumped behind to take cover.

Bleeding from the knick and limping, The Queen propped herself back up and switched the rifle to her other arm.

"I'd thought you'd learned more from me?"

The Queen grunted, "Should've known you were going for cover instead of trying to disarm me."

"I can stand back here all day," he called out to her. "Any chance you'll bleed out before I have to take a leak?"

"My friends will be along shortly," she said, steadying her breath.

"Friends? You learned nothing from me, did you?"

He stepped out from behind the tree and fired into the ground in front of her. Dirt and rock sprayed up, blinding her. It was enough of a distraction for him to step on the barrel of her rifle and smack the 9mm across her face. She dropped to her knees, grunting in pain from her torn patella.

"Like if you're going to waste a bullet, make sure it's for a reason," he said. He pressed the hot tip of the 9mm to the spot between her eyes. She gritted her teeth at the pain of the hot metal searing a circle into her forehead.

"Going to finish what you started?"

He pulled the gun back and swung his heavy metal toed boot across her temple. She went limp in the snow.

"Good luck explaining why you were up here and the only one to survive all of th—"

When Ray's body weight hit Reggie, the 9mm flew off into the woods.

"Ready to end this?" Ray asked. He sunk a fist into Reggie's kidney.

"Ever since I met you," Reggie bit hard into Ray's ear and took the top chunk off. Ray shrieked and backed off, holding the side of his head as blood ran through his fingers.

Reggie spit the flesh out into the snow and scrambled to his feet. "You taste like homeless shit. That was cooler in my mind."

Ray tackled Reggie through the door of his cabin and they landed hard on the wood floor. A few bees buzzed around them that had escaped through the bullet holes on the other side of the greenhouse. Reggie punched at the torn skin on Ray's leg where the chainsaw had nearly taken the leg off at the knee. At that exact moment, one of the stray bees stung Ray on the back of the neck. Unable to process which pain to deal with first, Ray was slow to respond as Reggie kicked him off.

Reggie pounced and grabbed Ray by the scruff of his coat. He rammed the top of Ray's head into the hard mahogany of the desk. The blow was so jarring, the glass top slid off the other side and broke into several pieces on the floor. Ray's vision doubled, his ears rang, and his focus disappeared.

"I promised I'd get that tattoo removed for you. I like keeping my promises."

Reggie gripped Ray by the scruff of his coat and dragged him over to the potbelly stove. He unhooked the handle of the door with his foot and kicked it open. He yanked Ray's coat off over his head.

"Time to finish what Deuce started in the trailer."

Reggie shoved Ray's arm in the stove and Ray immediately regained consciousness as the flames enveloped his arm. He could smell the burnt hair and sizzle of flesh as he screamed. His flight response took over. He knocked Reggie backwards. As he pulled away, he scraped his arm against the side of the stove, sloughing off a sleeve of black skin, leaving a raw, bloody mess underneath.

He raced out into the open air, plunging it into the snowdrift. For a split second, his logical mind took over, telling himself it was the stupidest thing he could have done, knowing he'd immediately get frostbite on the dead flesh if he didn't lose consciousness from the shock.

A kick to the center of his back made his next choice for him. The momentum of the blow pulled his arm from the snow and he rolled onto the hard ground, unconsciously using it to break his fall. Both of his arms were now essentially useless.

Reggie stood over Ray. A shard of glass from the broken desk sliced into his palm where he clutched it, but he didn't appear to care about what was happening.

"You cost me a lot of money, you son of a bitch," Reggie spit down at him. "I was a pubic hair's breadth away from getting out. I'd convinced Malkin we'd need that purple wonder in the 'dark days.' Keep people who didn't agree with us docile. We controlled the water and food. Played right into his fucking superiority complex. He didn't know he was my first test subject."

Ray's eyes darted toward where The Queen lay unconscious. This man had destroyed her. Led her toward her entire life on the streets. Ray needed some poetic justice. He needed her to play her role in the story and exact her vengeance on the man who'd done so many horrible things to her. She didn't need a man to save her. She was The Queen, for fuck's sake. He willed her to awaken and complete her story. It is what was supposed to happen.

She didn't move.

Shooting pain yanked Ray out of his reverie as Reggie shoved the pane of broken glass through his shoulder, pinning him to the frozen ground. A low howl escaped from a primal place inside him. The only thing keeping him from giving in, from letting the world become black and enveloping him was that he wouldn't give the piece of shit standing over him the satisfaction.

Reggie staggered back and laughed.

"You stuck? You fucking bug. Jesus Christ, you are a fucking cockroach. You should thank me, you know? I could've killed you a long time ago. As soon as you drove that Audi into town. But I couldn't do it without pissing him off. He thought you'd make a good little generalissimo as soon as you saw the light. And I still needed him in my good graces for a little while longer. But then I saw it. What a fucking cockroach you were! Crawling out of the fucking rubble of every nuclear blast in your life."

Ray wanted to say something. Wanted so badly to mount a clever retort. But he devoted every ounce of energy to continue breathing.

"The enemy of my enemy is my fucking pawn," Reggie pointed to The Queen. "You'd think she'd have learned better. All these years. Everything I taught her and she still didn't see the big picture."

Blood was flowing down Reggie's palm, spattering across the snow as he gestured.

"Why the fuck would I want to bring down the grid? How fucking stupid? I'm pretty sure life in the Stone Age was fucking hard. But all these assholes believed it. He said it himself. Faith is the most powerful thing there is."

Reggie gestured to the scattered bodies surrounding them. A carnage Ray promised, but hoped to prevent.

"Everyone is SO. Fucking. Predictable. She could have pulled the trigger and been done with this, but there was still some sentimental bullshit buried in her psyche for me." He smiled at The Queen, then turned on Ray again. "And how many times could you have walked away? So scared of not being 'free'. Well, guess what, asshole? You always were. The tattoo doesn't mean shit. If you'd let yourself get arrested, there was probably enough circumstantial garbage you'd have gotten off. But you had to be a goddamn cowboy. Thought you were Wyatt fucking Earp."

Ray wondered which one of them was going to run out of blood first. From the way his vision was blurring, all odds were on him.

"But old Wyatt was a murderer and a con-man and was real fucking good at manipulating a narrative. 30-seconds in Tombstone and he was an American hero. And from then on, it didn't matter what else he did. But here's where I differ from you, Mr. Earp. Unlike you, who keeps telling himself he wants to disappear, but can't seem to get out of his own fucking way, I'm going to disappear. For real. Done it before. Will do it again. So, FUCK Y—"

Reggie disappeared out of Ray's eye line. Once he heard the wet sound, he could get a good look at what was happening.

Boom. Left. *Boom*. Right. *Boom*. Left. *Boom*. Right.

Boom-Boom's eyes had fused into slits from the bee stings and most of his face had lost its shape. His tongue had swollen in his mouth and the words he was trying to scream at Reggie came out in the mumbled grunts of a madman mongoloid.

Boom. Left. *Boom*. Right.

It was sick. Horrific. Worse than what had happened to D'Arby.

Ray's stomach turned at the sight, but he couldn't look away. It wasn't a death he would wish on anyone, but it seemed a fitting end for someone who lived with no identity.

Each time Boom-Boom's fist landed, it took another piece of Reggie's head away with it.

Boom. Skin torn. *Boom.* Muscle ripped. *Boom.* Bone shattered.

Boom-Boom's grunts were becoming more labored with each punch. Ray could hear the air struggling to move in and out of his closing throat.

By the time Reggie's head was a wet pile of mush steaming in the snow, Boom-Boom was just punching through to the frozen ground.

The fists stopped their movement and Boom-Boom's arms hung limp at his sides. If his eyes could open, he'd have seen he'd finished the job. If his face still had shape, a slight smile would have formed at the edges of his mouth. And if his words still had meaning, Ray would have heard him whisper, "Sweets," before the bee sting's poison won the battle and Boom-Boom died in the snow.

51

Ray struggled to get to his feet, both of his arms hanging at his sides. Crying through the pain, he heard the quick crunch of footsteps racing through the snow.

He turned his head to see Nick, service pistol drawn.

"What in the holy fuck?" Nick said, shivering in the blizzard without a coat.

Ray looked over at what was left of the two men, a grotesque tableau of red stains in the snow.

It was over. He was free from these men who had manipulated him. Free from the meaningless tattoo buried in a blackened crust of charred skin.

"You're not... supposed... to be here," Ray said, breathing labored.

"I thought Boom-Boom was double-crossing us," Nick said, going to help Ray.

Ray stopped him in his tracks, lifting his burnt arm. Nothing was keeping the muscle from being exposed to the air and infection.

"You need to go before you... taint the scene. The blizzard will... cover your footprints. Don't touch anything. Walk away," Ray slurred.

"This is too big, Ray," Nick said. "The FBI will scour this place."

"There are... pieces of me in D'Arby's car... the chainsaw... the stove."

"Pieces aren't a body."

"It would at least... give me a head... start. Maybe some doubt I survived."

"You'll be running for the rest of your life," Nick pleaded.

"He's right. It won't work."

Both of the men turned to the voice coming from the ground. The Queen was awake and hadn't taken her eyes off of Reggie's corpse. Tears were flowing down her face. Ray couldn't tell whether they were tears of joy that the man was dead, or tears of rage that she wasn't the one to end his life.

"I'm not sticking around," Ray said.

The Queen stood and walked over to Reggie's corpse. She bent down and stared at the sludge where his head once was. The backpack had split open and spilled little baggies of purple powder into the snow and viscera. Ray could see it was taking every ounce of restraint for her not to spit in the remnants of Reggie's face. Instead, she tore a small patch of flannel from Reggie's shirt. She pulled out the burner phone, rubbed it as clean as she could, and shoved it into Ray's hand.

It took all of his strength, but he flipped it open and hit all the buttons with his thumb, remembering what it was like to text on the ancient keypad.

"I'm sorry," she said, "but a bigger part of you has to show up too."

In one swift movement, she yanked on the end of Ray's charred middle digit with the cloth. The fingernail tore free from the skin and Ray screamed out in renewed pain, dropping the phone in the snow. He instinctually went to grab his hand, but swiftly thought better of it lest he rip anything else off.

"Why the fuck would you—?!"

"Where?" she asked, calm.

Through clenched teeth, Ray answered, "What?"

"Where did he burn you?"

Tears were streaming down Ray's face as he nodded toward the cabin.

"Stove."

She limped through the open door of the cabin and emerged moments later.

"Okay," she said. Ray could see the narrative forming behind her eyes. "You said there's still a chunk of you on the blade of Malkin's chainsaw."

"And if you keep taking pieces, there'll be nothing fucking left!"

She turned to Nick, "You got here and Ray was already dead. You hid and watched Malkin chop Ray up, pack him into garbage bags and disappear. They took the stray pieces into the cabin for the fire. It'll explain why there are no bone shards or teeth. D'Arby's gang showed up. You did everything you could to stay out of sight. I hid the fingernail enough that it won't be obvious, but they won't miss it when they scan the room. It'll be a guarantee of identification, plus whatever skin you've already left on the stove."

"I wouldn't buy it," Nick said. "This thing is federal now. It was a goddamn massacre. I don't think they'll buy it either. The timeline on that text you sent won't match."

"Then it's your job to convince them," she said. "Something this big, they'll be looking for a straightforward solution. Wrap it up in a neat little package. Put that cop brain to good use. Use Solish as an alibi if you have to."

"Solish is dead. Boom-Boom must have gotten squirrelly. That's why I'm here now," Nick said.

"Even better," Ray said. His voice was shaking. He would be in shock soon. "Solish would complicate things. In Boom-Boom's Jeep, there's a laptop. Feds will find enough on there to connect Solish, D'Arby, Malkin—the whole fucking gang."

Ray watched Nick look him up and down. Energy was draining from him. The adrenaline that kept him standing was wearing off.

Sheriff's department sirens rang down the mountain in the distance. There was no condensation coming out of Nick's mouth. He was holding his breath.

"We have to go," The Queen said.

Three loners, haunted by the ghosts of the day stood in silence.

Choices made. Wrong paths taken.

Light snow fell on their heads.

"Look at yourself," Nick said. "I think your penance is over, Ray. I hope you can find some peace after all of this."

Ray wanted to say something back. Thank Nick for all that he'd done. Tell him that there was no way he could ever repay him for everything he'd risked to prove the innocence of a homeless man he hardly knew. All the actions Nick had taken based on nothing but faith in a kindred spirit. He knew all of this would never go away, not really, but the effort meant so much.

There wasn't time to say everything he wanted if he was going to stay alive and make Nick's decision to let him go worthwhile.

Maybe Archer was right. Maybe he had finally suffered enough.

"What do I... do now?" Ray asked.

"A friend of mine found a suitcase full of money a few years ago," The Queen said. "Might be enough to buy you a new life."

Ray shook his head. After all these years, Ernie would finally return the favor and save his life.

"Keep up the good work, Archer," Ray winced.

"You too, Cobb," Nick said, his voice cracking.

"Haven't you heard?" Ray smiled. "Ray Cobb is dead."

Ray leaned into The Queen and they hobbled toward the tree line.

Nick watched their figures fade from sight.

Then, they were gone.

Nick knew that there was one big hole in the narrative. He had the text attributed to Ray, but he couldn't justify being in the mountains already when he received it. There was something else he had to do or say. Something to shorten the timeline. He was on his own again.

He was staring at the mashed corpse in front of him. Didn't know who it was. Assumed it was Malkin, but didn't know why Lauren hated him so much. Why Ray had looked relieved. Why Boom-Boom had bashed his head into nothing.

There had to be some way to connect the Shadow Dance in the backpack. Someone in the story who couldn't refute Nick's testimony when he gave his deposition, but all the players in this tragedy were dead or gone.

He figured shit out. This is what he did.

But there was nothing. Nothing sounded real. Plausible. It was all so... contrived.

Nick screamed at the falling snow in a rage. Looking to take his anger out on the closest object, he ran at the backpack full of hallucinogenic drugs and punted it. He didn't get much distance on it and it spun about ten yards, scattering the purple powder in the snow.

He dropped to his knees and clutched his head, weeping.

What had it been all for? The lying? The deceit? Death all around him?

Nick wept for his life. He wept for his mother. He wept for the unknown future. The end of his life on the police force and maybe the end of his life as a free man.

The sirens were getting closer. Nick placed his service weapon in the snow in front of him and held his shiny LAPD badge for what he hoped wasn't the last time.

"Just wanted to make you proud, Ma," he whispered to the ground. The whipping cold caused snot to run to his lips. It dripped onto the chrome image of Los Angeles City Hall etched into the tainted shield in his hand. He tossed it into the snow next to his service weapon.

Chunk.

The badge hit something in the snow that sounded like glass. Thrown free when he'd kicked the bag. Nick tucked his hands into his sleeves as much to shield from the cold as to keep from putting his prints on whatever he found there and wiped the dusty snow away.

It revealed the image of an angry honey bee and a smiling bear giving a stung thumbs up with a criss-cross of bandages over its boo-boo.

X-Marks-The-Spot Honey.
All Natural. Locally Sourced.
Big Bear Lake, CA.

He'd found the honey guy. The connection. The map that led him to Big Bear Lake.

Nick was no longer careful about putting his prints on the jar because it had been in his pocket the whole time. It was his due north. The reason he'd gotten in his car hours before he was supposed to.

"Hands on your head!"

He hadn't heard the sheriff's SUV pull in behind him. He put his hands up slowly.

Saved by sweet, precious bee vomit.

The deputy grabbed his hands, shoved them behind his back, and pressed his face into the snow.

Nick tried to hide his smile from reflecting in his badge.

"I'm a cop."

If he had learned anything from his time in law enforcement, it was that the story can be more important than the truth. He'd spent most of his career reading people, both criminals and his colleagues. The task force they'd sent from the FBI was no different. They were nothing more than cops with federal badges. Different wrapper, same brand. They wanted their cases solved and closed, ready for the next one. Nick let them build the narrative with the evidence and filled in the minor details for them when something was missing. It was a lot easier than doing it the other way around.

They couldn't help but enjoy the tale they'd been told. A group of domestic terrorists make enemies with an international crime syndicate and they take each other out. The massacre was a gold mine for the media. On both sides of the conflict were people wanted in connection with dozens of crimes in the Los Angeles area. For the victims of those crimes, it was a righteous cleansing of sinners. Criminals destroying criminals.

Of course, it was more complicated than that, but Nick wasn't giving out more details than he needed to. He had to explain what he was doing in Big Bear. That was easy enough. He'd handed over his phone as evidence and the honey jar justified his hunch. He'd explained that he didn't inform local law enforcement of his presence because he didn't know what he was walking into. It hadn't been a lie. He wasn't expecting to find what he did. Solish connected the syndicates, playing both sides. When D'Arby found out about it, he went after Solish, but he found something else he wasn't expecting.

Nick told the story The Queen had laid out before everything went to shit. Ray Cobb had been part of the crew that had been the origin of The Bear tattoos. The laptop in the Jeep gave them Solish's address and information on Culp. D'Arby had already cleaned up the house in Panorama City. Culp was suspected to still be at large.

Deuce and the rest of the evidence at the hideaway in Topanga were gone. D'Arby's crew was efficient. It looked like it was ready for renters again.

When Solish's body was discovered, no one wept for him. The tattoo on his arm confirmed all the information Nick had given them to fill in the holes. Investigators connected the The Bear to Victor Mochulyak and Yuri Karsenov. Jimenez called Nick personally to thank him for taking the unsolved cases off his desk.

The one hiccup in the plan was that the feds asked for a deposition from Lauren Ashmore about her involvement with Dr. Solish. Nick wasn't privy to that conversation, but the whispers his friend Hank had heard in the hallway made it sound like it was a devastating story about a gang rape and a botched abortion. The conclusion of the interview was that she was a victim who wished to move on with her life.

On the day Nick got the all clear to come back to work, he didn't dress in the suit and tie of a returning detective. Instead, he wore jeans and a t-shirt. It was the uniform he used to wear daily when he was new to the RHD and shoved into the corner doing paperwork. The paperwork that started him on his long journey with Ray Cobb.

He didn't go back to the bullpen. Instead, he went straight to Jenkins' office.

"You want to get put back with Hsu or should I spare him the difficulty of having to work with you again?" Jenkins asked, not looking up from his computer.

"Put him with someone else," Nick said.

He placed the unsealed resignation letter on Jenkins' desk.

The lieutenant took off his reading glasses and flipped them down onto the blotter. He didn't make a move to take the letter.

"You heard you were cleared, right?"

"By the department, yeah."

"What's that supposed to mean?" Jenkins asked.

"You asked me if this was a job I wanted to do. You saw what happened up in those woods. Even though it worked out in the end, that's not how I want people brought to justice."

"That's why we need good cops like you who don't shoot first, then justify it after."

That one stung. Nick hoped Jenkins didn't see his ears go red.

"I agree," Nick said. "There are too many cops on the streets doing the wrong thing for what they think are the right reasons. We have to hold ourselves to a higher standard. But if we don't follow the rules we're supposed to defend, then why are we even bothering? We have to be what the community wants us to be."

Jenkins peered down at the letter, but didn't touch it.

"I'll forget I saw that. So Hsu or what?"

"Jim."

Nick never called him by his first name.

"This was a shit show, Archer. I know. But by going down that path, you got a lot of scumbags off the streets. And not just the assholes who died up in the woods. That girl you found in the clinic? The kid? The guy who got her pregnant was her Mom's boyfriend. Rapist. A registered sex offender who was working under an alias. That's one more pile of human garbage off the street."

Nick shook his head. He knew there would be a hundred examples. Endless justifications for bending the rules to make the world a better place. It always started with one slight step over the edge. Criminals had taught him that getting away with something is like a drug. And you don't get the same satisfaction from the rush unless you push the limit a little further until you can't come back from over the edge.

"I can't anymore. Not because I don't want to, but because I can't. It's time to get out. Before I become something I can't live with," Nick said.

Jenkins sighed a breath out and shrugged. He pushed back from his desk, his rotund belly scraping one of his shirt buttons against the pressboard. It popped off, exposing a stretched thin undershirt.

Nick snorted out a laugh.

"Well, that was fucking fitting. Was going to shake your hand and wish you luck, but that's not our style, is it?" Jenkins suppressed a smile.

"Hey, if you can get someone as hot as Carly Wentworth to fuck you with that gut, who the hell cares, right?" Nick smiled.

"I'll keep your secrets if you keep mine," Jenkins extended a hand.

Nick shook it.

"I'll call you if I need to get out of a speeding ticket."

"Fuck you. You'll pay your fines like every other civvie."

Nick walked out of the office and went to his desk. There was only a handful of personal items to grab amongst the piles of paperwork. He didn't even need a box. It all fit in his messenger bag.

"That's it then, huh?" Hsu asked.

Hsu hadn't seen the package in his inbox yet. Nick kept his gaze from settling on it. The outline of the firehouse bracelet in the manila envelope. The name Aelan Kham attached.

Aelan's blood came back positive on Ballantine's knife and now her name matched the tattoo on his arm. A DNA test would confirm the child's parentage. The newborn was already in the system, but at least she would know her mother's name if she went looking for it. It wasn't justice for Aelan, but it was something.

"I got you something to remember me by," Nick said.

He handed Hsu a small paper bag with something square in it. Hsu pulled the contents of the bag out and read it.

"Dirty Word of the Day Calendar."

"Sentimentality isn't my thing."

Hsu nodded, "Who knows? It might jar loose some pleasant memories we aren't expecting."

Nick smiled. "I guess I knew less about you than I thought. Take care of yourself."

"I hope your life is full of," Hsu flipped through the calendar and landed on a random page, "blumpkins."

Nick laughed. Hsu read what that was.

"Oh, God. Why would someone—?" he peered at the ceiling to think. "I honestly don't know if that's something anyone would want. Is it a good thing or a bad thing?"

"See you around, Hsu."

Back out on the street, Nick looked back at the building that had essentially been his home for the last three years. He was going to miss being a cop, but it never was what he wanted. It was the smart move when his mother got sick. Gave him purpose. Gave him focus. But he'd always wanted to be a private investigator. Now all he needed was a partner.

"Any tearful goodbyes?" The Queen asked. Her hair was up in a simple ponytail. She was wearing dark jeans and a forest green v-neck t-shirt. Her leg was in a brace. She looked unbelievable.

"My partner wished me an interesting farewell," Nick said.

"You ready for the next chapter?" she asked.

"First, I gotta figure out what kind of book I'm in," he said.

"What, like a mystery or a romance?" she gave him a smile that would melt diamonds.

"Or a psychological thriller," he said, not returning the smile.

"Am I missing something?" she asked.

"No. I was," Nick said as he threw his messenger bag in his car and shut the door. "Before we got the truth from Solish, who did you think killed Aelan?"

"Ballantine. Just like you," she said, trying to maintain her composure, but knew what he was getting at.

"And D'Arby just happened to find Ballantine the next day? And just happened to leave Ballantine alive after torturing him?"

He could see her thinking it through. Deciding whether to lie.

"I didn't do anything worse to him than he had done to other girls," she said under her breath. "Didn't matter that he thought he loved Aelan."

"It was calculated. Surgical. You took your time. He's never going to wake up. Doctors will pull the plug if no next-of-kin shows up. But you already knew that, didn't you?"

She didn't respond.

"My guess is that Burke didn't just knock on a random door after his confession, either. You were capable of that," Nick whispered.

"We're all capable of it if pushed far enough," she said. "There's a lot more of Malkin in me than I want to admit. I never gave you the impression I was a damsel that had to be saved or that I was a righteous defender of the weak. I live in a dirty world."

"We've both done things we aren't proud of," Nick offered.

"Don't do that," she snapped back. "Don't do what every fucking man out there does. Sees this strong, confident woman, this... Queen, and turns her into an ideal. It's how I've survived out here as long as I have. By using that to my advantage."

She was right. A beautiful, mysterious woman had appeared out of nowhere and he had developed a boyhood crush. He didn't know her. Hell, she didn't know him. Who would they be to each other tomorrow?

It didn't work like it did in the movies. No one should build a relationship on shared trauma.

He took a deep breath and extended his hand. "Nick Archer. And you are?"

She pressed her lips together hard and took a deep breath. He could see her making the choice. Deciding to put her trust in him.

After a beat, she took his hand and let it wrap around hers.

"Clarisse Montag," she breathed out. "Wow. It's been a long time since I said that out loud."

He held back the obvious Hannibal Lecter impersonation and asked, "Well, Clarisse, now what?"

"You won't see me again. I suppose I'm as guilty of stereotyping you. Came out here all flirty when really I was going to pump you for information and disappear. The next life for each of us is going to be hard. We both can't take the road less traveled by. We don't need to be saddled with something built on mistrust to add to it."

It was frustrating how her logic and confidence made him like her more. Maybe that was the problem.

"Okay," he opened the driver's side door. "Thanks for the adventure."

"Thanks for hoping I could live a normal life."

"You can. It'll take some time, but you can."

She leaned in and kissed him on the cheek. "Stay out of trouble."

"You too."

She turned and limped down the street. He watched her go.

"Stop staring at my ass," she called back.

He laughed and did what he was told.

There was no way she could have known one of his favorite books was *Fahrenheit 451*. He knew how Guy Montag changed after meeting Clarisse McClellan. Chose to take the road less traveled by. However brief their relationship had been, she was a catalyst to change his mind and his world. Even though she had disappeared from his life as quickly as she had entered it, she haunted the rest of his story.

Leaving Nick with one last secret seemed like a fitting departure.

"You got a buck?"

A young homeless man in a dirty beanie and threadbare shoes stood before him, the question asked like he already expected a "no".

Nick pulled out his wallet and opened the back flap. Empty.

"Sorry, pal. Fresh out."

The homeless man nodded and shuffled past him. "Thanks anyway."

"Oh, wait, hold up," Nick dug into the front pocket of his jeans, two fingers grabbing his informant money. He handed over the folded twenty. "Forgot my emergency stash."

"You sure?"

"Don't need it. We could all use a little help sometimes," Nick said.

The homeless man gave him a choked up smile, "Haven't eaten in two days. You're a good man."

Nick didn't know if he agreed with that statement, but there was new life in the homeless man's gait as he made his way to find some lunch.

He got into his car and pulled into the growing traffic on the 5 freeway, ready to see what tomorrow had in store.

Epilogue

Autumn winds blew hard along Lake Michigan, scattering the turning leaves along the vacant wastes of Lake Shore Drive. The early morning Chicago commuters hadn't started coming in from the various suburbs yet. In Grant Park south of Soldier Field, small encampments of people were waking up and making their way onto the "L" to start their long travels up and down the length of the city to beg for spare change.

Jeremiah "Look Down" Harrigan mumbled to himself, eyes on his feet. He hunched to a right angle, face always to the ground. Constantly on the scan for something he never seemed to find. But every time Lettie saw him, he told her he was searching for something new. His legs bowed into a permanent arch, forced to be the load-baring structure for his back, held straight and parallel to the ground. Lettie figured he probably had to fall into every chair he'd ever sat in because straightening his back would likely break it. Only thing Look Down was good for was noticing people's shoes. And sometimes that's all you need.

"Who is this guy?" she asked, bracing herself against the wind.

"Finds you things," Look Down mumbled. He held out his new pair of glasses, shook them, then replaced the straps around the back of his head to keep them from slipping down onto the concrete.

"How're you going to know when we find him?"

"Sorels," Look Down said. She'd gotten used to him identifying people by their shoes rather than their faces. Unless they ducked down to meet his eyes like they were looking at the undercarriage of a Buick, shoelace eyelets were as close to eye contact as Look Down came.

As they distanced themselves from the lake, the neighborhood changed. Abandoned buildings and vacant lots gave way to new construction condominiums. Every time gentrification threatened to restore a patch of old houses, there was another shooting and the neighborhood would stagnate. An old set of abandoned train tracks split ill-kept buildings and corner stores from beautifully restored brownstones.

In the break of a raised concrete wall, a man with scraggly grey hair and a big madman's beard sat on a crumbling step. He had a White Sox skull cap pulled down over his brow, but Lettie could see that one eye was drooping, either from a stroke or where the man's eye socket was broken. He was wearing a blue surgical mask, not uncommon in the waning COVID-19 pandemic.

Look Down took point heading toward the man, drawn by the smell of the Vienna Beef Polish sausages he was cooking over a small camping stove. He poked at them with a long fork, the fat dripping out. Juice sizzled in the small fire.

"Hey, Sorels. Got enough for three?" Look Down asked. Sure enough, Lettie could see he was wearing a pair of Sorels. He'd worn the rubber through the bottom. They looked older than her.

"Who you brought with you?"

Look Down leaned against the concrete wall, one butt cheek perched on the top of the makeshift stairs that led to the man's house, claimed with squatter's rights. The man used his left arm to pick up the sausage and place it on a paper plate sitting on the ground. His other arm was tucked into his coat and Lettie guessed it was missing for the amount of effort he was putting into not using it. He handed the plate to Look Down, who used it as a holder and bit into the end of the Polish. The casing snapped between his teeth and he chewed with his mouth open, steam billowing out into the cool morning air.

"This is Lettie," Look Down said, swallowing the bite and taking another.

"What you got for me Lettie?" the man asked. He didn't seem to care that the other sausages on the cooking stove were charring.

"Uh," Lettie had forgotten she'd even brought the thing with her. She pulled off her knitted gloves and reached into the pocket of her faded rainbow colored down coat.

She handed over a small MP3 player and headphones.

"Found it on the Green Line," she stuttered out. "Not the best, but it's loaded with stuff. The '70s and '80s, mostly."

"And what do you want in return?" the man asked. "I got a few things that would be worth this trade."

He placed the music player in his pocket without looking at it.

"My mom. She's gone. Not the kind to go without a say so. We're scared."

Look Down had finished his sausage and nodded.

"Damnedest thing," he said. "Thought if anyone can help, it's you."

"You got a picture?" the man asked.

The girl pulled out a small pre-paid phone and handed it over. The man took the phone, typed in a number and sent a text, then erased all traces of the number he'd just input.

"Got it," he said. "I'll find you when I find her. You may not like the result, so you know."

Look Down lifted off the steps and began his scoliosis shuffle back the way he came. Lettie didn't move.

"That's it?"

"That's it."

"Um… okay," she turned to follow Look Down back north into the city, but stopped herself.

"Who are you?" She stuttered. "I mean, what do I call you?"

The man looked up from the burnt sausages, pulled his right hand out of his coat, and extended it to her.

The flesh was scarred and pink. The fingers were smooth, and the nails looked fused into the flesh, save for the nail on his middle finger, which was missing. Under the sleeve of his coat, Lettie could see a hint of blue ink tangled in the charred flesh.

Without recoiling from his burnt hand, Lettie extended her own and took it. The man gave it a firm shake.

"Crispy," the man formerly known as Ray Cobb said. "Pleased to meet you."

Author's
Note

This book was a long time in the making. The first book came out in April 2012, the second April 2015. This one will land in your hands September 2022. Life altered a lot from when I first began writing it.

The political and social landscape has shifted since late 2015. The world changed. LA is no longer my home, though it holds a special place in my heart. A pandemic happened. My relationship with the story and the characters continued to shift and evolve. As my wife and I went through our own pregnancy story and loss, the tone deaf terror of what originally happened to Aelan and Imani had to be adjusted for my own personal reasons. Had I not made the rookie mistake of publishing a sample chapter of this book in *The Last Dance of Low Seward*, the pregnancy storyline may have disappeared altogether. But alas, I had already dug my proverbial grave and had to follow through. I think that's why it took so long for me to complete.

On that note, I feel that I must be clear that this book does not have an anti-abortion or pro-life agenda. Women deserve to have complete rights over their bodies, choices, and futures. Access to safe, legal abortions prevent places like Solish's clinic from taking advantage of women who feel they have no alternative. You don't have to like abortion, but no matter your faith, you should acknowledge that women have the right to make their own choices about their bodies. It doesn't matter what you "believe." If that alienates you as a reader, I don't give a shit. I don't want you in my club anyway, dickhead.

Then there was the matter of Ray's backstory. After some initial Hollywood "buzz" on *The Last Will and Testament of Ernie Politics*, I had several TV executives give me the advice that we need to dig deep into what makes Ray tick and slowly reveal it over time. Dozens of versions were written and abandoned. I finally settled on hints of his former life rather than chapters explaining where he came from. If Ray's former life finds its way into a different format in some unknown future, so be it. That's why I wrote this as a book first and not a screenplay. But the meetings got me in my head and gave me the brain jumblies.

I didn't want the entire book to be me revealing what motivated Ray just to say that I had done it. Recently I read a book by Jonah Lehrer called *Mystery: A Seduction, A Strategy, A Solution*. In it, he discusses the power of what literary critic Stephen Greenblatt called "strategic opacity."[1] Removing information actually makes the story better than explaining everything. We don't need to know everything that happened to Hamlet or Othello or why the *Mona Lisa* smiles to enjoy what the art is in the moment. Not that I would ever deign to compare myself to Shakespeare or DaVinci, but it made me realize that explaining Ray's origins and motivations in vivid detail did nothing to give the story more depth or make the reader feel more connected. Those details stole from the momentum of the story. Trying to explain away every choice made them less real.

Humans are flawed. We do strange things. Not all of them are motivated by a specific moment in our past. I've given you enough to know who he is as a man, but not so much that it stalled you from getting to *The End*. I hope your imagination filled in the gaps and no matter who I think Ray is, I hope you have a better version in your mind.

Thank you for taking this ten-year journey with me. Whatever book I write next, I hope it doesn't take ten more years to get to you.

— Brad Grusnick. May 2022.

---

1. Jonah Lehrer, Mystery: A Seduction, A Strategy, A Solution. (New York, NY, Avid Reader Press, 2021), 111.

Acknowledgments

Thanks to my early readers of The Last Days: Chuck Kreuser, Sean Gallagher, Mike Nelson, and Michael Williams. All of your insights and notes have helped make all of my books better and I am eternally grateful. You saw all the things I chose to ignore. Jermaine Johnson and Brett Sechrist are the best lit team a guy could ask for. Thank you to my parents, Robert and Nadine Grusnick for their constant support in all of my crazy endeavors. Thanks most of all to my wife, Sarah. Through all of the ups and downs of the past few years, you've always been my biggest champion. Now I will shut up about having to finish the book. And finally, thanks to you, the reader. Thanks for sticking it out through this trilogy. I hope everyone got a fitting ending. Without you, this is just a pile of paper.

About
the
Author

Brad Grusnick graduated from Northwestern University with a Bachelor's Degree in Theatre. He studied Comedy Writing at The Second City Chicago and is an adjunct professor at Columbia College. After 11 years in Los Angeles, he returned to the midwest to be closer to family, though he feels the pull from SoCal every single day. His other novels, The Last Will and Testament of Ernie Politics and The Last Dance of Low Seward, are also gross.

The characters in this novel sometimes make light of their situation on the streets, but homelessness is a real problem in the world. For more information on how you can help in the fight against the homelessness epidemic in the United States and throughout the world, please visit:

Nationalhomeless.org

ighomelessness.org

www.ingramcontent.com/pod-product-compliance
Lightning Source LLC
Chambersburg PA
CBHW051319190726
48290CB00001B/225